Red Moonglow on Snow

a RAVERY'S DAUGHTERS *novel*

by L. Nahay

Midnight Tomorrow Books

This is a work of fiction. All characters, names, events. and places are either products of the author's imagination or used in a fictitious manner.

For information, contact Midnight Tomorrow Books,1137 West Taylor St. #252, Chicago, Il., 60607

www.MidnightTomorrowBooks.com

Cover design and illustration by L. Nahay
Cover font *Metamorphous* designed by Sorkin Type Co
Faux Snow designed by Brian Kent

ISBN: 978-0-9910039-8-3

To all the women who can kiss their Others and tuck their children in at night.

And for all of those who can't.

For my monsters, who've endured this book-sibling constantly battling for my attention. Love you both immensely. Thank you for your support, your enthusiasm, and your patience.

Thank you, Thursday Linda, for being the first to read and critique. Helped a ton, as you can see!

Thank you, Daniel, for your insight, your time, and your help with the cover technicalities. You helped me out of a rut I would otherwise not have gotten through.

UNICORN

1

FOR A BRIEF MOMENT, I BELIEVE THAT I LAY IN THE ALCOVE, our small clearing within a cluster of trees by Lake *Mish-a-gun,* back in That Night I'd shared with Him. But the waves of the lake are slamming against the inside of my head as though the water has turned to metal and is trying to break free, and the air upon my face is harsh and unhindered, full of an anger and a violence that the lake air never once inflicted upon me, no matter what the Others claimed. My entire being feels weighted, battered, paralyzed. I don't feel right, as though I'm in a place I'm not supposed to be.

With effort, I locate two of my limbs. One leg bent over the other, and my left arm crossed over my middle. Where is the rest of me? My head and body feel elsewhere.

Eyes are closed, but I sense Him. All around me. Did he return? Did he leave me again?

Cardinals had guided me to the beach. I remember the sand between my toes, the smoky blue of the moving water, and the branches full of changing leaves over my head as I'd stood staring at the place where He and I had made our daughter. Today is her birthday. She's two. She's two and she's gone, just like Him.

I try not to, but I reach, seeking Him out, and sensation and awareness both begin to prick and tingle their way through my body as I struggle to move. I reach- and find the place beside me empty. Still. My fingers dig into the earth at either side of my body, trying to anchor myself to the feeble dream, but it isn't the bare earth of The Alcove that I have a hold of. The fleeting confusion of grass in my fists is chased away by the horrendous pounding in my head.

The sound of metal waves gives way to the sound of leaves being whipped into a violent wind, and fades further until only the sound of the wind battering me from the outside remains. Brightness shines through my closed eyelids, getting loud and present as the wind until I have no choice but to open them and accept the sunlight.

There's no trees overhead, only bright green blades shooting upward around my face and beating and scraping my skin according to the orders of the wind. Above me is blue that never stops. It's a blue that is too clean, too perfect, unmarred by the typically constant clouds. The wind, breaking through my skin and splintering my head, however, is neither clean nor perfect.

I do not smell the lake, feel or hear her. Where am I? This isn't The Alcove, the place where we'd made Talyn. Tears stray from my eyes down into the green holding me still. She's two today. Where is she?

My shoulder bursts in fiery pain, reminding me more so of her being gone and how, rather than the beauty today should hold......if......

I watch the green blades until their sharpness softens and becomes grass. The Alcove does not have grass. And nowhere does This Place, *Chi-ca-go*, have grass this green or sky so perfect blue and unhindered. Where's the wires, the street lights, the noise and the Others? Where have the clouds gone?

The wind attacks me in a strategic push, forcing me over onto my side. The coolness of the earth sends a shiver down my skin to my toes, reconnecting me to myself. A spot on my forehead burns as painfully as the rock in my shoulder. I remember that spot, a little right of my forehead's center. He'd kissed me there during the night. Almost three years ago.

The wind gathers up my hair and tugs it from all angles, jerking my head to make me look around. For a moment, I think nothing. Though my body has reconnected itself, what I see makes no sense. *Lake, trees, lake, trees,* repeats in my head even though neither are anywhere in sight. I wait for my eyes to properly relate, or my head to come back into alignment with the rest of me, but the vibrant green hills going on and on before me don't waver. The wind keeps pushing at me, continues to roar inside my head. I was at The Lake. I know I was. I had let the sand fall through my fingers, had stretched my palms out over the water as she turned her head to mourn with me. I remember the fallen leaves of the trees spinning around into mini tornados along the sidewalk. I remember The Alcove, I remember crawling around the depression our bodies had burned into the ground, the Silver Light streaming out through the memory of us, and the branches full and brilliant above me.

I glance down at my hand. Where is the Silver?

Silver Light, don't leave me here......

Mom's voice drifts quickly away in the wind, and the green moving hills and the infinite blue push thoughts of

The Lake away. Beneath my hands and legs I feel the retreating trace of winter, can taste the memory of snow in the air. None of this is right. It's Autumn, the ninth month of the year. It's Talyn's birthday, and I was nowhere near hills. Where am I and how did I get here? I attempt to pull my legs up to my chest in order to sit, but part of the dress is caught underneath my hip and I can't bring my legs completely up.

Dress?

The wind is roaring in my ears, pulling my hair out and whipping it around my face, tugging and yanking, jabbing at my throbbing shoulder. All I acknowledge, though, is the dress that isn't mine, draped over my body.

I look back out at the hills- rolls and rolls of hills, going on forever all around me- and panic begins to bloom in a force almost rivaling that of the wind. Seamless. This dress is seamless.

I untangle my legs from the odd- lavender? pale, pale blue? silver?- dress and set my fingertips on the spot on my forehead, which continues to tingle with the memory of His lips.

His clothes were seamless.

I left the house in pants. I was wearing clothes, wasn't I? All I remember is Silver, and The Lake, and her birthday.

Silver Light, take me Home......

The grass on the hills rolls forward and back, waving like water, and the angry wind withdraws as my mind searches and searches. Nauseous, I lower my face to the green. Mom's prayer wafts through my clogged head, reminding me of the Silver Light that grabbed her from

Home and then cast her on the *Mish-ah-gun* shores of *Chi-ca-go* before I was born.

The wind ends her truce and propels into me again, even sending her force into the earth below me so that it begins to tremble and groan. No Lake, no trees. Only green, only ear-splintering wind screaming something at me. Only lush, grass-covered earth under my face and body, under my palms with the faint, lingering smell of snow and the sense of winter retreating back to the earth's core; and the earth below me, trembling, rumbling, its growing frustration matching my growing fear.

Silver light, if not me, take my child......

Wind and grass. Angry and calm. Violent and serene. Beautiful, beautiful, green. Swaying and mesmerizing. Enticing me to close my eyes and go back to sleep, wake up and see another scene. But my head throbs and aches, and closing my eyes threatens to make my head explode. I frown. Wind and green. The memory of *silver* is throbbing in my brain, in my shoulder. I look again at the fingers before my eyes and see no tint of silver, no blanketing light over my skin, over the world. The ground beneath me is shivering, and I am trembling along with it.

Silver light, if not me, take my child and let her be......
......let her be......

Home.
The hills, the burning of His kiss on my temple, and instantly, I *know*. The night I'd met Him, he'd worn clothes without seams. Silver light had taken my mother from

Home, the world of her birth, and we've been waiting for The Wizard and that light to bring us back ever since.

Weeping, I look skyward and count one sun, two suns, with Home's ever-present feminine moon sleeping low and silent beneath and between them. The wind, angry and loud, is almost goading as she jabs into me over and over, almost knocking me down the hill I am crouching on, as if aggravated by my slowness.

I was born in that Other Place, have never seen my parents' birthplace, but I know where I am: I am in Home.

For several heartbeats, I sit paralyzed, trying to bridge the distance between The Alcove and here, trying to remember the journey, trying to comprehend. The whispers that had carried me to the lake trail on the air, carrying His promise back to me:

......*I'm taking you Home. In the morning when you wake, that's where you'll be. I promise......*

But that morning, I was not.

He *was* here, and he left me again. Again. Three years too late, He's decided to fulfill his promise and bring me here? Why?

I crumple into a ball and shake, trying hard not to cry. The wind is screaming, the earth is quaking, but the full impact of what He has done rises up and I bellow louder than either. "*Noooooooooo!*" I drag the syllable out until I have no more breath, and the wind pauses again, seeming a little shocked at my reaction. I lunge forward onto my hands and knees, digging my fingers into the earth and throwing fistfuls of grass still attached to their roots down the hill.

"*Bastard*!" The wind whips my scream back and turns my tears into slivers of ice it drives into my cheeks. "No! No! No!" I dig and pull and scream until my throat burns. The rumble of the earth grows more intense, nearly knocking me off balance. I dig my hands in deeper, the dirt severing the skin beneath my nails. My body begins shaking so violently I have to stop, try to think, try to calm myself. I don't want to be here anymore. I can't be here anymore. Not now. "Bastard," I whimper.

Why? Why now? Why not when He'd promised? Why not when His daughter was born? Or before she was taken? Why *now*?

And why here?

I'm not simply in Home. I'm in The Valley, my mother's blasted, specific birthplace. This is the region of her human mother Anin as well as Anin's Soldiers, the men who'd hunted my mother down and murdered my father, who'd attacked the home of Mom's foster parents and forced her foster father, The Wizard, to exile her to *Chi-ca-go*.

I stare into the impassive blue sky, seeing the distance between Here and wherever I was before stretch out interminably before me. Instinctively, I reach to my throat and let my fingers close on the emptiness as though my dragon charm is still there. He'd taken it when He'd left me that night. Can I find my mother's dragons without it?

The trembling in the earth is more demanding. I turn away from the place where the sky touches the hills miles and miles ahead. To my left, on the hills, a hoard of muzzled unicorns pauses not far enough away, with men astride their backs. Soldiers. And they've seen me, and they're stampeding full speed towards me. They are the rumble in the earth.

The wind holds its breath before screaming at me, almost as if he is yelling *RUN, Lira! Run!*. Yet I sit. Mom had said the wind is feminine, but it seems very strongly masculine right now, shouting and pushing me. I sit, my mind moving from the wind's gender to marveling at the pinpoint clarity that allows me to see every detail of every unicorn clearer than if they are right in front of me. Twenty eight hooves beat down the grass while hot steamy breath from seven mouths cuts through teeth and iron muzzles to replenish the wind. The raging stampede reaches my ears not in real time but from the echo off the hills. Mom would never paint a picture of a unicorn, she'd only verbally describe them to me as the demons they are; and yet, I can't stop my fascination, can't pull my eyes away and act on the danger I am in.

Soldiers. All my life has been a preparation of encountering them. No, not encountering: fighting them. They will take their time before killing me for being born female.

I am so tired of fighting, of the word, of the effort, of the attempt. I fought to protect my daughter, but what did it do? Those people still took her. I fought to maintain my faith and love for her father, but what did that do for me? And now, He's brought me Home at last. Yet once again, he left me before I could even open my eyes. Left me, once again, to fight alone.

I put my hand on the buzzing spot on my forehead. He kissed my forehead before he left me. Left me to die. Was that his intention before? Did he leave me on that beach in the dead of winter on purpose?

Snap of metal reins makes me blink and focus again. The Soldiers are leaning forward and shouting, hitting their demons with barbed whips that rip long new gashes into dirty, deeply scarred hides of brittle, sparse, worn fur. They're racing closer and closer. Unicorn grunts and growls escape metal muzzles that prevent their razor teeth from ripping into the human male flesh astride their backs. Unicorn teeth push out from thinned, cracked lips, saliva dripping as they gallop. Their eyes bulge thick with unspeakable hate and rage. There's the smell of man above them.

Smell of man *before* them: on *me*, *in* me.

Suddenly, the comprehension of RUN falls upon me with a too-late sense of urgency. I trip on the damn dress tangled around my legs while trying to pull off a strange bag strapped around my shoulder, getting tangled in the bag's strap in my panic. Once freed from both, I hurl the bag down the hill, not caring as what appears to be food tumbles free, because, I take off running as fast as I can. Though the wind seems to hold back in momentary respite, I stop breathing completely. Hoof beats abuse the ground so closely they upset my steps and make me stumble at every footfall. My back becomes singed by unicorn breath. I no longer hear the wind, I hear myself being chased. Feel not grass, not sunlight, but hooves clipping my heels, hands stretching out to grab me.

My lungs and throat burn, scorched dry as I pant and run so fast I have no awareness of what my legs and feet are doing. If I think, if I search for my legs I'll upset the rhythm and I'll fall.

I hike the dress that isn't mine up over my knees, secure it in the grass belt around my waist that apparently holds a dagger, and run up and then down a snow-covered hill, never slowing on the hills that follow, sometimes propelling myself away and up on all fours, using my hands to grab fistfuls of grass to help me clamber up another hill. The Soldiers have dispersed, splitting into two groups to circle around and cut me off. But the next hill is wider than they have calculated and I come out yards ahead. But only by yards.

There is no place to run to. Hills and hills and more hills. No shelter. No place to hide. No one to help. He'd sent me to The Valley for a purpose. This is that purpose. Bastard. I pull the dagger from its sheath and launch it. It sails through the air, turns slowly back and slides itself home into its casing.

Home. I am in Home.

I yank the dagger out and pitch it harder, grunting, screaming, crying. It returns quietly.

Just as I top another hill, I trip on the damn dress that has freed itself from the belt. For one brief moment I fly- it feels as though wings have sprouted from my back and suspend me, will glide me to safety.

Yet too quickly I crash into the ground and begin rolling. Twenty eight heavily muscled unicorn legs with blade-sharp hooves rip holes into the earth behind me as I somersault downward. Their hooves and legs are use to this terrain, use to running and chasing and attacking and killing. The beats of their hooves echo in my head, in whichever part of me that smashes onto the earth as I tumble and spin down the hillside.

I shut my eyes and protect my head, waiting to reach the bottom of the hill and for it all to be done with. Seven Soldiers. Seven sweating bodies lewdly growing more and more excited with the chase. Seven pairs of eyes already shredding me apart and seven revolting voices shouting at me from all around. I hear their voices now in-between crashes and rolls; quick escapes of syllables immediately inhaled and swallowed by the wind, which doesn't want me to hear what they're saying.

Abruptly, I stop rolling.

I lay still, unable to move or breathe, staring upwards at the double suns and the single moon, taking count of my body to be sure all of it has followed the descent. I hurt in places I never knew I had. My lungs have exploded and there's no use in breathing. But......two suns shine overhead. Two suns. Because I am in Home. I am in Home.

I hold the sob in.

[Are you alright? Just stay where you are! I'm on my way!] The panting voice forces its way into my head, jolting me into consciousness. I shake my head and swat at my ear. The voice leaves.

The Soldiers are closing in. I sit up and they're before me, no longer galloping or running or really even moving at all. A few Soldiers unhook barbed ropes from their sides. They are laughing, jeering, tugging their crotches, their lips drawn over snarling teeth as they kick their beasts to walk towards me. I know what Valley men are, how twisted they've become. I know what they'll do to me, and I know how much worse they'll do if they learn who I come from.

The wind lets out a long, angered yet helpless howl.

Cracked, bleeding, wind-torn Soldier lips move but what they spit out the air shreds and still won't allow me to hear. I can't feel my legs and I worry that since I've stopped running, I will not be able to run again.

The unicorns are completely crazed. They fight against the Soldiers holding them back, their eyes fixated madly upon me. There are long, metal braces around their necks to prevent them from turning their heads and attacking the men. Blood drips down the metal where the sharpened tips repeatedly stab them as they keep fighting to turn their heads. The only real way for them to release their immeasurable fury is to go after whatever they can that holds the scent of man. And now, that is me. In this part of the world of my parents' birth, with Soldiers and Anin and unicorns, I would be called Touched.

Which is laughable, as we had done much more than just touch. Bastard. Curse him for what he's done to me, for what loving him has cost me. I've already been cursed for it. But I will not be captured. I will not fall prey to anyone again, especially them. Mom had said the world has good it owes me, but they are all owed for what they've done.

I am not dreaming. I am in Home. He's cast me at their feet- as punishment for losing his daughter? Who gave Him that right? To continue to do as he wishes with me?

My fingers lightly caress the hilt of the dagger. I grit my teeth and unsheathe the blade that seemingly won't leave my side. The knife's sound- the metal sliding slowly against a metal case, like a hiss, a purr- dances through the wind. And the wind actually allows me to hear it. The old, sickened feeling returns to me with the sound: the repulsion, the regret over using a weapon; but the sound, the motion of freeing the dagger frees me from my own sheath, my own metal skin that's been keeping me weighed down. My blood is tingling, humming, knowing I have accepted that I'm going to fight. Again.

I'd fought against my parents' lessons to no end. As a child I had believed I would never be a warrior like they. Now, though, I know that I should've listened more.

Should have fought harder. I would have saved Talyn if I had. If I had killed them all.

The blade knows that I have finally accepted it as well, and it vibrates excitedly in my fingers. *Close your eyes and listen, Lira. Do you hear it? It's speaking to you,* was in one of Mom's early lessons, immediately after I had been taken when I was little. I'd been angry and instead of following her direction, I'd launched the blade into the wall and stalked off. My father, Mihn, had been pretty proud of that. From then on he'd insisted that knives were my weapon. And now I'm in Home, and one small knife is all that Talyn's father has left me with.

Who gave Him any right? He set me here for others to kill me for him. What about what He's done, what He's caused?

My blood is beginning to boil, gurgling back to life, feeding me. I allow the rush of pain that comes with feeling again. My body is screaming in agony, yet anger is a sensation we can manage. My eyes fix on those before me. My parents' distant voices flood the hills with instructions and encouragement. Fight. Fight. Always fight. Because of men like these, that's all my parents had known. Simply because my mother was born, and her birth mother, Anin, the Lady of Ravery, felt that her birth was punishable by death.

My body jumps up and charges without a shout or sound. The Soldiers and unicorns freeze, confused. Prey don't attack. I run straight for the unicorn and Soldier directly before me, leaping up and driving the dagger into the Soldier's side before he manages to grab my arms and attempt to catch me. I twist mid-air, my body sailing over the demon's horn and head, and keep flying by, bringing the Soldier down with me.

I think I lose consciousness for a couple heartbeats after crashing back-first onto the earth. As soon as I come to, I kick the man off of me, getting momentarily tangled in the grass and the damn dress while the Soldier struggles to orient himself. The beast-

[Hey!]

That voice again!

-turns around and faces us. Seeing us where we shouldn't be, he tries to turn his head to comprehend his empty back, but the bars on his neck prevent him from doing so. He turns his large eyes to me, questioning, unsure. The Soldier and I regard each other in much the same way, waiting for someone to make the second attack.

The demon rears up full, his deadly hooves inches above my head and sparkling silver and gold under caked mud. I flinch as he comes down, but to my shock, he unleashes his rage on his now former rider, pummeling what was once a man into the earth and grass, his grimy, mauve-colored fur now contrasted with brilliant red. *Finally*, the air sighs amidst the man's and beast's screams. *Finally*.

Dragons, I exclaim into my head, horrified. There is blood everywhere, vibrant as it beads down the edges of the grass around us. My eyes follow some drops' poetically slow descent, and the whole world pauses to let me.

More terrifying than the screaming is the following silence, when nothing and no one even thinks. The unicorn is panting, staring down at what he's done. I realize that I'm sitting, sitting very near the massacred, segmented Soldier and his newly-free, maddened demon. The beast remembers that as well and sharply redirects his attention to me. I shake my head clear and push to my feet, moving away very slowly.

The other unicorns resume fighting against their restraints, rearing and turning, their snapping teeth loud enough to hear over the wind. They twist and turn and rear, buck, but the Soldiers sit firm, use to such behavior. No longer concerned with me, the men beat their swords into the demons' skin and their heels into their sides, only making them scream louder and fight against them harder rather than succeeding in regaining control.

My heart relocates somewhere in my head, beating loud and strong and definitively in my ears. All the unicorns are facing me. Their lowered horns face me. Chaos and odor and lude voices and Soldiers and hooves and someone everywhere. The unicorns and the men are all screaming and shouting. The smells of beast and man merge and sting my nostrils. Convulsively, I launch the dagger into the nearest man's throat.

The Soldier yanks the knife from his right shoulder and flexes his hand, ensuring it works. How'd I miss so badly? Wind. I have to account for the strength and pull of the wind. How could I have forgotten that?

"Damn bitch! Get her now, Ernon."

Ernon, already on foot with his demon tethered tightly against another beast, is a tall, ghastly thin man. His stench precedes him as he approaches me. He smells worse than the demons.

[That's *enough* already!]

Voice again!

Greasy, long, ash blond hair sticks to the Soldier's forehead and neck and down his back in thinning, sickly vines. He moves in slow, precise strides, expecting me to cower, anticipating his overly-confident walk will make me buckle and lay myself at his lack of mercy. He only makes my fists clench and release in anticipation with every drawn-out step he takes. I take a half step back and bend my knees, ready to fight back. He grabs again at his erect groin and the wind growls. I think it's the wind. The demons are growing more anxious, pawing and grunting and shifting madly from side to side. Maybe I am the one growling. My legs are tingling with my defensive posture, but I hold it, thinking of my mother's dragons, of their strength, of their fury, for I am the daughter of Elaar, who is the daughter of dragons, and I won't die this way. Not by His or their doing.

He takes one step too close. My fist cuts through the wind and shocks it into silence before locking on stubbled jaw. The little needle-like hairs on his face slice through my knuckles. The snap of either my bones or his cracks through the hills. I don't care. He doesn't reel very much from the punch, but the fact that I had done it is the more effective blow.

[I'm right behind you! I'll be there soon! Stall!]

Talking again. Wordless chatter around my ears. Taunts. Frustration. Anger. Confusion.

"Something different about you, woman." The Soldier fondles his jaw. He says the word 'woman' as though it names a vile creature that slithers in the dark. His eyes devour me, rip through the clothes that aren't mine, through skin I no longer know.

"Ernon, stop playing these senseless games! Jix, shoot her already!"

Shoot.

Explosion so loud you don't hear it. You feel it as it rips through your body in that distant, odd, delayed sense of pain and injury. Your blood once vital and precious becoming sticky and grotesque. Vulnerable. Something tiny as a pebble so deadly, so costly.

The bullet in my shoulder ignites and throbs with thoughts of Talyn, reminding me of what I've lost and how I lost her. I won't be shot again. Won't be weakened by a tiny thing made from man.

Once so close and compact, nearly falling down upon me, now the Soldiers are spread further out, encircling me. An arrow is pulled taut, drawing my attention into its backward pull. Any second now it'll launch free, make the air sing in the pitch only target and archer can hear (wind allowing). The suns reflect off the point; I see it from where I stand. Suns and the one moon reflecting in a tiny bit of stone aimed at my chest. My shoulder is *screaming*.

The dagger is in my hand again. I don't question how as my father isn't at my side this time to keep me armed. My fingers tighten, ensuring fact and grip and surety. As the arrow begins to slip, I throw.

The Soldier's beast rears up at the same instant. I'd thrown for the man's throat, but the demon moved! Then, as soon as he senses the coming weapon, the beast's screams die and he descends in time for the knife to sink into the Soldier's ribs. Man sneers. Then looks down, sees his blood, and slips to the ground.

I stand relaxed and waiting for this second beast to come charging at me. *Touched. I'm Touched.* Hills and hills and hills all around. Talyn is gone. He- not the people who'd invaded our house- He has taken her from me. Him. Bringing me here, having me killed or not, he's taken her from me. So tired, so worn, so destroyed. *Stamp him out. Take all trace of him away from me*, I beg the unicorn. *Stamp him out of me.*

The center of my vision whitens out the monstrosity of hills and clear blue sky, and Talyn is there, suspended out for me. *Yes*, I cry to the unicorn, letting it feast itself on the agony that bleeds into my eyes and face. *Yes,* with Talyn all around, *Take His scent away. Set me free.*

Yelling, yelling, for this second unicorn is also now free. Ropes are being thrown over my head. But the demon's eyes are changing. Black and bloodshot slacken into something that understands pain, understands the intense desire for escape. Any escape. Black and red softening into silver and I begin to weep, *Pleeeeee-ase.*

Two more chains cross his neck, grinding against the bars around his throat. Just a little rise, but he turns away from me. Broken, muddied hooves hesitate over his rider only in my mind as I struggle to process that he's not attacking me either.

My leg feels odd. Wet. Hot.

Ropes flying. Men shouting. Unicorns angry. Wind howling. Grass bowing. Green, beautiful green grass. Under a sky too perfect, too false. The unicorn is already full into his attack, stamping his hooves down upon what remains of his former rider over and over while the restrained unicorns watch in glee and the Soldiers try hard not to see at all.

Two Soldiers dead.

Thin things tighten unexpectedly around me, pinching off my air, locking my arms against my side. Something about my throat, clamping tight. And a face, a too-white, toothy face under sticky greasy hair too close to completely see.

"I think that's enough," Ernon sneers, his voice low and toned with malice. "Get them tethered!" he roars, his fingers on my throat flinching, tightening, lifting. The unicorns are not compliant and they are short two men. The man I'd struck but missed struggles to stay atop his ride and the one restraining me leaves three to handle seven perpetually enraged unicorns.

"While I loved the chase, you can't run anymore. Feel that?" He reaches down and yanks on something imbedded in my leg, sending fire up my thigh. I gasp, choking on the scream.

An arrow is suspended in the air before me.

He twists it further in and I glare right back into his eyes, not flinching though the pain is nearly blinding and my head is going numb.

The point of an arrow is lodged in my right thigh......but the dress is now somewhat blatantly red, from the thin shaft of the arrow down into the grass blades that won't help cut.

No, it's not that the dress has decided on a color. It's my blood. The last Soldier. He'd hit me. There's an *arrow* in my *thigh*!

[You're *hit*?]

A cold foreign solidness begins to pierce into my awareness. The arrow has severed into my muscle, the tip is grinding into my femur. Nerves shoot pain down to my toes and up to the crown of my skull while ropes burn into my wrists, cut into my arms. My arms press into my ribs, constraining lungs that wish only to expand. But even if they could, the Soldier's grip on my throat is tightening and I can't bring air into or out of my lungs.

The sky around us is that even, detached blue, except where streaked by veins of night that never go away as the moon's constant presence keeps the suns from taking complete control of the sky. Stars still shine in the triangular segment of night, looking helplessly down at the scene below them. But the loss of air is making earth-bound stars dance in my sight much nearer than they should be. The blank-faced moon, the searing suns, the raging wind, the hills and brightening stars and loss of air and the pitch black unicorn standing before me- I feel like I'm suffocating in a jumble of dreams and nightmares.

Black unicorn?

The noise, the chaos, the pain ends after my eyes track back to my right where an eighth unicorn stands. Behind him is a deep canyon of exposed, dark brown earth scorched into the grass and hills. By his hooves?

"Now you're afraid, aren't you?" The Soldier leans in so close that his lips scrape over the edge of mine as he speaks. He then realizes that I'm not staring at him, that I'm not acknowledging him, and that the unicorns aren't grunting or shrieking, they aren't dancing from one foot to another. The Soldiers aren't struggling with them, and they aren't yelling at me any longer. Even the wind seems to have retreated. It is deadly silent.

He whips his head around and gasps, his head tilting back to see the whole of the new unicorn's head towering over us. Something as large and seething as he should surely have made some sound. By the layer of sweat on his skin, the unicorn had been galloping, though none of us had noticed him, heard him, been aware of him at all until he slid into the earth and stopped.

[That's a lie. You've been *ignoring* me!]

I know this Soldier-less unicorn. I'd had a nightmare of him just before Talyn was taken. That's also the name Mom would refer to him by: The Nightmare. And this panting, fuming nightmare stands before me now, snarling, his head lowered, his horn pointed towards me.

My brain has trouble processing him. He's wrong. His color, his body. It's all wrong. Blue sky and fresh green grass, somewhere behind me is snow. I remember running through snow at some point. Natural colors. Normal natural things. Under the dirt and grime and scars of these other demons, they bear normal colors. But The Nightmare is ruthlessly black. A black hole that draws in life and smothers it. In sharp contrast, his mane and tail are a dark red. Not the comforting red of my mother's hair or the rare beauty of the moon That Night, but......the color of something once vital and necessary turned sickly and grotesque.

Something about the *'drawing in and smothering of life'* tugs at me. Something Mom had said, but it was during......it was during The Void......

His chest propels air in short, quick bursts of hot steam. Like breath upon cold air, his scorches the warm wind. Thick, foamy sweat covers his black coat, giving it a burnt sun glow. Red mane, red tail, waving behind him like a flag, as if he needs an announcement. Each breathy growl escaping his mouth and nostrils echoes within my ears, threatening to shatter them.

The Soldier drops me, and the ropes around my chest fall to the grass. I control my gasp for air, and do not turn my gaze or let myself fall despite the exploding pain warring with the increasing weakness in my entire body. The Soldiers try to retreat back a step, but their unicorns manage to fight them and take a unified step in advance, attention fixed on the new unicorn, their god, ready to do whatever he bids.

"Why is he loose?" A Soldier asks shrilly, fear apparent in his broken tone.

"Where did he come from!"

I can't move. The absence of the wind's rage confuses me. This unicorn terrifies me as he had terrified my mother. A chain is thrown over his neck but he doesn't flinch. His eyes pierce through me. [Are you coming or not?]

I back away, unsure if it's the unicorn's eyes and prismatic, golden horn directed at me, his presence invading my head, or the thought of being nearer to him that fills me with terror more. "What?" I stammer. I think I stammered. Did I say it out loud?

[You prefer to remain here?]

"I'm not going with *you!*"

He's huge. My head barely reaches his shoulder. His horn shines like a sword as it juts upward into the sky, his teeth try to hide beneath parted lips. Eyes red as his mane. The ferocity that pulses out of him is worse than all of the others combined. And Mom's voice in my head, *Run away, Lira. Run away from him!*

He took the soul of my unborn sister. Is that right? Did Mom tell me she'd had children before me? Children that are scattered throughout The Forest here? I was so lost when she was talking, I couldn't hold onto the words as she spoke them.

My fate is safer made with the men.

"Ernon, he wants *her!*" a Soldier yells.

"Well he won't get her! Get him secured *now!*"

I bring my knee up sharply and catch the Soldier's groin as he charges me, quickly following that with a blow to his head with my clenched, bound fists. With a grunt he falls sideways. I turn and run, heaving myself up the hill I'd previously stumbled down, somehow managing to neither trip nor slide back down.

At first, I am flanked by a hoard of noise and bodies, but a few strides more, barely halfway up the hill, and I am completely alone.

"They're free! They're *free!*" The odd pitch in the yelled warning makes me stop and look down into the basin of hills. The wind has picked up only slightly, seeming delighted. The Soldiers are scrambling. The muzzles and chains that had once bound their beasts now lay lost in the swaying grass. Their neck braces are gone. The demons are somehow- The Nightmare meets my eyes dully, admitting nothing- completely free, and without any hesitation are picking off the men one by one-

The Nightmare slides into my view, cutting between me and the sights down below.

I can't speak. The screams-

[I will later discuss the insult of the terms 'demon' and 'beast'. Do you plan to just stand there? Get on my back!]

Abruptly, everything stops. My back is tingling, feeling as though a warm summer sun has broken through the clouds and found it. I turn to look over my shoulder, entirely oblivious to the massacre below me, and stare over the hills at the direction I had been running toward when they'd first begun chasing me. East. I had instinctively run east. It's ingrained so deeply into my bones, I can find my way through the hills and trees, through the scattered villages and rumbling lowlands, up the cliff walls to Kholsari, or preferably further to the mountain tops where my mother's family lives: the dragons. My grandparents, uncles and aunts.

Ama, the dragoness, saved my mother when Anin nearly succeeded in killing her, and raised her as her own. Now, after praying and waiting my whole life, now I stand in the same world as they. I feel the same air and am beneath the same suns and moon and sky. Family and safety. All that I've ever wanted.

But on this hill, with his kiss burning my skin, with all the dreams of my childhood a short journey away, my daughter, my lost baby girl, shines brightly within my consciousness, overshadowing all those dreams that no longer matter. I will never see her again, and she is all I want. All I need. What punishment does He get? What guilt does he carry around with him? What pain? Who gets to punish Him?

I close my eyes, letting the tears sting. If not for that one fact— He sent me to The Valley to die— I might do it on my own. Curl inward and welcome my fate. I'm Here. Even if I come to know where they're keeping her, I'm never going to see my daughter again.

The screams echoing off the hills reach my ears and I shiver, gag. That spot I first woke in. Can I find it?

[You aren't listening! They've begun now and they may not be able to stop. *Get on my back!*]

I have to get back to that spot. There has to be a way for me to leave, return to the Other Place. I can't be here without my daughter, without my mother. This isn't right. None of this is right and the screams, the screams-

I have to get back. There has to be a way. I touched our spot on the beach and it sent me here. If I can touch the right spot here, I'll go back.

[Lira! *Stop ignoring me!*]

Ignoring the monotony of the region, I struggle to remember which direction I'd run here from. Which hill did I start on? My body moans 'Not again' while nerves twitch, muscles tense, eager. I hike up the dress but it tangles on the arrow, jarring it horrendously, and won't reach the belt. I drop the hem, sickened, and spit out whatever has risen to my throat. The screams- *Don't look backward. Don't look down the hill. Tune out those sounds.*

I lunge, and sprint away.

[No! What are you-]

Get back to that spot, find the Door that brought me here. Go back. Go back and find my daughter.

The wind is silent as he works against me. The grass whips at my legs and rips away skin as I tear through. They are hands, hands reaching up to keep me here. I keep running. *Find the Door, the Window, the Bridge that'll get me out of here. It's too late. It's too late. I can't be here now.*

My back is on fire. Ghostly things are touching me. Behind me, behind me is east, mountains, dragons, trees. Calling me loudly, shouting that I'm going the wrong way. But this is the wrong place, the wrong time. I can't be here now. I want my daughter. I want Talyn. I just fought Soldiers. I can find my baby girl. Nothing will save those who have her.

The arrow in my leg dances back and forward, bobs up and down with every current and every stride and every single blasted blade of grass. The dress is tangled around my legs, pulling at the shaft of the arrow, shooting bolts of pain up my leg and into my lower back, up my spine, making my body throb with the pain. I yell out and stumble and roll a few times. Each strike upon the earth drives the arrowhead further into my leg, making it jab into my bone over and over.

When I stop rolling I lay still, panting, too stunned to cry. *Pull it out, keep running.* Except that my hands are still bound. I can't grasp my leg. I can't sit up.

Behind me is east, the place I've always wanted to go. Mountains and trees and Ama and Marr. Behind me is *East-*

The black demon oozes coolly onto the hill beside me. [Are you aware that you are going the wrong way?]

I curl onto my side and claw my fingers into the grass, ordering my body to rise, to keep going. "Get away from me!" Get up, keep going, don't stop till I find that spot and I'm back in that damn place.

[We need to leave this area, Lira. Let me help you.]

My legs refuse to obey! I can't get to my feet! "Why would you want to help me? Why would I want you to help me!"

[Because you Called for me to do so.]

"I did no such thing!" I try again to rise but the motion twitches the arrow in the wrong way and orders me back to the earth, trapping my last inhale midway to my lungs. With the pain, I can't draw it in, can't force it out. I can no longer tell where I am, which direction I need to run toward to make this place a bad dream. To make Home a bad dream- Dragons! How can I feel this way? "I don't want to be here. I can't be here!"

[But you are.]

"Make them stop screaming!"

[They have.]

"No they haven't!" I fall forward and throw my bound wrists over my head, using my forearms to plug my ears.

They won't stop once they've begun. I was Touched. Please, please take His scent away.

[I'm not really able to do that, though trust me, I wish I could. You reek of him and his stench is revolting.]

"Where are they?"

[They're gone. The Soldiers are dead and the unicorns are free.]

"The men are still screaming!"

[No, Lira. They're not. They're dead. The unicorns are gone. But we can't stay here. Please, come with me. There could always be more Soldiers. And once they discover the dead ones, or see the unicorns that are now free, they will search these hills in droves for an explanation.]

Blood. Blood everywhere, spilling across the hills towards me. Green to red. My red. My red made evil.

The hills fill with my agonized screams as I attempt to pull the arrow from my thigh. It's imbedded into my bone and won't budge. Dizzy, seeing spots with my head feeling numb and tingly, I fall onto my back and take deep breaths, let the tears fall from my eyes, down my cheeks, into the grass. When I've stored enough energy, I rise sharply up and break the splintered shaft almost near the arrowhead. My thigh explodes in livid, heated pain. I bite down hard enough to break my teeth but leap to my feet instead. I have to get back.

Blood, blood pools around my feet but the arrow's still there. There's a rock, a bullet, in my shoulder. What's an arrow in my leg? I need to run. Need to find that Door. Get back, wake up. Find Talyn.

The Nightmare's mouth clamps over my shoulder and he tosses me into the air. I scream instinctively as I sail through wind and land with a thud on his back. Before I can react, the demon-beast bolts forward. Instinctively, my legs press around his girth and my bound hands fumble through his mane to grab a fistful of red. "What are you doing!"

[You can't go back that way, Lira. And you can't stay here.] He sprints away from where I was heading, going forward in a great horrible lurch.

With short, jerky strides, he crests the hill south of where we had stood and then begins a quick, frightful descent down another hill, making my insides fly up into my throat. My fingers tangle themselves deeper into mane and I stare numbly through pointed black ears, shocked and silenced.

I'm trapped. I'm trapped in the dream that died years ago. Far, far ahead, just off to the right, hangs the moon with the suns at her sides, stretching across the horizon. Suspended in one long stride, I forget everything, my eyes captivated by that wonderful, welcome sight Mom had once danced beneath.

I'm in Home.

The hill and the beast beneath me —

[*Stop that!*]

—drop sharply, forcing my insides once again to go where they shouldn't be. I grope frantically for his mane. Every stride he takes reverberates in my head. Every rise and fall of the hills below us amplifies in my stomach, threatening to turn it and the rest of me inside out. And the screams......still bouncing off the hills......

Up and down, on and on and on, never ending, like rocking violently back-forth. *Back, slam, forth.* Down, crunch, up. And the nightmares. The nightmares.

IN THE VOID

I BALL MY FISTS AND FIGHT, punching and twisting, trying to keep myself from becoming restrained. I can hear her, hear Talyn screaming for me and I'm screaming back for her. She's being carried down the hall but hands and bodies are crowding around me, keeping me from running after her. When she disappears around a corner, I scream for my father: "Mihn! Mihn!" He doesn't come. There's chaos and clatter. Shouting and grabbing, hands pulling me away, tying my hands behind my back. Where's Mom! Men in uniforms again!

Mom charges through, elbowing and snarling her way......

"Lira, Lira, it's ok! You're having a nightmare. You're in your bed. This thing is poisoning your blood. I'm right here, love. I'm right here."

She vanishes. I drive the arrow through booted feet again and again, waiting for my daughter to drop from their arms back into mine. May, my childhood friend, is trapped under their feet, shielding her face......

"Elaar, if you won't call the police, I will!"

May's calling for more Soldiers! "Talyn!" I scream, fighting the hands that push me down. The explosion sounds again and something tears through my shoulder. It burns, and my ghost of a father is trying to dam the blood running rivers from my body.

"They are the ones who did this, May!"

"Those weren't real police! You have to take her to the hospital. They need to get that bullet out! She probably needs a transfusion with all the blood she's lost!"

"No, May! If it's taken out she'll die. I need you to sit with her. Do not let anyone inside the house."

I hear their voices- my mother's and May's- but I can't see them anymore. I can't see Talyn. I see uniforms and men, I see gold and blood. Not even my father can reach me here.

"Elaar, where are you going? You can't leave her here like this!"

"Call your grandfather, May. He'll know what to give her."

"Elaar, he's a Chinese herbalist. It's not real medicine!"

"How long has that 'fake' medicine been in use?"

"Centuries."

"As it's been used in my Home. As it's been used on you countless times. Call your grandfather. Do not leave her. With you here, she'll be fine."

"Elaar, you don't have a phone! How can I call him?"

"There's a phone downstairs."

"Since when?"

"Since they attacked her! The house did it."

"The house? Elaar, houses don't just-"

"I have to go, May. I have to find Talyn for her. Do not let anyone inside. If someone tries, use this. Kill them."

"Elaar! I can't-"

"Look what they did to her! They took her baby, May. They took her baby! Do you remember when they tried to take you, when they took Lira? If they come back, *you kill them.*"

Grabbing, pulling, hitting. Mom's sucked into the uniforms and disappears. I cry out for her not to leave. If she'd been here when they came, they'd have never stepped out of our doors again. Talyn's screaming, she's screaming......

My hand is squeezed and I try again to wrench free. Dragons, what are they doing to my baby?

"Lira, Lira can you hear me? I'm right here. Elaar will be back. You're safe in your bed, in your house and I'm right here.

"I remember them, Lira. I remember when they took us, took you. Your mom will find your daughter, Lira, and I'm going to stay here with you. Can you hear me? Lira, please don't die. You have to fight. Talyn will need you when Elaar brings her back. Don't die, Lira."

May's voice, Soldiers, uniforms, my blood- it all disappears and turns to green, vibrant green like my grandmother's scales, and I think, maybe, maybe she's come back for us.

But the green is not scales, it is grass, grass growing tall as my body. Sharp green blades that reach and grab and slice.

There's a city in the middle of green. In a flattened area below the hills. A sand-colored wall. A fortress. A manor. A tower. Ravery, my mother's birthplace.

Talyn's in Ravery!

I have to hack through the heavy doors bigger than the house with a sword until the doors bleed. Down the cobbled street with Soldiers making licentious gestures alongside me. Talyn's in Ravery!

Soldiers wearing blue uniforms and black boots and shiny gold five pointed stars surround me again. There's a black unicorn, a nightmare, standing behind them.

Talyn's in Ravery.

*

Back-slam-forth, a jagged rocking that pauses when back passes through nothingness and slams into solid. *Back-slam-forth.* This physical pain I can cause myself soothes the deadness, numbs, for a brief respite, the burning in my shoulder, the horror in my soul.

Moments, weeks, months. It's all a blur. I huddle on the bed and stare through the window, waiting for the first sign of red moonlight. He must come, He must.

When He does, I'll kill him.

Mom is drifting away, worse than before Talyn was born. Worse than before the night He came and found me. She can't find Talyn like she'd found me. There is guilt ripping across her eyes but I can't open my mouth to tell her......I can't hold onto a thought long enough to process speech and lack of blame for her.

Mihn is worried and I am drifting myself, away from Mom, deeper than her, and I stare out the window and I rock so that my back slams into something hard and strong and impenetrable. Today, if a today exists anymore, I no longer feel the pain.

Back-slam-forth back-slam-forth back-slam-forth......

Lost. She is gone, He is gone, and I am lost.

Mihn took and hid all the weapons after I'd set fire to His clothes in the center of the room. Afraid I'd harm myself. No one told him there's nothing. There's nothing.

Back-slam-forth back-slam-forth back-slam-forth......

Somewhere in a pause, Mom's voice flows to me from somewhere far away. It sounds like a song but she doesn't sing it, and the words sound as though they should be familiar, or maybe they are merely well-known to her. I've never heard them. She says it twice, three times, four, I lose count, until she sees that I'm struggling to listen, to hold onto the sound of her voice and her words and form understanding.

"When the single moon bleeds
and an age is at an end
The Year of the Dragon shall begin
guiding a man of ancient powers born
To the child misplaced.

"Two lives.
One breath.
Three.

"She who was raised in alien lands
Will one day return
with the touch to soothe the dragon
and the words to tame the unicorn.

"Love Him whose skin gleams red,
For he is your daughter's guardian
Whose life is forever entwined with hers.

"Lira, daughter of my soul. I know what you feel. I know it. It hasn't left me. You've been ripped apart and thrown back together. Your soul is now on the outside, bare and vulnerable, oversensitive and blistered raw and you can't cry or scream long or hard enough to make the ache go away. Blackness is so much more enticing. You pray it'll accept you, take you in, and let you vanish in its cover.

"When I came here, I wanted the water. It was your father's element. It was the first thing I saw when I opened my eyes. It was so large, that for awhile I thought I was in the water already, surrounded by a soft blue. Mihn felt so safe and secure near water, even if it was just a puddle of leftover rain or a sole drop of dew slowly traveling down a leaf. So much patience. He took pleasure in those simple things. They reminded him of the beauty of living, when our days were filled with mostly violence and chaos.

"I wanted that water, I wanted to wade in until I could no longer touch the ground and no longer know how far above my head the surface lay. I wanted to breathe it into my lungs. They burned, they burned so badly. I didn't understand what had happened, where I was. Where is Mihn? It's impossible that I should still be alive when he is dead. How can I breathe if he isn't mixed with my air?

"Every time the water touched my toes, you'd move. So I'd retreat back to the beach and stare, waiting for some sign, some communication to tell me I hadn't been cast off. I began to believe I'd caused too many problems, and they sent me away to finally have some peace. Without me, the Soldiers would leave the trees, and Ama and Draco, Aril and Hozar wouldn't have to be bothered with the troubles I'd brought them. They could return to their real families, their true offspring. I'd be nothing but a passing memory of a dream.

"And then you'd move again. No matter what, I had to ensure you'd get back to Home. I couldn't go into the water. I couldn't sit and stare and waste away. I thought of those words- *When the single moon bleeds*— I repeated them over and over again.

"It was the promise Hozar had given me to keep me tied to life. It was about you. And after you were born, I realized it meant that This Place isn't permanent. For you. You won't be here long, Lira, daughter of my soul.

"This isn't the life I chose for you. I thought, hoped— by my pain, by my horror— I'd relieve you of ever knowing this. You kept me from sinking into my grief in so many different ways, love. When they took me to Kholsari, The Wizard spoke those words to me just before the Soldiers attacked again. In that instant, for the first time, I felt you in me. I felt Mihn still alive, inside my skin, right then a complete part of my body.

"In those first and last days we had, I use to tell him I wished I could just crawl into his skin to feel him all around me, but in the end, it was he who came into mine. Did you feel that, Lira? Do you remember feeling that with Him? He crawled into your skin and produced your daughter. Remember that feeling, Lira. Draw upon it.

"I knew where you were going that night. I knew who you would find. I wished I could have given you the Preparation I'd been given. I didn't want you to be afraid. But He was supposed to take you Home that night.

"You have four brothers, Lira. You almost had a sister." I stop rocking. She keeps talking. "I didn't know what I was doing. I didn't know what to do with this body I even now feel so trapped in. It's wrong. It's all wrong. This isn't who I am. It's dangerous to be in this human, female body-

"Something kept driving me into willing arms and even at the last one I couldn't understand how a human child grew and then came out of my body. The oldest two are twins. And then another boy, and another. Mihn was so furious with me through those years, but we were both still merely children. He wouldn't speak to me for weeks each time I became obviously pregnant, nor for days after each one was born. But he always did as I asked and found someone from the fathers' family to take the babies.

"And then-

"Mihn's aunt was sick and I went to care for her. When it came time for me to leave, Mihn became nearly irate. I'd never seen him like that. I should have taken him up on his offer- I ran away instead, to prove him wrong, to ignore the other things he'd shouted at me. I knew I should've called for one of my siblings to carry me back home. I was due soon, but I was confused and I was angry. I was going to walk all the way to the mountains. But I ran into a unicorn who'd gotten lost in the woods, and when it charged I killed it. I turned and there was The Nightmare, the unicorn god. He just stared at me, sucking the life out of me and the baby. I ran until Mihn found me and carried me to Kholsari. And she was born, and she was dead.

"I'd never known grief until then. Regret. Fear. Cold. She was so small, so quiet, so still. I'd held the others after they were born, but I never felt like a mother. I never associated the act of making them, my growing body, or the pain of delivery to their irrevocable tie to me. They were human babies. Human babies who were going to go back to the human fathers who made them. I am not human. I could not be their mother.

"Holding her was different. She wasn't warm, she didn't move, didn't search for me, didn't make any sound. She'd come from my body. She'd moved inside me, shared every meal I ate. A human baby girl came from my body but she didn't move. In that instant, I was aware of myself, that I was not born from nor would I ever become a dragon.

"Aril cleaned her and wrapped her in a blanket and tied it with this thin pink ribbon, but her lips were blue. She was so small, so beautiful. She had red hair like mine. I couldn't accept that she was dead.

"The thought of cremating her in the dragons' way horrified me. I begged and pleaded with Mihn not to let it happen. So he took she and I into his arms and carried us away. He buried her beneath a large old tree near his old village. He use to climb that tree as a child with his brothers. He assured me she'd be a star in the sky, surrounded and watched after by his family.

"She comes to me in dreams. She looks like me. I still talk to her. She sees you, watches you, knows you as her sister. I think of the boys a lot. Being here makes everything final. Knowing I'll never see them has lodged into me with a menacing finality. If able to do things differently, would I have?

"I dream about the boys, too. I see them grown. I see them with families of their own. I wonder if they were ever told about me, that they came from my blood, that for a time we shared the same body. Would they know me if they ever saw me? Would they care about the woman who handed them away without any regret or any feeling? I hope the Soldiers never found them. I hope the Soldiers never found them. I hope the Soldiers never found them. I hope......"

I blink. Breathe.

"They were all born in my parents' cave. Except for the girl. She was born in my room at Kholsari. That's where Mihn brought the fathers' representative, in the little ante-room with the crib set up in the middle. Mihn always stood stiffly in the shadows. So angry. So upset with me. I never asked why the fathers didn't come themselves.

"Mihn, my Mihn, was there for her birth. He held me, cradled me against him. It was much later that I remembered how safe I had felt, how he'd molded himself around me. I never felt that before- so much comfort from a human body. I never acknowledged what I felt around him, and then when I did……

"It would have been like that with you, Lira. He'd have been with us through every moment. His would have been the first hands to touch you, to take hold of you and begin you in a life outside me. His would have been the first face you saw, the second heart you'd have heard beat, and his would have been the first kiss you received."

Mihn smiles sadly from the corner, streaks of tears lining his cheeks. His *was* the first face I saw, the first kiss I received. Though he was killed before I was born, his was still the second heart I heard beat.

"I wish I could've given that to him……"

Then my father is kneeling before me, eyes intense, inches from mine. The vibrant feel of his hands on my knees stops my shivering, my rocking. The only other time I physically felt him was when he was trying to stop the bleeding. Mom is still talking— low and soft— but my eyes are held locked with my father's as he signs to me:

Live. Fight. Don't give in. Talyn is not dead, is not lost for good. Daughter, my other love, do you hear me? Come out of this. Come out of this. He was deaf when he was alive, and while death has given him the ability to walk through walls and vanish into the air, he regards speaking as useless.

I stare into his silvery eyes, swirling like a tornado, not blinking, not breathing, the trembling in my lip the only movement to betray me. *I am lost. Do not find me. I can't be saved without her. I don't want to be.*

He grabs hold of my face in his hands and holds me in the present for what feels like too long, and too short. He releases me to sign again: *How can you be lost? I'm looking right at you.*

I'm lost. I'm lost.

"I never told you that prophecy. I didn't want you to think that your life was predetermined, because it's not, no matter what words are spoken or however they seem to be true. Hearing it now, I want you to see that nothing has ended. Life has more to give you. Has good it owes you."

My eyes shift back to the window, searching, waiting, and I feel the blow when my back slams once again into the wall, and I hear the wall splinter and crack.

3

I SEE NOTHING BUT HEAVY, SUFFOCATING BLACKNESS that drinks everything in without giving anything back. The wind whispers, howls, or screams around my head, yanking at strands of my tangled hair. I ignore it and stare, unblinking, ahead of me as though I can see.

A jagged horizontal strip of momentary brightness streaks across what I understand to be the line between sky and earth some miles ahead, giving a brief, doubtful view of something. Buildings? Trees? Why am I pointed towards it?

I inhale cautiously. The air is pungent with a wet earthy smell. Earth into sky, sky into air: Rain. Heavy, single, large drops of rain splatter upon my shoulders.

Something below me moves. A unicorn! "Get off me!" I twist and turn and fall sideways off the demon's back.

[I'm not *on* you,] a voice growls, agitated. The fall to the ground is further than I would have expected- if I'd had a mind to pay any attention- and the landing thrusts my elbow into my side, just under my ribs. I gasp from the added blinding pain from the arrow striking the ground as well, but struggle more to untangle my legs from something to get onto my feet. Damn dress!

[Are you done? That was a bit of an overreaction.]

"Go away!"

[If you can prove to me that you can care for yourself, I will.]

"I am perfectly capable of fending for myself!"

[I believe I said 'care', not 'fend'. Get up and walk. Find yourself shelter. Eat something. Then, I'll leave.]

I flatten onto my back, trying hard not to cry. Raindrops strike my face like malicious flicks of a finger. *Incompetent. Touched. Worthless. Abandoned. Thrown. A. Way.* "I hate you."

[I think we can safely say that who you choose to love and who you choose to hate have been ridiculously off.]

"No, we can safely say that I completely hate you, you evil, repulsive beast!"

The grass is long and sticky, coming over my head and sticking to my shoulders and arms, the sides of my face, wrapping around my legs. Thinking about my legs makes the right one begin to throb. I can't sit up to inspect it. Why is it hurting?

[You were struck by an arrow, remember?]

Don't talk to me.

Lightning pierces through clouds above me. I want to pick my head up and use the flash of light to inspect whatever lay ahead, but my hair has rooted into the ground and my head won't budge. "Are you here to kill me?"

[Am I allowed to speak to you now?]

"Are you?"

[No, Lira. I'm not here to harm you in any way.]

"You know my name?"

[I do.]

I can't feel my legs. I can't feel any part of my body.

[You ran and fought very hard. There's no question that you can defend yourself.]

I can't see anything. Dark and night have never threatened me before.

[It is quite black. But it's not threatening you. It's protecting you.]

Thunder races Lightning overhead. I can't decide who has won.

[Get on my back, Lira. I'll carry you to shelter.]

How long has it been? How long have I been here?

[Only a few hours.]

My thigh burns.

[You bled all over me.]

"Stop listening to my thoughts! They're mine! You kidnapped—" The word, the memory, chokes up the rest of my words. "Just, leave me here, please? Please just leave me here."

[You don't know where you are.]

"Does it matter?"

[Everything matters.]

"Leave me here!" I wish I could fade here. Close my eyes and drift away.

Movement beside me. I open my eyes and wait for them to help.

The boundary between night and the unicorn is a thin one. I'm in one big black ball of shadows within shadows. Night to camouflage a demon, how helpful.

[If you don't stop with the insults……]

The fragile boundary moves again. The large unicorn body steps partially out of the night and begins to sink down beside me. Long, muscled legs fold beneath his body. I jump. That horn. That horn- where's my knife? Will a dagger do anything against a unicorn?

"What are you doing?"

[I'm getting settled. I ran pretty hard too, you know. How long do you plan on staying here? It's going to get very wet and very cold. And just so you know, you look horribly fragile despite your behavior on the hills.]

His gold horn sparkles with a dim light. The prismatic raindrops holding onto it scatter at the next boom of thunder. I stare, transfixed, waiting for it to happen again.

Scents of earth, the promise and yearning for rain and the softening grass pull my head down, bombarding my nostrils and sanity. Cold, damp ground permeates through the thin dress and chills my skin with more than a touch of spring frost.

I close my eyes, bring my bound hands up to my collar bone and clasp my fingers together so tightly my knuckles throb. It's not spring. It's autumn. It's Talyn's birthday.

[It's been a long time since you've eaten.]

I turn my face away from him. Lightning comes again but stays longer. Through the grass I catch a better glimpse of whatever waits in the distance, but not enough to know what it is. "I just want to sleep. Sleep until you and everything else goes away."

[You can sleep all you want, but nothing will have changed. It's going to get very cold out here very soon, Lira. Get on my back. Let me continue to carry you. It's not far. It's just ahead.]

I roll over onto my side, but I can't pull my legs up to my chest, and so I keep falling forward until I'm almost flat on my stomach. "These clothes aren't mine. I don't want them on my body."

Lightning again brings a glimpse of what now looks like small, irregular mountains. Whatever it is leaps across the flatland towards me; calls out to me by my own name and a name— or a title— I'm not familiar with. I jerk back. The ghostly current carries Death's smell. I relax again. Can I answer? Slip into night soundless, with morning leaving no trace I was ever here? I don't want night. Night brings day. This will be real. I don't want this to be real. "Where are you taking me?"

[Just a place to sleep. Come, Lira. One movement at a time. And then you can sleep, I swear.]

I don't want to move, don't want to sleep. Want to sink into the earth and vanish. "Take me back."

[I can't,] the unicorn whispers sorrowfully into my head.

"I hurt."

[We'll see to your leg as soon as we can.]

"They took my baby," I whimper. Hearing me speak it ripples right back over me as though I'm kneeling and bleeding in the hallway again, screaming until my soul and every window in the house shatters. But this time I can't scream. I lay on my back and watch the blinding darkness, feel the same emptiness inside me. Where was I before I woke here, after she was taken? All I remember is darkness, like this, and feeling so abandoned. "He wasn't there, Nightmare, and Others came and took our daughter. And now I'm here. I hurt, unicorn. I hurt so much." On cue, my shoulder begins burning, the pain trailing down to mingle with the fire shooting out from the arrow. I'd had my arrow aimed at their chests but I'd hesitated. I had decided to call out to Him first instead.

[I'm very sorry, Lira. I'm here to help you, I swear.]

"Is a swear more reliable than a promise?"

[I take it the Ass You Reek Of made you a promise he did not keep.]

"It's too late. He's three years too late."

[You don't smell three years distant of him. His smell on you is *overwhelming*-] He must have felt my glare through the night.

"If I'm that revolting, go away!"

[It's not you. It's Him. But I think I'll be able to tolerate it. Eventually. I swear to you, Lira, that I am here to help you. And yes, a swear is more reliable than a promise.]

The night has given in to cold, and the large plops of rain fall more frequently. Unicorns rear and shriek inside my head, my arm is still throwing the dagger compulsively, again and again and again, pulling my arm into repulsive flesh with a sickening draw I can't control. Over and over. Blood and screams cover the maddening green and leak out through the blackness. Where's the green of my grandmother? Is she here? Would she know me? How will I convince her that I am my mother's daughter? Mom never kept her children, and I look more like my father than I do my mother. My mother has vibrant, wonderful red hair. The color of my alleged guardian dragon.

There's no stars. There's no moon. We're in the middle of something, in the middle of a storm, someplace in the void between thunder, lighting, rain and earth, in the void where life and worlds are born, where chaos is on pause.

[Lira. We need to leave this spot before the rain really hits. I need you to move. Crawl to me and get on my back so I can carry you. You need to let go of whatever you feel for me. We can't be out here when the rain hits.]

I don't want to move. I don't care about the rain. I do not want to go to him, to sit upon his back again and endure that nightmare of a ride. But I find myself moving anyway.

Who would think crawling would hurt so much? The cold has seeped into my bones and prevents my fingers from moving. That or I'd interlaced them together so tightly I broke them. Working with the coils that bind my arms together at the wrists, I plow my elbows into the earth and pull myself forward.

Moving is painful, the drive to do so is tiring and doubtful. Is this what babies endure in the instinct to rise onto feet and walk? I never got to see Talyn accomplish that. She'd been trying and practicing so hard. Was there anyone to encourage her, to provide arms to catch her?

I think of the people who have her, and the thought of them being loving and gentle with her is such an impossibility-

[Lira, Lira take a breath. Just breathe. Don't think that way. Keep moving. You're almost here. Breathe, Lira. Breathe.]

I scream. I can't rip at the earth and grass again, can't slam backward into a wall, so instead I rock back and forth on my knees and forearms, groaning, wailing, hitting my forehead against the ground. I want to hit something, punch something until my fists turn bloody and my bones shatter, but my hands are bound! And I probably already broke them. I howl again.

The unicorn stretches toward me. [I wish I could take you back, but I don't have that Gift and it won't help, Lira. You won't find her. Not yet.]

I press my face into the earth and sob.

[You're here for a reason. Get back on your feet, start taking care of yourself and find what that reason is. Then you'll find her. I swear. Except now, in this instant, we need to move before the rain comes. You have to get up. You have to walk or crawl toward me and get onto my back. Sit if you can or just throw yourself over my side. We don't have far to go. I won't be running so it'll be a smoother ride. We're in The Valley, Lira. Were you told about this? Lira, were you told?]

I nod, containing the sobs. The sticky blades of grass cut into my forehead. I nod again, just to feel the pain.

[We have to get you someplace safe. Then you can sleep, or scream, or cry however long you need. Reach for me. I'm not far from you. Lira? Lira, are you listening? Can you reach for me?]

I nod again. "Ye- yes."

My fists slap onto warm skin covered in a thin layer of damp hair. The skin underneath twitches, and then solidifies into a goal. My forehead falls onto the rope at my wrists and I breathe slow and hard, count, wait, try again, stop again. Arrowed leg against the unicorn's side. Wait. Leg over back. Wait. Use good leg to push body up and over. Wait.

I don't realize I've succeeded until my body ascends upward into the sky and I feel him beneath me. I tense, but he rises to his feet gracefully. My face sinks into mane. Red mane. Red is *my* color- Breathe, wait. He begins to walk as the lightning streaks the sky and again illuminates the strange shadows ahead.

I think I fall asleep, because the next thing I'm aware of is the sound of the hooves below me striking upon stone. I wake with a start and sit up in time to see two large, tall cylindrical structures jump out of the darkness at either side of me before diving back into the night as the unicorn continues on. I startle, duck. I look back but don't see anything, can't see where we'd come from or judge how long ago it was that I'd had to crawl back to him. It's so dark. My eyes are open as wide as they'll go, yet I still see only black.

Lightning, along with a searing headache, only allow me twisted images of some type of ruins.

The wind is mostly gone. Where are we? I can clearly hear the stone the unicorn is picking his way over; he walks much more carefully here (wherever we are) than on the hills. He pauses, considers and tests his footing before walking left or right in a circuitous way rather than a straight, decisive path.

I shiver, as much from the cold and the coming downpour as from the ghostly atmosphere. The wind is gone, as though we're enclosed in something. The air is heavy and sticks to the lining of my lungs like smoke. It burns my nose like ash.

After awhile, the unicorn finally stops. [We are done for the night. You can get down now.]

I glance carefully over his side again. It looks like we're inside the night and he's hovering within the black with nothing beneath his feet. If I jump, will I ever land or will I just perpetually fall? I want to take a chance and leap off and end the uncomfortable experience of sitting on his back, but, looking down, I am unable to see beyond my knees. Below that, my legs are just gone. At least, I can't feel or see them at all.

[There is a ground, though it's not particularly kind. I can't lower down. It's slick and I won't be able to get back on my own feet if I do. Just slide down. Hang onto my mane if you need to.]

My legs have been molded around the beast's girth so tightly and for long enough that they've forgotten how they should be. My knees refuse to meet and my legs collapse beneath me as soon as my toes touch upon something solid and cold and wet, introducing my body to a jumble of crumbled stone and broken patches of grass mixed in with a pebbled soil.

[I'm told that happens.]

Thunder rumbles again. I prepare for lightning, for possibly getting a quick glance in which to study my surroundings. Only no lightning follows. The unicorn walks off; I can hear his hooves upon the stone every so often. I crawl toward where he had last been, reaching for him, but he's too far away. I swallow and crouch, straining my ears, my eyes, any sense I can to figure out where we are. This dark is not comforting. I want the house. Who'd have ever thought I'd beg to be back in that house? I've hated it all my life, yet now I call it comfort.

My eyes grow use to the dark, and the blackness loses its monotony enough for me to distinguish changes in the density and begin to form a mental picture. There is some type of wall ahead of me. I take small crawling slides, stopping often to re-estimate my proximity, my ears straining, listening to the way the rain hits my surroundings in order to tell how close or how far I am and which way through the blackness to go.

The ground beneath me changes, becoming more solid and slippery. It's old stone, slimy by age and frequent spring rain and newly melted snow. My skin senses the nearness of something. The pitch of the rain is lower. My right side feels no drops. I take a breath and push out with my good leg. One long stretch and my right side edges up against a bitterly cold, dripping wet stone wall. I scoot my hips closer and leave my arrowed leg to lay flat before me. Somewhere beyond an unseen barrier, the wind is still howling. I track the thunder reaching closer, till it shakes the ground beneath me and the wall at my side. Feels like unicorns running across hills towards me. I close my eyes, swallowing the lump in my throat, and shiver back into a fitful half-sleep.

THE MORNING AFTER

A BRIGHTNESS PAST MY CLOSED EYES. I open them, frown at the white glow hiding behind a sky of clouds. Surely today calls for an exposed, glorious sun?

The night floods back into my mind, bringing a heated flush to my tired body. I stretch, inhale deeply, causing his warm cape to slip from its position around me. I fold my arms back up to my throat, curling the cape back over me and inhale again, a long slow draw of scent, of air tinged with him. This is the last moment holding onto last night, this morning. This is our last day, our last morning waking up in This Place. He's taking us to *Home*. Hopefully my father doesn't truly kill him. What else was he mumbling? Something about beating him into the ground being a lot of fun.

He's bringing us Home. He'll have to be forgiven.

Don't think about that. Smell, feel the air, the morning, this moment, him sleeping beside me. Inhale- why do I smell winter? Last night was summer. It was warm. I know it was summer.

Bare branches overhead sway and clash against each other in the wind. Winter? *Last night was New Year's Eve,* they struggle to remind me. *Today is the first Day of the*

Dragon. The cold wind hits me at all sides, running up my bare legs through a fold in his cape. I throw the edge of it further over me, sealing it shut, and turn to where I last remember him laying.

And turn to my other side.

And behind me.

In front of me.

Beyond me, past the trees.

Lake *Mish-ah-gun* stretches out to the horizon, a cold, gray expanse with bitter blocks of ice churning and colliding in the sharp waves. I scan the beach, seeing only a few people out in the cold early dawn. No sign of him. Where could he be? He must've risen much earlier. Maybe went for a walk. The gloomy sky and the cold are disquieting. I could've sworn last night was warm. And beautiful. I know I didn't dream it.

I stretch toward the pants the girls had forced me to wear, tugging them from the tangle of branches they'd been tossed into, and pull them on, standing to button them up. He'd been confused by these, by the way they fastened and zipped. It presented him with a challenge he was only too willing to conquer.

The memory seduces a flush-filled smile to play upon my face as another rush of heat swells up from my abdomen, dispelling the cold with a blossoming dismissal.

He'd worn a type of loose pants, drawstring, with no seams. They were so soft. A garment only wizards make; a garment demanded into being, rather than laboriously made and sewn. They're formed of want and magic and therefore seamless, material-less. But it's been centuries since there's been any real magic in Home. The families who'd been returned to the manors to protect Mom had only meager gifts. Nothing to be called magical or useful. Why did Ama think they could or would protect her?

His sweater, and the shirt he had worn beneath it, lay at my feet. Several feet away in the undergrowth await his socks and boots.

I look back at the beach, the falling snow, the shivering Others. Where is he? Without his boots, his clothes, his cape? Maybe it wasn't snowing when he left. But it's always bitterly, bitingly cold in This Place. Especially so close to The Lake. Is he so bold that he'd stride out completely nude? That's not allowed here. And then there's frostbite......

I pull on May's skimpy shirt and top it with his, and then his sweater and his cape. I clutch his socks and boots against my body, warming them up for him as last night replays in sensual memories made up of emotion and quick flashes of touches or words rather than a factual recording of time. I look out through the trees to the living lake, to the beach. How will I call for him? By what name?

The thought casts me back upon a tree. What does it matter, truly? I'll have him tell me his name every day for the rest of our lives.

I lean my head back upon the trunk behind me, pondering that prospect: every day, every night given to him. It took Mom half her life to finally accept Mihn. It took me only a moment to accept Him.

I pull away from the tree, smiling still, refreshed, and give my hair a quick ruffle with my fingers to set free any trapped dirt or leaves. Now I have to begin that promise. Everything had happened without hesitation or question, as though something larger than us was pushing us together, trying to ensure we happened quickly, sealing us together before we had time to ponder. Not as though Fate or Nature or Whatever had need to be so forceful. I chose my fate with one look at him.

Oh, when he spoke! His voice. My name from his lips took on another meaning. I close my eyes again, empty my thoughts, and gather in every last essence of this space- *The Alcove*. Our Alcove- listen one last time to the wind, the lake, and the strange surrounding quiet. I'd thought I'd heard birds, once, last night. But it's now so eerily quiet.

Stepping out of the trees is like passing through a gate that takes me from one world to a colder one beyond. It makes me shiver uncontrollably, but the shivering stops abruptly when I realize that there's no footprints. I trample my way back into the grove, stop briefly before the bare indent we had burned into the ground, and go out the other side into that thicket of trees. Nothing.

A deep, crushing fear rises within me, squeezing my throat shut. No, he wouldn't have left me.

Even as I think it, the lack of his presence consumes me. It's completely, undeniably gone. He's completely, undeniably gone. The air is empty.

Another deep breath and I pick a direction, pulling his cape tight around me and weeping from the smell of him suddenly upon me. He wouldn't have left me. Not here, not alone. He's taking us Home. He promised. He wouldn't have left me.

5

THUNDER BOOMS AGAIN SO LOUDLY that I startle awake. Before the echo has completely died down, the skies spread apart and the rain pours down; strong, hard, as if The Lake has just been upended over me. I bring my good leg in closer and hide my face in the alien dress that smells of Someone I Will Not Acknowledge. My thigh throbs. My bound wrists burn. The cold and the rain make my body tense up rigid and painful. And then there's the shivering.

I am in Home. I am in The Valley. I killed Soldiers. I lost my daughter. I cursed His lack of a name. This is the beginning of my punishment.

I try to keep from thinking, but thoughts wind around in violent spins within my head. I never ever envisioned my Home-coming to be like this. Am I so contemptible that only a unicorn wants me?

The downpour frees my strain and I cry along with the sky. The unicorn returns and the rain suddenly stops falling upon me. I push the hair out of my eyes, seeing only black, yet I know he is standing over me, shielding me.

"Why? Why are you helping me? You smell—" my voice cracks. I wipe the tears from my eyes, only to have the rainwater pour down my face. "I'm......I'm......"

[In need. I care not what your body has done, only what hurts your soul. This is where you are meant to be, despite the price you were forced to pay. You are safe now, Lira. I'm here to watch over you until you see that.]

His words bounce back at me strangely. An echo within the words whispers into my thoughts. Sounds of rain and wind and thunder are distant. He has formed a Shield around us. It will keep everyone away: Soldiers, the dragons—

"He brought me here."

Silence.

"You're keeping Him from finding me."

The unicorn shifts his weight upon his feet. [If I am?]

My thoughts carry me into another trance-like, sleepless sleep, comforted by the irony that a unicorn is keeping me safe, is keeping Him away.

*

"Yes mom, I'll eat before I go. Don't say goodbye. I won't stay long."

[What was that?]

The golden glaze that shades the hallway disintegrates like grains of sand falling through a sieve. Mom's puzzled face becomes accusatory as she stares at me: A unicorn! That unicorn? Mihn pulls out his sword but he is staring over my head. Did you not notice? He asks.

What?

Where, he corrects.

The grainy golden light fades, becoming thin, arching green brush strokes, and Mom is smiling forlornly, waving goodbye as she fades away......

[You talk in your sleep.]

A monstrous roar has followed out of my dream, further irritating the tremendous throbbing that has settled in my entire body. Mostly asleep, I reach beside me, but He's not there. My eyes are swollen. Where am I? I push myself up, my body aching as though I'd spent the night on stone-

My brain puzzles over the stone under my hands, the crumbling stone wall at my side. Past me it's green, except for what remains of a giant circular wall far in the distance. I try to kneel but when I lay my hands- swollen and painful- down for support they buckle under me. My right leg erupts in fire. I cry out and fall over to my side.

Why won't my body work? Where am I? My eyes burn. My head is uncomfortably swollen. Was I crying again?

Something like metal scrapes across something like stone. It's going to spark a fire. Off to my side, among two collapsed stone walls stands a placid, though not entirely patient, large black unicorn.

I flatten onto the ground, the cold and wet diving up into my back. *Yesterday.*

[You slept through yesterday. Soldiers were *two* days ago. Do you remember what's happened?]

"I'd prefer to forget," I scowl. The wind tugs at me: *Listen. Listen. Look:* green land beyond the broken walls. Blue overhead. No buildings, no wires, no poles, no metal things that rip across it. Just blue. There is nothing to impede my view, to separate me from the blue. It stretches on as far as the land below it, with tiny, unwanted me sandwiched in the middle. It invokes mixed feelings: do I sit back and admire, do I huddle and worry? The openness is too exposing, like I need to guard all sides at once. Any minute now, more Soldiers can come. He can come. How safe am I in these ruins? These ruins that reek of smoke and death.

"I don't like where you've brought me." Remembrance. A faint, buried memory in the earth and in me.

[Good morning, Lira. How generous of you to be concerned over my health. It really was a long gallop, with you slumped over my back, hacking and trying to vomit and screaming insults at me the whole way. It was absolutely no trouble to secure a good place for you to rest. Nor was it harrowing to stand guard over you the last few nights while you slept, ensuring no Soldiers- or Him- discovered you! *No need to thank me!*] he yells, stomping the front tip of his hoof so that it does spark upon the stone. His tail whips out at his side as he frowns down at me. He shifts his weight and abruptly turns away. The sound of his hooves, sometimes chiming on stone, sometimes making soft drum sounds on earth, is somehow entrancing. [You're not supposed to be hostile, you know!]

"I'm not hostile!"

[This is friendly?]

"You're a *unicorn*! Your kind is the one that's hostile!"

He turns his irritated face over his back. [With good reason! At least I wake in a better mood than you.]

"I don't know where it is I've woken!"

[You are in The Valley, Lira. You know this! Stop ignoring what's in front of you.]

The bright beautiful day stretches out before me, like a mirage of something that isn't there. Wind in my ears, whispering sometimes, howling others; gentle one touch, abusive the next. The wall, a bitter defiance, like He, standing there before me, daring me. Untouchable, whereas I was left to feel all his wounds and the wounds cast at us because of him. To make my life worse, He brings me here now, not when he had promised while holding me so lovingly close in his arms with the moon bright and full above us and the night so lovely we could only whisper. His heart under my fingertips and I had believed him. I'd believed him. Now. He waits until now, when my life and soul are gone.

[I went into those hills thinking I'd have quite a battle to contend with, only to find my new charge determined to fight off every one of the Soldiers before her, and their unicorns, and me, if necessary, all on her own. In this place where women are in danger- in this place where *you* are in greatest danger of all- you had no fear. Why do you let yourself be so victimized by him, when he's no longer around?]

The suns shine but it is so black, blacker than night. Blacker than the beast at my side.

[It's day. It's bright and clear and blue and I am not a beast! Lira, look at me. Turn away from the wall.]

"You know nothing about me."

[You have many nightmares. And they make you talk and scream in your sleep. I've learned a lot the last couple nights. Lira, no matter how well or how long or hard you fight, or for how great a cause, you can't always have what it is you need. There's so many other variants, so many other things that come into play. Your will is not the only one and therefore it's not always the strongest one. There's nothing different you could have done to change things.

[You're here now. You've survived through a horrible thing. But staying in the mindset of when that thing occurred will not be of any help to you.]

"Because you spy on my dreams you know what I've endured, what I'm enduring now? And you have the audacity to tell me that my reactions are wrong? How should I be behaving? What *will* be of help to me, O great unicorn?" I yell at him, not hiding my hostility.

[Me. I'm a Protector, Lira, as all unicorns are.]

"Protectors?" I scoff. "That's not what those others were engaged in on the hills yesterday."

[Two days ago.]

"Whenever!"

[These unicorns have been forced to become what they are. They killed those Soldiers, yes, because they are unicorns, but also because they were protecting.]

"Protecting? Who?"

[You.]

"That's absurd."

[You should find something to eat. Your bastard male didn't leave you any food?]

I remember the bag I'd been tangled in on the hills. "I threw it away."

[Would have come in handy.]

"I won't eat anything from Him!"

The unicorn gives me a half-disapproving look. [Well, this place we are in once had a great store of foods. Surely some seeds have survived the years and sprouted something edible this early in the year. He sure did pick a bad time to bring you here.]

I go blank, numb, thinking of all the better times he could've brought me here. So, so many other times that would have been so much better, would have changed so many things, would have saved and ensured so much. I can feel her small trusting hand in mine. Her tiny fingers, her nearness, the extension of myself, the blood and skin that came from half of me. And now the feel of her hand in mine is fading away.

My hands are no longer bound, but are crusted over in layers of dried blood, a fact that arrives into my consciousness impassively. I drop my arms down into my lap because my hands are empty and she is not in my embrace as she's supposed to be. My gaze shoots ahead of me again, over the earth that feels like a large open grave.

[I'm so sorry, Lira. It had not been my intention to cause you further distress.]

"I miss her so much it *hurts*. It hurts so deeply there is no end."

[I know, I know. We'll think of that later. Right now you need to find some food. Aren't you hungry?]

My stomach is past moaning, past the impulse of telling me it's time to eat.

I lean my body back against the wall. Tumbled-over walls are taken over by leaved, twisting vines, like hands stretching up through the soil to pull them back inside. This place is past emptiness, and, even with the rush of the wind and the flapping of a sole flag, filled with an awful, desolate silence. The silence of lifelessness, of old death. Maybe this spot was once completely paved, a thought that surprises me. The vision of a city as massive as where

I'd been, mixed in with this is somehow repulsive, even if this is the cursed, damn Valley, even though we wish it would all crumble away into nothing, taking its people with it.

Toppled stone walls and other ghosts of buildings stretch on for quite a distance, surrounded by the skeleton of an expansive wall. The smell of smoke strikes me strong and swift, making me gag-

An amber dragon plunges angrily down from the sky over me, forcing me to drop to the ground and cover my head as he spits out a hot rush of flame that scorches the ground so thoroughly nothing has time to catch fire. Screams, everywhere screaming. The city is a chaotic inferno, with smoke swelling so thickly that the sky has ceased to exist. Dragons explode out of the smoke that's so dense, they just seem to appear without warning, spewing more and more fire in never-ending attacks. Burnt air, burnt flesh. Smoke. Fire. *Screaming.* Everyone screaming, running. All around me are smoldering bodies: Soldiers and some unicorns and women. The smoke makes me cough so hard I can't breathe-

LEGACY

I CURL TALYN'S FRAGILE NEW FINGERS around my index finger. "The Lady Anin of Ravery threw your grandma from the tower when she was very young. She wanted Grandma to die. But Gwesana, the dragon who had been speaking to Grandma since she was born, was nearby. She dove from the clouds and caught her as she fell, then carried her home to the mountain caves and raised her as her daughter. The other dragons swarmed down on Ravery and burnt it to the ground for what they'd done. That is how we are children of dragons."

Talyn yawns drowsily, her belly full. But her changing eyes watch me, waiting for more. Cobalt eyes the color of her great-grandfather's scales now mix with crackles of amethyst, the color of her father's eyes.

I wrap her blanket more securely around her. So innocent, so dependent. Her life relies completely on me. What a responsibility. What a small, precious thing to make you feel so unconquerable and mortal and blessed and vulnerable all at once.

When I was little, I remember my mother pointing to each of her pictures on the wall and telling me stories, about life as the only child- the only human- on the dragon cliffs: the wind all around, the sea behind her, the Forest spread out before her and all the places she had walked through (*Flew*, my father would correct. He swears her feet left the ground when she ran). Her dragon siblings and her flights with them, the dares she'd take until they were too afraid to dare her anymore; the parents who'd saved and loved and raised her. Every morning, I use to find her seated on the floor in the upstairs hallway, smiling at the image of the river where, as children, she and my newly orphaned father had met.

But as I got older, her stories stopped coming, replaced by silence from her torment of still being Here, in This Place.

Talyn's life won't be like mine, and mine isn't like my mother's. Holding Talyn and feeding her and ensuring she grows and thrives has reinstated my faith in Him. So, I'll tell her those same stories because I need to remember, and we need to be ready when He returns.

"Our country is split in two," I continue. "In the west there's The Valley: green hills and Soldiers and Anin, nasty unicorns and their Bound women. The east, though, is where we are from: from The Trees and The Cliffs and The Lowlands and the dragons. East, Talyn, always remember east and trees and mountains. That will take us to the dragons. That is our home within Home." I drift off in my thoughts, staring at my daughter, thinking dreamily of raising her There instead of Here. What a life she'll have, with no memory of This Place. And I'll forget that I was ever here, and will drown myself in Home's air and soil, hide in her trees, on her cliffs, within the walls of Kholsari, and the arms of her father.

"The Lady had her Soldiers hunt Grandma ever since Ama took her away. The Soldiers were constantly coming into the trees, attacking villages to find her, but your grandpa fought them off." I look up and Mihn smiles at me, signing to me with his hands: *Go on. Keep telling her.*

"But this is the part I don't want to speak. And not with you here."

He shakes his head. *No worries. I made sure you understood when you were little. She needs to understand as well. If you tell her later, her ideals of normal male behavior will be too messed up to be corrected.*

"That's not funny."

Well, not all men are as great as I. We shouldn't raise her to believe all of us can walk through walls or produce fire according to our ladies' whims-

"Still not funny, Mihn."

Though now that I think of it, maybe we should. Get her to set her sights high-

Dad- I growl more than sign at him.

Really? What do you think I'm going to do when her father returns? Just hand you both off? Oh no. That man will certainly have to walk through walls- or be thrown through them.

He nods. *I'll throw him through several first.*

Alright, Daughter, tell your child my story, because it is yours, and now it becomes part of hers.

I swallow, keeping my eyes on him should he change his mind. "Soldiers killed your grandpa-" he doesn't flinch, not even a grimace. Long ago, when I was young, he had described to me the little field of gold in the middle of The Forest, where the trees broke open above them and for those last few nights, those very few nights after they were married, he and my mother slept under the sky without moving for days- completely unheard of for my mother. When Mom went to get food from a nearby village, the Soldiers came. He kept them busy to give her the chance to hear what was happening so she wouldn't be taken by surprise, so she- and I- wouldn't be taken at all. By the time she returned and brought them down, it was too late to save him. Her brothers flew her home after they set the area on fire. That's where my father's body is, mixed with the golden grass and smoldering earth somewhere in the trees of Home.

Lira, keep going.

I choke, stumbling on my words, unable to take my eyes from him. Talyn's eyes are on him as well, bright, happy, watching how the light from the window washes through him, how he makes it bend and ripple inside his translucent body, how the hues are altered in the gaping sword holes still visible throughout his shirt.

Habitually, his hand goes to cover the death blow that went straight through his middle, slicing his lower rib in half and cutting through his stomach and spleen, through his diaphragm and the lower lobe of his left lung before the blade split his main artery, and then severed his spine. They'd waited to deliver that one, waited until they and he heard my mother coming. They wanted him to know she would die and he wouldn't be able to do anything to save her. But they underestimated my mother's rage, and the speed and ferocity of her brothers.

"Ama and Grandpa Marr sent her back to The Wizard," I continue, tears trailing silently down my cheeks. "But the Soldiers attacked again, at Kholsari. Before they could reach her, the Wizard cast her here, in this world far, far away......"

Mihn looks away. *Forest,* he signs with his hands.

"But- I've never seen it."

He leans over his granddaughter and moves his hands slow and wide, tall and low, his fingers and hands forming his words, flowing like poetry, arching and reaching as he paints his thoughts in the air: *Trees so tall, so alive, they seem human, with bodies and feet and arms and fingers. Never stiff or still, they sway and hum, whistle. Shelter, food, fuel, and so much more.*

He describes their leaves for her: maple leaves that look like a young bird about to take his first flight, oak leaves that can cover his large hand, the serrated edges of a birch leaf that look like a plump dagger. The giant cottonwoods with the gnarled trunks and twisted roots, the tall firs. His favorite, however, are the needle-leaves of the evergreens of The Lowlands around Aril's and Hozar's- mom's foster parents'- old cabin, with the aspens that mingle just before the heart of the forest, whose branches go ablaze in reds and golds when autumn hits. He was born on the southern edge of The Lowlands, right where the trees transitioned towards the normal, seasonal type. He didn't have to venture far to find-

Kholsari, he reminds me, retreating back to his shadow.

I nod, pulling myself out from the entrancing beauty of watching him sign. People who speak pour their emotions into the sounds their mouths emit, yet his whole body moves and flows into each word he speaks with his hands. I had loved when he would tell me stories as a child, because his manner always pulled me right into the middle of his emotions and his words. Mom thinks I ignore her a lot of the time, but when he's standing nearby and mocking or arguing against her, it's hard to take my eyes off him and pay full attention to her.

I clear my throat as I readjust how Talyn is laying. "Aril and The Wizard were of The Forest, the Middle Lowlands, before Ama brought them up to Kholsari to assist in raising Grandma. Grandpa says Grandma was a wicked child."

He chuckles, shaking his head as he remembers.

"Ama needed a human couple to help Grandma retain her humanity, and had hunted the trees for months, watching the people below until finding and choosing Aril. Because they agreed, the dragons gave them Kholsari, an old cliff-side dwelling that had lain empty for half a century. Your grandma and grandpa say Kholsari was built in the clouds, high up into the side of a mountain, way, way long ago by the first Wizards. It use to be safe there."

Family, Mihn interrupts, adamant. *Your mother's foster parents.*

"Aril and Hozar? Aril was a healer. She tried to train your grandma and would take her on rounds whenever she could. No mother or child ever dies or falls ill when Grandma is near. She does that here, too. Midwife, they call her here. It started with May, then Rani, then me......"

Lira, my father reminds gently, smiling.

"The dragons call Aril's husband Hozar a Wizard. Not because he has any magical talents, but because all the men who lived in the cliff manors had been wizards. It was a title of honor, and he wore it graciously. If not for them and their insistent love, Grandma would never have known people to be kind."

Dill, he prompts.

"Aril and the Wizard have a daughter born nine months after Grandma came to live with them: Dill. She won't like us at all. She wanted your grandpa for herself."

Mihn rolls his eyes, shivers in not-so-mock revulsion. Dill was pretty. Unlike Mom she wore clothes, kept her brunette hair combed so that it hung sleek and gleaming down her back. Washed her face as Aril taught her to do, walked, didn't run. She had her father's blue eyes and Aril's grace, and was every bit the human girl mom could never be. Mom wandered the cliffs and trees at will from the time the dragons took her, and had no rules or boundaries, while Dill was kept within the walls of Kholsari and raised with human expectations. In Dill's head, she should have been the only child. Though my mother is older, Dill saw her as an intruder stealing what should have been hers: the dragons, my father, the interest and attention of Home. She should have been the one hunted and protected.

"Unfortunately," I sigh, "she is your foster-aunt." A solidness roots itself strongly into the room. I look up to discover my father looking at me pointedly. His gray eyes are piercing through the shadows. He wants me to pay attention to something. Something I'd just said? "All I said is that Dill is unfortunately Talyn's foster-aunt. Well......great......foster......"

Mihn shakes his head, waiting for me to continue and catch on. I scoop Talyn into my arms and flee the room. The motion is new to her, but like her grandmother she enjoys the speed.

Sam and Ella, mom's not-dragon lizards, scatter across the hall just before I collide with them. The pair hiss and inflate their bodies, walking stiffly away with eyes flung back towards me to show they are not appreciative of being so disturbed.

My foot lands on the top stair and I stop running, changing pace to frantically scan the murals that adorn nearly all the house's walls. I have been staring at these walls and my mother's memories all my life, yet now I can't remember this one crucial thing. I should have figured it out That Night.

When she first arrived in the house, Mom painted the surface of every wall with scenes and moments from Home. All the many memories and details she cherished. It began after she'd visited May's grandparents' apartment and spotted a shrine the family keeps, with pictures of lost and dead family members, and bits of cherished items from the country they'd fled. She ran back here and began painting frantically. My father said the color had just poured from her fingertips, that she spread her memories in a mad frenzy, as though by doing so, she was binding them to her, preventing them from ever fading away. Every wall, throughout the entire house, is covered. All but the walls in my room, which are reserved for my life and my memories.

I run down the stairs and then halt, going methodically through every scene down the first wall. Aril and The Wizard have a son. A son who was a toddler when Mom last saw him, making him maybe four years older than I. The son I was thinking of That Night, the always half-hidden toddler boy who has no name.

The boy who's grown by now. The boy become a man become......

Talyn's father.

Kholsari, Aril, Hozar, even a sneering Dill, all painted on our walls. I know all their names, know exactly what each look like, know their personalities, their demeanors and what they love and hate, but Mom's little foster brother was too young for her to say much about. He liked digging in the dirt for bugs and following Mihn everywhere he went, loved harassing Mom's brothers for flights while being doted on by her sisters. I use to beg

Mom to tell me about him because he was a child like me, and he was growing up in Home while I was not. And then I got older, and Mom began drifting, and I stopped wondering about him until I forgot him entirely.

But that boy grew up and somehow found a way here and then found me and made this child with me on that beach. That, I now know for sure. He had spoken to me in Home's language, had known my name, my mother. I never questioned how he knew so much, how he was tied to us at all. Just as had happened when I was a child, I never asked for his name.

I trace my finger over a picture of the manor built into the side of the mountain, with his obscured little face watching me through a window far away. Kholsari. How much time have I spent imagining I was walking those halls? Gazing out those cloud-high windows? This is where He is. "This is Kholsari, baby girl," I whisper. "This is where your father lives."

As a child, I'd pictured us as friends, running through those halls, laughing and playing, riding upon the dragons' backs together. I've had nothing else but these murals, these pictures. The girls that came here for Mom's fighting lessons could never understand me. But in my head, he did. Then I forgot all about him.

I lay my hand upon his house, wishing I could feel him, could reach him somehow, that the walls would melt away and I'd fall through, landing on his side of the worlds. "He'll be back soon. I know he's trying. We just need to be patient and wait and believe. He'll be back soon."

The not-dragon lizards stalk back towards me and flatten themselves across my feet after I sit down on one of the stairs. Kholsari stares down at me. Mom and Mihn have been decidedly careful never to mention his name to me. Have we always been predestined to meet? To fall so absolutely in love? The way my parents had behaved that night. Ten months ago. They not only knew he was coming, they also knew who he was.

Mihn walks slowly out of the front room and down the hall towards me. He stops a couple steps away and leans back against the wall, waiting. Mom's in the kitchen, just a few steps away. I meet my father's eyes, knowing that one quick simple question to either of them, and in a second I'll know Him.

I shake my head, turn away from my father and the painting. No. Not from them. He'll tell me everything I need to know when he returns.

Z

"THIS ISN'T THE VALLEY!" I scream at the demon before me. "You've brought me to Ravery!"

[Which is *in* The Valley.]

"You brought me to *Ravery*!"

[It is the only thing for many, many miles.]

"Liar!"

[I do not lie!]

"There's a great big place full of trees called a *Forest*! Not to mention it would be safer, and generally wiser!" I shout through the wind.

[Do you see any trees?]

"You claim to know all about me, yet you bring me *here*!"

[Hostile,] he admonishes. [I can't run with you out on the hills, not with as weak as you are.]

"I am not weak!"

[No, you just naturally sleep for days on end and look like a skeleton.]

"You and your whole big speech about knowing me and being a damn Protector! *'In this place where you are in the greatest danger of all-'* This is *Ravery*! I can't be here!"

[That is where you are wrong, Lira. Because of who you are, and what this place is, you need to be here.]

My hands ball into fists on the ends of my stiffened arms, flattening tight against my sides. The friction caused by pinning them against the damn dress- as soft as it is- pulls at the fragile new scabs that have been keeping the wounds from bleeding. Freed, my blood pours down the damn dress. Silver. I think the damn thing is silver. Was. No, no, a little lavender. No, now it's streaked with dark, cherry red.

Cursed beast! Bringing me to Ravery!

The demon shakes his head in agitation. [Can you not at least consistently call me 'Nightmare'? That seems to be your choice of name for me. It's more acceptable than 'demon' or 'beast'. I do not refer to you as 'the woman'. Or, more accurately, 'The Hostile One Who Bleeds All Over'.]

I glare, too angry to speak further.

[You need to do something about those wounds. Can't let yourself bleed everywhere. Ruin that dress you love so dearly. Shred the damn thing if you'd like. Wouldn't bother me. Might, actually, bother Him.] The *beast* turns away, his tail beating at his sides through the laughter of the wind.

More than a little too eagerly I reach down to the hem and make a long, complete tear in the dress, relishing the sound that echoes and conquers the wind, while glaring at the unicorn's rump, Him a distinct trace in my anger. I shred that strip a few more times, swearing and complaining, and bind the strips around my wrists with an overabundance of irritation. One second, the strips are the odd silver-purple-blue with the faintest stain of grass and the rained-out blood from my thigh. And then, near to magic, a pool of deep pure red appears. I stare, captivated, confused.

The sky above, the moon, are quiet. The moon is her normal ivory grey color. Not a hint of red aside from my own.

Everything is too muddled and hazy. My fists, now heavy with the wraps, fall back to my sides. The unicorn is watching me, waiting. *So tired.*

[Find something to eat.]

"I won't eat anything grown from this soil."

[I don't think you're in a position to be so incredibly picky.]

"Why did you bring me into Ravery?"

[Is there someplace else you need to be?] It's a leading question, buried in multiple layers.

The sights that greet my eyes are not mere ruins, and in no way do they 'greet'. They shout, they curse, they scream and blame me, blame my mother. Ghosts everywhere, reaching and grabbing, wanting to maul. The blatant smell of smoke, though it happened long ago.

"I want to be any place other than here." I almost take a step, wince and freeze. My nerves are such a constant river of pain that I've grown use enough to just ignore that it's not normal. The arrow scrapes everything open all over again with that small flinch of movement, forming brand new slices through my muscle and veins, the wound bleeding anew. I haven't the energy or the mind to cut the arrow out of my leg. Not now. I'm afraid to faint, to faint here in these ruins still burning with death. The stench of this place will cover me and the dragons won't know who I am.

The dress allows another strip to be torn from it, yielding without protest, as though anything I may wish it do, it will. *Disappear. Return to your master and tell him I'd rather be bare.* But that's like telling the knife to leave. It wouldn't even stay in the bodies I'd launched it into. At least the length of the dress is now shorter, so if I need to run again I won't trip. I bind the new strip of damn dress tightly around my thigh and what remains of the arrow's shaft, ignoring the brewing infection streaking across my leg and oozing from the wound.

The clouds overhead rage. Where's the blue? Gray, sometimes near-black storm clouds wipe across the sky like a herd of infuriated unicorns. Thunder and streaks of yellow lightning. A thick portentous feeling and smell. Something Evil Comes. Stunned, I watch the darkness fall over me like smoke-

And then the sky clears again. "This place is coming down upon me, unicorn. Don't you know what happened here? Why I should not be here?"

[Don't you know why you *need* to be here?]

"I *don't* need to be here!"

[You do, nearly as much as this land needs you here. What happened here, what continues to happen here, is part of you. If you do not acknowledge that, it will continue to happen, and you will be hunted as your mother was. The earth wants you here. The unicorns you thought wanted to kill you only want to be near you. They were racing after you on those hills to get to you before the Soldiers did. To do whatever they could to keep you from them. But the Soldiers were on top of them, and the frustration and confusion was driving them mad. The blood in you is old, Lira, nearly as old as the earth you stand on. It is blood that can right many wrongs.]

"I know the blood in my body and it is in no way part of this place! How can you think I'd care about here or anyone who lives out here? What about *my* wrongs and my mother's wrongs? Who'll help me right those?" I nearly begin to cry. I cover my ears with my hands, my head set to explode. Am I angry, am I scared, shocked, bewildered? Am I grieving? Who do I grieve for first: Talyn, her father, me? My mother and what happened to her here?

[Yet, in all this time that you've screamed at me for being here, you have not demanded or even asked that I take you someplace else. The Forest? The mountains? To the dragons? Maybe to who brought you here?]

"Take me to Him and I'll be sure to return this knife he so thoughtfully left me!"

[As appealing as that thought is, unicorns aren't really prone to leading their charges *towards* men, so I won't be leading you towards yours anytime soon.]

I turn away. "He's not 'mine'." I close my eyes and steady myself, letting my hand fall away from the dagger's hilt to grab hold of the wall only slightly more solid than I. I hear his voice in my head, whispering my name in the night. I can feel the smile tugging at his mouth as he teases me, feel his fingertips brushing across my cheek. How safe, how perfect, how whole I had felt in his arms. "I don't want to see Him."

[You seem fairly confused about that.]

I'm in The Valley, Ravery, and yet I feel Him so strongly here. I've gone so long without thinking about him, but now I can't stop. I've forgotten what His presence had felt like. This is not merely Home, my parents' and my home. This is His territory. He's everywhere here, all around me, hidden somewhere in the sky, the stones, the torn up earth, out there beyond the battered wall in the hills hills hills, where there's absolutely no place to hide.

Did he watch the Soldiers attack me? And he did nothing? Is he smiling, seeing me in Ravery, this place that only appears in mine and my mother's nightmares?

"Is it so easy to leave me to face everything alone?" Pathetic eyes search the unicorn, the instinctual man-hater. The wind has picked up. Why did Mom love her so much? She's harsh. My fingers feel the fabric of His dress beneath them and let go, coming back to lay useless and awkward at my sides before my fingers curl up and my arms cross over my chest in a way that keeps them from feeling.

[If I were to have had a part in him leaving you this time?] the unicorn asks me gently.

Unable to look directly at The Nightmare, I look at a spot of ruins just past sight of his head. Ruins, how fitting. I'm surrounded by ruins. I'm in ruins. I am ruined. I'm a castoff in a pile of ruins in the center of The Valley. So much time I wasted- that damn bullet keeping me sick and unconscious on my bed. And when I woke, I woke so numbed and shocked that my child- the being I created in one night of love, carried secure and safe in my belly for nine months, and set free with the magical ability of dispelling life out of such a small opening- I woke shocked and numbed by the understanding that my child, that anyone's child, could so easily be snatched away and that I- the daughter of Elaar and Mihn- would be helpless to prevent it.

"Should it matter?" I ask the man-hater brokenly, the wind settling down so that I can be heard. "He still left. Again." Tears and emotion damming behind my eyes have filled to capacity. At last, pushing my lip from my teeth, they burst free. "Nightmare, I don't want to be here!"

[Yet you are here.] A black muzzle stretches tenderly out, stopping upon my cheek. I freeze, mortified, pulling back. He takes another step closer, reaching out until his nose brushes once again across my cheek. Nothing's touched me in so long. After she was gone, I wouldn't even let my parents get close.

I close my eyes and hold my breath, confused about whether to run or fight or withdraw into a state of denial. Touch is brutal, all my nerves are screaming in agony. But he ventures closer, nuzzling me with more weight, and the contact, the physical contact from another living being, wedges into my walls and my body's confusion.

"In my dreams she is here, in Ravery, Nightmare. In my dreams I'm running through this place because she is *here* and I have to find her first, have to find her fast or she'll be lost to me forever.

"Except it didn't look like this. It was new, it was large and whole, filled with Soldiers and Anin. She's gone, Nightmare. She's gone. She needs me to find her, but I'll never find her here."

All the time I wasted, slamming against the wall, when I should have been searching, tearing that world apart building by building and person by person till I found where they were hiding her. I'm still slamming against a wall, but now there's nothing I can do. This world is a wall I'll never climb over or burn through.

[You are such a very strong, courageous woman, Lira of Elaar. Why do you wound yourself this way? It's been taken out of your hands and it is not your fault. This is where you are meant to be, for whatever reason. You cannot focus on things you cannot control or change. But sitting here for all eternity will do nothing beneficial.] He pulls away, waits, and then walks further into the remains of my mother's birthplace. I inhale deeply, my eyes burning. I reign in the need to reach out for him, to reconnect. I am grieving- for all of us- in Ravery, of all places. The tears bead down my cheeks in slow trailing caresses, hanging onto my jaw for one brief moment before they plunge to the tainted grass and broken stone below. He stops, returns and faces forward with his side against mine, and waits.

[Let me carry you.]

"No."

[Then let me help you.]

Reluctantly, I grab hold of his mane and let him support me as we walk.

Grass and low-growing weeds have pushed their way up through the stone that had once been a walkway or a market, and now tears that bear Talyn's name are being absorbed by them. Last night it had poured, but the wind and suns have long since swept the water away. Today I am raining, and the ground once scorched black and dry by dragons' fire is still hoarding every bit of moisture it can. Maybe it's just grabbing onto anything of me it can disintegrate.

Despite my resolution to appear strong in this place, to walk beside the unicorn with an allusion to dignity, I collapse to my knees and hide my face again, letting myself weep. I don't want to be here. I want my daughter. I want time to reverse so I can do things differently. I wouldn't wait for the next day when they came into the house: I'd kill the man right there on the sidewalk.

The Nightmare stays at my side and waits. I will never be spent. If I were to grieve for all eternity, it will never be lessened.

My body gives out before my tears do, and it lays me back out upon the cursed stone. Ravery's life-draining soil sucks my tears from my eyes before they weep free, pulling at them without ensuring there's an adequate supply, draining me quickly till I lay in a stupor.

SUSPENDED

IT'S THE MOMENT when you're mostly asleep, but can consciously make the decision to either wake up or fade back into your dreams. I'm still standing mostly in trees, and laying only partly in my body upon the bed. I feel the sunlight tapping tentatively on my back, the softness of my bed mixed with the earth beneath my bare feet, while His reddened moon shines warmly over our heads.

But thinking of morning makes me smile and happily leave my constant dream of him. I slide my hand along the bed, through the sheets and blankets, seeking the warmth that should be-

The trees vanish and my awake body crumples down into the mattress, as is the new morning ritual ever since I awoke on that beach alone. I had searched and waited for days, but never found a sign of Him. Mom found me in The Alcove and brought me back to the house. I'm sure Mihn led her to me as he had when I was taken back when I was little.

During the night I had dreamt that I couldn't find him. At times I thought that I had spotted him in the distance, and I'd begin to call out for him but his name would stay stuck in my throat, and he'd run straight past me. I stood

still and spread my arms out wide, waiting for those moments when I'd feel him fly through me. But He couldn't see me anymore, as though I had become invisible to him. I knew that all I had to do was call out his name and he'd find me again. Only I don't know his name.

I open my eyes and study the empty place beside me, remembering a moment in That Night when I'd woken and he was sleeping soundly, with the moon full and the red fading, and he was breathing so deeply, looking so beautiful in the night. I'd reached out and slid my hand over his chest, and as though it were a habit formed of years together, he rolled towards me and brought me in close, still asleep.

I felt perfect, held so securely. I felt perfect. This world, however wrong, was suddenly perfect. The two of us, that night and the suddenness of everything- I felt *perfect*, normal, and had drifted quickly back to sleep.

Where'd he go after that?

Rolling onto my back, I pull the collar of his sweater over my nose, breathing in what remains of him, and stare out the window. Outside, the wind is vicious, thrashing the frozen snow against the window glass in unnecessary fury. It makes a horrific, entrancing sound, soothing me back into a half trance.

Since returning to the house, I no longer sleep in the center of my bed. I sleep off to the side, towards the window. Every night I stare at the space beside me, so sure that should I wake during the night, or when the morning finds me again, He'll be there.

I sit up, entangling myself into the thick comforter, and gaze out the window some more. The songsbox turns on, sensing my movement, and begins scanning through stations until resting on one with subdued music. Songs of love and longing. I send it an annoyed frown and it quickly changes its tune.

It hadn't snowed all season before he came. Yet since He's been gone, it's been coming down with a vengeance.

I feel so suspended. Like I'm not here. Something's changed about me, and I'm not sure what. I miss him. I miss him so much. It makes no sense, and my mind is still swimming around in a daze. I never felt more comfortable in my own skin than I had in that one night. For the first time, I no longer felt like a separate species from the Others. I felt human. I had let all my walls tumble down, let my guards crumble away, and it felt so good. I don't want to return to the way I'd been.

And Him. One night wasn't fair.

Mom's body sinks down into the bed as she fits herself between me and the headboard. Her hand passes sympathetically down my arm. She smiles when I look at her, a sad smile that understands longing more than I do.

"The girls were mad when they left yesterday. What did they say?"

I pull the blanket's thickness more securely over my shoulders, relishing the way his sweater feels as it brushes over my skin. I plummet so deeply into my thoughts that it's a struggle to remember how to speak. I swallow, pondering the necessary movements and will, and find my voice buried deep in my throat. "They were more than mad. Inez had seen me leave with Him, but said we were gone by the time she got outside. But we had stood there for a long time. It was snowing. And the moon was so red."

I am so thankful she didn't find us. His cape was draped over my shoulders, and he was smiling at me, allowing me whatever time I wanted to bask in the moon and snow. I like the way he had stood beside me, the way he patiently waited, no hurry, no force. *Stop and smell the roses*. Rani's mother is fond of that phrase. Stop and feel the snow.

"They'd called their Soldiers- their *po-lice*?"

Mom growls at the mention of them. Her behavior toward them had apparently infuriated the girls. My lack of surprise had upset May further. She'd yelled that it was incredibly stupid of me to have wandered off with a total stranger. They'd thought they'd find my body somewhere.

My mind drifts, jumping from one moment of that night to another, in no particular order. Just anything I can bring to the front of my mind. His voice. Kissing him. His laugh. His touch.

My eyes close of their own volition and Mom laughs. When I turn my head to her, she is gazing out the window. "If Mihn were here......" she begins. But instead of cutting herself off and sinking inside herself as usual, she laughs. "He'd have been more furious than the girls. He would even have stood guard outside that door with his swords drawn, refusing to let you leave that night. Your He would have had many challenges to make him worthy."

Mihn is suddenly there before us, his arms crossed over the holes in his chest, glowering.

I throw my words at him: *Don't cross your arms at me! You knew He was here and you knew I'd meet him. You let me leave anyway.*

Because he was supposed to take you Home! he signs back. *When he returns......*

"Come down and eat, Lira. Scowling at your walls and sitting in bed won't help."

"Mom?" I twist around on my bed, catching her before she leaves. "Why weren't you bothered? I was gone for two days already when the Soldiers of Here came."

She leans back against the door frame, running her finger down the opposite side. Mihn materializes beside her with his back against the wall, arms crossed and sword resting easily in its sheath at his side, his eyes cast over his shoulder to her.

"I thought you were in Home."

She turns her eyes upward, avoiding mine. Her red hair against my plain white walls is the moon on snow. "I had prepared myself for not seeing you again. He was supposed to bring you Home, away from This Place. Why didn't he take you with him?" She whispers that more to Him, I think, than to me.

"Come down and eat, Lira." She pulls away from the door and heads down the back stairs. I wait and listen, being rewarded with the sound of the back door slamming shut. I glance at the window, at the ice and the cold and the angry, empty air beyond the glass. She's gone out to dance. She does that when she's upset, when she's scared, when she's surprised by a moment of joy, when she's mad. She dances naked beneath the sky quite often.

"Mihn?"

She's fine, Lira. Don't fret. He sighs, looking down at his feet while his hands play for a moment with the frayed edge of his tunic. *We've all had our notions of what our lives would be that next morning, didn't we? Now we have to rethink everything and accept that plans have changed, for whatever reasons. Go on, get out of this room.*

Lira? He adds as an afterthought. I catch the shine in his eyes and instinctively frown, crossing my arms in front of me, waiting for the Mihn-comment I know is coming.

Do Him- and the rest of us- a favor and wash his clothes. They're beginning to stink. How long have you worn them?

I reach behind me and fling my pillow across the room at him. With a smirk, he stands and lets it sail straight on through. *Ah, to see you with a knife would be great.*

Like a candle in water, his smirk drops and his eyes flare fiercely. Anyone who equates my mother with the demeanor of a dragon never gave my father his fair due. He only hides and controls it much better than she.

That's right. He has two hands, Lira. You make him do it himself when he returns. You make him work for you. You make him prove himself to you, you understand?

From childhood till he had pulled her into that village and had an Elder marry them right then, Mihn had loved to tease my mother with taunts of a domestic, subservient life. He really only enjoyed watching her temper fly. She was always angry and fighting, he'd told me once. Him or Soldiers or life in general. She'd never stayed more than a couple days inside any dwelling- from his aunt Na'el's small hut to her foster parents' huge Kholsari. The Trees, The Lowlands, the open mountain top where she lived with our dragon family- those were the only places large enough to contain her for any period of time.

Mihn told me that they were walking through The Trees in Home, as they'd been doing for a long time, and he'd stopped to ask her something, and she looked up at him strangely, as though he'd grown a third eye in the center of his forehead, or his face had changed its contours. She took a slow half-step towards him, and simply slid her hand into his. It was the moment he'd been holding his breath for all his life. He immediately turned around and charged her into a village, handing her over to the women to be Prepared. Within a day they were married. Within a month, he was dead.

After the Soldiers killed him, Mom's human foster father, Hozar the Wizard, sent her here. Her life was completely turned inside out and flipped upside down, and since Mihn died all she's wanted, and all she's lived, is this nearly domestic life he had once tormented her with. She scrubs the floors on her hands and knees until her skin cracks and bleeds. She stands before the hearth in the kitchen and watches her food cook until her hair is singed. And she restricts her life inside four walls and a roof rather than roaming and living outside like she'd once preferred. After all this time, she still has no idea he's still with her, watching her torture herself. This is not the life he'd have ever given her, for it kills him to see her contained and subdued. He loved her for her liberty, her tenacity, her feral spirit. Teasing her was fun, but he'd have never stripped her of those elements that made her who she was.

How can things of pure bliss be so abruptly, so cruelly ripped away?

Mihn is gone by the time I focus back on my room. I stand and throw His clothes into a corner. He can damn well wash them himself when he gets back here. I know what we felt, what we did that night was real. I know He's coming back for me. I know it.

9

THE DRAGONS ARE ATTACKING!

As I run through the streets, Ravery changes. Sometimes ruins, sometimes as it once was, with venders or buildings, or small little round houses made of stone.

"Talyn! Talyn!"

I round a corner and crash into the belly of a dragon. He arches his head back-wards over his neck, about to spew fire. I turn and flee from him, back down the street, tripping when it becomes ruins. I run right past her at first- Mom, sitting cross-legged in the middle of the intact street.

"Mom?" I stop running forward and turn to rush back to her side. She's staring upward, oblivious of me, hypnotized by the sight of the tower and the woman standing in the slit of its window. The woman in the tower screams again, then her screams become the agonized screams of a frightened, plummeting child, which then become the screams of Talyn as the Soldier/Po-lice run away with her out of the house......

I press my lips together and open my eyes, fighting the impulse to reach first. I fail.

[This is what sleep has become for you since Talyn was taken, hasn't it? We have to change that.]

Instead of the vibrant green grass I had almost been expecting, all I see is the massacred stone of Ravery. I close my eyes, press my face into the cold under me.

[Can you walk?] The unicorn's nose pushes against my side, nudging forceful but careful, and my body obeys without my consent, rising stiff and cold and empty.

I'm standing in Ravery, as though I'd jumped into my father's retelling of what had happened here and Mom's tie to this place. He'd pieced Mom's early life together as best he could from Ama's account, from captured Soldiers, from Forest People, and from a woman who'd fought with them. Mom never admitted to ever being here. She was just two or three when Ama took her away and the dragons burned this place down. Could she even remember?

I am standing in the middle of Ravery, not a tale, not a nightmare. This is the place my mother was born in, and I understand why she could never acknowledge this or the mother who threw her from that tower. Dead and vacant and forgotten, but this place is evil and always will be.

There's four mounds spaced evenly along what remains of the outer wall. Watch towers? One for each direction? We're heading north, toward what remains of the manor itself. All around us lay crumpled buildings, fighting desperately from sinking into oblivion. Weeds grow everywhere, keeping some of the ruins still standing. There's not one weed among the grass on the hills.

A flag has managed to survive the fire, wind, and time-forty years or so, I calculate quickly- and waves upon its pole atop one of the crumpled towers. The noise the flag makes is the only sound I hear above the wind. Under our feet lay what's left of the streets and walkways of an open market or Square. I mean Round. Ravery was circular.

Not even mice or birds or insects. Just the silence that comes from lack of life, of a haunted past, and the flapping flag and the howling wind and the sounds of the unicorn's hooves hitting the stone.

My feet leave no mark, no impression, not even sound as I limp along; but every time I separate a foot from the ground, it's like pulling out of mud, like the earth is trying to pull me in. I cannot stop. If I stop moving, no matter where it is The Nightmare may be leading me, if I stop, I'll sink. It makes me shiver. I should not be here.

We're at the great wooden door of the manor. Only it and its arched frame still stand, the walls and floors stripped away and scattered long ago. It's such a daunting sight— the doors intact when there's no longer anything to enter into. They're so stoically proud, fighting off oblivion, standing so grim and tense when everything else has already given up and fallen. No one will forget, as long as they stand resolute. I set my fingertips upon the petrified wood...... how different would things have been......? The wood is humming, vibrating, the wind is singing *Listen, Listen.* I quickly pull my hand away.

Beyond the doors all that remains is the skeleton of a tall stairway and a bit of the second story landing that has clung to it. Behind us, I can comprehend the former layout of the Market. It's frightful, nightmarish. A numbing sensation of something dark and dreadful leaves me feeling unsafe, so out in the open. The voices I hear in the wind are nothing good. Distant screams, revolting laughter. What if Anin is still here?

The wind is flying into my eyes. We are up higher now, and the fortress walls on either side of here have crumbled down to waist high. The wind from the green beyond whips around my head. Not violent, not menacing. Strong, but not quite forceful.

Sights from the Other Place merge into the ruins, piecing them together into what this place may once have looked like. Long ago, Ravery had been the sole city anywhere— Valley or Forest. Luckily, now, I don't think there's any city.

Walls and stone disappear and I am standing alone on a flat green prairie with grass to my waist, waving under my fingers, brushing against my body. I'm overtaken by peaceful beauty, the sanctity and purity of the hills. Blissful isolation and solitude; there is nothing but myself, a unicorn, sky, and endless hills. It's open and amazing. The sky spreads out an unrestrained blue above me, with soft, wispy clouds grazing contentedly overhead. The prairie explodes green and gold all around me, as though I am the point of origin. I feel so small, but not in a menacing way. Surrounded, I'm connected to something great and powerful, infinite and indestructible. There's no feeling of death, of people or ruin.

I spread my arms out from my sides, palms parallel to the earth, and relax into the way the grasses touch me. Back and forth, slow, steady, soothing earthen waves combine with the ebb and flow of the air. No slamming.

Then it begins to change. I regard the altar with a mixture of confusion and distrust. The altar spreads. Stone by stone, it becomes a platform. A building. The weeds and grass shrink back into their roots as the ruins reconnect. Perfectly rounded bricks move and shift around me. The manor rises, the towers. I immediately pick out the tower my mother was flung from. Flags with a unicorn emblem beat back and forth on renewed poles. Behind me, giant doors are closed and latched.

Small houses made of rounded stone dot the outer rims of the Round. The main and sole entry into Ravery is a gate two dragon lengths high on doors made of planks of wood from what was once the oldest and tallest trees. The road that begins at its threshold is made of sparkling stone, a pale, sandy color. It ripples and sparkles just like the sand by The Lake does on a hot summer day. It's blinding.

The main road, the one that leads to the extensive, rounded veranda I now stand upon, is wide. It stretches from the great doors of the city past the smaller duplicates of the manor behind me, through the Round, to the manor steps.

Shades of women in long flowing skirts and strips of cloth to cover their breasts walk back and forth through the city below me. I hold my breath, watching them. Tall and proud, feet bare, with only delicate, thinly braided bands of grass decorating their upper forearms and ankles, or woven through their hair and around their foreheads to keep their hair in check. A few carry a quiver of arrows with a bow nearly tall as they. A scant amount of others hold swords, and two have what appear to be whips made of braided dry grass tied to their belts and forgotten. The weapons are more decorations than weapons. A strange sort of jewelry. Looking at them, I get a sense that they know how to use them, but they've never truly had to. Most are not armed.

Unicorns abound; unicorns so strikingly different from the ones I'd met on the hills. These would never bring the terms 'beast' nor 'demon' into anyone's mind. Their coats are so immaculate they glisten nearly as bright as the main road, with silver manes and tails on beautiful white coats. Their eyes direct rays of light upon the women and girls at their sides.

As the women walk, slow and serene through the open city, more little houses appear around them. A little market forms in what becomes the city Round. I begin to notice the men. Men looking like farmers watch the warrior women pass by them with looks of heightening disdain.

The procession begins at the gates. A steady stream of women, but with each step, each change. Hair, clothes, faces, the way she moves, her smile and eyes- subtle changes. Mothers into daughters. Step by step, the generations approach me, a separate scene from the women, unicorns, and men that criss-cross the city. They hold my focus- the women in the procession- though I remain aware of what occurs around them.

The ratio of women to men alter, and all the while, more buildings. More men. Market flourishes, and then dwindles. Women once serene and elegant look wary and unsure, and now all carry weapons. Unicorns once the epitome of regal beauty and perfection seem to be crouching, looking more haggard, more worn, more threatening. And the line of women approaching me moves faster. Their brows furrow in frustration, there exists a sense of urgency about them. Their clothes have changed. No longer loose, airy skirts; now they wear shorter, stiffer, tighter garments, bodices that cover their torsos. Clothes to go to war in.

She lands soundlessly beside me- a blonde woman with plumes of wheat stuck in her banded hair. She raises her right arm into the wind, her spear held high, wailing a cry that is both a grief I can identify with and the need for bloodshed I can also empathize with. Though blonde, she looks like my mother.

The women in the procession and within the city run towards her, and they rush out of Ravery's gates on their unicorns' backs, carrying all manner of weapons. A unicorn stops and turns to me. Something about his eyes makes me think of the unicorn on the hill I'd hoped would kill me.

A small girl stands alone in the abandoned city, in the center of the main street and the flurry, watching me. I reach for her, but she's gone. All the women are gone, and the former farmer men in thick wool coats and woven pants walk back through the gates wearing stiff jackets, carrying bloodied swords. Chained, hobbled, and iron-muzzled unicorns are dragged behind them, mouths and noses foaming frothy bloody saliva. A bolt of lightning streaks across the clear sky, proclaiming its opposition to the happenings below.

The women return, but these are not the women from before. Skirts and shirts upon their beaten bodies are bloody and torn, if they exist at all. They don't raise their eyes. Instead of delicate golden grass decorating their bodies, chains made of iron drag them along the main road behind unicorns that once could protect them. Men once fathers, brothers, sons and lovers are now *Soldiers*.

I gasp when the scene changes again. Only men, dressed in armor now, walk the streets and alleyways while women scream within the dark walls of all those little stone huts until the screams begin disappearing altogether.

The gates open again. Things so large should make some awful, grating noise. But these don't, as though weeping in silence every time they're forced to obey men instead of their women. The carvings of women nomads and unicorns etched onto their fronts for all visitors to see are being sanded away, re-branded with men in armor conquering, enslaving, murdering, raping the women that once walked through those very gates. The violence and graphic depictions in the new scenes make me retch.

A new procession comes through the entry. Soldiers sneer, their leader proceeding them, looking smug and triumphant. His eyes so dark and frightful, filling my lungs with a suffocating, oily blackness. Evil bears no description, no clear warning you can see. But you feel it prickling your skin when it is near. You smell it, you hear it, you know it, you know you need to run but are afraid of attracting its attention. This man coming towards me is evil.

Behind him he drags a young girl, naked and numb, bloodied and irrevocably broken. Her hair has been hacked or pulled out and sticks out from her scalp in dirty, uneven protrusions that no longer represent hair. There is no way to guess its original color. She has vacant gray eyes that no longer see anything. She is beyond life, beyond hope, for though nothing good has happened to her on her trip here, it'll be worse once the gates close behind her. She'll never leave, and he won't kill her anytime soon, and she knows it. She's just a girl, a new teenager who should be more worried about dancing on the hills and spending long lazy days playing in the sun.

[Instead,] Nightmare whispers, [he'll torture her in ways so horrible her mind will shatter and she'll no longer be anything resembling human. That is Anin, Lira. Your mother's mother.]

Anin as a girl and Ravery as it had been both vanish. The women, unicorns, and the Soldiers all disappear. The rubble and wind return, and I realize that I am screaming.

[Any woman inside this place was a prisoner, even when the rein was still upheld by them. Your grandmother, Anin, is the last prisoner of Ravery.]

I glare at him, hating that I can't stop shaking. "My grandmother is Ama. Gwesana. *Dragon*," I counter bitterly, although not at all as convincingly as I try.

[Your mother was not born of a dragon, Lira,] he rebukes, as though trying to reveal common sense to a petulant child. [However painful her beginnings, this is where your mother was begun. This is therefore part of *you*. After Anin killed The Duke and escaped from here, she tried to hide, but this place had sunk into her. Her body may have recovered but her mind had been broken. She did order the attacks on your mother, and the murder of your father, but it wasn't entirely her fault.]

"Wasn't her fault? Then who's fault was it? You want me to love this woman? Have sympathy for her? She killed my father and caused us to be banished! It *is* her fault our lives are what they are! I should've been born in The Trees. My father should have been allowed to keep his life. My mother should have been allowed to live however she chose! How dare you bring me here! How dare you speak of things you have no knowledge about!"

[I understand more than you think. Elaar was the last remaining proof of many things. You see what happened because this land is in your blood, as Anin is. This place wants to be remembered. It wants you to know that you are part of it. It reached out to Anin but she confused the message. Now it reaches out to you.]

"The dragons are in my blood! It was they who raised my mother, they who made her who she is, they who gave her the life she had here. It was they who loved her. Because of them, I am here. They are my only family. I want nothing from these ruins that reek of death and evil-" I choke. The triumphant man dragging the teenage girl- dragging Anin- behind him returns to mind. Something about him clings to the inside of my skin. If my stomach was in any way full, I'd vomit. Instead, I cough on bile that sticks to my throat. I can't think it. I cannot think it. He can't be my mother's father. What was her life like in her three short years of living here? What did she see? What did he do to her?

[You are being reclaimed. You will see.]

"There is nothing to see. I know who I am and where I come from." The man and his sneer, his eyes saturated with the filth in his soul, comes again. We can't have come from him.

This is why being human equated something unimaginable to her. If Mom remembers this place, if she was exposed to things worse than I have just seen, this is the why of many whys. The girl I'd seen dragged up these very stairs is Anin. Is my mother's human mother. But a mother's sole duty is to protect her child. That is not what Anin did. Did someone fail in protecting her?

10

THE WALL THAT HAD SURROUNDED RAVERY is mostly gone, and the wind races in strongly. The earth has pushed up the cobbled ground in many places, making it uneven and very difficult to traverse. Soon, the earth will have completely reclaimed the ruins, and it'll become only a phantom legend. Not even their skeletons will remain. The sooner the better.

The wood of the closed double-arched door is petrified. Because of what it had been forced to helplessly watch, or because of time and weather? To my right, nearer the far back end of the manor, part of that infamous tower remains, holding itself up against time and weather and neglect. *Look at me. I will not let you forget me.* That's where Anin had tried to throw my mother to her death.

[That's where Anin was imprisoned.]

Even as far away as I am, I can gauge the height of the tower's window to the ground. What hate does someone need to possess in order to be able to pick up their baby and coldly watch as she falls that many stories by your own hand? To be so enraged when the child is saved that you pursue her through her life until you believe she is dead. How? How can anyone possibly hate their own child so much?

Are fear, horror, terror— is there anything to truly describe being thrown from a tower by your own mother, the woman who gave you life, who is supposed to protect you from all harm and love you deeper than anyone ever could? I can see it happening, feel the little feet cutting through sky and clouds as though they are mine, hear the wind screaming in her ears as she plummets closer to death. I feel the scream lodged in her throat, the insatiable need and childish belief of growing wings and saving herself, the impossible hope that the air will solidify and hold her.

None of that happened. Another unthinkable happened- a dragon exploded out of the sky and caught her, took her home and loved and claimed and raised her.

Hoof-steps in the distance echo sharply against the stone, cutting into my thoughts and bringing me back to ruins. My first thought is to ignore it, prevent another return into Ravery's past; except that The Nightmare's posture and demeanor has drastically changed. Use to be twenty or so long, wide stairs that rounded out across the southern front of the manor. Now, though, large sections are missing or are collapsed in many places. Past them, past the top of the black unicorn's head, down what use to be the sparkling main road, across the dilapidated Market Round to the remains of the entry, a unicorn with a Soldier on his back is trotting stiffly to us.

Every pound of each hoof echoes within me. Every bounce that brings the Soldier closer kicks at my middle. Mom would have stood here, excited and thrilled for the fight, her fingers teasing the hilt of the dagger as she anticipates feeding the Soldier to the blade. But I am not my mother. I'm not a fighter.

"You said no one would come here. Why is he coming here?" The gold of his armor nearly blinds me. The dagger is vibrating against my side and I want to scream at it to stop. I am not my mother.

As they come through the entry and into the Round, The Nightmare's nostrils flare out, and his breath escapes again in quick, short angry bursts. He walks stiffly towards them, pawing at the ground and bobbing his head, warning them away from the stairs. The Soldier pulls back on the reins quickly, his unicorn threatening to rear, but with another tug on the reins he forces his unicorn's head to the right, distracting him. The unicorn grinds his teeth together over the metal bit in his mouth.

I don't know who makes me more nervous: the man or his unicorn. Is there anything left in that mangled unicorn head? Beneath the chains, the dirt and grime, the changes time has forced upon them, is there anything left beside rage? Am I looking at my own prospect- after all the tears are shed, after the grief, the anger, will there be anything left?

In those large, aquamarine unicorn eyes- the only thing of him that is clean- waves of coherence are followed by waves of insanity. He is focused completely upon me, and I forget where we are, what time period we're in. We're alone on Ravery before it was Ravery, when it was just pure, flat green, tall grass, beautiful blue, and women Bound to unicorns.

The Soldier shifts his weight and the unicorn becomes incoherent again. Dragons breathe fire but unicorns exude it. This new one *hates* the man on his back, *hates* the metal that enslaves and forces him to submit. Dragons live for centuries, but they do eventually die. Unicorns are immortal. How long has this one been enslaved?

Horrified, I remember the vision I'd had, with the unicorn who'd looked back at me from the gates. He'd reminded me of the unicorn on the hill I'd pleaded with to kill me. Dragons, they can't be the same.

Mistakenly, I meet the man's eyes. "I will find Her later. I watched you on the hills. You will be fun," the Soldier drags out his last word, showing only teeth. His sense of fun is something that must be avoided.

The Nightmare scrapes at the ground beneath him, his hoof screeching horribly across the scattered stone. When the Soldier doesn't back down, he rears halfway up, grunting and neighing, tossing his head. Perfectly balanced, he walks forward a few steps on his hind legs, his front pair suspended sharply at perfect height with the man's head. The Nightmare crashes down on stiffened front legs with a sound like the first crack of lightning.

The Soldier doesn't react. "He puts on a good show. What about you? You did well surrounded, but how much better a show will you provide for me alone?"

The wind leaves me and propels her full force against the Soldier, leaving the air around me acutely, oddly silent except for the ringing in my ears the violent shift creates. The man shouts again, but the wind apparently likes him even less than it does me. It devours his words, capturing them directly from his mouth, letting only the indecipherable echo travel to whoever might care to know he'd had the audacity to try and speak. The wind bombards him, trying to toss him off his mount's back. The unicorn beneath him knows this, and its anticipation of him falling is rippling across the surface of his skin. A Soldier is helpless on the ground, as I have already seen.

My fingers play lightly upon the dagger, my body tingling, preparing. Only one this time. Only one. I should be able to fight just one more. It's four against him; Nightmare, myself, the other unicorn, and the wind.

The Soldier gives off the same vibration as the shade-Soldier in my vision who'd been dragging the girl. He has deeply hooded eyes that indicate perfectly clear what he's gazing at. Though he makes the proper motion, he does not smile. He's a predator prematurely tasting his next prey. There is something, something in the air that surrounds him that sends chills up my spine. He hides it well but it's strong enough that it seeps out and perverts his surroundings. It oozes out from every minute motion his body makes.

He's the black-haired Soldier chasing me through Ravery in my nightmares, the one who's trying to get to Talyn first.

I take a small, involuntary step back.

"Give me a show!"

Thunder jolts through the ruins, shaking the ground and making it moan. My eyes shoot directly to the skies, but they're bright blue and cloudless.

The Soldier glances at the sky as well, confused. The Nightmare rears again, the impact of his feet striking stone beneath him shoots sparks of miniature lighting and makes that thunderous sound again. The Soldier kicks his unicorn, forcing him to walk around The Nightmare in a wide half-circle, back and forth, over and over. The unicorn snarls, fighting against his metal restraints, trying to stop, to trip or fall. He watches The Nightmare, the Soldier watches me and I can't break his gaze. Yearning teeth flash wicked and sharp under his sickening smile. In that flash of teeth and intent, I realize that I am being hunted. The Soldiers from before hadn't quite dripped this type of threat. What came from them I could ignore. But the way this man looks at me is inhuman.

Mom taught me to hate this region, its people, its unicorns. Hating Soldiers is easy. They took Mihn from us. Predators- like everything else- develop tastes for certain food sources. This man's tastes are gender driven, but not for love or even lust. Is this what the women here faced? Is that what The Nightmare's trying to get me to understand? The vision I'd gotten here takes on new meaning. How do men turn on women? How can they look on us with such vehemence, wearing their plans to seek and destroy so openly?

Where are Valley Women now?

In a different life, in a dark, snow-enclosed space, His eyes upon me were filled with love and only love. Standing out in the open, tendrils of that poke demandingly at my skin, warring with the residue oozing across the ruins from the Soldier. His may have been filled with love, but the look in this Soldier's eyes is the absolute opposite; an opposite that should not exist. He doesn't want to play a game, he doesn't wish to conquer. Among much more, he wants to maim, devastate, shred the humanity out of me only because I was born female.

He kicks the unicorn beneath him with his heels, being sure to dig into the bruised muscle, and forces the beast to advance. It doesn't occur to the man that the wind and the two unicorns are soundless, synchronized allies, all headed towards one implicit goal. The Soldier tries to make his ride continue as The Nightmare advances, but his unicorn cements his chipped silver hooves to the scattered stone underneath. This time the sky truly does yell out- a loud explosion of thunder that erupts directly overhead. A flash of lightning pierces the blue sky heartbeats later.

The other unicorn is bracing himself, lowering his head, squaring his stance, gritting his teeth to prepare for an impact. What are they planning?

The Soldier is staring at me, devouring me. I pull the dagger from the belt and hold it at the ready, locking my jaw. His lack of words is becoming terrifying. Plans are forming in his dangerous head. He's studying us, looking for weakness, for gaps, for a costly mistake. He kicks his unicorn more harshly. His teeth grit in frustration when the unicorn refuses to listen. He pulls at the reins, trying to make him back away, but the unicorn lifts his head and then swings it abruptly downward, pulling his chains from the Soldier's hands.

The Nightmare lunges in an unexpected fury, slamming his side into the other unicorn. The sound of his collision silences any thunder. It sends a quake through the ground, and the remains of the manor behind me creak and moan. The unicorn is so firmly planted that the shudder of the impact courses through him and flings the Soldier off his seat.

The unicorn immediately whirls on him, but the Soldier has regained possession of the reins and as quickly as his toes touch the ground, he leaps back onto his beast's back. Enticed with the idea of being free of him, the unicorn continues to try and throw him, and the wind picks up force and gives assistance as The Nightmare watches, lips parted over teeth that glisten white.

The other unicorn glances at me, a quick flash of beautiful lucid eyes on either side of a long silver horn; his eyes suddenly void of rage and full of compassion and need. Unwittingly I step forward again, but in a flash the rage returns and he turns away from me, galloping the Soldier out of Ravery so fast I don't think his hooves ever touch the ground. Unicorns are immortal, but there's no way his body will survive The Nightmare's impact. He won't get but a few miles. He knew this, and he allowed it.

We stand there— The Nightmare and I— watching, breathing with heavy chests as they become spots on the hills, and then after the hills stand bare. I struggle down the stairs and across the grass to The Nightmare then, laying my hand uncertainly on his side. I ponder each and every short, velvety hair that rises up to greet my skin, surprised at their softness, at his warmth, at the fact that I'm willingly touching him and not very upset about it. I close my eyes and rest my head against his shoulder, feeling shaky and unsteady. The heat and rage shooting from his skin keeps pricking my own. The rush of adrenaline- his and mine- is going to leave me even weaker than before.

His chest rises and falls in slow, soothing swells. The Soldier is gone and I want out of Ravery and the whole damn Valley. Away from unicorns and Soldiers and evil air. Trees. I want the trees and mountains my parents had sworn to me.

I begin shivering uncontrollably. "Take me to The Trees. Take me to The Trees. Now. Please. Take me there now."

[You can't run from this place, Lira. You are part of it. If you turn your back as your mother, and as Anin did, it will follow you until you agree to acknowledge it. That Soldier will not leave you be.]

"Take me to the Trees, Nightmare. Please." In my mind, I'm standing in the hallway of the house, the house I had been born in, the house my mother found after waking up on that same blasted beach. The green of the grass dances on the outskirts of my sight. I focus on the walls of the hall. Specifically, on the murals my mother had painted. Mountains, The Trees, the dragons, Kholsari and the cliffs, and the aunt and uncle who'd raised Mihn after the massacre of his village. Eastward places. Over and over, my parents had pounded into me to go east, to seek out these places, these people, the dragons, that dragon. I'd worn that charm every day until That Night. When I woke in the morning, he and it were both gone.

East, they'd told me and I'd agreed. *Go east*. Yet I am here, in The Valley, beside not just a unicorn, but *this* unicorn.

Unicorn, the wind yells at me, bringing me back to Home, to The Valley, to the ruins of Ravery. *Unicorn. Unicorn. Unicorn.*

My fingers hover over the spot where my charm had once lain. They close around the empty air and hold on tight, remembering the feel of the small silver dragon that use to lay just at my collar bone. My father had made it for me when I was born, and now I know it was because of the Wizard's words to my mother before he banished her away from here.

Love him whose skin gleams red. Is he here? My hand tightens around emptiness. *Find him*, Mihn had told me often. *Find this red dragon. He will always help you.*

The thought, the image of that dragon has been my only constant, my strongest comfort, my security all my life. What if he is a lie? What if he doesn't exist? What is left if my last remaining thread of hope is taken away?

We're facing south, but I look instinctively east. The wind is swirling around me, caressing my face, playing with my hair and I'm frozen in dread. All I see are green hills, and I want them all gone. Now. Past them, east, will be trees. And through the trees, mountains. On the mountains, our dragons. Thinking it, standing here in Ravery, they're so close, so within reach. I can whisper out to them and the wind may carry my voice and they might hear, they might come find me. All this time, waiting for this, and I can't move. They're so far away.

Because through the hills, in the trees, before the mountains: He'll be waiting. If I whisper out, He'll hear first and he'll come first.

[So, you'd prefer to stay here after all?] the unicorn calls when I don't move.

"I'm wondering exactly which direction we'll be heading."

The Nightmare studies me, sorting through his plans and thoughts. [Yes,] he answers. [We must first go east. Will west or south bring you to the trees?]

What is worse: there, closer to Him, or this valley, this place? It's all the same, just different types of danger.

[I can't exactly go without you. If you've changed your mind and would prefer to take up residence here, I think that would be slightly wiser.]

"I'm not staying here."

[You're not moving, either. One step at a time, Lira. You want to leave here? We'll sort out the don't wants of that later.]

With the adrenaline and fear fading quickly, my body is beginning to tremble again. I want nothing more than to lay down and sleep. Sleep it all away. But not here. Not one more moment in this place. I take a breath, refuse to take even the swiftest glance at the ruins, and place one foot before the other until I reach the unicorn.

"Take me to the Trees."

[Alright. But I'm carrying you, and you are not going to argue about that.]

11

THE WIND HAS SLOWLY EBBED AWAY, lessening her intensity the further from Ravery we move, while The Nightmare's pace intensifies. His silence, his constant upward glances, the tension in his back all tell me he's worried. I need water, food, the arrow removed from my thigh- according to him. I don't care either way. What's an arrow in my leg? I want the reminder. I've gone too long without food or water before I was brought here. I'd rather have a silver tree. Anything but more hills.

I can physically feel Talyn slipping away the further east we go, as though I'd set her down on a hill, turned my back, and walked away. I try not to think. My wrists and thigh burn, the bandages soaked with blood act like magnets attracted to the earth, which tries to pull me into it. I want my parents' trees. I want them now.

When The Nightmare stops, I make an effort to sit up straight and look ahead, to make sense of what my eyes think they see. The wind travels up the hill to where we stand, gentler than ever, but whispering caution. I squint my eyes in the bright afternoon light of the sunsmoon, my jaw clenched so tightly my back hurts. My hair moves in and out of my face, and the dress wanders up my thighs, wanting as desperately as me to just float away.

I'm not completely sure of what I see. Depending on the direction the wind takes, the sight becomes either solid or hazy, or clearly fictional: a desert of green, a lake of emptiness, the mountain Kholsari is built into, a fence of multiple Hims, Moms, and Mihns, or another fortress like Ravery but built from the trunks of trees-

My eyes focus yet the image doesn't waver. It *is* another fortress. An intact one made of trees. "What is that place?"

[Unicorn camp. What UnTouched Unicorn Bound women there are left live only in camps, Lira. Women and men have not co-existed peacefully in The Valley in decades. Contact- as you understand now- is violent, and the women and girls don't usually survive. Touched or not, many will risk everything to get themselves, or their daughters or someone else's to a camp. These few women and girls are the last of Valley women.]

It's a fortress built round like Ravery, the wall made with hundreds of thick tree trunks stuck into the ground to stand upright. A large gate faces us, but no road or path leads down to it. From the rise we have stopped upon, we can look over the edge of the wall and see inside. Not smart planning on their part. What keeps the Soldiers from just burning it down?

[They haven't found it yet. Being nestled down in such a basin, it isn't noticeable from far off. Soldiers pass by and never know.]

"I want to go into there as much as I'd like to return to Ravery."

[We have to go in, Lira. Not merely because they've seen us.]

Fifty or so small tents are spread along the inside western edge of the camp, with unicorns wandering free on the eastern half's pristine open pasture. The unicorns there shine like earthbound stars. They're grazing lazy and serene, a few lift their noses and look in our direction. I stiffen, knowing that my body is betraying me and giving off a message I do not want known: He was here.

[He's not here now. They won't attack you.]

I do not belong to Him, can they smell that? Can they smell it was only one night long ago and that it will never happen again? "Let's just go around them. Look, trees. Are those trees?" My vision goes hazy again, and I'm not sure, but the hope that I had seen our destination, our safe haven out of The Valley and away from all of its creatures and people lift my spirits- which is a strange, unwelcome feeling.

[I've already made sure they see you. If they are what they were, they'll be sending some warriors out to escort us.]

"What! Why would you do such a thing! I don't want to go in there, *demon!*"

[The unicorns won't betray you, *Woman*. And you are entering the camp with me. Regardless, you need to be seen to, and you may not last until we find some Forest People.]

"I don't care!"

[But I do, Lira of Elaar. I care.] He couldn't have said anything else that would have shocked me more. [If we stand here long enough, that Soldier will find you again. He will hurt you, Lira. We have to go in.]

"No we don't. I don't't!" My stomach turns and moans. My head scrambles to think of a way to avoid the camp. *Run*, but there's no way my body can comply. Something in me is screaming that he's leading me into a trap. Mom had said never to trust unicorns, specifically *him*. But there's no place to run to or hide.

I close my eyes while my instincts go to war inside me. The tired, uncaring one tells me to just give in. Another begs me to run. My faintest, in Mom's voice, suggests quite eagerly that I fight the whole damn camp. What's the worst a bunch of shut-in women can do?

Miles away, behind the camp, begins the trees of The Forest. The more I stare at them the more solid and real they become. The sight of trees, of Mom's and my father's Trees, my trees, pulls at me evocatively, *Come here. Come here to us.* I'll be safe in there, sheltered by wood and leaves, among Forest People.

East, to people that I know, to faces I long to see, to air I need to breathe.

I want it again, I want my parents' trees so much. All the need I'd felt for them before He came, that I lost after Talyn was taken, floods back in a frenzy. The relief of having a unicorn as a Protector is no longer so desirable. Send me the dragons, take me away. Send me Him for all I now care, just get me out of here, away from these people.

The Nightmare scowls over his shoulder at me. [Really?]

I shake my head to clear it. The thought I'd just had: Him again.

The Nightmare begins to walk, to trot. I pull back on his mane like I'd seen the men do, but he only growls and yanks my arms forward with a toss of his head, trotting onward anyway. I tighten my legs around his girth and pull at his mane again. He breaks into a gallop. I contemplate letting go, falling off him to the ground. I don't really care how many bones I'll break, I'm not going in there!

The gate coming closer opens and two lean, stern-looking women charge out from the slightly open doors and begin to gallop full speed towards us on unicorns the crisp clean color of- not white, not blue, not grey, not purple, but a color somewhere in between, a color that belongs only to them. They move almost too slow— every hoof coming down in elaborate detail, making soft thud-smacks on the grassed earth which echoes up through my body rather than traveling across the air into my ears. The echo is so clear that it prevents any other sound from reaching my ears, even blocking the wind.

Their tails and manes appear to flow underwater, trailing up when they are down, and falling down strand by strand when they rise back up to take another long stride. These unicorns move so differently than the ones ridden by men; these are beautiful. One woman holds a sword in an outstretched arm while the other holds a bow, both watchful and war-ready. The beauty and grace of the unicorns become obsolete. These weapons are not decorations.

Nightmare, they're getting too close! Stop! Stop!

[Lira, you have to relax. You have to trust me. We want them here.]

No we don't!

"Hurry! You're almost safe!" a Unicorn Bound yells above the rise in wind. As the others increase their pace, The Nightmare increases his. They may as well be trampling over me. The sound of their hooves is worse than when I was running from it. It's everywhere. The unicorns are everywhere, including beneath me, carrying me along and I can't make any of them stop.

The archway is waiting like open jaws. Just waiting. *Patient, patient. Prey is coming. Closer. Clooo-serrrrr.* Trapped. I'll be trapped. They'll close those giant gates behind me and I'll never get out. What if I'm never allowed to leave? Forced to stay there, with people I detest. Impossible. There's no way I can-

[You don't know them enough to claim you detest them. They are a product of the cruel turns life can take, same as you.]

They are not like me!

[It is only for a night. For you to get food and more rest. For your wounds to be tended to.]

Don't you remember what just happened at Ravery, where you said I was safest?

The beast doesn't answer.

They'll let me leave as easily as they let me in? If it's as dangerous for women out here as you imply, how can I believe you that I'll be allowed to leave?

[We'll figure that out later.]

How can you tell me it's safe when you haven't thought beyond getting me inside! Bringing me here has nothing to do with helping me, does it?

[What? I'm insulted!]

I should be the one who's insulted. You take me from Unicorn men only to deliver me to Unicorn women!

[That's a very interesting way to put it. I'd laugh if you'd release your grip on my *skin*. Aside from the Soldiers, when was the last time you were in the company of others?]

The night I'd met Talyn's father. Three years ago.

[And Bastard was the only human you've ever encountered that was......No, no. Forget that. Have you never had a group of women who would help you?]

No, I answer immediately, but before it leaves my head, memories of my childhood friends remind me that I am wrong. Rani, Inez, Zara, and of course May- girls my mother had delivered into that world, girls who spent most days in our house. Girls who brought me to that damn club.

There's no time for memories. Women my age and older and a very slim amount of girls are waiting just behind the doors, watching me intently.

Jaws, waiting.

[They are waiting to greet you, not devour you. To them you are Unicorn, you have escaped what they all know and fear from the moment they are born. To them, you've just escaped their nightmares. I know you can't stay in there, Lira. But please, don't make it so obvious.]

A few feet through and the giant doors behind us are slammed and bolted shut. I nearly scream, but The Nightmare pretends to startle, rising up on his hooves to make me scramble to maintain my balance. Soldiers are vulnerable at the feet of unicorns. I am vulnerable at the feet of these women, and we're surrounded by about thirty silent, shocked faces. I stare right back at them, somewhat crossly. Is there something wrong with the way I look?

What do I look like? I don't even know anymore. Suddenly self-conscious, my emotions dwindle from antagonized hostility to awkward unease.

[You look like you've been through several wars and haven't quite come out of it yet.]

Wow. Thanks.

The two women who'd herded us into the fort walk their unicorns to us. One reaches out and runs his muzzle over my leg. I can't help it- I jump and try to pull away from him. A murmur of questions from the watching women reaches my ears, but I'm too afraid to divert my attention from the unicorn. He looks up at me with something stranger than compassion, but doesn't come closer. The other advances a careful step and I cringe, feeling cornered and very vulnerable. Outnumbered.

The Nightmare actually stays silent, but more importantly, he stays still. If he so much as breathes in deep beneath me, I'll throw myself off him and break through those doors. I close my eyes briefly, trying to drown out the sound of screaming, to wash away the sight of the unicorns ripping the men apart.

"You're not use to unicorns," the second unicorn's rider observes, though I imagine it can't have been hard to figure out. By the way she sits, the way her voice carries, it's clear she's higher up on the Unicorn Bound hierarchy.

I match her posture and attempt to mimic her appearance of ease. "No, I'm not. This one is the first- there were others but they......He rode here pretty hard."

The woman smiles. "The first ride has become the worst for many. They know what we face without them and the smoothness of the ride is not as important as getting their charge to safety is. He brought you here?"

"He did."

[It'd probably sound better if you left the bitterness out of your voice.]

Another murmur waves through the watching women: I keep hearing *'UnTouched'*. I am apparently well past the age of normal virgin hope. Unbeknownst to them, I am more than just 'past the age'. How old am I? I don't remember. I haven't thought about it. I'm young, I should be considered too young. Twenty... twenty-something. I can't remember.

"You are our fourth this week. This is very unusual. Are there others coming? Do you know?"

The woman advancing nearer appears to be close to my age, and even at our odd stance atop unicorns she is striking, tall. Her long auburn hair is braided into hundreds of small plaits that hang down to her ride's back. When the suns hit her head just right, her hair explodes in copper brilliance against the pale gold band of dried grass encircling her forehead with its ends woven through her hair. She wears a simple, pale yellow dress that is bunched up around her hips from the run. Her skin is tanned almost as copper as her hair, and just about sparkles like gold. She sits with a straight back, but easily, her legs hanging loose down her unicorn's sides. When he looks back to see her, her face breaks out into a beaming smile and she runs her hand down his neck lovingly. A quiver of arrows is strapped to her back, peeking out amongst her hair timidly while the bow almost as tall as she is tied docilely to her belt, as though it hadn't been raised and raging moments before.

Her unicorn doesn't stand as tall as The Nightmare. He, like the others, is thinner as well, with a coat clean as crystal, and the bewildering color of an opal. His eyes are clear and intelligent, relaxed, making he and the rest of them appear to be an entirely different species than the ones who'd chased me down the hills; than The Nightmare, even.

The woman studies me as carefully as I her. She catches sight of my wrists, not completely hidden in The Nightmare's mane. My fists are still clutching tightly to his hair, my wrists still wrapped with the torn fabric from my dress. She has undoubtedly seen that my own skin is pale, not tan, meaning I am not from their Valley.

[Your skin is not so much pale as......well, you don't look very well.]

Thank you. So much. I can't say I'm feeling very well, either.

[How badly are you feeling, Lira? I feel you shaking and I know you better than to think that you're afraid. Your skin is burning mine and your balance is off.]

"My name is Nykka. This is my camp. What is your name?"

I steal a moment to think, to gauge her and debate on whether I should answer, but my head is swimming from the ride and the abrupt stop.

[You weren't born here. There is no way to tie your name to your parents.]

It takes some more thought before I agree to answer her, somewhat hesitantly: "Lira."

My hesitance seems to elevate her estimation of me. Her features soften. She kicks her leg over her unicorn's back and slides to the ground, never losing her balance or weight, her knees maintaining their function. How does she manage that so easily? It makes me pretty angry.

[Jealous.]

Angry.

The other woman is already aground. She wraps an arm under her unicorn's face, hugging him to her. She smiles up at me and approaches closer, laying her hand accidentally on my injured leg, about to say something. When her hand falls on the splintered end of the arrow, she yanks it away and looks to Nykka with her hand motionless mid-air, not sure what she had touched. The scream is caught in my throat, but they've seen my body stiffen and the pain overpowering me is undoubtedly plain on my face.

Nykka walks over and pulls the damn dress over the broken shaft. The pain of the other woman jarring the arrow has made every muscle in my body contract, paralyzing me. I can't stop her, kick her away, however unwise that may be. She carefully takes in the protruding shaft, the dried blood covering my skin, and the oozing infection before reaching through Nightmare's red mane for my wrist.

"The Soldiers *found* you. They captured you! But they didn't Touch you?"

I shake my head, which releases a gasp of air.

"Unicorn brought you here in a hurry for a reason. I'm so sorry. Thank the suns that you've found us. Lira, you are safe here."

Unicorns and Unicorn Bound when my trees are only miles ahead. All we had to do was avoid this. A day or two of more travel, but then I would be completely safe. I'm fine. I could have gone a few more days.

[No, you couldn't have.]

"Era? Era?" Nykka scans the crowd, but can't spot whomever she is looking for.

"I'll find her!" someone shouts.

"Have her meet us at my tent. I'll bring Lira there." Nykka turns her attention to The Nightmare, running her hand across his cheek and down his face. Beneath me, his body shifts closer to her. I just about kick him, wishing him to go away and live happily ever after with the sacred virgin, rather than stay stuck with smelly me.

The unicorn laughs. [You are *jealous*.]

I am not. You are both absurd.

"Will you follow me, Unicorn?" Nykka whispers to him. "Let's take her to my tent where she can be seen to and rest."

[And she talks to me so nicely, too.]

I grind my teeth. "I can walk."

[No you can't!]

Watch me!

Like she had done, I kick my left leg- the good one- over his back and slide down, careful not to rotate the arrow into the beast's side and praying to my unseen dragons that I land steadily. Could I please also land gracefully? I keep a tight grip of his mane in both fists-

[Ow! It's meant to stay attached to my neck, Woman!]

You brought me here, Beast.

My toes touch packed earth and my solid leg wobbles but *holds*. I want to cheer. I want to jump for joy. Instead, I carefully shift my weight to a leg and a half. A leg and a quarter.

"Are you sure you can walk? Your leg does not look well. Neither do you. Your skin feels fevered."

"I'm fine. It's fine."

[It is not. Your skin scorched a crater into my side. And you are turning greener than grass and shaking more than you were when we arrived.]

I'm fine. Wounds from weapons are nothing in comparison to other traumas. Heal Talyn's separation, and everything will be better.

We start moving, the entire camp following almost on our heels. I can't see anything except Unicorn Bound faces staring at me. I wind my fingers further into The Nightmare's mane. This isn't good. This will not turn out well. Safe? There is no such thing as safe. And definitely not here.

I study everything and everyone we pass, trying to assess them, trying to find flaws in their enclosure, a place to hide. Though this place was built to hide, there's no place to hide from the other women. The tents are spaced well apart, making visibility around them pretty clear. The fortress built solid to successfully keep all unwanteds out also keeps the inhabitants locked eternally within.

My leg and shoulder feel like they're on fire. Every limp sends bolts of pain from arrow to head and toes, ricocheting over and over.

Nightmare, I don't feel so good. I can't walk much more.

[Let me carry you, Lira.]

No.

[That limits your choices then, doesn't it? It's not much further. Whatever your reasons for walking, you've gained their admiration and respect by doing so. Use me, Lira, I'll hold you up.]

It's unusually large inside the camp. From the outside it would never appear so. Unicorn heads lift into the air the closer we come, catching my scent. Catching His. I wait for them to go into their rage and come charging at me, but nothing happens, just as The Nightmare had said. Their content eyes fall lightly upon me, sparking with strange recognition before they immediately pretend to ignore me.

[Why don't you believe me? We've gone over this many times. No unicorn will ever hurt you. It sounded like you'd begun to accept that back in Ravery.]

Stop talking about that place.

Is there some sort of truth in The Nightmare's words? Or is he controlling the unicorns so that his words appear true?

[You are alarmingly paranoid.]

And you are too trusting when you're surrounded by virgins.

[By the way you bring up their chastity, I think you may envy them. Would you wish for the opportunity to give up that one night you dream about so frequently and live as they, never to have the Touch of Him on you?]

I stop walking. Would I?

Nykka comes to my side, laying a hand on my arm. I cringe. "Lira, are you alright? Do you need to rest?"

"I-"

Beyond her and the new Others are round, opal-colored tents set in neat circular rows. Yet it's not the tents that catch my eye, but several little girls running among them, peeking around corners and ducking back when they notice I'd spotted them. They giggle and abandon their attempts at stealth. Their skin is smooth and golden under the sunsmoon, the gentle breeze is playing with their hair in maternal affection, and I'm reminded of Talyn's blonde hair bathed in sunlight on the beach the day before we were attacked, the way the air had played gently with her just as this air does to these girls.

Nykka follows my gaze and smiles. "Our little treasures. When I was smuggled in, there were girls coming in monthly. And then a couple times a year. And then none at all. I use to worry, but then I find relief: if there's no more girls being born, then there's also no more women out there......enduring. I'd come to truly believe that, and then a few days ago a woman shows up and leaves three of her five daughters. She'd begged us to take her son, to raise him correctly, but, we can never have males in our camp. How would that have turned out? We'll have to turn him away in a few years before puberty brings out his aggression and he attacks one of us.

"The woman's oldest daughter had been Touched. She was barely a teen. Her face- her face was as battered as her mother's. One of the younger daughters refused to leave them. And the mother was heavily pregnant. She hurried away once the three middle girls were safe inside our doors.

"We haven't fully recovered from the shock of their arrival and now you've appeared. Where were you before here?"

"I don't know," I answer automatically, watching the smallest girl.

"Who kept you so well hidden?"

"My mother."

"Where is she now?"

"I don't know."

Nykka squeezes my arm, nodding understanding. I stare after the girls even after we resume walking, turning my head to keep my eyes on them, stumbling just a little. The youngest girl smiles shyly, beautifully at me and waves, and I smile back with hot tears in my eyes, my heart crumbling.

"I worry what will become of us. We're stuck inside these walls, and we're dying out. Many of the women have the drive to reproduce......but our memories of what that entails will never allow for that to happen. It's tearing their souls apart and we don't know what to do. They fight over tending the girls, but the little ones are slowly becoming not so little. They won't need the type of tending these women yearn to give.

"I think the original intention of this camp's placement was to be close enough to the trees that women could take their chances and abandon our hills and unicorns entirely, and try to lead that other type of life with the Tree People," she continues. "Except no one who's come in here for as long as I can remember has ever wanted to risk leaving, no matter what their bodies are crying for."

These women won't ever know that love exists between the sexes. They won't know how beautiful life feels......

[And they won't know how much it hurts when he betrays them, abandons them, shatters his promises.]

The unicorn's words are like air washing over the trees, and right there surrounded by Unicorn Bound and hills, I lay back down in The Alcove, our alcove, and push myself tightly to Him with his warmth keeping winter and snow and Others and that whole entire world at bay. They'll never know that love and sex are not acts of violence, but splendor. Magic.

[Which fades in sunlight. There are many forms of love that luckily don't require the inclusion of a human male.]

I give the beast a reproachful glare. *It was not merely sex, unicorn.*

He winces. [Do you have to say that word? Is it necessary to keep reminding me of what did occur?]

We left the club and walked for hours. Walked and talked. He wanted to know about everything he saw. I was born there and everything scared me. He comes from here but was un-phased. It amazed me. That world became less scary when I let myself see through his eyes. He wanted to jump into one of the monsters......a......a car......and try and control it himself.

The Others, their clothes, the way they talked, the buildings, he asked so many questions that I couldn't answer. I was suddenly the ignorant visitor. I'd been raised to know that my life There was only temporary. So nothing mattered to me, except then, when I wanted to be able to answer his questions and keep his interest.

We sat on the beach and watched the water. It was the largest body of water he'd ever seen, and I was so proud to have been the one to show him something he quickly loved. He pulled me up onto the wall and brought me in against him and began to hum, and we finished our dance from the club right there on the beach.

He's humming beside my ear again and I feel the waves' rhythm sometimes contrasting and sometimes flowing with his body's sway. I close my eyes and feel his tune vibrating through me. The tune I'd turned into his daughter's lullaby.

I think more about what Nykka has said, hating her for drawing me in, for making me feel sympathetic to them, because they'll also never feel a baby grow inside their skin, or labor her into life, or have that first sight, that first cradle, that first nursing. She was a ball of suns and moonlight, and I couldn't soak up her rays fast enough.

[They won't know what their mothers, and you, felt like when-]

No, I whisper to the unicorn. *No, please don't go there. I wouldn't trade the few months I'd had with her, Nightmare. If I could wish, I'd wish that these girls know love and have babies one day. At least, that they are shown the choice.*

[There are many ways to be a mother, Lira, and once born, you are always a daughter. When those girls there arrived, these Bound Women became their mothers, and they became daughters a second time.]

She is my *daughter, unicorn. Mine. She will never be someone else's. And I will only ever be* her *mother. No one else's. I could never love another's child the way I love her. What these women feel for these orphans- it's not at all the same.*

[You are wrong in that, Lira. Was your mother not loved and raised by one who did not make her?]

It's not-

I can't finish. I think instead of these girls' fathers- rapists and murderers all of them. But in order to be here, in this haven, these girls were rendered motherless. Do they understand what they've lost, to be this way, to grow up Unicorn-Bound? Did they ever get a chance to know their mothers? Do they crave her touch, her warmth, her love? Her smell? Do they crave her at all, yet not know that they do? Do they miss her? Do they realize how necessary she should be to them, and what they lose in life without her? Do they grieve over her sacrifice? Sending them away to safety must have given their mothers a tremendous sense of unshakable peace. If only I had had a safe place to send Talyn to. To know that she'd be safe and cared for and forever out of Their reach. I could sacrifice myself or my security easily, gratefully, eternally.

The mothers of these girls— are they dead? Are they alive somewhere, forced to endure some private torture while thinking constantly of the daughter they won't ever see again?

I am like them all. In order to be here I am both motherless and daughterless.

It takes me several heartbeats to realize we- myself included- have stopped walking again.

"In another time, our lives would be vastly different from what we've been left with. We can only be grateful that we live, and continue to remain apart from the men," a woman beside me says, her expression forlorn.

I don't care about their troubles. All I want right now is to sit down somewhere out from under Valley suns, away from all the devouring gazes and frenzied whispers I've been able to mostly tune out until now. The excited chatter going on around me is buzzing like unwelcome guests in my head. It feels like they're all falling down on top of me. So many Others......their weight adds to my own and I'm struggling to hold it all up.

I shift onto my left leg, allowing my right to lay loose and limp to the ground, and lean against The Nightmare's side, laying my arm over his neck for support. My stomach is rolling and churning and cramping tight, and my shoulder and leg are *throbbing*. I pour my weight into The Nightmare, and the space between us fills with his concern.

[Lira?]

We're standing outside Nykka's tent, and as much as I need to sit down, now that we've stopped and I can, all I want more is to keep moving.

"Let me help you inside. I shouldn't have allowed you to walk." She doesn't allow me to protest, coming up to my side and wrapping her arm around my waist, pulling me away from The Nightmare. "He'll be fine, I promise. Hope will guide him to the pasture so he can graze and meet the others."

It's not the unicorn I'm worried about, though. He sees the terror in my eyes and tries to nuzzle me, but I startle as his horn comes nearer. [You'll be fine, Lira. Let yourself be cared for.]

But you said I needed to start caring for myself!

[Which you can't really do when there's an arrow in your leg and you haven't eaten or had anything to drink in days. There are exceptions.]

Why is it your *decision?*

[Because you'd have decided to die on those hills rather than ask these women for help. Go. I'll check on you later. It's alright.]

No, no it's not.

He lets an older woman- Hope- guide him away with only her hand on his mane, and I stare helplessly after, shocked to have been left behind.

"He'll be fine, Lira," Nykka attempts to reassure me, giving me a courtesy nudge. "Alright, ladies, please give Lira some time to adjust and rest before coming to meet her." The women around us smile and wave, calling out welcomes and good tidings, peaceful sleep and dreams, and again telling me how safe I finally am. With that, Nykka pulls me into the tent.

She stops just inside, allowing my eyes a chance to focus within the dimness. The round tent is plenty tall enough to stand, the domed center being close to twelve feet tall with an opening for heat and smoke from the central fire pit to escape. Out from the heat and brilliance of the suns, I forget where I am and who with, and relax.

"How do you make the tents?" I ask, wondering at their odd color, reaching out to the entry way and running my fingers over the fabric. It's cool and smooth, softer than worn, favored fleece.

"We brush the unicorns every day, and spin their hair, and then weave them into cloth. Feel how soft. You'll never wear or sleep under something softer." And yet it doesn't compare at all to the damn dress on my own skin. Bastard. "We'll get you your own home and clothes and blankets in the next couple days. For now, you'll stay here with me."

A couple women walk up behind me, making me startle, and coax me to sit down on some pillows. "We understand that you're jumpy, Lira. Trust takes time."

They prop up my injured leg while Nykka carries over a bowl of water. Her braids swaying over each other make the strangest sound I've ever heard. It's fascinating. "We have a well where the unicorns graze. Everything we need is here, including safety. Ceal, will you go see where Era is? She should be here by now."

A few more girls come in as Ceal leaves. One comes close and combs her fingers through my hair, trying to untangle the knots. "You don't look good," she confides. Her face has a large, newly healing gash that begins at her jaw on her left, crosses her off-center nose, and ends just over her right brow. Purple and yellow bruises dot her face, and her arms and throat show the red welts left by a man's hand. She drops her gaze, her freshly washed raven hair falling over her face.

"This is Raven. She and her sisters were the ones to have arrived just a few days ago," Nykka introduces.

I glance at Raven, seeing the grief and the terror for her mother still haunting her. The lie of this 'sanctuary' makes me bitterly angry.

[No, Lira. Stay quiet.]

But they sent her mother away! If the unicorns aren't troubled by me, how can they fault a pregnant woman, a raped child, and one young boy whose only other option is to be raised into his father? They shut their gates and left them out on those hills to fend for themselves! What chance do they have? The Soldiers will find her!

Her. The one from Ravery had said he'd find 'Her' later. I meet Raven's eyes and take in her visible injuries with a horrible new understanding.

[These women are governed by their fear. Fear can spur you to act, but it can also condemn and cripple.]

"You should eat, Lira. Eat just a little. You can't eat too much when you haven't eaten for awhile. Your stomach needs time to adjust. We'll get you something more substantial later."

"Here's some bread and some grains." One of the girls who'd come in with Raven lays the new things at my side, within easy reach. She steps back and beams, proud of her contribution.

I snap my mouth closed and switch my attention from Nykka to the child. "Thank you, sweetie."

My stomach rumbles and I understand that I am hungry, but I stare at the food in my hands, the smell and the warmth of the bowl neither comforting nor appealing.

"Era! Where have you been?"

Behind me, a woman- Era, the Bound's apparent Healer- enters the tent with barely a sound. She holds her head high, and dips her eyes alone instead of her head to look down at me.

"This is Lira," Nykka continues, rising. "She was attacked by Soldiers a few days ago. There's an arrow in her thigh. Her wrists may need attention as well. Lira, this is Era, our Healer."

Within my answering nod I take the Healer's whole appearance in: her hair spirals up in defiant twists from her headband and ties like a wild grayish monster. She's wearing a long, faded green cape that crisscrosses over her chest and is secured behind her neck, leaving her shoulders bare. Beneath her cape is a simple, faded pink sleeveless dress. She's somewhere in her fifties, though her graying hair contrasts sharply with her flawless golden skin. If you look at her any way other than directly, you'd think she was younger. Her eyes are as green as the hills, as green as my mother's, and a vibration emanates from her skin; a vibration, a charge that stings, singes my skin, drills into my bones.

"I'm sorry. I wanted to see the new unicorn she's brought us. You are newly Bound?" The Healer kneels down and reaches for my right wrist.

[Say yes.]

The Nightmare's unexpected presence in my head makes me flinch. Era pauses to meet my eyes. "I am The Camp's Healer, Lira. Do you not trust me?"

While I ponder that question, she undoes my crude wrappings. I swallow down the wince of pain when she rips the last layer free from the scabs it had sealed into. The wounds open and begin to bleed again. "Who did this to you?"

"You did," I answer through a clenched jaw.

[Lira!]

"Yes, I'm sorry. I need to evaluate the damage. This is from a restraint. A rope. Who did it?"

It seems an asinine question, given who she is and where we are, given that they are hiding from the same threat, and that Nykka has already told her. "Soldiers. A few days ago."

I pull my hand free and begin rewrapping it, resenting that my blood has fallen to their soil as well as Ravery's. I want no piece of me left here when I leave.

"Don't cover it just yet." The Healer takes some items from a bag strapped around her waist. Raven retrieves a mortar made by a stone with an indent ground into its top.

"I think we'll all leave you to your work, Era. Come on, Raven."

Raven gives me a tight hug before she leaves. "We're safe here, Lira. They won't find us or hurt us ever again."

With only the Healer in the tent with me, it somehow becomes very small and stifling. I push myself up straighter and remove my leg from the pillows. She flicks her eyes towards me as I shift, but continues to cut her chunks of roots and dried plants and adds them to the mortar. "How did you manage to escape Soldiers?"

The implication of her question makes me bristle. There's a bit too much emphasis on 'you'- *How did* you-you of all people- *manage.* "I killed a few. And the be—"

[Careful!]

"—unicorns took care of the others. And then Night-"

[Unicorn Bound probably wouldn't name their saviors 'Nightmare'!]

Saviors? Really? What should I rename you, then, dear savior: Flower? Ladybug?

[See? You're hostile.]

"Night," I continue, "came and brought me here."

"*You* killed Soldiers?"

I don't care what I may appear to be to her, I am the daughter-

[Stop!]

I grind my teeth. "Soldiers are merely men. They can be killed."

The concept seems to surprise her. Had they never thought to fight back again? Regain their freedom, their part of the country?

I don't care. My body wants to give out- the state I was in before coming here, lack of food, water, real sleep is consuming me and I don't have the mind or the patience or the desire to talk or explain myself to her.

"What were you doing on the hills, alone?" The Healer's eyes are passive and seem neutrally interested. But she isn't smiling, and her posture is too stiff to be friendly.

What was I doing on the hills? I am the daughter of Elaar, born in a world very far removed from yours. My long ago love brought me here and dropped me on the hills at the feet of Soldiers so that I die as punishment for letting Others steal his daughter.

[You can't say that.]

Really? Would she not like that?

[Your sarcasm is quite funny. Answer her, but not like that. There are many versions of truth.]

Get out of my head! "I don't know. I woke up there and in that way."

"Where were you before?"

"I don't know." Irritation puts an edge to my words. The woman holds my gaze long and hard, but then she smiles. "I'm sorry. Please understand, we haven't had a new Bound in a long time. Especially a grown woman who's managed to keep herself UnTouched. And then Raven's family, and now you. It worries me that something is afoot."

She withdraws another piece of something from her bag, smells it, and places it on the mortar, grinding it into the other things she's already made into a powder. "Your unicorn is a beauty, Lira. It's so rare to come across one with absolutely no scars, no marks of restraints or Soldiers. Actually, it's never happened before. Where was he before he found you?"

Nightmare, get me out of here.

[Lira, everything is fine.]

No. No, it's not. Get me out of here now.

There's something about this woman; as though I know her, as though I should know her, as though I don't want to know her.

"I don't know where he was or from where he came. It didn't really seem to matter then, or now."

Her nearness is disjointing. I labor to my feet and limp to a sort of table made from stiffened unicorn cloth and suspended from the tent ceiling by thin braids of grass and unicorn hair. The Healer follows me, moving much too fast. I spin around and she nearly knocks me over. She grabs my wrist, digging her fingernails into my shredded skin. I try to pull free but she is stronger.

"She should never have been born. How were you?" she hisses venomously. "You are not wanted! Neither of you are!" Her eyes are appallingly vile, a complete contrast to the controlled coolness from just moments ago. "Why would you think to come here, to me, for help? As though I would ever help something as evil-made as you!"

I'm too stunned to speak or shout or move.

"I know the blood in your veins," she continues harshly. "The curse it put on her. The stain. That *thing* was never meant to be, she should never have lived, and neither should you. For the pain your mother and now you cause Anin to endure, for what you and the Other One will one day do-" She brings her closed fist up, uncurls her fingers, and blows the powder she had made in front of me directly into my eyes.

I scream and shove her away, my face on fire.

"Because she lives, you die."

I crash into the tripod and fall along with it to the tent floor, onto the coals that had been silently burning. Rolling quickly, I don't even feel the arrow or my swollen leg. The pain in my eyes, my face, my throat, my head, is immensely greater.

"Nykka!" Era screams, her voice echoing shrilly inside my head. I try to put distance between us, but my legs won't lift me up and I crash into something else. The pain!

"Don't touch her, Nykka!"

"Era, what have you done?" the camp matriarch demands. Their voices pierce holes into my nerves. I move my hands to cover my ears, falling again.

"I hope I just killed her."

Nightmare! I scream in my head, unable to make my mouth move.

"Why would you do that?"

"Do not help her, Nykka! *That* is the daughter of Elaar."

The ground below me topples and turns. The powder's a poison. I can feel it coursing through me, invading me, changing me. My veins are burning! I can't open my eyes to see.

"That's all true? How is that even possible? I would never- How are you sure?"

"Am I not your Seer as well as your Healer?"

[Lira, what is going on?]

The pain! I can't produce a functional breath. My body tries desperately to flush the stuff from my eyes, but I am suddenly barren of tears. I have to get out of this tent. I force an eye open, and through the blur and pain, I find the door and ingrain the distance before my eyes clamp shut. Oh, Dragons! What did she do to me!

"Why would she be here if that were so?"

"I dreamt of her last night. She was standing in a new Ravery before Anin. She had her daughter with her, a daughter who will-"

I lunge. Pause only enough to take another breath and leap forward again, propelling myself through the tent until I break through to the outside. The bright sunsmoon brings on a new wave of pain, but I don't stop. I push through women and girls not yet catching on to what's happening, running into tents, until finally I collide against their fortress wall and collapse to my hands and knees.

I think back to the layout of the camp as I'd looked down upon it before we'd entered. The wall is round. If I'm fast enough, I'll eventually come to the doors. I'm going the right way. I have to be going the right way.

Instead of doors, I run into a body. A small, child's body.

"Lira? You're bleeding!"

"Raven," I begin. My voice sounds like a whimper. But I don't have time to worry about that. "Raven," I gasp. "Help. The doors." Every word is a choke, but I get them out. I think I get them out. I think in a way that's understandable.

"You didn't look like that before. What happened?" her voice is rising, afraid.

I let my head hang and breathe slow, as slow as I can, though my heart keeps racing, the bullet keeps burning, my leg keeps throbbing, and my head keeps screaming at me to run, run through the girl and get to the doors. "Help," I choke out.

She is so silent for so long that I think that she has left. "The Soldiers," she whispers. "Him……" Though her voice drops into a whisper, the fear in her words is shrill.

I reach forward and find her wrist. "Raven," I try again. "My mother-" How does Era know my mother? And why would the Unicorn Bound hate her as well? I thought it was only Anin, only Soldiers.

Mentioning my mother makes up Raven's mind. "Keep your side against the wall," she whispers. "I'll walk at your other side so no one sees. My mother will have run to the trees. Go to the trees, Lira. Go where the men won't find you. Find my mother, please. Please?"

I nod.

Trees. They are so close. I know I can make it. I am the daughter of Elaar. I can run blind and on one leg. I can run just enough to get within my parents' trees. And then I'll be truly safe.

Raven struggles to lift the planks of wood bolting the double doors shut. Her breathing quickens as she panics. A board falls from her fingers with one end still in the latch, but she quickly rights it and slides it free.

"Lira, this isn't a good idea! Maybe they're sorry. Maybe they didn't mean it."

I get to my feet and hug her quickly, and then pull blindly at a door until it opens enough for me to fall through. Now the hills have become freedom. Lovely. No, they're a passage. I'm going to the trees.

[Lira! Don't-!]

As always, the wind is strong. I try to get to my feet but the wind pushes me to my knees several times.

[Lira!]

When I finally get my balance straightened and reorient my sense of direction, Raven screams and something grabs hold of my throat before slamming me up against the outer wall of the camp. I feel the body before me stretch towards the doors and Raven screams again. She is flailing, striking at someone, and he is both laughing and panting as he brings her and himself closer.

"Where is Her?" he growls. I can't open my eyes or speak, but I recognize the voice. The Soldier from Ravery. At first I think he's speaking to me, but his voice is muffled. His head is turned away from me and towards Raven. She screams and screams and then her voice catches and she's struggling to breathe. The marks on her throat. He's choking her. "Where is my son, Little Bitch?"

I release my grip on his arm and strike at his face with my fists. My strikes are weak, but I hit again and again to at least distract him. I reach to my left with my other hand, but unable to find Raven or where he's holding her, I return to punching at his face, kicking with my stronger leg.

He swears and pulls me toward him by my throat before slamming me back into the wall. He does it again, ensuring my head hits, and then a third time. My head and body go numb. "You are for later," he growls. He releases me and I fall. There's a crash beside me as Raven is flung into the wall as well. I fumble with my hands and find her foot, but she's not moving.

"Where is Her and my son? You better tell me, Little Bitch, or I will ensure they don't take you back into these walls before I throw you to the garrison. Do not ignore me!" He is fumbling at his clothes, and I realize he has every intention of making good on his threat. I grab onto her foot and pull her towards me, covering her body with mine. His own daughter!

"Get off!" he orders, trying to wrench us apart, but I wrap my arms around her and refuse to let go. She begins to return to consciousness.

"Lira! It's Him! It's Him!"

The Unicorn Bound have arrived at the doors and are screaming. If they release the unicorns, we'll all be dead. Where's Nightmare! Arrows are falling around us, but they must not yet know that their Seer wants me dead, or they'd undoubtedly be less careful of their aim to strike him down. And with one Soldier in sight already, they probably won't venture onto the hills to save Raven in case there are more.

His belt is off and he whips the buckle onto my back. He's going to rape his own daughter, and they'll think they can't stop it. "Run," I whisper into Raven's ear before lunging my body into his, hoping I've pushed him far enough away from her that the others will grab her and lock the doors behind them.

The doors slam shut and I can't remember how I got onto my stomach in the grass. Fingers dig into my hair and my head is yanked back. "Are you offering yourself now? It seems they don't want you, anyway. There's only one reason a camp won't accept a bitch."

I kick and hit backward with my elbows as best I can, but I know that my energy has been spent and my attempts are nothing, and I begin to panic. In my ear, the Soldier laughs. "You've gotten between me and Her, and now me and what belongs to me. You'll pay until they do. Time for my show, woman." His free hand claws into my breast before slicing down my abdomen- my adrenaline spikes enough that I flail and scream, with no doubt that the unicorn or anyone else can hear me. *"Nightmare!"*

"Yours has just begun."

Nightmare!

[Lira!]

He yanks me along behind him by my hair. The grass tangles around my legs and I trip. I cannot allow myself to be on the ground! Only I can't hold my weight or match his pace, and my body falls again. He swears and yanks hard on my hair before hoisting me up with an arm tight around my rib cage. The armor covering his chest crushes into my back.

I refocus, concentrating on my other attacker. *Leave,* I order the poison, walling it off. It stops, pulsing in paused intensity somewhere in the center of my chest. *You don't belong here.* It forms a loose, powdery ball. *Leave,* I command again, and it begins to slowly dissolve.

I try to push out of his grip, try to wrench free, try to kick him, but enough of the Seer's drug has hit me and my earlier fight with him has sped it along.

To my terror, I pass out.

12

WEIGHT OF BODY ON MINE. Body heat that snarls and growls, wants to attack and maim and take what it cannot have. Presence of something that takes its own form in my head. A distorted face with jagged teeth that drip blood and drool. Sockets empty of eyes. A haunting, terrifying black emptiness. Threatening, revolting touches. Claws that scrape down my body, trying to shred fabric that refuses to give in. This is not The Man the damn dress obeys-

My swollen eyes shoot open. The Soldier's heated pair stare back, a scant few inches from my face. His mouth is on mine and he bites down hard on my lower lip, breaking skin and drawing blood. His body is pressing down onto mine, his armor off, his pants undone. I gasp and bring my right leg up into his side, jabbing the arrow's splintered shaft into his flesh. He yells and slaps me before clamping a hand down on my throat. He uses his other to try to pin one of my arms down by my face. No! No! My eyes clamp shut again. I slap and hit frantically with my free hand, keeping it difficult for him to catch. My head is swimming with poison. *Do not black out! Do not!*

He claws at my chest, my sides, trying to shred the dress, to pull it apart at the seams.

Except there are no seams. The dress holds tightly together around me.

"I will show Her what happens. I'll show you right now. Don't you ever decide you can flee from me. I will always find you, no matter how far I have to hunt you down. And once I find you, you'll never try and flee from me again."

I stop breathing and just fight. His body on mine is thick and horrible. I can't scream, can't speak. He is heavy, and stronger. I kick and rock, not allowing him a chance to get too comfortable. I slap wherever I can land a blind strike. The dress won't give and his frustration is overtaking him. He releases my throat and begins pulling at the fabric with both hands while I begin scrambling backward. He grabs my knee and casts the back of his hand across my jaw again. I kick his in return. He is set on maiming, destroying, shredding. Raping. How can I kill him if I can't see? I stop thinking and fight, move, ignoring the pain. I'm poisoned and I'm blinded, wounded and drained, but he's not going to touch me.

Then my body is beneath his again. His knees press my arms to my sides while his ankles cross back over them, and I know that I am trapped. He laughs. "Her stopped fighting a long time ago. I think I've forgotten how fun it is. She stopped screaming, too. What makes you? It's this leg, isn't it?" He finds the arrow and wrenches it up. All my pent up breath escapes in a scream too forceful to silence.

He sighs, ecstatic. "That is *excellent*. I could have taken you right in front of that camp, made them watch. But this time I want no audience. I am Ealin. Say it. Say it!" He grabs hold of the arrow's shaft again when I refuse, and yanks it so hard that he rips it out. But I don't scream for him this time.

"Scream!" he orders, pressing the point of the arrow into my throat. "You'll produce sons for me, won't you? Her kept giving me bitches and only one son. I bet the thing she's carrying now is another bitch. I'll kill it right in front of both of you. She finally gave me a son after I snuffed the thing born before him."

The knife.

Just like that, it's in my right hand. I can only bend my arms up, which is the only direction I need to have right now. I jab the knife into his under-thigh as far as I can. He howls and goes limp enough that I continue to push upward, grabbing onto the knife with both hands as soon as my other breaks free, and push until he sails over my head. His blood is pouring down my hands and snaking through my fingers, but I don't think, don't pause. I roll so my feet and face stay pointed towards him, and launch the knife after him before I've stopped moving. My palms slam down onto earth-

The Soldier, everything else, just ceases to be. I inhale, I stretch out my awareness, my hearing. Earth and baby-new leaves. Earth and thin, low, sparse grass that grow only beneath the shade of trees. The smell of trees, of damp. Sound of wind high, high above me, soft and gentle, rattling branches. I gasp. Branches! I hear branches! Trees, there's trees over my head. *Trees.*

"Bitch!" Under my palm, the knife again, solid and sure and able. "Her was just 'Her', but you will be 'Bitch'."

I can't open my eyes. My chest burns. But the knife is under my palm. My ears track the sounds of the Soldier ahead of me, struggling back to his knees. Where's Nightmare? Am I in The Trees, my parents' Trees? I need my mother's dragons.

His foot crunches loudly to the earth beneath him, holding his weight. As his other, his sliced leg, slides up beneath him to join the first, I throw the knife again.

He howls, enraged, again. With a string of curses and another grunt, I know the knife is being withdrawn. I pry open my eyes but they pour bloody tears that blur the tripled vision spinning in mad, sickening circles. The knife has landed close to his heart, in his shoulder. The face that turns to me explodes with rage. My eyes spasm shut again.

The knife is under my palm. Shocked, maybe now even frightened, he makes no move except to swallow. I force my body to stand, yielding the knife ahead of me as a warning. I am gasping so hard I can't even growl.

Light and trees and earth, Soldier and knife and my body are a kaleidoscope of images scrambled and jumbled back together, spinning, turning. But there's trees. That's all that matters. I'm in the trees.

"Do not......" I begin, but my throat shuts down as well and I cough so violently I taste blood. I back away. The air is laced with the sharp scent of blood- his and mine. Though his words attempt to sound threatening, I feel his eyes studying the knife, and me, in uncertainty. He had watched on the hills, must have seen, but now beside me it's unmistakable that the knife always finds its way back to my hand. That must be somewhat unnerving. I embrace a new respect, a new pride and need for the dagger, and my fingers loosen their frantic grip.

"This is quite the show. You have some tricks hidden in that damn dress, Bitch. But fabric can always be torn, and women will always be caught. Run if you want. There's nowhere for either of you to go. I will find Her, and I will find you. None of you will be safe forever, do you hear?"

The ground beneath me rolls like those wicked hills. The air feels dark and thick, full of the Soldier. I stumble a few more careful steps back, listening. He doesn't move. He's still hunting me as he had on the hills. Today or tomorrow, he's sure he'll have me. I use the tree beside me for support and curl around it to limp further into the woods. When I can no longer keep my steps controlled and deliberate, when I don't care if there is a safe enough distance between us or how costly it is to turn my back his way, I fall to my knees and crawl frantically on.

Nightmare! A unicorn to keep men away. Him and Soldiers. *Nightmare!* Where's my father? I want Mihn, but I'm calling for my mother's enemy instead.

*

I don't know for how long or for how far I stumble away. Sometimes I walk and sometimes I crawl. Have I really gotten anywhere? Lightheaded, I fall against a tree, holding my trembling knife-hand against my forehead, trying to steady myself, trying to think. Sweat floods into my eyes with a hot dry wetness, trying to rehydrate my burned eyes. But the sweat only reconstitutes the dried blood. While the droplets are cold, my skin is icy hot. My eyes, face, and throat are blistered raw. What did she use on me?

Confronting and fighting Soldiers had once filled Mom with exhilaration and purpose and drive. She'd have laughed at the Unicorn Bound and turned and *walked* defiantly away and no one would have made a motion to stop her. Blind, she'd have still known where that Soldier's heart was and would have aimed correctly.

Air made within the souls of trees takes hold of my senses. I choke, holding back the sobs. Home, but I'm under attack. Suns and moon and sky and trees mix with Valley and unicorns and Soldiers. Knives and blood and running mix with exquisite smells- how my soul, my body, my blood, has yearned for *these* scents and the feel of *this* ground beneath my feet. The rough bark of this tree against my face. I'm Home. I'm in Home.

I take a deep breath and bring in as much air and smell as I can, ordering my lungs and throat not to clamp shut before filling to capacity. The air is so inexpressibly magnificent, nothing at all like the air I have been breathing in the Other Place. Eyes no longer functioning, my other senses strengthen, and I identify everything around me.

Trees. Suns above me. Moon in between. Hundreds and hundreds of tall trees stretching up to the sky and out in all directions. Trees filled with life. Trees that breathe, that speak and think. Surrounded. Surrounded, sheltered by sounds and creatures. No more endless hills!

Think. Think. Birds are singing. Soldier is not here.

A faint, familiar thread of scent makes me stumble and crash into a tree before falling backward into the understory. Him. Or, He had smelled of this. My face turns toward the origin of the strand. East. The mountains, the foothills, the dragons. Him.

I make an effort to ponder my options. I'm shaking, I can't see, and everything hurts and burns and throbs. How do I know the Soldier isn't standing in front of me? What if there's more? What if I walk right into Him? Where's The Nightmare?

I'll go north. The air ahead of me is tingling, sparkling through my eyelids. That is east, I'm sure. I alter my direction and crawl, sometimes almost walk, tree by tree, taking a breath only once my side touches against bark. My father is deaf but he hears with his whole body. So I listen, seeing with my ears before taking another step, sliding my hands carefully ahead of me so as not to crunch through any undergrowth or snap any branches, keeping my head ducked, and ready to change direction should I ram into anything.

The birds hush behind me, warning me of the Soldier. I quicken my pace.

*

My hand slides around the curve of the tree's trunk, and then I lose the power to keep my arm up, and it falls to my side. My shoulder takes its place and becomes the only thing keeping me upright, aside from the tree itself. I can't walk anymore, and won't be able to crawl much further either.

It hurts more to realize that the beast is not going to come to my aide. Why would he, now that he's inside the camp with women who truly adore him? My hip and forehead fall onto the tree as well.

One more step. Just one. I can't stop yet. My leg feels three times its size. At least it's no longer arrowed. From my hips to its torn hem, the damn dress is soaked and sticky. How much more blood have I lost? I choke, remembering Mihn trying to stop my bleeding before.

I inch my leg forward to take another limp onto my good leg, and then push my body forward against the rough bark. But the tree ends too quickly and I fall sideways, knowing that once I crash upon the earth, I will not be able to move again. I lay there face down, sure the Soldier will fall down upon me at any moment. It doesn't matter what he does to me; I won't be alive to see morning anyway.

I inhale, breathing in more moss than air. The air is muffled, more muffled than a buffer of trees can provide. There is only moss beneath me, not dirt. I pry my eyes open, breaking the scabs that had formed over them, and blink constantly to clear them. Everything is a dull black. I lift my head and look behind me, seeing night and trees and low-growing brush through a crack in the world. I hold my breath, confused, before realizing that I'm inside the tree.

I lay my head back to the moss, close my eyes, and think of the wind, think of her enough that she takes on a form. A white......dragon? I want them so much. Travel east, remember Mom's secret route to the mountain top, and walk into my grandparents' cave. I know exactly how to get there, precisely which mouth of which cave is the entrance to their in-mountain cavern. Will they accept me, or do they love only my mother?

Wind in her white, nearly discernable shape weaves and dances before me. After everything, I am Here only to die. At least I'll die in the belly of a tree. I'm so sorry, Talyn. So sorry. *Baby, baby, baby......*

Wind twists and turns and becomes a transparent little girl. She's just entering toddler-hood. How long is her hair? Does it still curl just at the ends or did she inherit her grandmother's full waves? Eyes would now be more so His than they were when she was a baby. Those miraculous purple eyes. I have only to search faces to find her.

She holds her arms out to me: *Mama! Mama, find me! Don't leave me here!*

I sob in reply, *Here is only all my fears,* and reach forward for her so strongly my arms feel as though they've dislocated themselves.

"Talyn! Talyn!"

A branch cracks just outside my shelter. Talyn is whisked away into a fold of the air as its shape disappears. The Soldier's head- dark as night- sneers into the tree. My fingers flinch around the dagger's hilt, but it's useless now. All he has to do is blow a soft gust of air upon me and I'll crumble.

He grabs my ankle and pulls me out of my shelter, and I can't even lift my head. "What doesn't rip should certainly burn."

Thunder. I hear thunder.

[Lira? Lira, can you hear me?]

Through the lids of my eyes, I see a long black face come towards me, preceded first by a long gold horn that lights up the night like a lantern.

[Blessed stars,] the voice gasps. [Oh, Lira. My Lira.]

Nightmare? My eyes open. His horn floods the space over my head with a subdued, warm golden glow that is somehow not the wrong color. His horn is transparent, filled with sparkling stars the color of gold that float free, suspended within. Like fireflies......

Fireflies, spewing out May's glass jar. Little spots of softly blinking lights, *This way. This way.* Regrouping, spiraling up......and up......and up......

[Lira?]

"Fly," I nod, and drift away with the bugs.

SILVER LIGHT

TIME IS NOT A FRIEND. I will not think about how much of it has sped merrily by.

Morning creeps in, reverent and unnoticeable. I open my eyes to silver light that sparkles and shimmers off the edges of every object, in such a way my eyes can't focus. I pull my head back, turn it to the side to look out the corners of squinted eyes, only to find no real improvement. It feels like someone has inflated something within my body. I can't hear a thing. My head is both heavy and light, my body the same. I hold my head over my legs, hold my legs to my chest, and just wait. I wonder if it'll ever snow again.

She was born just after dawn, seems so long ago.

A leaf floats past my window, carried along by the wind. It makes no sound as it scrapes across the glass, but somehow I hear it. In the corner, beneath the shadows, it still smells of night. I wonder what the air tastes like.

The silver glares hold me entranced. What's wrong with my eyes? My legs are cramped. They tingle in that stabbing way when I uncurl them. Do I remember how to stand? The change in position, the sudden height makes me dizzy. I gasp, wince when my head becomes too heavy and dark, and plant my hands on my trembling thighs until the spell passes. Where's the humming coming from?

The silver glimmers haven't gone away. Standing in the center of my room, I stare in awe at the songsbox and the dresser it's stationed upon......at the window frame, the seat, the bed, the little bitty cracks between the floorboards, the knots, the grain, my skin. Everything is lit with silver around the edges, dusted over surfaces.

I rub my eyes.

She was born this day two years ago. I hear her breathe, smell her, feel her in my arms. Is she here? Was it all a horrific dream?

The sunlight bending around the house is visible in silverish rays. I turn my hands over, silver caressing my fingers and the lines in my palms. I outstretch my hand into a strong silver ray; is it warm in the sun?

My shoulder hurts.

Does she remember me? Does she know she is mine?

"Your name is Talyn. Talyn, I am your mother. I am your mother. This is the day you came from my body. I am your mother and you are mine. Please, please, tell me how to find you."

Nothing. Only silver.

I open the door of my bedroom tentatively. Silver light streams in through cracks in the shades of the hallway windows and through the open bathroom door. The doorframes, the borders between the walls and ceiling and between the walls and floor, the patterns in the carpet, the railing and the edges of the stairs, the pairs of candles before each door, before the stairways and set upon each stair and the little flames burning perfectly, reverently still- all gilded in silver.

The floor creaks when I step out of my room. I slowly place my foot into the hall, extending the noise as I shift my weight. I wait. No rush of water pours down the hall to whisk me away. I take another step, wait. The floor doesn't collapse and leave me plummeting forever downward. Take one hand from the doorframe behind me. The other. My room doesn't wither and die. My legs and hands tingle with a sharp, prickly heat. I blink, bring the silvered air into my lungs. I can't focus.

I struggle downstairs as though I step both up and down, right and left. It'll be dark by the time I get to the floor. The moon will be red.

In the kitchen, Mom sits in the early morning darkness sipping some tea, the non-dragon lizards at her feet. The birds in the rafters overhead meet my eyes with the same confusion. They should be screaming, but I can't hear a thing.

Dark crescents rim Mom's lower lids. Her feet are lined with mud. She holds the mug frozen to her open lips, looking at me stunned, disbelieving that I have just walked into the room. The candles become aflame when I sit across from her. Two candles every few feet. My daughter is two and I don't know where she is.

I lower myself into my favorite kitchen chair as though it's still normal. The last time I was in this room, I had made us breakfast. I don't even remember what it had been. Talyn was practicing standing, her hands on the arm of this chair, giggling and sputtering and shrieking at me. She'd bounced and stomped her feet, slapped her hand down on the seat. I didn't know. I didn't know that it was the last time I'd hear her laughing, that it was the last time I'd be human. Mom left the house and I went into the front room, our favorite room, and while Talyn played, I fell asleep. When I woke, there were people in our house, and when I woke a second time, she was gone. Can I wake a third time, and find her here?

I know I am slowly wasting away, and I allow it. I welcome it. I want it.

Like Mom.

It's so bright.

I close my eyes, will my soul to fly away. Reach, search, find someplace else.

What will Talyn be doing today? No one but we know it's the anniversary of her birth.

As I open my eyes, the sound of water lapping at the beach comes clear as moonlight. The smell of fresh air, sand and snow again beneath my feet like when we- He and I- had walked along the beach. Silver red light but the vision doesn't leave. I know I'm in the kitchen but I can't see it anymore. Mom sits in the bend of a tree limb drinking her tea with our rafter birds nesting in her wild hair. The hearth is there, wall-less and burning in the midst of trees. His and my clothes are strewn throughout the undergrowth, tangled in whatever they'd landed in as we'd playfully stripped out of each layer, one by one, a taunting, teasing cast-aside of each. It snows and then it's that bright green of new summer. Snow and summer, white then green. Behind me the waves are singing, crashing on the sand and pulling away. Crashing on the sand and pulling away. Crashing-

Something. Something's whispering to me.

"Lira?"

I hold onto the vision, entranced, tuning Mom out to try and hear. She opens her mouth but her body fades away. The hearth rumbles with laughter, warm, heated laughter that melts the remainder of the snow. Summer green, all around. And the waves, saying my name. *Lir-ra.* *Lir-ra.* Crash-and-fade. *Lir-ra.* Crash-and-fade.

What is The Lake saying? Green and blue and silver stretch on in every direction as though we're at the edge of the world. Are we? What if Mom had listened to that voice that tried to call her into the water? Would it have carried her to the shore on the other side? The shore that is maybe Home?

Wind swimming through the trees. Leftover leaves falling from their branches and collecting, swirling away in a tiny tornado, as Love- two spinning so wildly together you cannot see where the seam that holds them together lay. Seamless.

It's new summer again and the leaves are grown.

Autumn once more. Winter's coming. The leaves break away, cascade downward like feathers. The wind picks up and catches them before they crash, holds them alight and suspended before nature has her way and pulls them down and apart.

Summer and the air is playful, joyful, teasing the leaves where they hang feebly onto their branch.

Now they lay like shattered glass, fragile and brittle, crunching under malicious feet, unable to be what- all together- they had just been. Whole.

I was once whole.

A long, long time ago.

"Lira?"

Mihn hides behind a waterfall of blue-gray fog, watching me in a thoughtful way. I feel suspended, held on some other plane of existence. I'm mildly aware of him and my mother beside him, calling my name. Part of me is fearful, wants to reach out to them. But The Lake calls out to me again-

Mom's voice, pleading, so far away. "Silver light, if not me, then take my child and let her be-"

Go for a walk, daughter. We won't be far behind.

Okay, Mihn.

Mom's hands grip the mug tightly. She's going to shatter it in her hands.

Reaching. Something reaching for me, and my body trying to push herself closer into His grasp. Already in the kitchen doorway, staring down the hall towards the front door. The foyer door is open, showing the double dragons etched onto the outer doors. Spiraling upwards, aiming themselves towards freedom. Almost there. In the distance, there's screaming. My screaming. The silver holds the wave of my blood at bay.

"Take some food, love."

"I won't be gone long." I start down the hall. Mom takes hold of my arm and holds onto me.

"There is good that you are owed. You are the child of my soul and you deserve more than what this place has given you. Remember, I cannot go back now," she whispers. "I'll be here, Lira. I'll be here and I'll find her for you. Take care of you. Go find her father. Go be with Him. I'll do the rest."

I stare at her, bewildered. The Lake calls to me again.

The sky above is bright clear cloudless blue. I squint up at the brightness, wondering if my feet are hitting the pavement or if the wind is carrying me. The sound of the waves in my head is like the heavy steady breathing of perfect sleep, lulling me along.

Whispers. Guiding me, calling me......

A breeze passes by. Do I know that smell? My feet stop and face me into the air. Whispers are stronger. Enchanted, I follow, strain to hear, to see, to understand.

Everything now has a red tinge to it. Where's the silver? I walk, heedless. Trees, homes, Others pass me by. I close my eyes and taste the red-silver air on my tongue and my lips. Why does it seem so familiar? So long since I walked in the air. Cars and people. I cover my ears, keeping them out. Don't lose the whisper.

Sand under my feet. I open my eyes and look down. Sand. Then I hear The Lake. The beauty I have kept myself away from holds me mesmerized. Pure, beautiful blue spans out before me. The rising sun sparkles across the gentle ripples like dancing diamonds. I had thought for sure the water would dry up, be sucked back into the earth as the river where my parents had first met had done when Mihn was killed.

I know exactly where my feet have led me. I turn to my left, where the line of trees begins. Four steps in, and I'll be in The Alcove. I find myself walking there, pulled there.

The difference in seasons does alter the feel, the atmosphere. Fall has a lightness, a warmth, as much as it holds the first real chill of the year. That difference makes this part of my past faceable, unintimidating. Numbed, I walk in.

I notice everything, every falling leaf, every fern, every bug and blade of grass. The first time I was here, it was summer in the dead of winter, the first day of a new year, the Year of the Dragon, the very moment a new year, a new life is supposed to begin. Now, somehow, the outside air has found a way in but still I feel Him, all around: in the air that touches me, in the air I breathe, in the untouched ground beneath my feet. I want to wave my arms in the air, down my skin to get him out, off, away. But I can't move.

Just a few steps away lay the clearing that had lent us that night. After all this time, His presence remains so strong. I've tried so hard to forget him, forget this. Now I'm glued, like a ghost has decided to borrow my body to remember how it was to feel, to see, to touch and remember. It makes me move my feet, forces me to walk in.

The wind that sings of him plays with the leaves. But feeling of all kind has long since been numbed from me. There— where we had last been together, where our daughter was made— pulsing now with silver threads- is the depression we had formed. I stare warily. *Two lives. One breath. Three.* Should I have come here on her birthday? Does it matter? I came here the day before she was taken from me.

I crawl into the clearing, veering around our depression. Two naked bodies roll and move, a fleeting remembrance. An illusion. Laughter, so pure, so real, pierces up into the present, firing into my heart. Only one tear. Only one can fall.

Apprehensive, I crawl over to the spot where we had lain.

......Can I let you go now?
No.
I'm taking you Home, Lira.
If I said I was getting cold again?
I love you, do you believe me?
I do.
Always.
Where are You?
Where are you?......

The whispers grow, getting louder and louder till they are no longer a whisper but a tingling, a something I can feel as well as hear. It becomes strong, like it originates from that spot. I inch closer. *Let me go. Please, let me go.*

His laughter in that crowded club, holding onto me so I wouldn't fall away. Those brilliant, sparkling eyes. His voice in my head in my ears in this air, so clear and real.

But he left.

"Goodbye." I reach out and set my hand—

DRAGONS!

The silver threads that followed me from the house explode in a screaming, scorching, tear-apart light that inhales me at speeds so fast I can't catch my breath. Clamping my eyes shut doesn't protect them from the blinding light. I flail, unable to find my ears to protect them from the piercing roar. I can't feel anything below my feet but rushing air and currents of light.

I scream. I think I scream. Some other invisible thing then grabs hold of me and yanks. I think my back is broken but I'm spinning, tumbling, falling-

14

"Am I dead?"
[No.]
"Can I be?"
[No.]

Dead, I can go anywhere I want. I can go back to the Other Place. I can find my daughter, and Mihn and I can guide my mother to her. And then I'll find Him, and haunt him worse than he's haunting me.

[I'm so sorry, Lira. I should never have forced you into that camp against your will when you were so certain something bad was going to happen there.]

She'd be found, and safe. If only I were dead.

*

"It's whatever......you are doing......to the water......isn't it?"

[What?]

I cough for several minutes before able to speak again. "Unicorn Seer......poisoned me......somehow knew ......who I am-" My throat spasms shut and another painful bout of coughing attacks.

[Lira, just rest.]

"Should be dead. Leg is sore......should be worse......"

[Go back to sleep, Lira.]

"You're drugging the water......"

*

I can't fight it. I reach out, completely sure the space beside me is full. My body and mind is *certain* his body is curled around me, that his breath is on my neck, that his fingers are entwined with mine. I reach, so hopeful, so needy, so sure- I *smell* him. Smell the earth and trees that house him.

When his body does not reward my fingers, all sensation of him vanishes.

I roll onto my chest and lay nearly flat upon dew dampened earth, wishing my body would just sink all the way down. My right palm lays flat upon the world's pulse, and with my ear down in the earth, I am made to listen. My eyes level with ground, I see the area as a newborn seed would see its new world. My vision sparkles with tears, casting an ethereal shade upon everything that meets my gaze. Sunsmoon above slips down to where I lay, spreading warmth upon my back that seeps through my skin and pours nourishment through my veins. The smell of rich soil, so pungent and clean rises from below, filling, comforting.

I return my back to the ground. Brand new leaves bright green and perfect wave above me. I stare in disbelief- I can see again. The leaves, how light shines through their skin, how water and food travel through their veins as it does through mine. Leaf, holding my stare, whispers, whispers so softly in a language that may have been familiar, generations ago. My eyes travel through transparent green, a leaf-shaped window to some distant world. Window I can *almost* see through......

My lips shake, and I drift back to sleep.

*

"Dragons."
[What?]
"Where......dragons......"
[The dragons don't fly here anymore, Lira. Not since your mother's been gone.]
"Dragons......"

*

My eyes flutter open, locking on the gnarled trunk of an elm ahead of me. From its roots flow the stream I cannot see from where I lay, though it's only a few yards away. I feel it traveling unseen beneath me until it reaches that opening beneath the elm and bursts out into life and day and air. I want it, want some water, but I can't move. Rooted to the ground not like a tree growing upwards, resilient, searching for the sunslight, but like moss, never more than an inch off the floor, hiding unseen in the shadows of greater, more confident beings, crawling outward.

My lips tremble. *Don't cry*, I plead with myself. *If you start, we won't stop.*

The earth groans, stretching beneath me. What feels like a hand presses against my palm. Beside my face, moss and last fall's leaves twist and fall away, and the soil beneath takes the shape of a wrinkled, grandmotherly face. Large lips and a thick moss of hair, ring of fallen leaves for a crown, pebbles for a necklace and earrings. Deep, speckled brown eyes turn to me and blink.

No shame, she whispers back.

I don't belong here. Not without my daughter. I want my daughter.

The face of the earth smiles placidly. Trees bow low over me, listening. The breeze they create disturbs the heat coming from above, but my body can't shiver and doesn't care, so it doesn't matter.

Everything matters, the earth rebukes.

I want my baby.

The face lowers her eyes and shakes her head, fading back to earth.

I want Him. I want to feel whole and safe and held.

Nightmare grumbles, a bird perched between his ears. He frowns at it and shakes his head to send it off. Unicorn. He's still here? Did he go somewhere?

The Earth's voice rumbles, soft and deep. Each syllable spoken with immense care and clarity, it commands attention by her gentleness and the complete ideal of 'Grandmother'. Does my grandmother speak in such a way? The sound of her voice more important than the content of her words?

Earth's face appears, clearer, closer. I blink, pull my face back slightly in order to see.

Earth Whisperer, she continues. *What is done cannot be undone. But your trials were not put upon you with no chance for recourse. All will come right in time due.*

Heal me, I cry into her embrace.

Heal me, she whispers back. I seal my eyes and fade away again.

RAW

A SOLDIER WITH BLACK HAIR stalks me through the halls, but I run up a grand stairway, heaving myself up with the railing, taking two stairs at a time. Talyn's in Ravery and Anin is going to kill her! I have to find her!
Talyn! Talyn!
In and out every room, screaming her name. She doesn't know who I am. She won't answer.

*

My head lifts up from the floor, eyes swollen and raw and now painfully dry. So weak. So vacant. My head has a heavy sickness lodged in it.

Across from me, on the floor and partially against the wall, Mom sleeps with tears falling from her eyes. She always cries when she sleeps.

The house rings and hums and screams with its and our emptiness. Walls that should echo with a little girl's giggles and new songbird voice shoot back only stark silence. Little bare feet learning to walk. She'll be running by now.

The sun streams in bright and unforgiving. Mom stirs, sitting up. Our eyes meet but we say nothing. My father stares out the window, the light making him glow.

Numbly, I want to tell the light, the day, to go away. They're not wanted here anymore. Night isn't welcome, either.

I set my head down and escape to blackness.

*

Ravery's on fire. The blaze nips and burns, jumping out at me like angry hands. The tower door is barricaded closed. I have to find a unicorn to break the lock.

*

Legs to chest. Can't move. Can't blink. Sit in corner. Stare, only stare. Rain chimes against window and immediately washes away. House is tainted. Touched by an evil hand. No wind blows. So silent. So dead.

"Lira, I've brought you some food."

Legs to chest. Can't move. Can't blink. Only stare ahead. Window not in front of me. But I can still see.

"You have to eat."

Eyes close. Window. Sun to moon to red to Him.

"Will you at least try? Please, you need to eat."

Dark and secure in this corner. Detached.

Door click soft— Mom's left room.

Trees by Lake whisper and play. *I hear you calling. No one's here.*

Station on songsbox changes. Want to reach throat, but it's bare. Not even my charm to soothe me. He took it with him. If I'd had my charm, Talyn wouldn't have been-

Song on songsbox forces comprehension into my head. Blink again. My darkest hour, and His smile, and my love for him-

Snap!

A hot, red rage claws its way through me, boils its anger through my veins like a dragon spreading her wings and ready to burst into war. Feeling surges through me like a river, burning and painful, consuming as well as altering.

I charge the songsbox; snatch it from the table and throw it across the room. Panting, yelling, I watch it crash against the wall, a myriad of shattering voices and different components and materials falling pathetically to the floor. I scream, whirl, grab whatever I can and hurl it across the room. Another something and another. I scream again, tear the pillows from the bed, shove the mattress to the floor, send an innocent table flying.

"Lira?"

Finding one of my boots, I close my eyes and fling it. It leaves my fingers slowly. In my head, the air parts and ducks out of the way, letting it glide through. Air stopping and splitting, fleeing. Shoe turning, suspended, traveling so slow.

Shattering glass and cold and icy rain bite my skin, making me gasp. Is it winter again? How many winters have passed? Two? Three? Seeing the broken window surprises me. The momentary stillness lets me sense Mom's presence.

"Lira?"

I look back to the jumble of things on the other end of the room. I want to set it on fire. Set the whole world on fire. Set myself on fire. Set Him on fire. I want to feel the heat singe the outside of my skin the way my soul is being seared away. I want the sky to turn so black, so thick with smoke that everyone here shudders and cries. I want That Woman and her men to understand that I'll cut them to pieces when they're found. I want Talyn to know I- I want Him to know-

My legs collapse.

"Lira." Mom rushes to me, but I crawl away from her to the toppled bed. I pull myself onto the slanted mattress and bury my head. "I hate Him," I moan. "I hate him, I hate him, I hate him."

Mihn quickly repairs the window and all the other broken objects, placing them back in their spots. The songsbox clicks back on, singing a different song till Mom orders it to be silent. She lays down beside me and holds me close against her while she runs her hand hypnotically down my back and hums. She hums softly at first, and then she sings while I sob. Hours. Old tunes of Home I haven't heard since I was a child, when her own dreams of returning had not yet been broken. The sound of her signing is as effective as it was when I was little. I hide my face under my mother's chin, feeling small and helpless and dependant on her all over again.

She stops singing, takes a breath, and then whispers her prayer:

"Silver light,

Take me Home
Where I can fly on Wind's swift wings
Where rainbows are winged, loving things
Home to skies always powder blue
Home to all I hold as true

Silver light,
Don't leave me here
Here is only all my fears
I want to go Home
to the earth that I know
to faces I long to see
to the air I need to breathe

Silver light,
Please, take me Home
I want to dance to the tune I know
amongst the ghosts who had come before
I need to get back to the land they roam
where only our suns can keep me warm

I need my stars
I miss those souls
To where my body can rejoin her own
Home is where I need to go

Silver Light,
If not me,
Then take my child and let her be
Home in waters that once quenched my thirst
Home in the place of her bloods' birth
Home where the morning will be her closest friend
Home where the night has a gentle hand

Take her down the paths of her father's steps
To meet the air that came from his breath
Show her the life she should always have lived
And all the things Home has need to give

Show her the moon who comes out to talk
Late at night after a long day's walk
Show her mountains who surpass the clouds
And trees that love to sing and bow
Home where the rain laughs as it falls
Home to answer all her calls."

*

The Nightmare, my mother's enemy, makes
Ravery's door explode into fireflies.
Anin's hair whips around her face. The wind is
howling. Anin, my human grandmother, holds
my daughter in her arms, a knife to her throat.

*

I keep dreaming about that damn unicorn.
"He came for you once. I know he'll come for you again."
    "The demon......"
    "No. Your Him. Talyn's father. He'll come back for
you."

"I keep dreaming about that unicorn. He's in my nightmares." I think it's day. Grey. Winter's gone. I think it's raining. Washing down me like I can feel it. A waterfall cascading down my back. Slightly warm, wet, nourishing. Caressing my skin, making it tingle and yearn for more.

"The Nightmare is not real. Your He is, Lira. Think of him."

Shut my eyes. Shut my eyes.

Black.

Retreat.

Don't feel.

"Together the two of you made her. It was a shared passion, a shared love that allowed you both to give yourselves to the other. Nothing can erase her or take her from you. You cannot be kept from her. She is your love embodied. You are that child for me, Lira. My love put into a form I can see. You are my reminder that he was real and I loved him ferociously, and that he loved me just as strong."

I've allowed myself to be reached.

Day, as dark and bleary as it is, shoots small darts of light and awareness through my closed lids. The rain rings in my ears as I become more and more aware. I try to retreat, to shut my eyes tighter. Would clamp my hands over my ears if it didn't mean unwrapping them from my legs. If it didn't mean moving.

"You are the daughter of my soul, of the man who is your father, the man I found my purpose in. You have not lost everything."

I open my eyes to piercing life. Screaming, menacing life. Life Here. I glare at everything; despise the bed, the walls, dresser, songsbox, window, day for being in the same room.

My eyes fall upon Mihn, watching behind my mother. Mixed with my sight of him is Mom's bloodshot eyes accentuated with her words: daughter of my soul. Meaning him. She calls him her soul, which crumpled up and died with him as mine did with both Talyn and her father.

I glare at my father and he shrinks back to his corner, stunned. She needs him. She grieves for him still, yet he is here, and he won't let her know. He lied to me. They both lied to us. Promised us forever but then ran far away.

"He got what he came for, Mom," I scowl. The sound of my voice makes them gasp. Saying it hurts so much. If Life refuses me peace, if I am to be forced to endure this torment every day, then I won't do so quietly. The need to rage is filling me, giving me substance after evicting me from my safe oblivion.

I push my way through the weight of Mom's words, watching as everything clicks into place. Her pain is different from mine. She knows my father loved her. What do I have? I thought I loved him and I gave myself up to him because I believed his words and what our bodies were doing, but I'm still in This Place and we're slowly drowning and now I don't know where my daughter is or if she's alive or safe. There is a ball of poison metal lodged in my shoulder, burning constantly to keep me from ever feeling peace. Where is he, if he loves me so?

Mom's remaining thought of her love is love. Mine is hate. A small part of me feels guilty for dishonoring him, but the truth began to sink its roots that day she was taken.

"Lira—"

"No, Mom. My daughter is *gone!*" I push up to my feet and they hate me for it, but I order them to hold me. They tingle and my legs burn, wanting to crumble under the scant amount of weight my body has somehow managed to retain. My arm flings out to the corner where my father always is, making him flinch. "He watches you grieve and die for him every day and yet all he does is watch! My daughter was ripped from my arms and He's sitting in his safe Kholsari as though I never happened!"

"Lira—" she tries again, reaching out to me.

"No, Mom!" I scream, backing away. Mihn reaches out for me as well, but I dodge him too. "My daughter is *gone*! We were banished here and no one cares! Your Wizard never had any intention of bringing us back. As *He* never had any intention of bringing us back. We'll never leave here." My voice cracks with the scorching pain that rips through me from the inside out. It doubles back and shreds what remains. "What am I supposed to do? How long am I supposed to just sit here and wait for someone to save me? Who's saving my baby!"

My chest wants to explode. I hear her......I hear her *screaming*......She's screaming for me but I can't answer. I don't know where she is! I don't know what they're doing to her!

"I know him, Lira. I held him in my hands when he was just born and I knew we were linked by some great purpose: you, Lira. You are that purpose. I loved that boy. I watched him grow and learn-"

"What should that mean to me, Mom? Where is He now?"

16

......*LIRA......LIRA? WHERE ARE YOU!*......

My heart racing, my body shaking, I wake, spin quickly over to my side and vomit before collapsing to the ground again. I point my eyes upward, breathing hard as my heart threatens to explode from my chest. Trees separate me from a bright blue afternoon sky, littered by only a few passing white clouds. I shield my eyes, take deep cleansing breaths to clear His effects away, and the wind obliges, carrying him from me. Only the easternmost sun is visible from this spot, and he tries with all his might to stream down upon me only, tries to make me warm. But I turn my eyes and body away from him.

Heedless, daylight pretends to move on and play with the weaving mist. All around is color. Is music. Underneath me, the Forest floor- made of fallen leaves, ferns, thick patches of grass and moss- is a thick soft cushion, and I lay, trying not to allow myself to feel comfortable.

An odd feeling- a lost dream?- tugs at me. I turn my head, but beside me is layers of forest ground. No face.

A branch from somewhere behind me snaps loudly. All at once, I remember where I am, and what had brought me here. The Camp, the poison, the Soldier. Dragons, it wasn't a dream- he pulled me from the tree! What has he been doing to me! Frantic, I sit up and look down, run my hands down my chest and legs, seeing blood and bruises, knife wounds and mangled skin, the damn dress in tatters. But as my mind accepts that none of that truly exists, that my body is whole and intact, I notice Nightmare, the beast, the unicorn, my Guardian waiting for me to realize that I am safe.

My body doesn't agree with him. My back and sides ache from where the Soldier had whipped and kicked me at the camp's wall. My jaw, my lip, my leg. My brain is swimming inside my head, my abdomen is cramping up again, and I see three more Nightmares than there should be. I curl myself over and lay back down, praying I don't vomit again as I cup my hands alongside my face.

Nightmare doesn't stir, doesn't speak. When it becomes clear that I'm not going to fall back into unconsciousness again, I swallow, and attempt to speak. "Where ......are......we?"

[Where you want to be. In The Trees-]

Please don't shout.

He lowers his voice until it is barely a whisper echoing between my ears. [I wasn't shouting. Is this better?]

I nod- Ow. I shouldn't do that.

[I carried you out of that stump several days ago, remember? No, you probably don't. I found you just in time, too. That damn Soldier had his hands on your legs and was pulling you out from the hollow. He'd made a fire and was planning- It's alright, though. I think he's going to leave you alone now.

[Most of my time with you has been spent agonizing over your health while you lay unconscious for several days. This isn't fun. I've been so worried, Lira. How do you feel now?]

"Poisoned."

[Are you thirsty?]

"Why? I know-" I bring myself half upward onto my hands and wait until the coughing stops. I ignore the spots of blood spraying from my mouth to the dirt, which soaks them up. I speak quickly, afraid I won't be able to get all the words out. My voice is hoarse, my throat swollen and on fire. "You've been drugging my water." My throat spasms shut just as I finish the last word.

I keep checking, but it is still bright and sunny and day. I want it all to go away. I want to sink back into my poison-induced delirium. Did Mom drug me after Talyn was taken? Is that why I was the way I was? In that corner, all those nightmares.

[We've been in this spot for a few days. It would be nice to move a bit, wouldn't it? If we move deeper into the trees, we may come across a person or a village.]

"Benefit of that?" I whisper.

[The benefit of people and villages is food. Do you remember what food is?]

Your insults are not amusing, unicorn.

[We're back to that, Woman? It does no good to move a little only to park yourself on the ground for several more days after.]

With a stomp of his foot, the fire he'd set beside me dies with not even a curl of smoke to show it had ever existed. My eyes and shoulder are burning. I retreat back into a ball, shutting my eyes tight.

Remnants of dreams that have been plaguing me since I came here creep back up upon me. I don't have the strength to ward them away. He wouldn't have sent me to the hills to die, would he? This stupid knife. A bag of food? The dress that wouldn't give under the Soldier's hands. I open my eyes and focus on the first distracting thought that pulls me from thoughts of Him:

I like how it feels to lay on the forest floor with the dirt against my face and in my hair. I like feeling so low, so even and level. Like watching the way the trees move. The sound-

Nightmare's fire tentatively flashes back on, small, only four inches high, testing how I'll greet it. [All we have to do is go more east, find a village or a house. There's always someone who'll supply a traveler. And you especially.]

"Me especially?" I wait for some clarification, but he gives none. "No one in the trees will know who I am."

[They'll always know.]

"I hope-" Coughing again.

[Easy, Lira. You don't need to speak. Go drink some water. And yes, I am drugging it. You need it.]

I hope you are wrong. That Seer knew who I am and look how helpful that turned out.

[It's not the same. I swear.]

Your swears no longer reassure me, Unicorn. I require more specific details from now on regarding any 'swear' or 'promise'.

He turns away, shaking his head and rolling his eyes.

I curl myself up tight, the nausea increasing. Is it sickness or is it an empty stomach? I don't want to move, I want so much to just sink back to sleep, but for the first time in days, weeks, months, my body is going to refuse.

I groan, swear under my breath and heave myself up to my hands and knees. It's not as bad as when I woke on the Hills. I don't feel like I've been ripped apart and put haphazardly back together. My limbs quiver and shake, but they hold. I take a hesitant reach forward but stop to look down at my leg. Partially sitting on my left side, I pull up the hem of the damn dress to glance at the arrow. A little late, I remember that the Soldier had ripped it out. Do I want to know what my leg looks like?

Yes. I need to know.

Where there should be an open, infected wound is only a healing injury that's merely bruised. An ugly bruise from deep in my muscle, topped with a shiny scar lighter than the color of my skin and the exact width and length of the arrowhead. It's barely even swollen. I question the unicorn with a puzzled look.

His only response is a swish of his tail- a spray of brilliant red cascading hair by hair by infinite hair strand through the air and forest backdrop.

Drugged water. "Thank you," I whisper. He nods.

It's a short but laborious crawl to the stream. I'm coughing and my head is spinning madly once I reach it. My eyes begin to ooze blood and I instinctively lift my hand to rub my face clean.

[Don't rub, Lira. Your skin is blistered and fragile.]

I sit on my ankles and splash the drugged water from the stream over my eyes. The sharp coldness is instantly medicinal. I pull my legs out from under me and set all four limbs as much into the water as I can. The sharp tingles of cold and water against my arms and feet help to release me. *Nourish me*, I plead. *Hold me here. Wash Him away.* I avoid my reflection, not wanting to see.

Nightmare walks around me to the base of the stream and pretends to drink, but with a slight twist of his head the tip of his horn touches the water before he puts his mouth back over it.

The water swirls, caressing the shape of my legs. It ripples around my fingertips, casting off halos that grow until they get too big. I think He got too big inside me, and I became the ripple that needed to fade away.

The water is gentle and sympathetic, turning her ears upward to hear my woes.

I think I called out to him, Nightmare, and that's how I came here. What if— What if this is my fault? If I'd called out to him sooner, gone to that spot and really made sure he heard me, he'd have come back, and Talyn......

['What if's' are dangerous, Lira. They bring more pain and confusion than is necessary. If he was able to bring you here earlier he should have. He didn't. It's not your guilt to carry. Neither is the loss of your daughter. It is His.]

"I should have fought harder." *I should have killed them all.*

[You did what you could but the outcome was out of your control. This place is your peace, Lira. It's time for you to forgive yourself.]

I'll never forgive myself. Or Him.

The little stream weaves its way through the ground and fallen leaves like a snake on a secret quest. I rest my head on my knees and watch it go, with the corner of the dress caught in the current, pulling at me as the water-snake tugs it. *Come on, just wander along with me. Leave all worry behind.*

If this water was larger, I'd strip off this blasted dress and dive in and never come out. It's Mihn's blood in me. He had so loved the water. This water. This clean, refreshing, beautiful water. The water of Home. Lakes and ponds dot here and there throughout The Forest, known only to those who'd unintentionally stumbled upon them while on a journey to someplace else. The Hidden Lakes, they're termed. At least by my parents.

But I cannot slip out of this skin and disappear, cannot break free of my chains and float away. I bring my head up again, stopping the lure of remorse and guilt and longing before it can envelop me too tightly. My eyes peer through the trees as though they can locate the direction to the nearest lake. Oh, I so want to sink myself into some water. A bath would do so much good. Wipe away this stink. Wipe away everything.

Nightmare's reflection somehow fits inside the shallow, narrow stream, which holds his image amidst constant disruptions. The water softens his reflection, makes him appear natural. The gold horn with the stars inside floating free as lightning bugs......

Mom had called him The Demon of Demons:

> *'He scared me so. My body went cold from the outside in, seeing that black horn growing longer and longer, trying to reach my heart, steal my soul. And it was going to him......and it went......'*

In all those years, never once did she mention that she had been pregnant then. I could have had a sister. How many brothers did she say I have? Oh, my head is so jumbled. Nothing makes sense anymore.

When I was in that corner, back-slam-forth, Mihn had told me that after her first daughter, my sister, was stillborn, he had led our mother through the woods and she had followed him numbly, did what he said with not even a nod or blink. She was like a child, needing to learn how to feel and function again, and he merely took her by the hand and led her along, telling her to eat, telling her to sleep, to stay by the fire and keep warm, to smile, to walk-*right foot, left foot, watch your step, tuck you in for bed*. He'd tried to do that for me, to lead me out of that dark place, but I wouldn't let him reach me.

Mom had the childhood friend who would become my father, I have the very unicorn who use to haunt our nightmares. Why did my life get turned so upside down? How? What did I do wrong?

How am I Home?

I rub the water over my legs. I move my toes and watch the water flow between them. "You tried to kill my mother."

The Nightmare sighs, as though he's been waiting all along for me to bring it up. [I did not. I had not intended to frighten her at all, but she would not listen to me. To either of us.]

You attacked her. In the trees.

[That's how she saw it, but it's not what was happening.]

"What do you mean 'either of us'?"

[There was another unicorn there.]

"The one she killed."

[That didn't happen as she saw it, either. Like you, she thought unicorns were demons, that they would kill her. That unicorn recognized her from when they were both in Ravery and ran to greet her. It didn't see the knife in her hand and ended up running right into it. But it does take more than a small knife in the throat to kill a unicorn. I tried to tell her that it was alright, but she was so terrified, she turned and ran.]

"How could that unicorn have recognized her? She was little more than a baby when she was in Ravery. And, she was in Ravery. When would she have had contact with a unicorn?"

[The woman who saved your mother's life would hide her in the stables with the unicorns.]

"What are you-" My entire body spasms, and for a moment I can't breathe or speak.

[We can talk another day, Lira.]

I want to know now. What woman saved her life?

[Both the duke and Anin tried to kill your mother at birth, and many times after. Another prisoner, the woman who acted as midwife, interceded each time and saved her. She suffered badly for it, but she kept your mother alive for as long as she herself was alive.

[For people here, your mother was a symbol of something surreal yet not past their grasp. She was hope. She was innocence and beauty. Something endangered and sacred. They came together for her, to protect her, to fight for her. She had a spark in her soul that few possess, and it made everything want to bend and please her. Life poured itself into her with a selfless desperation.

[Even when she had the smell of man's touch, she retained her innocence. She was something between child and adult, human and dragon and unicorn, earth and sky and magic. She lived so strongly.]

I take that in, trying to repaint how I know her. "She's not that way anymore."

[Yes she is. But grief changes you. If you allow it that power.]

"How-"

[Lira, stop trying to speak. Drink some more water.]

I'm disappointing to you.

[Not at all,] he whispers as he approaches nearer. [You have a beauty and a gentleness inside you, all around you. You have yet to see what I know you can do.]

I don't want beauty and gentleness. I want rage. Revenge. Hostility.

[You've had rage. And you exude hostility, believe me.]

"Revenge."

[This is your revenge, Lira: you are not so easily defeated. You have strength, Lira, a remarkable amount of strength.]

How do you know these things about my mother?

He looks away, seeing through the trees to someplace else. [I have been visiting your family line for generations. No one has listened to me. We cannot change what has passed, so let's focus on you caring for yourself again.]

Quiet, so quiet and peaceful and beautiful here. I can't truly be here, in these trees. Sitting by a stream in my parents' Forest, sitting beside a unicorn and discussing my mother's stolen life and my own wreck of one. So beautiful here. So perfect. "I wasn't like this before, Nightmare," I blurt, my lip trembling. I cough more, and begrudgingly swear off speaking aloud.

I know it. I remember being different, feeling alive and strong. I no longer feel beautiful or gentle. I feel broken. Tainted. Repulsive. It's so hard......so hard to......She and I should have been born here.

[But you weren't. Do you think you're strong enough to move, Lira? I think it time we leave this spot and move further into the trees. We're still too close to The Valley border.]

I don't respond. I trace my finger lightly over the water's surface. The cold of the water- soothing just moments before- attacks me with chills and shivers. I deserve it though, don't I?

The unicorn sighs and walks up close to me, so close that the heat from his body makes me feel almost warm. I close my eyes, denying it from him as I'd denied myself the warmth from the sun. [Lira,] he whispers, [if we stay here for too long, He will find you. We really need to move.]

Was it easy for Him to find me the first time? Why'd it take him so long the second time? I lift my head and look ahead of me through the trees, feeling for a moment that I am back in that alcove where we'd made Talyn.

[You don't want Him to find you.]

What does it matter? I'd said goodbye and he'd found me. But he never stays.

ENTWINED

MY HEAD FITS PERFECTLY HERE, with my chin on top of my hand, which lays on top of his chest, right below his shoulder. People surround themselves with invisible boundaries, a safe zone, an aura they guard. But now, I'm laying in his and he in mine. I'm swimming in his, basking and flying in the warmth that vibrates off him.

He's sleeping, and his face is turned away. I pull my hand free and touch his face, his hair, his jaw to his chin, in love with every inch of him, with how his skin feels beneath mine, with the structure of his bones, the contours of his body. I let my fingers fall down his throat and across his chest before tucking my arm against my own again, letting my face fall to the side, in love with the way his heart has sped up and given his awareness away.

"It is way too soon for you to be awake." His face is still turned away and his eyes are still closed, but the muscles around his cheek twitch, telling me he's smiling. Dragons, that smile of his. It gives me lovely chills and a rush of heat all at once.

"Tired, are you?"

He chuckles defiantly, twisting toward me and bringing me in closer. Oh, his eyes when he looks at me.

He is gloriously transparent. No caution, no part of him held in reserve, his thoughts and emotions right there for me to see. They are heavy and full and vibrant. I rearrange my body and legs until they all fit into him. He presses his lips to my head and pulls the edge of his cape over my shoulders and up to my jaw. "Are you cold? Do you need to get dressed? Or, halfway dressed?" That fire dancing in his eyes. And that blessed, tilted smile.

"I'm just perfect."

"Good." He laughs lightly, taking me by surprise with a great, solid kiss. I close my eyes and settle deeper into his warmth. Mom's talk of Home and dragons and Soldiers and unicorn beasts have kept me so unable to belong anywhere. All her talk and training of fighting, all her warnings of Soldiers, of the dragons who are my family because they are hers, the trees and mountains and cursed hills of Home. None of that holds any bearing, any importance any more. I am not of This Place, so I don't belong here. Yet no matter how detailed my accounts of Home are, I don't know it, so I don't really belong there. But here, skin to skin against Him with our legs still entwined and our arms wrapped around each other, I've discovered where I belong. The need to leave Here has encompassed my whole life, but it has completely dissipated in our one night. One night with him. Finally I feel at peace. Finally I can breathe.

"You're crying." He shifts and cradles me beneath him; brushes a tear so lovingly from my eye that the tear is followed by a friend.

I remember my father's behavior just before I'd left the house, how he had paced back and forth in the parlor, swearing and swearing damage to someone. He then countered those graphic details with how my mother would not be happy if he did beat that someone into the ground. Now I know Mihn meant him. My him. He's mine.

I smile, despite the words I accidentally blurt out. "My father wants to kill you."

"Your- who?"

"He won't. Don't worry." I turn my head under his shoulder, looking somewhere over my head, hearing the distant waves but unable to decipher the upside-down images. "Did I tell you that this is where the Wizard sent my mother?"

"Right here?"

"Not here precisely. On the beach somewhere. We use to come here a lot, she and I. Waiting." My eyes wander away, captivated still by everything they see, by everything I feel. Above us, the moon is almost back to being silvery white, though the edges retain a faint red hue. The leafless trees between us and the moon rock softly in the wind, and somewhere beyond us the lake is washing her waves tenderly on a snow-covered shore. Winter surrounds us, snow falls everywhere but the tiny space we're borrowing among the trees. It falls slow and straight right over us, and just before the flakes should fall upon our skin, they slide away and arch around us, never making contact, as though we lay beneath a clear dome. The sky is hazy, reflecting the street lights from the city.

"It's snowing," I whisper. I blink every time a flake falls near, even though I know it won't land on me. It's hypnotic, watching from directly below.

He laughs. "You are watching the snow as though you've never seen it before tonight."

"There's a lot I haven't seen or felt before now, I think."

He shifts, encircling me with both his arms. His fingers glide through my hair, igniting another excited tremble. "Wait until you see real snow," he says, stretching my captured lock of hair out, spiraling the end around his finger.

"This is fake?"

"Oh, yes."

"It's snowing There now?"

"No. The seasons Here and There are not in sync. You'll arrive to summer, warm and brilliant. I'll show you everything, take you anywhere you want to go."

Those flashes of places I'll see with him replay. I shut my eyes and nestle against his chest. "Where first?"

"I think I'm under a mix of obligation and threat to bring you to the dragons first."

"Then what?"

"Then we'll be the second pair of humans allowed to swim in the sea. We'll wander the trees, explore all there is to explore. Stay in bed all day?"

"Mmmm. All day?"

"And night." His fingers dance along my collarbone, bringing up a shiver. I flash him a daring smile. "If only it wasn't so cold."

"You're draining my energy keeping you warm, you know," he scolds, inching closer.

"Maybe we should skip this 'all day and night' thing and go Home now. If you're too drained."

"Ha ha. So funny. But we wouldn't get very far if I were to try right now. It's a long jump, and it's not entirely effortless. Or painless. It wouldn't be safe or wise to try. Not until I'm more rested." Those eyes, those beautiful, daring eyes of his.

"Aw, so abused," I tease.

"Not nearly enough." Kissing him is finding my soul. Though the rest of the world sleeps, there's music in the air, there's life being reborn, returned, found.

"It's snowing," I point out, an invitation, a question.

He settles his body down upon mine, easing his torso between my thighs, making me sigh in response. "Keeping you warm is going to be an all night endeavor, isn't it?"

I snuggle down into the warm loose earth below him, remolding myself. "Oh, but you're so tired."

He bends his head into my neck. "And abused," he reminds me, his lips and breath upon my throat sparking more shivers.

"And abused!" I gasp as his fingertips bring forth some heat. "Where have you been?" I gasp between kisses.

"I got here as soon as I could," he whispers breathlessly. He smiles as his lips return again to merge with mine-his-ours. I grab onto the smell of him. Trees and earth and warmth and Home. How can a man smell so beautiful? He kisses me again and I cling to it, stretch it out longer and allow him no chance to catch his breath. I wrap my legs around him and bring him back into me easily, smoothly, and smile when he releases a groan from deep in his throat. I stretch my body against his, tighten my leg around him- not as if he'll stop or leave. I focus on his hand spread out on my back. My fingers in his hair. His mouth brushing over my brow. My core and his. His fingers embracing my thigh. My lips at his throat. His trembling arms enclosed around me. My teeth against his shoulder. And dragons, I do not want this to ever stop.

He rolls back to the ground, pulling me over him. I laugh wildly before willing myself into all he is until there is no me, no him, only us.

*

In the aftermath, we're nose to nose, eye to eye, holding ourselves as close as we can while waiting to catch our breath. I trace my thumb across his lips, and he smiles, silenced, and lets me.

"You're smiling," he whispers, amused. He bundles the cape around me......again......his grin crooked. "This is not why I came here for you."

"Oh no?"

"Stop teasing. I'm serious. I don't want you to think-"

"I very clearly remember making up my own mind. And controlling my own body."

"Mmm." He kisses my forehead, a new habit, and settles down into the earth. "Go to sleep, love. Come morning, we're going home."

Home, I sigh, ready, eager and yearning once more. Mom and I will finally be free of this place. All this time waiting, and it'll be over in one more night. She won't have to suffer any longer.

Easily, dreamily, with a smile exuding from my whole body, I close my eyes, snuggle against him, and do as He says. Tomorrow, we'll be Home.

18

THE ~~DAMN~~ DRESS, TANGLED on the branches
He's thrown it on, waves in the pre-sunsrise
breeze beside us. It's a flag, a banner. I look at it
and smile, removing 'damn' from its name
because it's off, because He took it off, and now
He's laying nose to nose beside me. I tuck my head
under his chin and burrow closer, and he wraps
his arms tightly around me, combing his fingers
through my hair and running them down my back
over and over.
"I'll never let you go again, I swear. I swear," He
repeats.

Then He and the dream are gone.

I reach. Nothing.

My eyes open and see it: morning. Warm and bright and day. I've survived the night, survived the dream, but more alarming, it is morning and I'm not scowling, not sobbing, not laying here full of trepid denial. I'm not turning my head and damning it all away.

It's a morning like I use to know, when I would lay still in bed knowing that the light brings a world of possibilities, that the sun's warmth will seep into my soul and stay with me for days, weeks, months.

Where has my torment disappeared to?

Dragons, I think I feel my soul again.

My hand rises up to rest upon my collarbone. I know it's bare. Still, I wait, but the sorrow, the anger, the loss, doesn't re-ignite. I watch the way the branches above me move, marvel at the distance to the sky far overhead, pretend I lay on a cloud passing slowly along, like a boat without oars in the middle of The Lake. The sound of those far away waves matches the sound of the leaves immediately overhead. A constant hum, a constant soothing sound.

I am grounded and centered, as though at some point during the night or within the last few days, I've been returned to my body. I've been gone for a very long time, and being trapped within skin is new again. Is lovely again. Air kisses me and I feel her, feel the softness of the damn dress, draped as it is over most of one leg while exposing my bent left leg. Hadn't I shredded it? The earth beneath my back, how the grains shift if I move. The flood of smells, as though I'd been holding my breath for years to stave it off.

I'm not shutting my eyes and curling into a ball, hoping it all just goes away. How can this be good? How can I be ok?

Nightmare makes the small fire beside me grow. I sit up and hug my legs to my chest. And the feeling doesn't shift or fade. The fire dances, trying to engage, but I stare, lost again. How can I be ok? How can it be ok that I'm ok?

I woke up to bright, warm day and I didn't turn away. I dreamt of Him, and I didn't cry, I didn't scream or punch

Him like I've said I'd do should I ever see his lovely face again.

I brush my dirt-smeared hand across my face and allow the fire, the sunsmoon, the 'ok' to sink in.

[Good morning,] offers my guide, my guardian, my savior. Every morning since I began recovering from the Seer's poison, Nightmare has told me to get up and walk, and I've done so without a fight. When did I stop closing my eyes, my lungs, my soul, and allow Home to flood herself into me through every pore? I've been eating plants and roots grown from her soil, have been breathing air made from her trees while running my fingertips along the trunks and playing with leaves as though I'd never seen one before. I have tried to retreat, to drop those leaves, to walk without acknowledging where I am, to ignore that Home is taking root inside me.

And today I wake and I'm residing in my body again, and my body resides in Home, and I'm ok.

Ahead of me, all around, are trees. Each trunk is a different hue, has different furrows running up and down their surfaces in different patterns and directions. Leaves are subtly different. But trees, trees, trees and trees. Between two you see another, past that another, another. They stand still and silent and stare back at me. If a cloud passes overhead, they're either in shadow or light. When I look behind me there are more. Trees in every direction, surrounding me.

I rise to my feet and reach out for the nearest one, set my hand upon it and then let my body fall against it. I press my forehead to the bark- this one smooth- and shut my eyes. The tree is warm, like a being, it's life humming beneath my hands, thrilled with the touch and the recognition. In return, it's supportive, caring, concerned. Honest and sincere. The tree is how people should be.

"*Tree Hugger*", is what May would affectionately call my mother, as Mom use to scold them all if they pulled on a branch, broke a leaf, or threw things at the trees surrounding the house.

I open my eyes and look back the way I think we've come. I'm fairly sure that's west. It gets brighter the further out the trees go. The space between them will widen and grow until suddenly they're gone, giving way to green hills and Unicorn Bound and Soldiers and Ravery.

I can only walk. Touch each tree and pray that each step gets easier. Sitting anywhere won't help me or Talyn. I'll figure it all out later.

[Which way would you like to go?]

His question stuns me. We argued about it, I think, in Ravery. But since leaving the stream, we've just walked. I don't think I've cared about where we were heading. Now, being asked, everything I know whips through my head-maps and scenes and images, my parents' stories, Mom's murals, their instructions, my dreams. I know I should go straight east, know I should seek out the dragons. The ache for them grows every day, but I can't go that way. Not now. Not yet. I need more time to get myself oriented.

"North," I answer, although I am looking east. It's where I'm supposed to go. It's where everything is supposed to be made right. Except that He is east as well, and nothing can ever be made right.

Nightmare is right. I don't want to be found by Him again.

[Then north we'll go.]

With each step, spring leaves, allowing summer to rise from the earth, come down from the sky in tentative exploits. My feet sense the sinking snow deep within the earth's soul, and my shoulders feel the coming heat of summer. It's more warm than cool, and the light spring rains have already stopped.

Trees grow so high here, unhindered by humans and pollution and buildings and so many other ands. So tall, I can't reach their lowest branches. There's a silence beneath them, a heavy calm, an aura of safety. They're fairly spread out still, and so I walk upon a spongy carpet of green dotted by bright, unusual wildflowers. At first I pick the best blooms, carry them for a few hours, eat a few and set the rest down. Eventually none are left to set down. I'm *hungry*. And being hungry and eating feels so good again. White petals, purple clusters, green-blue leaves and green stems now course through my body, making me part of the landscape, making me begin to believe that I belong here. That I exist within my body again.

The wind is singing. She's not howling in pain or screaming in anger or whispering warnings. She sings as she skips ahead of me, taking on that distinct white shape with the long, draconic tail trailing behind her.

The Forest hums. Every insect, animal and plant lends a note. And the trees far above- waving back and forth on long sturdy trunks, as though they sigh, content that they are what they are, that they are where they are- the trees provide the harmony.

I stop and stare upward at them. My bare feet sink down into the softness of earth, sinking, growing roots of their own while my body lengthens, growing upwards to match the height of the trees around me. I bow along with them, sigh and hum, close my eyes as the wind winds through my hair. My arms unfold and stretch outwards, my fingers together, holding onto the air a brief number of heartbeats longer before spreading to let it through. I become a tree. Birds fly past my face; this flutter of feathered wings and little beating hearts, high-pitched greetings of friendship and companionship.

A noise interrupts the reverie. For a moment there's nothing to see. But then an odd species of creature alone in a community of grand beings darts through the trees, and suddenly I am human again, on small fragile human legs with small human eyes.

The young girl bursts out from the trees ahead, long, matted red hair bouncing behind her as she sprints. She comes upon me quickly, not seeing me, her arms spread wide, face tilted to catch the air and warmth of the suns. She continues, closer and closer, gaining speed. I take a step back, open my mouth to speak......

And she runs right through me, skipping, laughing, holding out her arms as she waits for the wind to pick her up and carry her away. I whip around to watch her, but the wind catches her and she vanishes.

"Mom?"

I turn back around. Nightmare stands still, waiting patiently. [Wind-]

"The wind did that? Made my mother appear?"

[It was just a memory.]

Wind sings a pleasant, happy tune in my ears. Around us, the trees are bowing unnaturally low, their branches and leaves brushing against each other, hovering a few mere feet over the ground. I gasp and take another step back. "The trees are *bowing*, Nightmare."

[Welcome home, Lira of Elaar.]

"I—" I want to say that I'm not home, want to deny how desperately I still yearn for this place, this country, this world, this life. But I can't.

*

Over the last week, the Forest has been changing. No more ghostly memories, no more bowing trees, but the further we go, the more different everything becomes. Today, the air is heavy and thick. It takes a different type of effort to breathe. Maybe effort is the wrong word. It's not difficult to breathe, but somehow you have to breathe differently here, wherever here is.

I pause to looked around, inhaling deep, exhaling slow. The forest has darkened, but not because of time of day. The trees now grow much closer together. With one palm upon one truck, I barely need to reach to touch the trunk of another. Branches are even lower here, too low to even bow under. Shielding my face, I move gingerly through the branches, moving them carefully out of my way with the unicorn picking his own way just before me.

There's nothing growing over the tree roots, nothing covering the ground except for soft brown earth. The trees make a *whorling* sound, they don't rustle, they don't hum or smile or whoosh. The silence beneath their sound isn't harsh and angry like at Ravery, it's just silent and still.

[The moon shines directly overhead.]

"Is that why nothing grows? The suns don't touch here."

[This is the area many believe is the center of the world.]

An indistinct remembrance, a stowed away instinctual memory, pulls at me faintly. "There was something about children in this part of the trees, wasn't there?"

The unicorn nods.

"And trolls. Were there ever trolls?"

[Every one I've encountered thus far has absolutely sworn to me that they were truly men.]

I ignore his sexism and kneel down to touch the earth. Children, trolls and the center of the world- beliefs that stem from people who don't even live within the trees. The Northern Peoples. In order to maintain prosperity, every season they use to abandon a newborn here, feeling their eventual death would fertilize the earth and ensure their survival all the way through to where they live.

"I'd forgotten about that," I whisper, pulling my hand back. Maybe by now they've learned: when you sacrifice your children, nature enacts her revenge and eventually your people die out.

But what about me? What happens when you don't toss your child away? Will either nature do anything for me? Will this world avenge the wrongs of the Other?

A cold wind travels up the dress and scrapes along my spine. I turn and stomp onward, my mouth clamped tight. I want out of these trees, out of thoughts of people who can throw away their children so easily when there are mothers who can't be mothers. How many bones of how many infants are buried beneath my feet?

I run, and Nightmare, understanding, ventures no comment, jogging along behind me instead. My pace picks up, going faster and faster, and soon I can't see what I pass. Everything blurs and I run harder. I jump over logs, whip through brush, dodge trees. Bark scrapes against my palms as I set them upon trunks and quickly shoot past.

Years of twigs and dried leaves and other odds tickle the soles of my bare feet. My lungs burn, my heart pounds, my chest is full and my body is light as air. I'm racing air and wind, racing a unicorn, racing the worlds.

I close my eyes, not losing pace. In my head, I see the forest and can avoid trees smoothly, sail cleanly over roots and bramble, can locate Nightmare and see how his legs move, how he doesn't break a sweat, doesn't pant, doesn't seem at all bothered by the pace. He's beautiful, galloping so smoothly. His colors, the forest colors, blending smoothly. He is a thing of nature after all.

I push my body, run faster. My lungs no longer burn, my heartbeat slows to a normal pace. The sunslight is somewhere ahead, teasing my face, reaching out to touch my throat, my chest, and the tops of my legs. My eyes are closed but the sky above me is blue and I remain in it, let myself believe that I'm flying, not running; that the wind has grabbed me by my arms and is lifting me up, carrying me above the treetops, away from the places that take children or abandon them to die.

Nightmare slides to a clean stop when I do. I open my eyes, glance at our surroundings, and go straight to him, throwing my arms tightly around his large neck. I bury my face into his mane, his beautiful red mane and hold myself to him, and he says nothing, which is what I needed to hear.

19

WE WALK WITHOUT A WORD. I don't know which direction we're heading to but I don't particularly care. What I do know, without question, is that I trust where the unicorn is guiding me. The camp and the Soldier were accidents he had not foreseen. He won't lead me into any trap, won't lead me anywhere towards Him. He came after me as soon as the gates of the Camp were opened for him, and since then, he'll never let me out of his sight again. It is an unbelievable relief to have someone beside me that I can depend on.

Lost in thought, I walk right into the unicorn's side when he stops without warning. He doesn't flinch or grump back at me. His nose is lifted high into the wind. Smelling deeply, eyes half closed but ears pointing forward, he strains. He glances at me. [Do you hear that? Do you *feel* that?]

I shake my head, the motion making me dizzy and starting up another fit of coughing. "What is it that you hear?" I attempt to listen, to try and locate whatever is calling him, but can't detect anything above the breeze and trees. His ears rotate in different ways, trying to tune into whatever sound he hears. He walks again very slowly, very deliberately, stopping more frequently. We move silently, me keeping behind him, letting him lead.

"Stop! Nightmare, I hear it! I hear it!" My skin breaks out into a cold, tingling sweat. A big chunk of ice lodges in my throat as my bones freeze me motionless. The sound, however muffled and distant and faint, brings up a frightening primal reaction. Vicious. Visceral. I grab onto Nightmare and take one painful step after another. I want to go mad, cry and scream and tear the trees to shreds to find the source and soothe it. It's hard to breathe, hard to resist the urge to run as hard and as fast as possible. *Toward* that sound. To go barreling through the trees ready to fight for it. I should know it. The more we walk, the more frantically I search, struggling to place it.

What is it? What is it about that sound that strangles me? As we draw closer, it becomes louder, becomes a cry, a wail, a heart-shattering scream of terror and need-

NEED. Talyn reaching out to me from that man's arms, doing her reverse wave. *Mama! NEED you!*

The air explodes and sounds like windows shattering. Not so far away, partially hidden by some vegetation, tiny trembling limbs appear to break out of the ground. Dragons-

"It's a *baby*! Nightmare, it's a baby!" The infant's cries shred through me. I sprint heedlessly, ripping through branches and roots that strike and hit from all sides, all levels, that then rush past me in a blur. I'm anchored to the sight of a baby alone in the woods, screaming shrilly. Screaming for me. *Have to stop the crying! Someone's hurting her! Talyn, I'm coming!*

The maddened rush that had propelled me forward suddenly withdraws inside itself. And is puzzled. Talyn is not a boy.

His cries muffle into long moans that make his lower lip tremble, make his chest pop in uncontrollable hiccoughs.

I drop to my knees. A baby?

He's not even a day old. There's dried blood and mucus and other birth debris covering his skin. Dirt has adhered into it and he's grimy, looking like a troll with his small shock of blackened hair covered in filth. He's been separated from the placenta but it's laying within sight, and his umbilicus is tied tightly with what looks like a long lock of hair. My hand goes to his face, hovering just over his skin, unable to complete the touch. His face furrows into a heartbreaking frown, his chest lifts, trying to make contact with my hand. He flinches every time my tears fall upon him- flinches, holds his breath while debating whether a tear drop is something to fear and cry over, whether or not to wait and see.

A strip of cloth is on the ground just beside him, leaving him naked. He is shivering in the chilly, spring forest air. Tiny clenched fists nearly blue with cold hold still, arms splayed out beside his head. His breath comes quick as his new mind works, trying to figure out if he's saved. Is this someone going to help, is this someone going to hurt, or is this person going to just simply leave as his mother did?

His thin lips are cracked and bleeding, so dry. How long has he been here? Screaming? I lift my head and scan the trees for movement. Are his people here? Are they watching? How could they just leave? Are they close? Could we track them down and force them to- To what? People who want their children don't leave them abandoned in a forest where no one will find them.

Just as my ache has begun to subside, just when being here has begun to give me some peace, I find myself kneeling before a baby. It's been forever since she was little like this, lifetimes since I held her. Why? Why take mine when she was so heavily wanted and loved? Why not the child whose mother doesn't want him anyway?

I try again, but can neither speak nor touch him. I snivel back air and tears just as he does. Long, drawn out whimpers escape our parched lips. We both want me to touch him, say something. He needs to know that he's been found, and I need to physically find him, but I can't do anything. I can't move. His face is a dark red; swollen eyes are almost clamped shut. My body is too far away to feel, and too far for him to see clearly. I bite my lip and stop my sobs, becoming silent.

Silence and distance are something new once you're born. Before birth, you are encased in touches, in sounds: your mother's body touches you all ways and always; and then her heart beat, the sound of air filling and leaving her lungs, her voice traveling through her skin, even the blood pumping through her veins gives you constant companionship. Then you're born and there's nothing but frightening silence and distance in between touch, and jerky, unbalanced sound.

He can't wait any longer. His pause ends with a long, piercing wail; the kind that skids, like a chatter, originating from the same primal place that my maternal instinct- in answer- reactively fractures free from.

Throwing him against, into, through my body is the equivalent of stabbing myself in the heart. The feel of him is intoxicating, the relief that is washing over me is excruciating. I'm holding a baby. This, this is what I have been yearning so strongly for: the feel of her in my arms, on this place against my chest. This isn't her, this isn't my daughter. I didn't help make him, didn't carry him in my body, didn't give birth to him, but he *fits*. He fits too perfectly. How remarkable a thing this is- baby snug against mother. No matter that he is not my baby nor I his mother, we are two broken pieces that make one.

He continues to cry, but the sound is different. It's a cry of relief, a cry chiding me for taking so damn long. I hold him tight, my body stiff in shock. Little by little, though, my body sways, finding courage to pick up momentum until I am rocking side to side. Not back and forth, not slamming, not needing a rhythmic pain to remind me how empty I am, to keep my break from healing. I'm rocking. Smoothly, soothingly, as emotions locked far away slowly began to bubble back to life.

A baby. Something endangered. Threatened. Something people can steal, can throw away. Something I need. I close my eyes, bow my head, cocoon myself around him. *Baby*. An interrupted connection I have not been allowed to retain.

I rock mindlessly, trying to soothe away his fear, his screaming wails. I've endured centuries without feeling, and the sensations of touch and feel return in a raging flood, roaring through my soul, into my pounding heart, spewing out vibrant blood that feeds me with the key to being alive. The fire courses through my veins, my limbs, through my lungs starving for air and arms starving for Talyn. And when it is through reclaiming my body, it returns into my soul and builds up until it pours out again without stopping to ask first.

Everything becomes silent, becomes clear and still. My heart is beating against another chest, a tiny little chest that curls itself into that beat, into that feel. Nine months inside our bodies, the sound of our hearts must be so distinguishable to our children. Would Talyn remember me if all I do is hold her? They're expelled from our bodies and we hold them against our hearts, and they have this sound again, soothing them to sleep, making them well when they fall ill, chasing away nightmares that wake them in the night. What do they feel when this sound is taken permanently away? How confused? How anguished?

I hold him against me in that brief moment of stillness, just before the flood escapes my soul and makes me sing my daughter's lullaby to someone else's son. It's been so long since the song last passed through my lips. It was born from His tune, just as his daughter was:

"As I rock here back and forth,
with you cradled safe and warm
Feel my heartbeat on your ear,
You lie here with none to fear

"Suns have dimmed so Moon may rise
You breathe soft with sleepy eyes
Magic spells and dragons' wings
Fading fears make worries flee

"Night draws close so rest your head
Dragons watch so don't you fret
Safe and sound you'll ever be
Protected by the love of me

"Dreams abound go on and play
dreams to follow into day
A smile to stretch across your face

Where many kisses I will place......"

My voice trails off. His wails have finally ceased, replaced by soft, thirsty gulps of air. The baby curls himself against me, clenching and releasing my dress in tiny hands, scratching my skin with his baby sharp nails, his mouth open, searching, needing the one thing I am not able to give him. Dark, black-blue baby eyes peek upward at me. More black than the typical baby blue. Those eyes, those large, beautiful eyes that are too old for the body they aid. They're suffocating, pulling everything in, studying all though they can't quite see.

I can't look at the unicorn. "How could you put this on me?"

[I didn't do this!]

I run my thumbs down the sides of his nose, along his gaunt cheeks, down his jaw to his chin. His skin is cold, moist as from fever. My touch is creating rivers of almost clean in his grime. My lip trembling, I go down his neck, his thin shoulders, his unwrinkled arms. His fingers don't have the strength to catch or hold mine. He doesn't stretch into my touch. He's just so relieved, so drained, he just lay there.

> *......I slide from her hold and continue down her legs to her feet, which I raise up to kiss the soles of. "My daughter."......*

My whole body begins to ache again, to sob. I cradle the boy under my chin, overwhelmed.

TALYN

THERE'S ABSOLUTELY NO HINT OF RED in the sky. Not even yellow. The Year of the Dragon is nearly gone.

The contractions turn me inside out, pull my head down into my body. I feel like I'm with her, so much so that I can see her, compact and squished with her arms crossed over her chest as she waits for me to push her out. Her head turns against my pelvis, and with a jolt of pain I am forced back inside my own head.

My body is being sliced into a million different places along lines and boundaries I didn't know existed. I am not going to sit on my bed all day like this. She's coming out *now*.

As a child, I went with Mom when she was called upon to deliver babies whose parents also originated from lands far from here. Sometimes the fathers were a wreck, pacing back and forth, apologizing profusely. Other times they just wanted to be far away. But when Mom directed, they slipped into the bed with their wives, held her against their bodies while whispering encouragements and words I couldn't hear but understood nonetheless. I had watched them together, amazed, awed, saddened. When the child they'd made was born— the living display of their devotion, their love— the men were there, holding their wives, holding their child. They were *there*.

Is that what other children are brought into? Is that what other children have? Why was I- why are we- not allowed?

I shake my head.

Even Mihn had been here when I was born. Nothing could ever drive him away from us, not even death. It was my father's hands that I first fell into, his kiss on my cheek was the first I received. So where is *He*? Where is the father of *my* baby? Why hasn't He come back?

Another contraction. I lay back and try to relax.

My daughter's birth should be like the births I'd witnessed, not like mine, when Mom was physically alone and terrified. It shouldn't be my ghostly father biting his fingers and pacing the room. Our daughter should not be born Here, made part of this world as I am. We should be Home. He should have taken us Home. He promised. He promised.

"Lira, relax, your body knows what's she's doing."

Mom enters into the room, a single candle igniting for her. She brings with her a bowl of warm water, blankets, and a glass of water for me. She puts the water to my lips, telling me to sip slowly, taking it away just before another contraction hits.

"I don't think it'll be long now. Are you doing alright?"

Another contraction. I breathe in deep, exhale slow, digging my hands into the sheets around me. I nod to her when I can and take another breath.

Another contraction.

A driving need consumes me. *Push her out.* "Mom."

"Ok, then. Just like I told you."

My daughter will be born here like me. But her life will not revolve around a dream we'll never find or never have. I'll push her out, bring her into my arms, and call to Him. He'll hear, he'll remember. He'll be at our side.

I focus, find the muscles, stretched and sore around my belly, and push, feeling her move and displace the inside of my body, feeling my skin tear as she leaves me.

Just like that, we're two. Just like that, and my body is changed. The body of a mother. My breasts are swollen and full, my belly empty. My daughter is no longer contained within my skin. She's out. She's out I have a daughter I'm a mother.

"Lira! She's here! Your daughter is here!"

My arms move of their own mind, stretching out for what they were made to do: hold a baby, my baby, born of our blood, our skin. She passes from her grandmother's arms into my embrace smoothly. Mihn looks down at her and instantly she is clean of all the debris of birth.

Another bond invisibly sealed with just a touch; a deep, settling weight; a bond even more instantaneous than the one with her father had been. I'm speechless. What do I say to her? I don't want to speak. I want to look at her, study her, breathe her back in. I had thought there was nothing in any world that felt so natural and necessary in my arms as He. How good it feels to be wrong.

I did this. I *made* her. I pushed another life out of my body. I hold a brand new person in my arms. Such an unfathomable idea, though she rests in my arms. How do bodies create this miracle?

She isn't crying. Her narrow blue eyes are open, pondering me in as much wonder as I fix down on her.

Her cheeks are pink, full. Hair his light brown color adorns her head.

I'm a mother, just like that. I made a life, a being that breathes and feels, has a heart that beats, eyes that see, body that senses. How is this possible? How do we just appear within our mother's body and then appear in her arms?

Just like that, now we're two, and everything's changed. He's here again. He's in this amazing little girl who is His and mine and ours, making us one though we are three. It's been so long since I was with him that he's begun to fade. But now, now......

"Two lives, one breath, three," Mom whispers, echoing my amazement.

I cradle my daughter against me, and then instinctively bring her to my breast. Nursing introduces me to a brand new sensation. Fleeting pain and discomfort settle quickly into a rhythm that is hypnotic and soothing. I cradle her closer and rock side to side, humming the tune I'd heard him hum until words form.

> *"As I rock here, back and forth*
> *with you cradled safe and warm*
> *feel......"*

Why is weight such a blessed thing? The weight of her. Smell of her. Feel of her so-new skin against mine. Holding her is like holding a glass ball that offers glimpses of what the future will now bring. Laughter and giggles, bright little girl smiles and late night whispers, bare little feet racing along the floor and dancing outside with her grandmother. Tiny sun dresses to bring us our missing second sun. And He there with us. Soon. He'll be here with us so very soon, and like before it'll feel as though no time had gone by.

I run my thumbs down the sides of her nose, along her pudgy cheeks, down her jaw to her chin. Down her neck, her narrow shoulders, her wrinkled arms until her fingers catch mine and hold them tight. I smile and her breathing quickens. She had stretched into my touch and now that my fingers are trapped, she's growing frustrated. I slide from her hold and continue down her legs to her feet, the soles of which I raise up to kiss. "My daughter," I whisper to her.

He floats into my mind again and I smile, filling my head with the sight of her and the remembrance of Him, of making her. I feel his arms encircle me, as though he's looking over my shoulder at her. I'll commit this to memory, how she smells and how her new skin feels and the way she looks, so fresh and new, so that when I see him, I can tell him.

21

[LIRA? LIRA, YOU'VE BEEN SITTING there for too long. Boy's too quiet.]

For a moment, I don't know where I am or what I've been doing. Holding. I think I'm holding.

The baby's skin is so cold that I begin to panic. I pull him away from me, and his face falls to the side, eyes half closed. I catch the scream and trap it inside when his chest finally moves, very slightly, very weakly. I shift the way my hands hold him, struggling to keep myself calm and steady, and he turns his head and searches for me. He's exhausted, dehydrated, starving, and so very cold. But he's alive.

I grab the scrap of fabric beside him. It's clean, but only large enough to use as a makeshift diaper. He's so cold. I set him down in my lap and reach for the bottom of the torn dress that's not a dress but a mark of territory, fashioned to appear as a dress women somewhere here wear. But it's not a dress because it is not fabric and was not sewn. It was placed upon me as a mark, as a reminder that he still thinks I belong to him though he's nowhere in sight. My hand shakes as it holds the corner up, thinking of Him making this, dressing me, while my other arm cradles a child that is not his.

I shred the fabric, take it between my teeth and tear. For a moment it resists, wondering where it had failed. And then it gives, coming apart smooth and quiet. Somehow it's large enough to wrap several times around the foundling. My foundling.

Nightmare's head lifts into the air again. He grumbles what sounds like curses. I tense and scan the trees for threat. [We have to move. The air is changing in too many ways.]

The baby sinks his head against my collarbone, laying his left hand softly against my throat. I want to cry out at his touch, but banish the urge away. At the touch of a foundling, those emotions of losing her are threatening to pounce on me again. Why lose one to gain another?

Nightmare is already obscured in the trees but I can't move. I don't want this. I want to put the baby down and run as far from him and this place as I possibly can. He's not mine. I want *my* child.

My arms, however, hold the foundling secure. My foundling. So, so long have I been craving this feel, the warmth and smell and feel of her in my arms. He is slowly becoming part of me, and I can't stop him from taking root. I do not want this. I don't want another woman's child. Yet, the thought of letting him go, of leaving him, of turning away makes me horrified and possessive. Horrifyingly possessive.

I inhale, readjust the boy in my arms. My nerves are at hyper-attention and I feel as though I'm shaking and drunk. Nightmare's face is just visible within the shadows of the trees ahead, nervously waiting for me.

[We must move. Quickly, Lira. Even if I must carry you both.]

"No! I can walk. I can carry him."

*

Afternoon ages slowly to evening. The light is beginning to dim, but only slightly. I follow slowly beside the unicorn without blinking, without feeling or thinking, just clutching the child that is not mine, that someone else had thrown away. This world gives me a child when the Other One forbade mine from me.

We stop in a small clearing where the grass once again grows, where rain or dew has collected in a small basin in the earth. Nightmare- no longer trying to be discreet- puts his horn into it and declares it clean. I kneel down and dip my fingers into the water and rub what remains on the baby's parched gums. His infant instincts and reflexes will not allow him to drink anything that does not come from a nipple. He no longer has the strength to make a sound or move.

"What am I going to do? How do I save him, Nightmare? How can I feed him? What if he's too......?"

The unicorn lowers his head, nuzzling me, softly touching the boy's exposed chest with his velvety soft lips. [He doesn't smell so bad. Even though he has several types of filth.]

"Is that all you can say? Make a comment on his gender?"

[Lira, it will be alright.]

"Details, *unicorn*! How and when is it going to be alright? For who? And don't you dare speak all wise and condescending again. All is *not* right! Nothing is right." I rub my eyes dry on his face. "I don't know what to do."

[He's just a baby, Lira. You *know* how to care for him.]

"Only until someone rips him away from me. I cared for her. I could not protect her. I can't handle that loss again, Nightmare."

[What happened to your daughter was a random, horrible event. It won't happen twice.]

"All I remember of my life is that day, Nightmare. Everything before is hazy, everything after is dark. Being on the Hills, the Soldiers, the camp, everything after is muddled, as though I don't really know that it occurred. Maybe it was all a dream. Maybe I'm still dreaming. Maybe Home isn't a real place, or The Other Place isn't a real place. Now, now......" The boy sighs, a huge gulp of easy air. His eyes are locked on me, watching, waiting, listening. "It feels as though I've opened my eyes after a long nightmare, and there's a baby in my arms and I can't quite remember how or why. He's going to make me remember what life use to be like, and I don't know if I want to."

[You remember more than that day, Lira. You just won't allow yourself to hold onto anything that once made you happy.] He scowls, [except for......ug. Never mind. Drink some water.]

I fight against the wall that wants to protect me from the baby in my arms by focusing on him: the sound of the air moving through his nose, the fact that he is real and in my arms. Every time I glance down and see him, I *see* him. His reality isn't wavering.

I look away and inhale, and study something less frightening. I've already assented that Home has sunk her roots. I may try to buck her influence out, but that would be like swearing off the necessity of breathing. Baby green stalks of new grass grow along the edge of the little purified puddle. Illuminated, sunlit reeds. *Suns.* I turn my gaze to find them, listening to my body's awareness of them high over each shoulder in a clear sky, and feel a longing for their warmth. Before, I'd hid under the shelter of the trees from them, not wanting their touch. Sitting by this pool feeling very close to exploding in a rage of emotion, I call up for their warmth, feeling their steady rays settle me and hopefully flow through my skin into the baby. He and I are so cold. *Suns, suns, I'm sorry. Please see me.*

Suns. Sky. Grass. Pool. Trees. Unicorn beside me. Silence. Peace. Wind through branches, wind through leaves, low-laying grass and even some wildflowers. Baby sleeping in my arms.

If the baby dies, I'll never forgive myself. I'll surely call on Him and make sure he feels my pain.

The unicorn curses, turning his backside toward me. [*I'll* ensure he feels pain regardless! Does He have to be part of everything?]

We're surrounded by maple trees. In autumn, the leaves will be red. In the summer, they'll spit off seeds shaped like wings that'll spiral downward as they fall. Mom called them 'Dragon Wings'. The Others called them something else, one of their flying machines. I remember being young and standing under the large maple planted in front of the house, getting showered when the wind broke their anchors and set them free. It was the only time

I danced. How amazing this spot, forested only with maples, will be in summer and autumn.

My parents never did tell me how to make syrup. Everything else they crammed into my head, and they never shared something so simple. Fire cakes would taste so good with some syrup. Fire cakes would taste good if I had some flour, some water, a pan......Tea. Oh, I need some tea. Dragons, do I need some tea. Nice hot tea warming my hands even though summer's almost here and it's already warm. I'm hungry. I'm so hungry.

[Lira. *Lira-*]

Something about Nightmare's tone makes me clutch the baby spastically and whip around, scanning the trees before answering. "Nightmare?"

The ground beneath is groaning, and then it starts shaking and rumbling, roaring like thunder. Like hooves coming down the hill.

I stand. "Nightmare?"

He turns to stand in front of me, his side against me. I tighten my arms around the baby as my heart drops and freezes, my mouth falling open. Two, three, four. Four Soldiers on unicorns, with Ealin in the lead.

"I thought they no longer enter the trees!"

[They don't!]

"I thought you had killed him!"

[He ran off! I didn't think he'd return! Not here!]

There's a baby in my arms, upon my chest, against my heart. I am overcome by the awareness of him and the terror I had felt while fighting for Talyn. The cost of failure- again- is too great and unbearable. I can't lose this child, too.

[Lira, *run away*! Get into the woods and hide!]

I'm back in the house surrounded by four people who move and speak and look like these Soldiers. I can't run away because there's no place to go and hide, no way to escape. And my daughter, my daughter in a Soldier's arms. That sound, that pop, that crack, and my blood, and the man running away with her, sneering, and she's screaming. My daughter's *screaming-*

TAKEN

I DON'T LIKE GOLD, BUT THE DREAM is bathed in it, and it's a different kind of gold. More yellow, transparent, with flecks of refractile blue. I sit in the midst of it, holding Talyn on my lap while the flecks float around like stars. The gold is like a gelatinous Shield cocooned around us. Talyn gurgles and giggles, reaches out to the gold.
I frown. It should be silver.
A fleck darkens. Not the beautiful blue it had just been, no longer floating. I watch, too suspicious by the gold to feel enthralled. Now the blue fleck is black. Now it has a face, legs with solid gold for feet, a long horn that siphons in the gold gel until it's gone, contained inside the horn atop the black unicorn's head.
Nightmare!
[Lira! Wake up!]

I jump awake on the couch in the front room, startling Talyn who'd fallen asleep on my chest. I dreamt of that unicorn Mom hates. Dreaming of him always ruins the rest of my day. I look around dazedly. The sunlight coming through the window behind me has cast everything in gold.

Mihn is throwing things, trying to grab my attention. He's spinning around the room and finally stops with his face directly before mine.

I frown. "What?"

Lira! Get up! Get up now! he signs quickly.

The front door is opening. It's not the way Mom opens it. It's tentative, tries too hard to be unnoticed, and then it waits, moves a little more, listens and waits. I put my feet to the ground and freeze mid-rise from the couch when a black boot touches the hallway floor just outside the front room's doorway. My breath catches. As I quietly rise, a man turns into the room. The man from the beach. The man from the sidewalk.

I stand, Talyn in my arms, unable to move unable to breathe. The man edges step by step into the hall, peering into the parlor across the hall and then into the room where we are. He stops, finding us, relaxes, straightens, and smiles cruelly. The smile is satisfied, victorious, eager. A smile that quickly becomes a sneer as he turns to the woman coming from behind him.

"She's here, Edna."

"Lisa-" the woman begins, but I'm not listening.

It's been so long since I last saw her. Even so, the instantaneous recognition brings on a childish panic. When I've tried to think of her, I could never remember what she looked like. But here she is and I immediately know her, remember the way her perfume had given me a headache, and the name she'd called me by that had made my skin threaten to turn in on itself.

She'd come here once before, when May and I were children playing in the front yard. They burst through the hedge gate, grabbed us both, and tried to run. May was not a fighter, but my parents had trained me to be one. I got us both free, but she was behind me as we ran to the house and they grabbed her again. I forced myself between them and she made it up the stairs, through the front door, and into the house, screaming for my mother. But by then they had dragged and thrown me into their monster......their car.

Why is she here again?

Under my palm is a dagger. My eyes flick over to my father, standing at my side with his sword. He pulls it from the hole in his chest and launches it at the first man, over and over again. On the fifth strike, the man grabs hold of his chest and turns pale, coughs a few times but then recovers.

Mom should be back soon. She'd gone to get some food from May's grandfather's little shop. She'd gone for food when Mihn had died, too. But when he was attacked, he'd made noise to alert her. All I have to do is stall and find a way to forewarn her. She'll attack from behind. Everything will be fine. This woman hadn't succeeded in completely taking me from Mom when I was a child. It'll be impossible for them to do so now that I'm an adult.

Talyn clings to me, knowing something's wrong. She's nearly pulling my shirt off my shoulder, her nails have made little cuts in my skin, and her little legs are wrapped as much and as tightly around me as she can manage. "It's ok, baby girl. It's ok. Don't worry."

I keep the dagger out of sight by holding it beneath her. "I think you have the wrong house. I don't know who you are."

The woman's face twists in anger. She clutches at a gold necklace hanging from her neck, a charm with two crossing lines. Her eyes find the walls, the dragons painted everywhere. "Blessed baby Jesus," she exclaims, making a motion with her fingers, quickly passing from her forehead to her chest to her shoulders. "It's worse than I thought. Look at the demons painted on every single wall! I bet you dance naked in the moonlight as your mother did. Oh, I tried. Lisa I tried to save you from this. But you are following in your mother's misguided footsteps. Another bastard child. Surely you see that all our salvation comes in rescuing your baby? You see that, don't you? You know she must be spared your life?"

A cold, numbing realization slowly spreads through me. This has nothing to do with me this time. She's here for another daughter. For *my* daughter.

"Every day for over twenty years I dealt with people like you. People who *should* be the ones that aren't able to reproduce so easily. I believed in my job and cooperated with the system and tried to save so many helpless children- but the system kept failing! Do you know what it's like to scream at the top of your lungs, trying to protect something as precious as a child, and no one listens? Do you know what it's like to hold a child as she dies in your arms, the night after being ordered by the court to return her to that house and her undeserving mother? You don't know what that's like!

"There are so many perfect families that can't have children. Why should anyone struggle through a flawed system designed to fail all when it's easy to find the children that need to be saved and pair them with better parents? I tried to give you to one of those perfect families. Do you know what I went through knowing you were coming back to *this*? I won't go through that again. You have no right to destroy that perfect, innocent baby!"

"Get out of this house! Get out now!"

Rage flares into her face. They'd held me in a small room in some small, dirty house. A cold, inhuman room with couches covered in dusty canvas, set on gold carpet, with aged shades drawn down on every window. The sunlight coming in was golden. I hate gold. Silver. It's Silver Light that sent Mom here, that brought Him here, that'll bring him back and take us all home.

But the room was gold, and she and some tall man were standing over me, trying to drill a new name into my head. I was throwing things as I always do when I'm furious, and the man had tried to pin my arms to my side. But I'd bit him, kneed him in the groin and shouted everything my parents would do to them when they found me, for I had absolutely no doubt they would come barreling through the door and kill them all.

It hadn't turned out to be quite as dramatic as I had fervently wished. Mom had appeared in the doorway with their daughter held hostage, her dagger making the teenager's blood run in a small stream down her throat.

And then we were walking down the street, and then we were back here, as though it had never happened, and we never talked or thought back on it. Except that both parents drilled fighting into me harder than before, and May's parents and then the other girls' parents begged the same for their daughters.

"Women like your mother and you should never be allowed to have babies. Sleeping around indiscriminately, raising children with no fathers!"

Mihn rises up and whips around the room so furiously he loses form and is just a flash of air with an odd hue. How is it our fault that he was killed? How is it mine or Talyn's fault that her father is not here? We are not fatherless. Neither my mother nor I chose the life we are living. If we were allowed any choice-

"You probably don't even know who the father is, do you? All you worthless women doing nothing but having more fatherless children. It sickens me! You can't keep that baby! There's a family who deserves her, a family with both a mother and father. They're educated, well-bred, wealthy. What can you possibly offer her? That baby is leaving with me. Ron, go." She makes a quick motion with her arm towards me. The man takes a step and my right hand flies free, releasing the dagger in one swift motion before he can finish his first step. My stomach spasms with the sound of the blade slicing through his body; the sound of the silver guard hitting the wall of his chest, unable to sink any further.

I set Talyn behind the couch and force a calm, reassuring smile to my face. Her eyes are large and round and I have to pry her fingers and legs free from me. "Shh, baby girl. Everything's fine. You stay here and don't make a sound. Stay right here. Mama will be back."

A bow and arrow are in my hands when I turn to the others in my house. My eyes shift over the room until finding my father's air coming back together to show me his nodding form. The others have yet to understand that their friend has been struck by a knife and is dead even though he hasn't yet fallen.

I can't believe how calm I am. How quickly I've reacted. All those horrible lessons after I was taken and my insistence that I could never, ever harm someone. *Teach me all you want, Mama, but I'll never be a fighter. I'm going to go live in the caves with the dragons. I'll never fight. I'll never kill. I won't have to if I never see people ever. The Soldiers will never know I'm there.*

I stare down the shaft of the arrow, off the point, targeting That Woman, seeing the space between her ribs where her heart can be hit and stopped. I hear it, know exactly where it lays. I see my arrow leap from the string, push through the air and sink through her suit. Her face is gray, her mouth open in suspended terror.

Suspended. I've been counting the moons. I've been waiting nineteen months. Where is He? Why hasn't he come back by now? There's people in my home and a bow in my grip and my eyes jump off the tip of an arrow and I suddenly see how long I've been waiting for him. I have been waiting not patiently, but stupidly because He had *promised* to take me Home. I've had every reason to doubt him. Now the months, the weeks, the days fall behind me in an interminably long, meaningless line.

I swallow a sob. How could I have been so stupid?

That Woman is yelling, the second man who'd remained behind her until his companion fell is now kneeling on the floor, pulling his fingers back from the lack of a pulse he'd just discovered from his friend- but my daughter is behind me and the only thing keeping her safe is me and one arrow. Her father is never returning for us. He never intended to. My father is whipping about the room, crashing into the walls, making the glass of the windows rattle and shake and consider shattering. The fireplace sparks a small fire every time he passes and goes back to ash as soon as he leaves. But my father is a ghost. What can a ghost do?

That one night I gave to Him has been etched into my soul as the most beautiful night I'd ever experienced. I knew there'd never be another night like that one. But it was a lie. Nothing about that night had been even a partial truth. How stupid I've been to be so trusting! To not even ask his name! Is that why neither parent has said anything to me about it? Out of shame over my behavior? My only beautiful forever is hiding safely behind me.

"Are you listening? That's murder! You just killed a Chicago police officer! Do you know what the penalty for that is?"

I'll be here forever. We're never going to leave. What did we do to them that they would banish and abandon us here? What did we do that the people *Here* hunt us like the Soldiers had?

"Your life is abhorrent. She's better off dead than to be raised by you!"

That night was powerful, it couldn't have been a lie. He kept me against him all night with one or both arms always around me. I love him. I love him so much it *hurts*. He made promises that burned into both our souls and produced a daughter. A daughter I have to protect. He'll come soon.

I pull the arrow back against the string. "My daughter is the granddaughter of Elaar. She is the great-granddaughter of dragons. She has a father. How else could she have been born, you ignorant bitch? *My* father is in this room. How am I alive without him? Do you feel him? Do you feel his anger, can you sense his thoughts? He was a warrior, but that's nothing compared to my mother or my daughter's father or how they will respond to your presence."

She makes some sort of movement. Her eyes? A flinch? There's someone else in the room.

I whip around and a man is behind me, leaning over the couch with his hands out to grab Talyn. I- My stomach punches in on itself. I can't breathe. They want my daughter, my baby, my only link to the man who is my soul. He *is* my soul. I do love him. He loves me. He's coming back, just as he promised. I have to stall. All I have to do is stall. He'll hear my screams for him, he'll feel we're in trouble and need him now. I'll guide him back to us. He'll come soon. I just have to stall.

My thoughts are on a rampage, thinking, strategizing, struggling to bring to mind everything my parents have taught me. They grilled fighting into me with such insistence I learn, enforcing their weaponry skills, their methodology, tactics, trying to ingrain it all into me. But I'd hated the thought of fighting. I hated confrontation. Being told I needed to be able to kill someone without thought, without hesitation had encompassed me with a fear I was too young to accept. But I want it now. I *have* it now, the ability to do whatever necessary. There's a man reaching for my daughter; I've become something more primal, more terrible than just a mother. My child is being threatened. I'm a mother with the angered blood of dragons taking over my veins. They'll have to kill me. They'll have to try to kill me.

A thick, heavy thing is spreading through me, stifling the scream deep in my soul that wants to escape. Me, Talyn, my father, That Woman and a man behind me, the dead man on the floor, a man before me reaching out to take my child. No one else. No sense of coming, no sense of acknowledgement, no sense of anything else occurring but this. He's not coming back. He had- and has- no intention of coming back. I can scream at the top of my lungs and he won't be coming back. Not to save his daughter, not to aid me, not to ever bring us Home.

The men in Mom's and my lives have abandoned us both. We are alone, and all we have is ourselves. I was only a night to him. What a fool I was to believe it was love. If he was coming back at all, he'd have done it long ago. He'd have never left. Talyn is *my* child, and they will not have her.

I lift the arrow and launch it. A strange sound echoes back to me too soon. A pop, a crack, a loud *boom!*, a smell of something burning, and a flash of nearly formed wind, all wrapped within one quick moment. An explosive pain tears through my left shoulder and knocks the bow from my hand. I think I hear Mihn yell as I grab my chest and fall to my knees. On impact, my breath bursts out as though it had been held back for ages, yet I can't retrieve another gasp of air. My vision blurs, thoughts of Talyn are replaced by a wave of terror released from its waiting spot in my center. There's blood, everywhere. Everywhere is red. Red is my color. Is the dragon here at last?

I begin to fall, so, so slowly......

"Get that baby! Now! Get that baby!"

"No!" I'm being pushed out of my body, out of this room, as though it's happening somewhere else, at another time, to another mother. The man has Talyn in his arms and she's crying, wailing, trying to fight, punching and pushing, but the man is unrelenting. She begins to hyperventilate, reaching for me with her backward wave. *Want. NEED.* I try to cry out, but can't. I try again to think of Him saving us, but the vision fades before it truly forms.

No! She's mine! They can't have her!

That primal being within me explodes, giving me one last burst of life. I retrieve the fallen arrow and drive it through the man's black booted ankle until I feel the tip lodge into the floor behind him. He howls and I wait for Talyn to fall from his arms back into mine.

But something slams against the back of my head—

*

A dull heaviness rings in my ears. I can't hear a thing, yet the silence is painfully amplified. My eyes struggle to open. My shoulder throbs and is wet and hot and horribly sticky. Something is pressing down on it and it *hurts*.

I'm on my back. Where am I? I can't make sense of where I am or why I feel so disconnected, so worn. I blink, stare at the embossed white squares of the ceiling above me. Am I on a floor? Am I sure that's a ceiling? Am I sure I'm on my back? I try to see around me, to remember why I should be on the floor. Why am I bleeding? Why is my father crying? Why can't I move my left arm and- Dragons!- why does it hurt like that?

Where's Talyn?

There were people, there were men in the house, wearing blue uniforms and black boots. I killed one. Where's the body? Where's my daughter?

"Talyn!" I try to sit up but something against my shoulder pushes me forcefully back down. I flail with my hands, screaming my daughter's name. Where am I!

A hand appears above my face, moving frantically until I make out the words Mihn is trying to sign one handed. *No! Still! Still, Daughter. Lira, no move no move no move.* He never minces his words. His anguished face leans into view and I realize his other hand is the pressure upon my shoulder. I've never seen that expression on his face and it's terrifying me.

"They took Talyn! They took my daughter!" I can't hear her, can't smell her, can't sense her. I roll over, fighting Mihn who keeps shaking his head 'no'.

"Lira! Lira, lay back. Don't move. Dragons. Stars. Earth. Trees. Home. Silver Light......" Mom falls to my side and puts her hands over my father's. Her eyes are swollen and red. Her body is jerking heavily as she tries to control her sobs. "Don't move. Don't move, baby girl. Don't move. Don't move."

There's something in my hand. I look down. Talyn's blanket. Talyn's blanket smeared with blood. Whimpering, I lift myself up and scramble out of the room towards the front doors banging open and closed, *back-slam-forth* against the outer wall. The emptiness of the house, the complete lack of her spills out of the air. I stare, uncomprehending, at the banging doors.

It begins. From deep, deep within. A feeling there are no words for. It grows and grows and grows till it reaches my lips and I can no longer hold it in. I scream, long and hard. Glass of all the windows shatters into millions of pieces, raining down to the floors in metallic chimes that echo throughout the house. My soul turns so cold it crumbles up and dies. I stare out the door and scream, and scream, and scream......

<u>23</u>

THE SCREAM BUILDS UP AND ESCAPES not through my mouth but through my soul before I can stop it. In response, the air vibrates, quakes, sends out a ripple that immobilizes the world. I hold my breath as something unseen explodes. The wind charges away from me in a backdraft, whistling, roaring shrilly. I feel as though I'm standing in the center of a tornado, except nothing's happening.

It isn't my momentum I am hearing.

[Lira, you *didn't-*]

Trees and trees and trees. A hallway of trees. A passageway. Leading only to me. Straight to me. I can feel Him, I can feel him charging towards me, and it is too late to stop him. Soldiers are before me and He is behind. I'm pinned.

The Soldiers come to an abrupt simultaneous stop, and I whip my head back to them with the enlivened wind swirling around us, the hallway of trees racing up to me. Don't they feel it? Don't they feel Him coming? The bitter wind of Ravery can't reach here, but my ears are ringing with a similar roar.

"Bitch." The Soldier speaks in a mix of hiss and purr that might have wrinkled my skin, but He is on his way and He frightens me more.

The three men behind Ealin hold their reins nervous yet firmly, swords drawn and held in ready hands. The unicorns before me look more belligerent than that first group out on The Valley. They can smell Him in the air, can smell him on me, and they are turning frantic and anxious. The dagger's in my hand, my body's hovering in a ready crouch, shielding the baby. Events I have never seen flash through my head: Mom fighting Soldiers, Mihn fighting Soldiers, dragons attacking, villagers who loved them both dying, Mihn dying- Here, here on this soil I am standing on. And this baby, this baby in my arms, against my breasts-

I will not let her go again. They will not take her from me again. I'm in that day and I'm holding Talyn in those last moments but this time He's coming and I don't want him to.

The three companion Soldiers battle their unicorns for obedience. There are kicks and stabs, small, barbed whips ripping into hides making small, curvy red rivers down their flanks. I look at the red, transfixed. There's red here. There's red to draw Him here.

The Soldiers disperse, fanning out to surround us. Behind me, behind me through the millions of trees between here and the cliffs-

Dragons. Closer, faster. This time He's angry, enraged. He's not going to just walk up with an outstretched hand, all smiles and charm and warmth. He's going to come barreling through me. This time when he leaves, there'll be nothing left of me.

My nerves are on edge, tingling and alive and I want to be sick, want to lunge, attack, scream, run away. I can't allow Him to find me. I need to make these men and their unicorns go away, and then I need to hide. I'm holding a child that is not His.

I turn from the trees to the Soldiers. If they won't leave, I'll make them. I won't hesitate this time. I hold the baby like a charm, a new talisman, and he fills me with strength. Tall, tall like the trees. I am a tree. I have roots that grow deeper than theirs, these men of hills and grass. The bodies I come from, my dagger and a baby to their armor and swords. I am the daughter of Mihn. I am the daughter of Elaar. I am the daughter of Elaar! "I am the daughter of Elaar!"

[Lira, no!]

I stare blankly at the unicorn, not sure what I'd done wrong. Dragons, had I spoken aloud? Something's happening. The trees hold deadly still and tremulously wait, the wind vanishes. His propulsion towards me dies. My courage suddenly falls as Ealin's face turns pale white. The wind slowly returns with the shrill sound winter makes. The trees start to shake, the leaves to whine and wither.

My words have created a ripple. I stumble back, waiting for Ealin to explode in rage. Instead, a slow, lethal smile pulls at his mouth and it's worse than his rage. It's the tongue-flick Mom's lizards do just before they attack any rodent or large bug that strays into the house; so calm and still, at that moment so benign while they appear to lazily watch another creature's movements. But they're calculating, trying to predict which way their prey will try to flee. Their eyes sluggish and placid, but all the while they are tasting their decided victory and glory. Right when their prey's initial fear turns to curiosity, they'd lunge with sudden vibrant eyes and there'd be a crunch of bones, a tail sticking out of their mouths followed by a lick from that forked tongue. In that quick, devouring flash, they make it unquestionably clear that they are purely predator.

Nightmare leaps forward on stiff legs, his back arched upward to make himself appear larger and more deadly, but all eyes are on me.

"The daughter of Elaar is mine and mine alone!" Ealin commands his band. He holds his sword tightly at his side and all four kick their spiked heels into the unicorns' sides to make them charge.

Nightmare's yelling at me to run, but I can't move. He runs ahead of me and rears, expelling a part-neigh, part-scream, part-growl. The baby starts to whimper. Hooves pound within me, the Soldiers' open mouths are shouting, and the propulsion from the trees begins again. But it's suddenly, immensely different: It's not Him at all.

The trees and earth explode all around me and the baby and I are thrown to the ground, a large weight pinning me flat down. The Forest is screaming as she's being ripped apart. Trees are being shattered. They fall with a deafening tearing sound that fills my head as they crash downward, smacking into other trees they sometimes take with them. Earth and leaves erupt upwards as though I lay on land with hidden volcanoes that have simultaneously decided to detonate. Maple leaves shower down......

An enraged roar-scream makes the wind stumble and retreat. It's a sound more substantial and frightful than anything I've ever heard, followed by a crackling bellow that sounds like rushing fire. I'm sweating. I feel on fire, like the world's become engulfed in flames.

The immense weight over me presses down closer, flattening me further. I can't breathe. I sink my body deeper into the earth and forcibly curl onto my side as best I can. My legs- flattened between something both hot and cold, between the ground below me and the weight above me- fight to draw up around the baby to cocoon him into my body so that the weight above rests fully on me and doesn't smother him. I cover my head and the baby's with my arms and we are sealed. My eyes are shut, but I have a visual certainty of red. Of lots of red. The sound of the whole forest crackling echoes off the form above me. I clamp my hands tighter over my ears to drown out the overwhelming noise.

Another roar. It's worse than a roar. Wordless rage surrounds me, mixed with fierce intensity. Once expelled, the weight above me lifts. The baby's looking up through a small opening between my bent arm, mouth in a wonder-stuck 'O'. I look up sharply, dazed, seeing nothing but vibrant, dazzling red. Like the dust of a million rubies compacted into one great slick and faultless wall.

For a moment, confused, I stare at the perfect, rectangular scales rising and falling above me, so smooth and shiny my reflection bounces back at me in every one. I turn my head to look forward: two thick, muscular red legs connect to a red chest and a long, red neck glistening amidst the fire that's being propelled forcefully out of two strong jaws. Red, red, red jaws.

> *"Love him whose skin gleams red,*
> *For he is your daughter's Guardian,*
> *Whose life is forever entwined with hers."*

Mom's words weave through the haze in my head, becoming solid now that the dragon she'd told me of is before me. Over me. I catch my breath, mesmerized by the sleek red chest heaving over me. Dragons-

A dragon.

My dragon.

The dragon's heart pounds in my ears, inside my head. The force takes over my body and I freeze, focusing on that one sound, that one feel. I've been waiting for this sound all my life. I use to dream of my dragon, before my dreams became filled with Him. Mihn had dangled that charm over my head from the time I was born, telling me: *You must look for him when you go to Home. It's important, baby girl. He's your Guardian. Look for him when you go Home.*

I lay my hand on the baby's chest and turn my head sharply upwards, staring at the red dragon chest. There's a dragon standing over us. My dragon is here and He, thank the stars, is not. I'm safe. I'm completely safe.

Everything will be fine now.

The hissing roar of intense flames fills my ears. Smoke that suffocates the air catches in my throat, scorching the linings of my already raw trachea and nose and I can't stop coughing. I pull the baby's damn-dress-blanket loose and cover his head with it to protect his more fragile lungs.

The heat of the fire and the sudden unexpectedness of a dragon has sent the charging Soldiers rearing quickly backward, barely escaping the scorching flames. One turns around and keeps on running. The dragon quickly spins on the ones remaining, his tail whipping through the air. It's a different pitch of hiss, more commanding than the known sound of arrow or blade. The Soldiers stop and stare and dumbly wait, held still by that terrible sight and sound.

The dragon's tail splits more trees until it meets with a Soldier and makes a sickening thud just before it sends him flying. The Soldier's unicorn tumbles and rolls once across the ground before shaking his head clear and staring at the dragon. The dragon's head disappears from my sight for his neck is stretching backward over his back. His body fills as he draws in large amounts of air, pulling the front of his body up, onto the tips of his fingers. I scoot the baby and myself forward where there's more room to breathe. The unicorn turns and gallops away, barely escaping a small stream of orange-red fire with streams of black that lick at his tail. The dragon roars with rage that he had missed. I cover my ears and duck my head.

The dragon turns to Ealin's last remaining companion, whose blood leaves his body before he pulls the reins and disappears into the trees like the first Soldier had done. Now all that remains is Ealin, and the dragon's face whips back to him, his lips taut and trembling in a wicked snarl, showing teeth the length of my hand dripping with saliva so hot that it sizzles and burns the ground wherever it lands. Above me, the dragon is drawing in enough air to cast an inferno.

Mom had told me that the wind is born in the cliffs, and before she explodes free every morning before dawn you can hear her rumble and roar around within the confines of her den as she builds with excitement. The sound of the air filling the dragon's lungs is exactly how I'd imagined Wind sounds, whirling around, building momentum within her chamber for her race across the earth.

The dragon's belly is growing while his chest is flattening. His back and neck are arched high over the ground while his head remains almost level with Ealin's. His teeth glow under parted lips and smoke billows out from his nostrils. I collect the boy in my arms, wondering if I should try to scramble out from beneath the dragon's body. In the end I can't move even if I'm told to.

Ealin shouts, dodging a propulsion of fire. The smell of burning hair and flesh fills my nostrils as his unicorn shrieks, maddened eyes bulging. I search from my crouching position for Nightmare, shocked to find him glaring with more intensity at the dragon than he'd had towards the Soldiers.

"Just because you called on the winged demons for help does not mean it ends here! I will hunt you down every day of your life. Your life belongs to me! Daughter of Elaar, I'll-"

The dragon spins and I flatten myself back to the ground, throwing my body over the baby as the great tail gains horrendous momentum. My mind and heart are racing each other, my ears and head are screaming. I can't seem to breathe but I can't look away, either. This was not part of any dream I had fabricated in my whole life. But what part of this or the things that have occurred already have been part of anything I'd anticipated?

Ealin yells as his ride intentionally topples sideways just before the dragon's tail reaches them. Synchronized allies, always. The unicorn plants him in the ground close to the dragon's front and rolls back to his hooves. The dragon turns. Just before he lets his fire loose, the unicorn flees, his hooves making sparks on the ground as he runs. Ealin grabs hold of the stirrup as the unicorn jumps over him, and allows the beast to drag him away.

It's suddenly very quiet. There's no yelling, no screaming, no fire. I peer through a break between the dragon's legs and his head turns slowly. The rustle of scales all around me is magical and chime-like. I hold my breath, captivated. But his head continues to Nightmare, his lips stretching back more and more, further displaying frightful dragon teeth. Smoke seeps out into the air again, two twisting ropes of smoke that snake seductively around the dragon's face, ready to do his bidding. His belly is slowly re-expanding. Nightmare squares himself to the ground, lowering his horn, pointing it at the soft plates of the dragon's neck as his own lips part in a menacing snarl.

I scream. "No! No, stop!"

Images and emotions from the dragon's mind flash inside mine, and bursts of fear, rage, confusion fall into my head in a cyclone of second-long flashes. The expanse of his emotions are too powerful. My own thoughts, my own feelings are expelled from my body and sink into the earth below me. I can't remember myself. His adrenaline pumps through my veins so loudly I hear it, feel my vessels expanding to support the overflow.

He's swearing at Nightmare, vowing vengeance for me.

With my name he remembers me and his mind is abruptly quiet. His heart slows till I no longer hear it pounding over me and his breathing turns normal. His belly recedes and I can almost stand beneath him. Slowly, smoothly like a snake, his neck arches around to his side, and his head peeks at me from between his front and rear left legs. His warm air pricks at my face. The boy coos and weakly reaches out for him. I glance down to him, momentarily lost, and then back to the dragon. He stares at the baby and me with a look of bewilderment that must mirror my own.

I walk slowly out from beneath him, planting each foot carefully down one before the other. Our noses remain almost touching and I stop as soon as my head clears his side. He has me pinned and neither of us move. Around us the trees that use to be upright and blooming are mostly splintered in pieces and smoldering, most nothing but ash. We're encircled by a plumed wall of grey smoke wafting to the clouds.

"You killed my trees," I blurt.

His lower jaw snaps against his upper. Beautiful, swirling, blaring red eyes make the whole world fall away as though it had never been. The whole of his eyes are red-iris to the sclera. Mom told me that their eye color bleeds into the white when they are angry. And it's safe to say he was fuming pissed enough to weep blood when he'd arrived.

His thoughts remain fast and heavy, but this time they're blocked from me, tumbling around me rather than through me. His brows raise in surprise, meet together in a partial scowl to hide his alarm. My eyes drop, knowing my face and throat still bear the scars and bruises of my last fight with Ealin as well as the Seer's scorching poison. But I look back to the dragon quickly, needing to see every inch of him.

His nostrils are flared but not in the same way they were before. Smoke is seeping from them again and his lips are trembling, pulling back in an angry grimace. My alarm rises and he immediately over-relaxes into an almost-frown.

He's stumbling, fumbling around in his thoughts. {Who did that to you? When?} His lips wrinkle over his upper teeth and he glares at Nightmare, his belly rumbling and filling.

"No he helped me! It was that Soldier you fought off. Several days ago. And a Seer before him. Nightmare helped me." I'm trembling, and thankful I'm pressed up against his leg. I can't stop drinking him in. My eyes continue to travel over every inch of him. His color, my red, a wondrous, vibrant red, dotted by miniscule silver specks that shine and create their own light. He's not an obnoxious, bright apple red, nor as dark and dull as cherries, but deep and perfect, the color of rare pure rubies.

The Ruby Dragon. That's been Mom's title for him. Aril always wore a ruby pendant passed down to her from her mother and so on. Mom said it was the most beautiful hue of red she'd ever seen. As a child, she'd sit in Aril's lap and just hold it, just stare deep inside, allowing herself to get lost in the red.

His chest begins to heave again. His eyes are deep, holding knowledge and vibrance and a something I can't reach. Though Nightmare is large compared to the other unicorns, my dragon outweighs my unicorn by at least four times. His presence is still as powerful as when I'd been trapped beneath him, and yet he's non-threatening. I take a step forward and his neck begins to retreat, allowing me space to move. I want to see all of him, so I continue to walk until I stand before him. He takes a half step in retreat to grant me more room. He's sleek, and moves so smooth, so graceful, a combination of smoke and water.

The bridge from his nose to his eyes is long, four hand lengths. His fervent, ruby-colored eyes continue to devour me and I watch as the red begins to retreat back by threads into his irises, leaving the equivalent of a human's white part of the eye a deep, soothing pewter grey that contrasts nicely with the ruby. His brow bones end in two spiraling silver horns that arch backward over his ears and neck. Only males have horns.

Long, thin ears sit just behind his eyes and beneath his bony ridge of eyebrows. They flick back and forth, around and up and down, sometimes together, sometimes separate entities, not quite sure how to rest, where to focus.

Just before his ears, beginning at the center of his brow and running backward along his spine is a crest, appearing like useless spikes not sharp or stiff enough to cut through warm butter. I linger on them, knowing that moments ago they would have been raised and would have been much different; strong and deadly as swords. At ease, they flatten to small braided ridges that end at his tail. His giant wings, now folded elegantly against his back, have a clean silver talon at the main joints.

The sight of him after waiting so long renders me speechless. The chaos and fear and uncertainty of the last few days, weeks, years- the terror of moments ago- the pain of the last couple years all melt away just by looking into his eyes. All the answers of the world and my life might be found in them.

None of Mom's memory-murals or tales and descriptions or any of my dreams compare to standing before him and seeing him real and breathing before my eyes. The Ruby Dragon, my Guardian. No more do I miss my charm or feel its absence. Seeing him, I know why Mom loved his kind so much more than humans.

"Are you here? Are you real?" I yearn to touch him yet I'm terrified that he's illusionary, that he'll be whisked back into the air like Mihn likes to do. I stare pleadingly into his softening red eyes. Streaks of silver are bolting through his irises, almost like lightning. Watching them helps me calm myself.

{I'm here. I'm real.} The whisper arrives in Nightmare's way, in my head, but thick and smooth, rolling like calm heavy waves, strong like the oldest trees. All my tension, fear, worry hisses out of me. My dragon is here.

24

HIS RED SCALES LOOK AS THOUGH they should be cool to the touch in comparison to the unicorn's skin, only they have a different force of warmth, as though he'd soaked up the suns' rays and is reflecting them back to the earth, back to me. I unwrap one of my arms from the sleeping baby and reach up to touch the dragon's cheek. My touch somehow startles him. His eyes grow wide, swirling so madly the red takes over once more.

"What's your name?"

{Karr. My name is Karr.}

Karr's eyes abruptly darken and narrow and I pull back. He lifts his head sharply over mine, growling, a billow of smoke escaping his nostrils, making me cough. He takes a turning step towards Nightmare. His words quickly withdraw from my mind, coming back only in fragments when their intensity is heightened. *{-accuse me!......What about your care?......Her face is burned!}*

The end of his tail is jerking back and forth like the cats would do after they'd come into the house. They'd spot the birds flying in and out and think they'd come to a feast, only to be told by Mom that they weren't allowed to eat any of the animals within our walls. They'd sit on the floor and stare up, or at the floorboards at the mice scampering to and fro, seething, their tails betraying their outward assent.

Nightmare? I venture, growing nervous.

{Nightmare? That's his name? From here on, Nightmare, *I am yours.}*

[You think you'll be around long enough to have an effect on me? That's comical.]

{You forget where you are and who she is and that I, a dragon, stand before you! In my *territory!}* The sudden animosity between the two swells to overpowering, souring the air as it continues to grow. The baby whimpers. I run my finger over his face and he nestles into my touch, shocking me. His mouth is so dry he can't shut it, and his eyes are heavy and sleepy, sinking back into his head. He's cold, even though I'm sweating. I bundle him tighter into the shreds of fabric and bring him closer to me, which draws the dragon's attention sharply away from the unicorn. He stares. *{There hadn't been a baby,}* he murmurs, sounding both confused and worried.

I nearly fall apart. I don't move. I stare at the dragon but he's still pondering the baby. I shift my eyes to the unicorn, unsure, breaking. Yes, there has always been a baby.

[Does it make a difference?] Nightmare retorts.

{Where did he come from?} Karr asks me.

[Same place all babies come from,] the unicorn grumbles.

Sex, I shout at him, intentionally making him wince. "We'd only just found him," I explain to the dragon. "In the woods. He's not well. I don't know what to do. I don't know how to feed him. He needs his mother. He's too young-"

[Lira, you're doing fine. He'll be fine.]

"Details!" I shout aloud at him. "I'm not doing anything, Nightmare. He's going to starve while I hold him!"

Karr scowls at the unicorn. {*What would a demon know about human babies?*}

[Ah, a dragon knows much more. Is that what you're saying, dragon?]

{*Dragons raised Elaar's mother, or have you chosen to ignore that? Lira. I can fly you and the baby anywhere.*}

Fly. That one word holds me captive. Mom had flown on the backs of her siblings and parents. When I was little, she'd take me to The Lake when the wind was strong and set me standing on the edge of one of the retaining walls. I'd do as she'd say and close my eyes and spread my arms, and she'd hold onto my waist and whisper into my ear how it had felt. *Details*. With her voice, the wind pushing through my hair, and the water sounding like a forest of leaves rustling, she'd gently shift my balance side to side, forward and back, and I'd believe that I was flying on her dragons' backs.

{*Let's leave here. Let's get you both tended to. Climb onto my back,*} Karr instructs.

A few trees still smother, their cores red as burning coals, but now that Karr has downed the majority of the nearest trees, I can see the sky, can hear its call louder than the trees'. How Mom had loved to fly. It freed her, she said. Fly, so simple, so quick. I can find the baby food, get us clothes. He won't die. Because Karr is here.

Nightmare wedges his body between us, forcing me to stumble back away from the dragon.

"Nightmare! What's wrong with you?"

The dragon's chest lowers, his haunches raise, and his tail betrays that slight but deadly warning. A deep rumble gurgles in his throat. A growl. A laugh.

Both bare their teeth; Nightmare's even, flattened ones and Karr's pointed, carnivorous double rows. Nightmare and his long, star-studded horn; Karr and his size, his whip-like tail, his fire-filling middle. Their once invasive presences abruptly withdraw from me but their argument plays out on their faces.

The baby starts to cry, clawing at my chest with arms so weak I don't notice till I look down to see him. "We don't have time for this!" I shout. Damn, I'm getting dizzy. "I need to be getting him food!" Neither hear me. Things are changing. Tempers are rising too far. "Nightmare! Karr! Stop it!"

Nightmare suddenly rears, whipping his head so that his horn catches the dragon's throat and draws a stream of blood.

I scream. I lunge myself forward, flatten my hand upon the gash. The dragon's blood trickles down my arm, the exact shade of his scales and glistening just as bright, too. I lean into him, as though my miniscule human body is enough to prevent him from meeting the unicorn's attack. The dragon's scales twitch and tense under my hand but he allows himself to be restrained.

{It's nothing, Lira} he growls. {He is only a territorial demon, trying to posses what he has no right to.}

[Oh, that's not what you're trying to do, though, here in 'your' territory?] Nightmare rants, making another quick lunge forward.

Karr's head drops quickly down, forcing the unicorn to back away. Snarling, Karr yells back: {A woman can't be *possessed and hoarded. Keeping her blinded is not the same as keeping her safe!}*

[Aren't you the genius? What is it *you* are trying to accomplish by being here?]

{I'm here to make things even.}

I hold my breath, but although his belly rumbles and stirs, the dragon does nothing more, not even pulling away from my hand still on his neck.

Nightmare snickers. [This is making things even? Just you being here? Go back to wherever it is you came from. You won't be leaving here with her.]

{Neither will you! You aren't needed here, unicorn!} Karr's body now pulls away from me, filling.

"Stop it!" I throw my back against Karr and shoot my hand forward to the unicorn's neck causing them to anchor me against the other. Karr's jugular beats against my spine, Nightmare's against my palm. We're all three breathless. They're enraged. I'm frightened. Karr's scorching breath races down my head and neck and shoulders, making my backside fiery hot while my front remains cold. And the baby, the baby lays limp in my arm once again, drained from the brief burst of life he'd expelled and lost awhile ago.

"That's enough! The two of you can stay here and fight out whatever troubles you have with each other, but I'm not staying here. This baby-" I choke. So cold, so quiet now. How he'd screamed when we'd first come upon him. Split my head in pieces, shattered my ears, drilled into the space where my heart use to be. But that is better than this.

I clutch him against my breast. If only I could somehow nurse him myself. Use my body for what she'd been intended for. How I miss that.

"This baby-" I begin again but cannot finish. My arms and legs begin to tingle, little explosions at all the nerve endings in no particular pattern- right wrist, left arm. Left hand, right thigh. Neck, shoulder, lower back. Rapid-fire jerks and nauseating, blinding vertigo. I'm going to faint.

{Lira?}

I collapse back against Karr and slow my breath, hoping neither notice. Just breathe, just focus. I won't faint.

{You're in the trees, love. Tell the unicorn to leave. He doesn't belong here. I'll take you where you need to go.}

I shake my head and look up over my head to him. "No, Karr. I need him."

[Goodbye, dragon.]

"No, Nightmare. I need Karr, too. So far, he's the only thing of Here that is true." The unicorn seethes, and the dragon grins down at him smugly. My face softening, my eyes pleading, I try to catch Nightmare's eyes. "I need you both."

[Both?] they both protest.

"Will you make me choose?" I challenge them.

Nightmare grunts, turning away. [No, I will not make you choose.]

{You know you'll lose.}

[It is not I who will lose.]

The dragon moves his posture slightly, and that slight movement no longer keeps his body shading the suns. Their glare attacks my eyes. I gasp, my head going thick and fuzzy, my vision blackening, my skin tingling sharply. I hold the baby frantically, hold my head, and counter every attempt my body makes of buckling. Oh, I need to get something to eat. Something better than forest plants. Mom's tea- how that always made everything better. Mihn's hot biscuits. Bread. If we don't start moving soon,

I'm going to crumble into the ground and then I'll never get up again.

{Lira? Are you ok?}

Deep breaths, deep breaths. Baby, baby in my arms. I cannot drop him. Karr's scales rustle as his head moves closer to me. I strain, trying to focus on him, on the softness of Nightmare's muzzle pressed against my burning forehead, the weight of the child in my arms, and the rhythms of all of their breath.

{What's wrong?}

[Perhaps you should just rest?]

{What's wrong?} the dragon demands again, his voice rising, echoing.

"No, I don't want to rest. I just want to move. I want to leave this spot. I want you two to stop arguing. I need you both to help me. Help this child. Can you do that? Can we go now? I don't like it here."

Though my body is shaking, I have to move. I'll find some food. I'll find someone who can care for this baby, and everything will be fine. I'll figure out the rest after. I don't need Nightmare telling me what to do. I can move, I can make them both follow me. I'm perfectly capable of caring for myself. For a child. Deep breath, lift my head, take a step. They'll have to follow me.

North, to be safe, I decide. I cast a glance over my shoulder to ensure they follow. Karr's glaring scornfully at Nightmare but is first to move. He turns slowly, his tail barely missing the unicorn as he circles around him and walks to meet me. To the unicorn's credit, he ignores Karr's attempt and follows along.

{Where do you want to go?}

"No one can take me where I want to go."

[North,] the unicorn interjects quickly. [We were going north.]

*

I can't walk anymore. My head is spinning, my stomach is cramped into a tight ball, my body feels as though it has been attacked by all four unicorns. And the Soldiers. And Karr. And Nightmare. All at once.

I stop to hold onto a tree as everything turns black. My eyes are still smoldering the poison's toxic touch and the tears that I can't weep are like sandpaper against the healing burns around my eyes. I tighten my arm about the still-sleeping baby. I can't let go. I can't ever let him go. I can't be sick. I have to care for him. Why is he still sleeping?

Karr's concern permeates into me. {*Lira, are you alright?*}

I'm fine. The fact that I don't speak aloud doesn't escape either of my beasts.

[She's not eaten.]

Karr's temper reignites. {*Well shouldn't that have been of greater concern than my presence?*}

"I'm ok! I'm fine! I just tripped."

{*You did not trip. You reached for that tree deliberately before you collapsed into it. Let me carry you —*}

[Most certainly not!]

Instead of a heated retaliation, Karr lets out only an amused chuckle, which still manages to irritate the unicorn. {*You are so afraid that I'll fly her away from you that you'll force her to walk in the condition she is in?*}

[Lira, I will carry you. Allow me to do so.]

I fail at an attempt to laugh. "No! After the first and subsequent rides on your back, I'd much rather walk."

{Well, you can't walk, love. Shut up,} Karr instantly rages at Nightmare. {And just so we are clear, flying her away from you is my exact intention. She doesn't trust you to carry her, she can't walk, you refuse her my help, and yet you prevent her from going to where she'll actually be cared for. I'm not going to stand here and allow her to starve while you watch, so I'll leave-}

"Karr no!" The idea of the dragon leaving, of him not being here brings on a strong panic attack. Only a few hours since he's come, but it does not feel that way. Nothing went right after my charm was stolen. I got lost. Something bad will happen if my real dragon leaves me.

{I'm not leaving entirely, love. I'll fly to the nearest village and bring you back some food. I'll be right back.}

"No. No, I'm ok. You don't need to leave."

{You're not ok. When was the last time you ate?}

"I don't......I don't remember."

{When was the last time you drank?}

"Before you came. Before the Soldiers came. There was a pool of rainwater in the earth."

{Blessed stars. I'm killing her? We've been walking for hours!} he yells at Nightmare.

[Yes, not moving- thereby inviting Soldiers to find her- would have been a much better plan.]

{If you hadn't interfered in the first place, she wouldn't be in this situation at all!}

[Your interference does not, and will not, make anything right.]

The dragon raises his lip but turns back to me. {You can't keep walking, Lira. But since your demon friend is concerned only with his own issues, I'll go.}

He stretches, first his back, arching like a cat while straightening his legs. I gasp at the span of his wings when he unfolds them from his back and extends them upward. Catching the sunsmoon, they cast red glittering reflections throughout the air and trees, as though his wings are made of crystal. He glances down at me but catches sight of the baby, who kicks his leg and makes a brief cry right then. Karr's face goes quiet, flat, as though he'd forgotten the foundling's existence until just now and isn't sure of his plans anymore.

His wings collapse back to their resting places and his whole body shrinks down from his former pre-flight readiness. *{We haven't named him yet, have we?}*

['We'? What do you mean 'we'? He doesn't involve you.]

{Oh, because you're fully invested in the care of a male infant?} Karr's head falls lower, studying the baby in my arms. *{He sort of looks like a troll, doesn't he? A little hairy, with that black mop on his head, and just strange. He's too thin. Not appetizing at all. No wonder the trolls didn't devour him.}* The baby hiccoughs.

{Look at those eyes,} the dragon muses, moving closer. The two of them become lost in private whispers while his own eyes vibrate tenderly as he looks down, the silver blending with the red and turning nearly purple. *{Dark, and deep. Ancient and ageless. But, there's brightness there. He's the blaze that will keep your dark away, love.}*

Blaze, I think, trying out the sound, marveling anew at the baby in my arms. *Blaze.*

A little shocked at himself, Karr pulls his head up sharply and shakes it. *{Blaze,}* he repeats. *{It's draconic. That's a perfect name for him.}* He turns to Nightmare, *{Now I'm involved.}*

[Don't you have someplace you need to be? They're going to starve while you stand and watch.]

{I can't wait till you leave for good,} the dragon growls before softening his voice and reassuring me. *{Love, I won't be long. Stay here with our little Troll-boy. The beast can't take care of you but he can at least guard over you while I'm gone.}*

[You arrogant piece of-]

"Where will you go? How will you find us again?"

Karr's head drops down, his eyes swirling red and grey reassuringly. I try to clear my vision to watch them, but it's too hazy and the movement of his irises is beginning to make me more dizzy.

{Lira, I'm a dragon. I can always find you: by scent or sound or even sight from far away. You won't lose me no matter how hard he tries.} He presses his muzzle into the hollow between my cheek and ear, *{Do you believe me?}*

I nod and he reluctantly pulls back, walking several paces away and circling, his eyes skyward. All his weight transfers to his hind legs as he balances and prepares to propel himself into the air a second time. He presses his body to the ground and with a giant leap catapults himself upward.

How can something so large float with such lightness? Why can't people? Why can't we sense a good current, leap, and stay there?

The gushes of air his wings make sweep up all manner of forest and earth, but I don't cover or duck. What if he doesn't return? Everything that leaves me never returns.

He hovers over us a moment, wings spread out to their fullest, blocking out the sunsmoon's glow. The current keeps testing his balance, making him sway and readjust his position to stay airborne, though the reluctance that falls from the sky leads me to believe that he'd prefer to remain grounded again anyway. *{I promise.}*

Promises never go so well.

*

The fire Nightmare built is small, but creates an unexpected amount of heat.

What do you do for an orphaned infant? There must be something. Oh, I can't think. I need to eat something as well.

The baby is quiet, lying limp in my arms. His face is against my breast, and if I look down, I remember. I remember being a mother once, the feel of nursing, the second time I felt comfortable having my body exposed. I dream about nursing often. I'm grabbing infants and trying to nurse each one but we don't fit. They aren't my Talyn. I remember holding her to me, feeling part of me expel into her and watching her grow because of that. It was another amazing thing my body had found the ability to do.

Blaze is so cold, so still. Karr hasn't returned. What if the baby dies? I'm sitting as close to the fire as I can, but he's still so cold, so quiet. I pull the front of the dress away from me and tuck him inside, against my skin. His cold body makes me gasp and instinctively want to pull away, but if nothing else I can at least fill him with my heat.

A baby placed on the bare skin of his or her mother doesn't produce heat alone. Mom had always instructed new mothers, myself included, to do this- skin on skin- and in my youth, I had never understood how such basic contact could be so important. Then I got older, and He taught me what simple touches can do. Just his fingertips on my cheek or mine on his arm, and I felt powerful or stilled. Grounded or intoxicated.

I did this with Talyn. She was never far from my skin in those first months of her life outside of my skin. It had helped to bind us and to initiate her feelings of security and warmth and comfort in association with me, before I failed in my most important responsibility as a mother: to protect her.

I lay down on my side, bringing up my legs to envelop Blaze while scraping up some earth to pack behind him. I hold him closely against me and soon, his skin and his breath upon my heart match my own temperature. We stare at each other. I'm close enough that his eyes can see me. I stroke the side of his face. *Don't die, baby. Don't die.*

Again, I'm helpless. Worthless. I can't save him. I can't help him. Why allow me to find him? Why not someone else? Look at what I'd done to my daughter.

I close my eyes and clutch him against me. He'll die while I hold him because I'm powerless, useless. *Don't die, baby. Please, don't leave me.*

[Lira, settle yourself.]

This worthless body I live in. She couldn't protect Talyn and now she fails with another. What do I have? Can I sacrifice myself to someone to save them both? Tell me who. Tell me who, tell me where to go. How could Karr leave me alone with him?

Food. Food! He needs to eat something!

Trees. Only trees and weeds and dirt. What do the Unicorn Bound do with their foundlings? The Other Place had stores, canisters filled with powder that provided food for babies whose mothers couldn't feed them. For babies without mothers.

She was small like this. New. I was tired and sore from her labor, but energized and eager for her. I held out my arms, and I brought her to my breast. So quickly. It all happened so quickly. I had looked into His eyes and claimed him as mine, and my body knew what to do with him from there. And then she was in my arms, and I knew what to do for her. So quickly, and they both were gone.

This *damn* body —

Blaze is pushing at me with weak fists, but his mouth is searching. My breasts are tingling and burning and feel like they're swelling. The air halts in my lungs and my heartbeats race over each other, suddenly unsure of their path: forward or back? I pause, wait. It's not possible. He's not mine. But what if I can feed him? I remember how......

I barely move him. His mouth finds my nipple and he immediately starts suckling. How he fits, how the tingling expands, how his need is overwhelming me and I *have* to feed him. So small, like she once was. His body is curled into a ball, showing how new he is. He needs to eat, or he'll die. There's nothing else, but me, but my body and that amazing thing she had once been able to do. I close my eyes, curl around him, and pray, drifting through bright, happy memories. *Relax, Lira. Your body knows what she's doing.*

Then, it's happening: I am nursing a foundling.

My foundling.

My son.

[You see, I told you it would be well.]

Looking down on him, on Blaze, my Blaze, my light, my son, I'm awed. I am flowing into him. I can almost see the life flickering beneath his skin, can almost see the spider web of possibilities branching out. He'll live. My body did what I had wished it could, and now this baby will live.

I find his hand and uncurl his fingers, pushing my thumb into his palm and bringing it to my lips. His suckling pauses, and he smiles. I pull him away, get him to burp, and sit up to switch sides, cradling him differently than I'd held him up till now. I *cradle* him, hold him and feed him like he's mine, as though I have every right to. It feels like so long ago, yet I remember so smoothly, slip back into being a mother so quickly.

Everything happens so quick.

Suddenly I'm nauseous, overwhelmed, shaken. I pull Blaze out from the damn dress when he is done, burp him again, and set him inside a pile of loose warm earth. I wipe my nose with the back of my hands and ignore my running eyes. I rub at my temple hard with the heels of my palms.

[Where are you going?]

"I need......I need to..."

[What am I supposed to do with him!]

"I don't-" Nightmare scoffs but I have already turned to run into the trees.

What have I done? What has my body done? Am I truly so needy, so desperate, that I latch onto the first baby I encounter?

I run until I have to stop, knowing that I've only accomplished going in circles. I can't run away. What I've done frightens me, but it also binds me. My fists clench tightly against the sides of my head, waiting for the upheaval within to settle. Around me the air spins, sings, plays with my hair. Moon is so bright directly overhead. This is the first time I've fully noticed her. Female moon.

Female moon shining brightly on me on this day of all others. This day, when I missed my daughter so wretchedly that I nursed another woman's baby.

The moon holds my face in her hands, holding my chin up to her light, keeping me from turning away or ducking my head. A breeze whispers through the trees, softly touching my face, and instead of wanting to cry, I fall completely at ease, feeling only the cool warmth of the moon and the loving, gentle touch of the wind. Beneath my bare feet every grain of dirt and sand and fallen leaf and branch and twig and the softness of moss and ferns tingle against my soles; the damp mixed with the dry, the dying mixed with the living. Everything coexisting, working together to make this place what it is.

My fingers relax and uncurl, letting the wind flow through them. The dress pulls away from my skin, dancing out beside me, joining with the air like two little girls holding hands, spinning and laughing.

The air finds my skin and weaves down the inside of the feeble dress, around my breasts, down my ribs. My body relaxes and lets go, and my head falls against the current and I am still and silent, suspended, listening, feeling, letting the wind take over. I'm enveloped, being hugged and held and accepted and taken back.

Around me the trees bow and wave and my ears fill with the sounds of the leaves. The leaves hold onto the security of their stems, attached to their anchor the tree branch; they play with the thought of letting go and flying, attaining that higher level of existence. But it's still spring here. The time when roots are strongest, when they grow; when it's time for birth and rebirth.

The wind leads me, and the trees and their leaves and the ghosts that fill the air are whispering. I keep my eyes closed and release control and my feet float on the current, no longer touching anything earthbound. My body— pulled along by the wind and the earth and all those silent things that live invisibly— is still. But my mind— never allowed the rest of peace— races. The image of Blaze spins around with the fading image of Talyn, becoming stronger as she grows more distant, tearing my heart, my soul, in two.

This world that I want and need, and that world that I feel condemned forever to. Torn in two. Like everything around me: dragon, fighting a unicorn; my mother, dying with the guilt of living; my father, living with the guilt of dying, watching with a soul that remembers his life and is reluctant to relinquish it. And Him. Always Him somewhere in the midst. Me, me always caught in the middle.

The earth meets my soles again. My body is heavy and so, so tired and I continue to fall until my head rests on my arm. All I want is to sleep, to escape somehow, and the wind urges me to do so. *Sleep, sleep.*

<u>WANTED</u>

THE WIND WHIPS AROUND, but never touches me. I sit with my legs crossed on the retaining wall made of large round stones that encircles a section of The Lake. There's no beach here, and there's signs everywhere warning people not to jump into the water, due to the imperceptible boulders and other dangers just under the roiling surface.

The wind is teasing the water into a fit, and the waves have formed the large chunks of ice into perfect circles, like hundreds of full moons floating on a dark, watery sky. The wind is careful not to touch me, not to push me over the wall and into the churning water before me. The grove of trees, with Our Alcove nestled discretely within, is far to my left, but I stare ahead into the horizon, never once shivering.

The police came to the house again this morning, as they have a couple times since That Night, since May and the girls had called them, believing I had been taken against my will and harmed. It's alarming to me that they continue to come, since I'm clearly alive and was never harmed, and back in that house, that damn house. Especially with as hostile as Mom is to them. *They look and move and talk like Soldiers,* she's warned me. *Do not ever trust them.* Too bad they couldn't see or hear or feel Mihn. That would have been gratifying.

I dreamt I was back in The Alcove last night. Even in my dream, I waited for Him. I held my breath and just stood, hoping and hoping. When I sensed him, though, it was not anywhere around me, but within me. I looked down and saw that my hands were around my middle, and I woke up.

I've been sitting here all day. Sitting here, wandering the beach. I even walked up to the trees, but couldn't walk in. Where is he? Why has he been gone so long? Why did he leave me? I want to call to him, I want to stand on top of this wall and scream his name so loud that every single world can hear me, not just Home and Him.

"Where are you?" I whisper, wiping the tears from my cheeks. Three moons have passed. Three months. Was there something I was supposed to do? Did he tell me something that I forgot in the heat of everything else? I don't understand what it is I'm supposed to be doing. Why is it I'm back to waiting again?

Dragons, I'm pregnant. I don't know how to handle this. What will he think? He'd care, wouldn't he? He'd be happy?

Being pregnant is odd. I rolled over this morning in bed and felt like there was a ball implanted into my middle that hadn't been there yesterday. The police knocked on the door and my immediate reaction was to grab the stray sword beside the old hearth in the kitchen and defend. When Mom charged down the hall and began yelling at them, that's when it set. My dream, my middle, my reaction: I'm pregnant. I couldn't look at either of my parents. I grabbed his cape and left the house, came here.

What is she doing, this baby forming inside me? How big is she? Does she know my voice, the rhythm of my heart yet? Maybe she'll have His eyes. My eyes are my father's gray. Mom looks at me and sees him, I know she does. Attached to that is the sadness and the grief that's always been a part of my mother, and I don't want that. I don't want our child to see that longing, that remembrance, that grief and the 'if only' every time she looks into my eyes.

When she was pregnant with me, did I ever soothe Mom, as this child soothes me? Did I give her hope at all, that life could still be well? Mihn and she say nothing about the time between his death and her being brought before her foster father and waking on this beach. I don't even know how much she remembers after finding him in that field. But if I had held this one's father as he lay dying, knowing that as his heartbeat grew weaker hers grew stronger, could I connect to her the way I am now?

"Daughter, I am your mother," I whisper into the air. "And you are wanted, and you are and will forever be loved. You were made in love, and you will grow in love."

I turn and set my feet on the pavement, ready to begin the long trek back to the house.

<u>26</u>

MY CHEEK IS WET.

For another breath and heartbeat, I believe I'm waking up in that little clearing by The Lake, but after I reach over for His body beside mine and realize that He isn't there, I remember. I am Home, I am in The Trees, and it is early evening, not very long after I had ventured away from the baby and the unicorn.

I push myself up onto my arms. I can't have slept for very long, and yet it feels as though I'd slept for centuries. Disoriented and drained, I discover that the trees and the wind have brought me near a clear little pond that lays silent and patient, as though it was formed just for me and has lain here knowing I would eventually come to it. I'm sure I'm surrounded by tiny invisible onlookers but all I hear are the whispers and the music of the trees. It is nice to bask in the silence, no one talking, no one shouting or fighting. For the very first time, my mind floats from one thought to another, with no frantic images bombarding it, finally finding the time to organize through my shattered mess and set some things to right.

The wind pushes at me so I crawl forward, pulling my legs beneath me when I stop at the pond's edge. My reflection on the surface of the water jumps out at me, making me gasp. I was once so hopeful, so dreamy, so strong. Had this face really once known how to smile? Had this body really once known bliss?

He had found me beautiful, but now I'm a shadow with dark red welts around my sunken eyes and cheek bones that show too much beneath my fleshless skin, hidden by limp, tangled hair.

A dip of a finger in the water and my reflection is cast away on the outward ripples. I am streaked with dirt, the damn dress is smudged and shredded, the body beneath is so wretched, so foreign to me. I'm a skeleton. I clutch at the bodice of the dress with my fists, feeling the shadow of a body that hides beneath its cover, with breasts newly swollen laid atop nothing but bones. My face contracts with a forceful sob. Nightmare was right. I can fend for myself, but I don't know how to care for myself anymore.

The pool ripples, and when it clears there I stand, with a body full and healthy, and a face glowing with joy. In my arms over my head I hold my daughter. I remember that day. We were happy and safe and so full of joy and certainty. I was a mother. I was still in the heat of love with her father. She was my bright little sun and He was our warm, wonderful future. I want to hold onto that time. I want only to remember those days of unquestioning happiness. The hope I had felt in that moment had been so strong that now it rains upward out of the pond into the air.

Her baby face is becoming so faint, and my arms are still boulders aching to hold her, my body to nurse her and love her. I was alone then, but I had my girl, and the return of her father was complete surety. He loved me, then. He was coming back for me. Then. I was in love, knew that it flowed two ways. I had the start of a family, the thread of hope for a better life. A life Here. With Him.

But there's no chance for that anymore.

The pool ripples again and I am on the floor of the front room, crawling up the hallway, reaching, bleeding, screaming. Screaming and screaming and screaming. The pool fills with red and I watch, a prisoner, and sob, gasping and choking. And then it clears, and my current self is before me again. Desolation and grief are all that show now. If the tears I've shed had been collected, they'd drown both worlds I've lived in. I miss who I once was.

It hurts, knowing it is time to let go, to give even a temporary goodbye. All around me are soothing whispers, consoling, understanding. It is time to let go.

The dagger slips out of its sheath smooth and placid, making a long scraping sound against the silver metal holster inlaid with tiny dragons. It surprises me. All this time, I've forbidden myself to touch or look at it, to acknowledge it. I assumed the sheath was made of grass, like the belt, and assumed the blade was a boring blade like the one my parents had trained me with. But neither assumption is true.

I turn it over in my hand, the moon shining directly upon it. It's not even metal. It's almost crystal clear, with a milky blue-gray hue. With nothing but sudden surety, I know the blade is made of diamonds. Not the sparkling, flashy things set in the windows of jewelry stores back in the Other Place, but raw diamonds, which look like a fairly unremarkable rock when first pulled from the earth.

A knife made of diamonds. This is why it cut through armor. I open my hand flat with the knife set balanced on my palm. It's not merely a knife made of precious stone, it's been intricately molded and sculpted, etched with designs. It's curved, like a dragon's tooth. Or a dragon's talon.

My heart wails quietly.

The inside of the curve has tiny serrations. On the body of the blade itself are delicately carved dragons in circling flight. The handle is simple, with only a very small hand guard. Etched in red, that at first glance looks like scales, are two inscriptions spiraling around to the bottom:

> *Love Him Whose Skin*
> *Gleams Red.*
> *Forever Entwined.*

I study the shape again. With the handle, and the inscription that looks like scales, it is a talon.

I bring His diamond blade to my throat, my hand trembling. In the pool are two images: one of me holding Talyn, and another of me holding Blaze. The wind is in my ear, saying softly that it is all right. *Let go, bring in.* It encircles Talyn as it carries her away, whispering that she will never be gone. It lifts Blaze and holds him out to me, telling me to take him. Tears fall soft and quiet now. I've reached the bottom of my chasm and it is time to climb out.

I hold out a handful of hair at a time, sawing until I've cut through. The wind carries some of my fallen hair away, letting other clumps fall into the water and float like rafts, and other fistfuls to fall upon the ground around my legs.

When the last handful of hair falls into my lap, my body springs forward, freed, and I cry into my hands. The wind's nodding, telling me: *Good. Cry, get it out. Cry hard, cry complete, cry true.* I can't remember how long it has been since I was in The Valley and that frightens me. But I know it's been just over one year since she was taken from me. Several lifetimes since she's been taken from me.

My hair bounces up to my jaw. The cool early evening breeze kisses my now-bare neck. My face lays upon the ground by the pool's edge. I have stopped crying. My tears are shed. I play with the edge of the pool, my finger tracing tiny streams my tears have formed in the mud. I'm afraid to get up, afraid of leaving. Of forgetting. But tears are spent and the pool is now clear. Talyn is There, but she is also deep inside me. Beside her, but foremost, is Blaze, and he is Here and he needs me now.

The water offers a hand and asks me in. I pull off the damn dress and obey, sitting in the center of the pool. *Heal me*, I beg. *Heal me, heal me, heal me.* He made me feel whole and then he ripped me to shreds.

The water is not cold, not warm. It reaches only to my waist. I wash my face and my newly-shortened hair as I work to detangle it, while the water washes down my body and returns to its pool. My mind drifts again to Blaze, and how it'll be time for him to eat again. My body shakes, but the tears and the guilt are gone.

I dunk the dress into the water and scrub it between my hands, realizing I can never cleanse it of what it symbolizes. I need to find other clothing and get rid of this. He has no business being anywhere near me, even if, especially if he's in the form of a dress, in which case he is on me, all around me. He has no business doing that.

Rising, I reluctantly pull it back over my head. I stand in the center of an unknown pool in a world far away from my daughter, and I am spent and afraid, but I have a son who needs me.

I walk back the way the wind had carried me, but then stop and return to the pool's edge. The dagger waits eager and motionless where I'd dropped it, glowing under the moonlight, knowing I'd return for it.

I slide it across my palm and wait for my blood to realize that it is free and fall to the ground. A few drops tentatively peer out through my split skin and descend. I collect a fistful of dirt and mud and my cut hair and hold the mix tightly, watching the moist parts of the mixture wash through and find their way back to the earth.

"Earth that I belong to, hair and blood that is me, I want you to remember me, remember my blood, remember my shames. I leave this spot, and I will cry no more, but I will not forget. If you want me here so greatly, then you must remember this blood I give you, for it runs through my daughter. I'll stay here, I'll raise and love this boy you've given me, but you must call to my daughter and guide her back to me. I bind you to this promise."

27

I PAUSE. NIGHTMARE, BLAZE still sleeping where I left him, but no Karr. Nightmare spins around. [Where have you been? How am I supposed to care for this child? I don't know what to do!]

"Did he cry?" I ask, in as short a mood as the unicorn.

[No.]

"Did he wake up at all?"

[No.]

"Then what are you complaining about? Do you know what I have done? Do you have any idea at all about the extent of *my* complaints?" I kneel beside Blaze, so tense and shaky that I fear the currents of anguish buzzing off of me will zap him awake. Only instead, the calm that has settled over him since I last held him, since I *fed* him, flow upward towards me until my nerves settle back into my skin and my worry, my guilt, withers submissively away.

His little fists are loosely made, resting contentedly upon his bony chest. The moonsuns come to light his face, and he is beautiful and sweet, lost in a forest of dreams that will finally now be full of a future. I run the back of my cut hand across his face, drawing him in, knowing there's no longer any need to worry. He'll grow strong and healthy.

I wake him and bathe him with the still-wet dress. His diaper is dry, but I won't worry. I nurse him for our second time as the sky darkens deeper, Nightmare trying to make me speak about where I'd been and why I was gone so long. I don't answer, remaining in a state of silence that only includes me and this new child.

My body still has barely any to give, and Blaze is fretful and frustrated, but I rock him and sing his sister's song in a low voice until he returns to sleep. My eyes fix on the sky, my ears straining for that profound sound of dragon's wings Mom had so often whispered about when she was in those downcast moods that made her think she could hear her mother and father or siblings coming to bring us back. Where is Karr? He's been gone so long.

[He'll be back soon enough,] Nightmare grumbles. [You were by water this afternoon? Is it far? We should walk there, perhaps. You should drink more.]

"But Karr—"

[He'll find us, unfortunately. How about the water, Lira? Do you remember how to get to the pool?]

"I never said it was a pool."

[You didn't need to. I see it when you think it. Can you get us back to it? You need to drink more of that water.]

I nod.

[What did you do to yourself? Why did you chop off your hair? What did you do to your hand? What happened in there?] He waits for me to answer, taking me in, watching the way I look and hold Blaze.

And then he nods, understanding. [You need to bandage your hand before you lose too much blood. The dragon will smell it and throw another fit. Have you not noticed that your new friend is more hostile than you? He'll ask questions. I understand, Lira, but I don't know that he will.]

The trees are darker and don't look at all like they had when I'd come through earlier, but I know where to turn and where to head, and we find our way without any trouble. There's no sign that I'd been here already. No blood, no hair. The pool doesn't move, the trees don't bow, the wind doesn't even whisper through the trees.

I kneel down and wipe some of the water onto Blaze's dry mouth and then lean over him and bring some to my own mouth, drinking long and hard, like I can never get enough to sate my thirst. I don't realize how thirsty I truly am until I pull away and can't count how many handfuls I'd gulped down. My body isn't shaking quite so much anymore, and I feel better. I'd forgotten the toll nursing takes on you. And I don't have the benefit of leftover pregnancy fat. Of any fat that can be burned off instead of my scant needed weight.

The moon is almost completely in her place for the night and the cool nighttime wind is starting. I lay Blaze down and go about gathering wood despite the unicorn's protests. I am fully capable of doing things. I can take care of myself. The purposeful movements do further to settle me, anyway. I set down my piles and step back to watch as Nightmare turns them to fire.

"You are fairly useful, I guess."

The unicorn glares. The fire he'd made falters and pops. I smile, knowing I hadn't upset him enough that he'd really take it away.

[Lira,] he begins, noting my constant checks on the sky. [Why don't you go to sleep? At least sit and rest?]

I sit close to the fire with Blaze in my arms, and stare into the ever-changing color of the flames. Blaze wakes for brief moments, his eyes fluttering, making sure I am still with him, that he hasn't been abandoned again. Every now and then he whines, when he has stored up enough energy to do so, and I smile, knowing he's getting stronger, hopeful for the day he releases another full blown wail.

I let myself get lost in the fire, hoping my thoughts just stop. Karr's been gone so long. I turn my head and am back in the hallway, gazing out the door, waiting for Mom's students to leave so we could slip back into our lives and our makeshift world, locked inside our house. The warmth and the security I hadn't realized the house had once given me returns across the unfathomable distance, weaving out to me from among the trees, letting me know I had not been forgotten. Mom rounds a corner to come out of the parlor and my presence somewhat startles her. Her face breaks out into a delighted smile. I want to run to her, want her to catch me like she'd done when I was small, hold me like she had after they'd tried to take me from her.

I blink back tears. Oh, I need her now. What would she say to all of this? *Relax. Relax, your body knows what she's doing. So let her.* And she'd give me tea to help make me feel better, like Aril had done for her whenever she was upset or scared. Tea, oh I want some tea right now.

In the shadows of the hall, behind Mom, is Mihn. How powerful my father has always been, not needing to say or do anything. He was always there or around and I knew everything would be fine, he was watching over us. There were so many stories he'd tell to lull me to sleep, or stories he'd complete because Mom had said it wrong or missed a few key events, according to him. I'd wonder what it would be like if she knew he was there, and to watch them argue and tease, smile and touch so that I'd have grown with a less fractured sense of my parents' love for each other. I wish I could have felt him hug me or throw me in the air as other girls' fathers did.

Counting down the minutes. I know this term. I keep repeating the countdown from the Other Place, the one they'd said when I'd run from the club, my hand in His, but Karr doesn't return. I waited so long for Him to return. Is He near now? Is He watching me?

[You still love him, after all he's done to you?]

I shoot the unicorn an angry glare. "Get out of my head!"

The unicorn's tail whips his side. [You're not denying it,] he complains.

"I'm not admitting to anything, either. When I screamed today, I was so terrified that He'd somehow heard me that I thought I could feel him coming. But it wasn't Him, and I'm so grateful. I'm *grateful*, Nightmare. And I'm grateful to you for finding me, saving me, staying with me. But Nightmare, I don't want Karr to know."

[Know what?]

"Anything. Everything. Him. I'm not broken, and I don't want him to see me that way."

Nightmare softens. [No, you're not broken, Lira. But you have to tell him something. He's a dragon. He wants to bring you east. And it's always possible he knows this Him of yours, or may run into him at some point. If you want to limit what He knows, just remember that your dragon Karr does appear to read your head and your thoughts more easily than I.]

But where is Karr? The stars are slowly becoming visible. Small white balls beginning to shine here and there around and between the three larger orbs.

Nightmare rises to his feet. [Here comes the bastard dragon now.]

I am stupidly giddy as a little girl and conversely hushed into awed silence by the sound of Karr's wings announcing his approach. It's exactly as Mom had said. That sound, the best lullaby anyone could have. What is it? A rush of air, of fire, of water? All those sounds at once, with the dulled, distant chime of his scales. A sound that harbors good things, home, family, love. It's a sound you can place all your trust in. And I'm finally hearing it.

Karr circles, dancing in between the suns and the moon and stars. Only he's angry. Nightmare's gums draw back and I pat Blaze's back absently. "Is he mad that we moved?"

[He is. Didn't help us loose him, though.]

"Nightmare."

Karr's voice enters into my head. *{I cannot land there. There's better space not far away and I'll walk to where you are. I'll be there shortly.}*

I return to the fire to wait. Again, but this time my fears are gone, replaced by that excited, ridiculous childish giddiness. I can't sit. I can't stand still. I pace, I rock Blaze, I sway, rubbing his back. The stars have multiplied greatly. Their swirls have become more noticeable. So many stars, and so close that they group in large spirals, like a flock of seagulls in a tornado. They give off the sense of having millions of onlookers, keeping tabs. Are they truly the souls of the dead? Is that what our struggles and our trials in life attain for us? In the end, is it worth it? Mom believes Mihn's star is in the southeastern corner of our sky, over the village he'd been born in. But it's not. It's right beside her.

From the corner of my eye, I spot Karr emerging from the trees- a breathtaking escape of red from a night-blackened forest. His body relaxes at the sight of me, and his pace sharpens. I want to smile, but so much has happened in this one day that I nearly cry instead.

Starlight and moonlight hit the side of my dragon's face, displacing the red of his scales in another completely new way, like looking at beach sand when it's scorching hot, and the steam rising from the baking sand distorts your vision. {*You cut your hair,*} Karr blurts, confused. {*Why did you cut your hair?*}

Nightmare snarls. [You were gone a damn long time. Did you even remember to find her something to eat?]

Karr nods slowly, still studying me. Can he sense that everything has changed? Nightmare was right, then, about his ability to read me better than the unicorn can. And Nightmare's been annoyingly perceptive.

Strapped around Karr's neck is a large canvas bag. How odd- a dragon carrying a bag. Where did he get something so big? It's large enough that I can probably fit inside fairly comfortably.

{*Well, since the beast won't allow me to fly you around, and you won't let him carry you, I thought he might at least allow you to sit inside a very large bag so I can carry you.*}

This time I let myself smile. "That's not what it's for."

{*You don't believe me?*}

"That you're going to stick me in a sack and carry me around?" My body tenses when he looks at me in wide-eyed silence. He's going to stick me in a sack.

He drags the silence out a moment more before laughing. {*Truth is that since The Beast is too proud to alleviate your burden, I decided to find a way for me to carry your supplies.}*

"My supplies?"

{Yes. You're not really doing so good without anything. Took the man awhile to make a bag suitable for a dragon. His hands wouldn't stop shaking. It's been a long time since anyone's seen a dragon, you know. Since your parents roamed. I didn't think my presence would have this effect on them. As if I'd eat him or set his whole place on fire. I only do that to Soldiers. Unicorns if you'd allow.}

I cast him a warning glance before changing the subject. "My supplies?"

Seeing a dragon sit is quite an amusing sight, and to see one struggle with too-long talons to reach a bag and disconnect it from his body is enough to make me do more than smile. I laugh. The large sack drops to my feet and I kneel down, tentatively lifting a corner to peer far inside.

{Dig in, love. It's all for you.} The dragon inclines his head, noticing Blaze's bright-eyed gaze intently watching every move he makes. *{The youngling looks......different. What did you do?}* He lowers himself onto his belly, resting his neck upon his arms as he brings his face down close to the infant below him.

Could this have been my life? Would I have been the newborn in my mother's arms as she showed me off to her family? Would they have gazed down upon me now as Karr does to Blaze? If He had brought me here when he'd promised, it would have been my daughter in my arms beneath Karr.

{Lira? Are you alright? You went someplace very dark. I couldn't even sense you.}

I fumble through the contents of his gifts. There's a large gourd filled with water and a smaller of milk, dried berries, some grains-

{Your dress is...... tight...... er. What happened?}

"It must have shrunk when I washed it this afternoon."

{Shrunk?}

"Rice!" I shout. "You brought me rice!" And oats. Flour and sugar, bowls and a cup. There's two pouches stuffed full of herbs. "Tea!" I exclaim even louder, pulling the little sachets to my chest. My eyes well. "You brought me tea."

Karr basks in my delight. He lifts his head proudly to Nightmare. *{She likes me more than she likes you.}*

The unicorn shakes his head and stomps away, mumbling a long string of unrepeatable curses.

There's a loaf of bread and a slab of cheese. There's an actual quilted blanket for Blaze, and some strips of cloth for more diapers, of which he will soon need, and a little shirt.

I smile, my words unable to convey the gratitude I truly feel. "How did you think of all this?"

{Scared the life out of a few villagers. I've recently learned that fear sometimes gets you where you need to be.}

28

CRISP, CLEAN, BLUE. DARK AND PERFECT. Starlight, moonlight, even sunlight. Night is so different from day. Night and day Here are so different from night and day There.

To the unicorn's disdain, I leave my spot and settle myself against Karr's side. His scales gleam in the night's varying lights, casting a sheen of red over my skin. "You're as beautiful as this night."

{I can think of many other things aside from myself that equal this night, if not make it dull in comparison. Did you eat enough?}

"I did. Thank you." It's been so long since food has offered any attraction or taste for me. This meal, in all its simplicity, could not have been any better- even if the pot Karr brought me has a crack that leaks liquid into the fire. Good thing I have a dragon and a unicorn to restart my cooking fire- even if they turn it into a war of who can get a better flame started first. The dragon lost his temper at one point and there was something of a raging column of flames instead of a small, safe, in-the-woods type of fire. Once the fire and the fire starters had all settled down, I boiled the pool water and made myself some rice, adding some milk and some dried berries as an afterthought.

"I'm making oatmeal for breakfast."

{Yuck. That's just boring. I'll have to do better my next food trip.}

I'm in the trees, in the air and the perfect dark blue night, nestled against a dragon before a fire. I can look across the fire and smile at the truest friend I've ever had: a unicorn, my once greatest fear and supposed enemy. (I smile though he is still scowling and cursing. Jealous beast.) Today, I was given a son. Today, I was given Karr. This is a perfect night- and if I don't think too far or too deep, this will stay a perfect night. Above us, the sky is ablaze with stars and the moon. If I turn my head in either direction, I can see the tops of the paled suns. My body sinks further into Karr's. "Thank you."

{For what?}

"For coming."

Blaze wakes and immediately focuses on Karr. The dragon blows warm air out of his nostrils and the baby wiggles and grins. He's swaddled in the little gown and the thick blankets Karr had brought; he's fed and warm and claimed, abed in a crib of pulled grass and sifted earth. He looks like a little mouse, dwarfed inside the blankets and further dwarfed by Karr and Nightmare. One arm dangles outside his wrappings. He has five miniscule, insanely tiny fingers. The other perfect five are partly uncurled, up at the side of his face. Tiny perfect lips keep together as he breathes smoothly through his nose. Cheeks pink, flesh normal healthy thriving baby color. What mother would just leave him as his had done?

The flames of the fire jump as a log collapses. Sparks fill the air like firecrackers- those noisy things of the Other

Place that filled the sky with bursts of explosive color. Blaze scrunches up his face. He turns his head to the fire and hypnotizes himself back to sleep, a perfect little foot peeking out from the blanket. Five little toes. A little leg. *I kissed the soles of her feet. My daughter. My son.*

I curl myself around him, sandwiching myself between him and Karr. When she was this age, I nursed her almost constantly. But she and I were in a healthier state than he and I are now. When my body is built up and can give him more, his strength will improve and he'll want to eat more. He is still too weak and spends more time sleeping than eating. But I'm caring better for myself and soon we'll both be in a healthier condition.

With him snuggled tight against me, I take his small fist into my hand. His face turns to me but he doesn't wake. His skin is baby smooth. And clean, and warm now, the way it's supposed to be, with good color a little flushed from the fire. He's thin, but he'll chunk up soon. Be a normal little boy all smiles and laughs, romping through the trees and earth with me. He won't grow in a house, with a roof and walls and floors and ceilings. He's going to grow in the trees. He's going to be a little boy who's constantly smiling face will also always be streaked with dirt. He'll learn to speak to the wood and air and dirt and forest life before he speaks a human word. For a father, he has two: a dragon and a unicorn. No one on any world will be able to take him from me.

She was once this small. She was once this close against me, where she had once been safe. My soul would pour out through my skin watching her, so overfull with love was it, so grateful.

The fire catches on my skin; igniting and washing over my chest as my breasts fill again. In unison, Blaze wakes. I pull him toward me and let him nurse, studying him in silence. Eyes open and seek me out, lock on me, claim me.

{*Oh! Oh that's-!*} Karr scrambles to his feet behind me, withdrawing backward. I look over my shoulder at him, caught between laughing or crying. His neck finally arches over my body to look down, shocked. He blinks. Hard. Blinks again. {*I thought- He's not- He's not yours. Right? How is* that *possible?*}

"He's mine now."

{*That's not really what I meant. I thought- Shouldn't you need to be a mother first?*}

[How insensitive can you be?] Nightmare yells, stomping his feet and charging forward. [Has she not become his mother by what she has done and by what she is currently doing?]

{*I didn't mean that either! But* how......?} the dragon can't finish his question. His final word hovers for a few moments.

[At least I'm not fool enough to claim I know how women's bodies work and what they can or should not be able to do. She's feeding a baby! Stop staring!]

"He needed me. It's only nature and instinct, Karr."

{*This is what happened while I was gone. But- you're crying.*}

"I am not." I wipe my eyes and sit up, bringing Blaze to my shoulder.

{*Why does it make you cry?*}

"It doesn't."

{*It is.*}

Nightmare stomps his foot down so hard it echoes up his body and produces a loud pop of an explosion from his horn, complete with a red and gold ribbon of smoke. It has a paralytic effect, reminding me of the pop from the gun.

My shoulder screams out in memory and I forget to breathe while waiting for something to strike.

It's nothing, I repeat over and over. There's no guns here. There's only a dragon and a unicorn. However much they hate each other, I'm safe between them.

Karr recovers from his own shock of me nursing Blaze and curls his body back around mine. *{I'm sorry. I didn't mean to upset you. Dragons don't do that. It's amazing, love. Please forgive me.}*

His plea nearly pries all my truths from where they are locked away. His neck wraps around me so that he can place his swirling, enthralling eyes before mine. I think it's the first time he's been calm and settled since he's arrived. The reds of his eyes are not rubies in sunlight anymore, but are darkened to where it doesn't hurt to meet his gaze. They shock me out of whatever I was about to say. A breeze wafts through the trees, soft and warm as human fingers, traveling across my exposed neck. I gasp, a shiver following the touch, and am momentarily back in the club, just before He'd arrived. I shift my head quickly, scanning the trees, but as before, I can't find His hiding place.

{I'm sorry. I should have brought something warmer for you,} the dragon apologizes, mistaking my shiver. *{I'll get you something on the next trip. A coat? A cape? A blanket? The man was taking so long and I was so impatient to get back to you. I can't believe I forgot.}*

"No. Don't leave again. I'm fine as I am."

{Where are your shoes?}

"I don't have any. No-" I stop him. "I don't want any. I want to touch the ground."

{It's not touching you back as gently as it should. Look at your feet.}

"Don't look at my feet. We feel fine, Karr. Please don't leave again. Beside you I'm warm."

My charm dangles behind my eyes, my father holding it in the air over my head. *Hey, baby girl. You remember this beast right here. He is the rarest of colors. The color that warms you just by being near it. It's a special color. He's an extraordinary friend. Stay close to him. Promise?*

I push myself closer. "It'll be summer soon."

{*I'm bringing you shoes and something warmer anyway. But not tonight, love. Don't worry. I'll stay here and keep you warm, and we won't walk anywhere just yet so your feet- and you- get some rest.*}

Karr's heart beats heavy and slow against me, a strong, steady, massaging beat upon my back. The cliffs are there ahead of us, even if I can't see them. I envision my family flying over them, and Mom's voice replaces Mihn's. She's holding me against her, whispering in the night about her home:

> "I'd wake sometimes when everyone else was asleep, just before dawn, when it was still dark and quiet, and the moon was level with the suns. I'd hide behind a boulder and watch the suns rise. The ocean behind me sang in waves, in encrypted whispers in a language only I understood.
> One by one the dragons would come out as day hit in one glorious burst of heat and light. That's what I waited for, the rainbow of their bodies emerging from the mouths of their caves, as though the earth was pushing out her rarest gems. They spread out over the rocks. Some held their wings straight up, like transparent towers that

transformed the light like sun catchers; some
stretched them out along their sides, like rivers
that have been brilliantly dyed; and some held one
wing up, one down. Everything not directly
covered by their scaled bodies would be draped by
their reflected, dazzling colors.
Then my sisters would find my hiding place and
bring me back home."

"Do they know I'm here?" I ask Karr. "My mother's family? Why was it only you who came?" I roll back to see him. "Why is it that *you* came?"

{*You screamed and I heard. I don't know why they didn't. Maybe I'm the only one who's meant to hear you. Just like Sana and your mother.*}

My mother calls her mother 'Ama' but the dragons affectionately call the dragoness 'Sana', a shortened version of her name, Gwesana. I'd forgotten that.

{*Do you want them to know you are here?*}

"Yes. No. Not yet. Is that wrong?"

{*Do you think it is?*}

"Why do you answer my questions with a question?"

Karr laughs. {*I don't know how to answer you without knowing exactly what you ask of me. You have not been responding the way it was expected. It was never anticipated that you would be so......so......*}

"Hostile?"

{*Hostile!*} He laughs heartily, his body moving so much that it vibrates like an earthquake against me. {*Why would you say hostile?*}

I grin. "Nightmare says I'm hostile."

{Well, good! He's a demon, after all. Does being here upset you?}

I'm silent a moment, unsure and certain at the same time. "This isn't how I'd pictured it."

{I'm sorry. I'm very sorry.}

"It's not your fault, Karr."

Again, that surge of warmth, that undeniable feeling of being safe and secure radiates from him into me. I open the door between he and I and let it all in. Will that sense of security leave me if I move away from him?

{I want to know what happened before I came to you, Lira. I can't change it, I know. Maybe I can ease it for you. I won't let anything happen to you again, I promise.}

[She doesn't trust promises,] the unicorn retorts drily.

{I promise,} he repeats, emphasizing it. Coming from him, it sounds solid and unyielding, stronger than a swear or a vow or an oath. {Please.}

And so I tell him. I recall the flash of blinding silver light, the feeling of being ripped into pieces, the heaviness of my body when I'd opened my eyes to angry wind and green, green grass in my eyes. For him, I again feel the pain of running up and down those hills, the fear, the echo of the unicorns' hooves in my body, the snow, the suns. I feel the arrow lodge once more in my thigh, the Soldier's hand around my throat, the ropes cutting into my wrists, Nightmare slicing through the hills towards me, and the Soldiers' screams bouncing off the hills as I try to run away from all of it.

Then, "Nightmare took me to Ravery."

The dragon recoils and I am bombarded by instant cold. {Are you insane? You took her to Ravery?}

[She needed to see it, to accept it so it no longer holds such fear.]

{Says who? Did you at least warn her first, or did you just throw her into another shock as you saw fit? I'm assuming you 'promised' her it'd be fine. You're not as blameless as you seem to believe.}

Nightmare doesn't respond. He doesn't make a motion or a sound, and Karr doesn't press any further. His point had been made. I feel no blame toward the unicorn. He did not put me in those situations in order to wound me. He'd told me that some wills are stronger than your own and that events transpire that are beyond your control, and so I've accepted his apologies and have given him the same forgiveness he wants me to give myself.

"I saw what had happened to my mother there, Karr. I saw what happened to the women before she was born. I felt the evil of the place on my skin, saturating my lungs. All my nightmares take place there. I'm always running, searching-"

[But you saw that it's not the same. Ravery is dead.]

I pull Blaze in close, nodding. Karr's head drops down over me, his lips pulled back. He snarls at the unicorn, who follows my earlier plea and turns away. "A Soldier followed us there- the one you chased away earlier. We left Ravery and came to a Unicorn Bound camp. The Seer knew me, Karr. I don't know how. Something about a dream. She poisoned me with a powder she blew into my eyes."

{Where were you while she was attacked, demon? How could that Seer have possibly known who she was?}

Nightmare's frown deepens, but his posture doesn't revert to an offensive or even defensive one. He seems only annoyed. [Quite possibly, she knew who Lira was because she was, in fact, a *Seer*. They're known for that sort of behavior.]

{Luckily you were satisfied after *she got poisoned and decided to take her to where she belongs.}*

"The Soldier took me to the trees," I correct reluctantly. Fury fills my head in one quick, powerful flash, causing an instant, yet very powerful headache. I sit in order to quickly put my hand on his leg, the closest, quickest part of him that I can reach. "The Soldier didn't do anything, Karr." It's only a partial lie, but I'm afraid he'll lunge at Nightmare and truly harm him before leaving me to expel the rest of his rage on each and every Soldier still alive on the Hills. "Your temper is not making this easy for me, Karr. It's done. I'm here. You're here, and Nightmare did what he could. Believe me in that please."

The dragon swallows, bringing his emotions in check and bottling them into a very fragile container probably housed dangerously close to his internal fire. *{Then what?}* he asks tersely. *{Nightmare found you again?}*

"Yes. And then we found Blaze. And then you found us."

{Did I find you today with the same Soldier who took you from the camp?}

I chew on my lower lip, stalling. "Yes."

{How is that possible, demon, if you rescued her from him before? Why wasn't he dead?}

[Did you kill him?]

{How are they in the trees? Why are you?}

[Why are you? Aren't the dragons keeping to the cliffs these days?]

Karr grinds his teeth. *{Why aren't you with a Healer?}*

"I am with a healer. Nightmare drugs my water. I thought I'd never see again. I looked much worse, but whatever he's doing is speeding up the healing."

{And your leg?}

"My leg? Oh, the arrow."

Karr's nose brushes over my thigh gently, sending a soft flow of warm air over the healed wound. My skin wrinkles in hot/cold shivers.

"Because of Nightmare, it healed when it shouldn't have. I don't know what I'd have done without him, Karr. Please. Please," I beg him. "I need him."

{That's unfortunate,} he snorts.

Blaze stirs. I bounce him in my arms, humming distantly, staring east at the non-visible cliffs. The suns are slowly on the rise. The dragons will be leaving their caves as soon as the first lights of morning hit their doorways. Come out, stretch their immense bodies out to soak up the heat. Way up high, on top of the world. Away from all the human sorrows and pains. I think of Mom's murals, of Karr leaving those places to instead sit grounded by this fire with me. "Are you homesick?"

{Homesick? No, how could I be? Home is a relative term. Is it a place? The place you were born and raised? Is it someplace else you long for? Is it merely wherever the ones you love most dearly reside?}

I pull away from him to try and see his face, but in the night with the shadows made by the trees around us, it's hard to find. "Am I keeping you from something?"

{No, love. No. I want *to be here with you. I need to be. Beside you, I know the answer of home is the latter question: my home is right here with you.}*

Nightmare snarls.

My eyes, though dry, burn. I close them, rub my forehead and then hug Blaze closer against my chest. Karr moves, and it's a strange, beautiful and indescribable sound. *{Why do you cry when you feed him?}*

[Why wouldn't she be upset? After everything she just endured, now she has a child.]

{*How much of 'everything' was caused by your nearly lethal stupidity? If she'd gone where she was supposed to, none of it would have happened to her!*} Blaze begins to whimper. After a contemplative pause, Karr takes a gigantic dragon breath and settles himself.

"I'm upset because I've lost control over everything. What does being here mean? What will it do? This place is Home, but it's not *my home*. I have to go back. I'll always have to go back. But now there's Blaze. I was so afraid he'd die, and I had nothing to give him, no way to save him, and then my body took over. I can't not feed him. But how do I have any right to him?"

{*How can you think you don't? You saved him. If you didn't take him into your arms, or to your body, he'd have died. What your body does to ensure he lives is amazing, Lira. Disregard my initial reaction. I've never seen it before. It's something of a myth to us. Only human women have this ability. Well, you and animals, I guess.*}

[Cold blooded creatures like you can't be expected to comprehend the caring nature of warm blooded ones.]

{*Dragons rear their brood and form tight, life long bonds, ass. And yes, dragon blood may need help from the suns to warm it, but come here and see whether my blood is cold or not.*

{*Lira, you did something only you could do to save a youngling who needed you. Why would you cry over that?*}

"I wasn't prepared."

{*Are we ever prepared for the greatest moments in our life? If we expect them, if we prepare for them, then they wouldn't be the times we cling to the hardest. What you are doing is more than just nature and instinct- as you put it earlier. You found a starving, abandoned child cast off in the middle of a forest and you knew that somehow you could save him. It was your choice that started nature and instinct.}*

I turn my head up to his, amazed. He pulls his gaze away and stares east, toward his home and family.

His eyes dart down toward the baby who's only sleeping at my breast. *{I've often thought of having my own offspring,}* he says matter-of-factly. *{Although regurgitating our food into our younglings' gaping mouths seems a little violent now that I see what women do.}*

"Ha," I laugh lightly. "I suppose so. Nature and instinct, though Karr. It makes you do things that previously seemed strange and cringe-worthy. Have you attained breeding status?"

{Not yet. Maybe one day I'll be allowed such an honor. Have a nice big clutch scampering about terrorizing their draca and me. Should make life interesting.}

"Is there a certain dragoness for you?"

{I have one in mind. Though I never voiced the offspring idea with her— thought that might be too bold, too soon. I don't want to scare her off. Not yet, anyway.}

The dragon having something of a love-life is extremely entertaining. It brightens the night. It lightens our shifting moods. Nightmare and I started off pretty badly, and my pair of males even worse. This- something that doesn't involve myself and won't anger Nightmare- is a distraction we all need. "Does she at least know your interest in her?"

{I believe so. But she is keeping me at a distance.}

I nod. "We females like to do that. Especially when we are afraid."

{Afraid?}

[Or when males are blatantly without a brain.]

Dragons. More appropriately: *Unicorns!* There went that attempt.

{All unicorns are male, aren't they? No wonder you're so frustrated all the time.}

Dragons!

"What does she look like, your hopeful?" I raise my voice pointedly. Thinking of her, Karr's thoughts bleed the radiance from his soul into my head, which is brilliant and more effective than the thickest blanket or the largest fire.

{Gold,} he whispers. *{A beautiful, blinding gold. She steals light from the suns and outshines the moon at night. Just to see her is enough to end all my troubles. Her voice is enough to melt my heart. Whatever she asks, I will do, no matter the consequence to me. I love her truly, more than she could ever know.}*

Nightmare coughs and spits at our fire.

Karr's unabashed tenderness more than merely amazes me. He laughs, delighted. *{I've made you blush! Have I embarrassed you?}*

"I'm not blushing."

{I see in the dark. You're nearly as red as me.}

"Am I keeping you from her?"

{Not at all, love. The time is not right for us. So I am here, as you need me. I am your Guardian first, her lover later. Ahh, that shade of red looks lovely on you.}

"Leave me alone," I pout, turning away. "I think you rather enjoy that you made me blush- which I'm not."

{My beautiful proclamation embarrasses you. How will my love react?}

"You did not embarrass me."

{Mm-hm.}

"You didn't! I just......I think I believed in love like that. Once."

{You don't believe in it anymore?}

"I see it around me. In a way. I know when my mom is thinking about my father. I see it in her eyes and the change his memory elicits in her whole body. She is lighter and she breathes easier and she glows. There's smiles in her eyes if not on her face. And I see the same with Mihn's when he looks at her, when he is quiet and just *sees* her. I hear it in the way her tone alters when she says his name, how her voice drops suddenly when he enters her thoughts. I notice how Mihn's motions transform when he's signing and thinking about her. The expression on his face and on his entire being. I can even see it in the air around them.

"And I feel it when my mom talks of her parents, and when either talk about how Hozar and Aril, and my father's Aunt Na'el and Uncle Roone, were towards each other. But I don't know any of them and my father is dead. And He- He-"

Karr is silent a long time, as though what I'd said is hard for him to digest. I realize what I'd done but don't know which mistake he'll call me on. I've never told anyone about Mihn before. How could I? But the dragons knew him. They'd understand. But, Him. I did not want to ever speak of Him with Karr. He'll fade away to nothing eventually.

{You see your father watching your mother?}

His question fills me with relief. "He watches her all the time."

{I don't understand.}

"You're more a romantic than I am. You knew them."

{Yes. But.}

"He could never leave her. Nothing, nothing could ever keep them apart. Not even death."

He's silent a moment more. The moon has just found a spot in the trees where it can bleed through and rest upon him, and in a way I have red moonlight again. His eyes are swirling and then still, their color altering hues every moment that passes as his thoughts turn and influence them. When he is angry, or impassioned, they blaze red. The rare moments he's calm, they're either pewter grey or swirling. When he's happy, streaks of silver shoot through. That's all I've been able to decipher so far.

{Elaar talks of The Wizard? And Aril?}

"Always. She loves them. She misses them."

{And......she talks of their son?}

I stiffen. He'd caught my lapse. "She never told me his name. Neither did He."

{It wasn't his intention to-}

"I don't care!" I shout, before the breadth of his words settles. I spin around, stunned. "How do you know what His intentions are? Do you know him? What else do you know?"

{Do you want to know his name?}

[You need to back off,] Nightmare growls, no longer on the other side of the fire but there before us, his horn pointed at the dragon's throat again. Karr doesn't flinch, doesn't fly into a temper.

{Back off? From what? I want to know why you're around, why she feels she needs you. Yes, love, I know this 'Him' of yours quite well, although the story he tells seems to vary significantly from what you're radiating.}

"He set me in The Valley! He left me-"

{That's not true. You're possessed by a unicorn. He's tried to get to you several times but wasn't allowed.}

I scowl. "I am *not* 'possessed'."

{*Not anymore. He came to me for help, Lira. He could do nothing for you in The Valley except get you killed. The Wizard had spoken of me and your 'He' thought I'd help more than he could. He was holding a necklace in his hands and I understood that he was right, I was the only one to save you. When you screamed he charged off towards you first, but I stopped him and came instead.*}

"He was coming," I whisper to Nightmare.

[But he didn't. He sent something of an envoy, though.]

"Is that what this means?" I withdraw the blade angrily from its sheath, holding it up in the moonlight so the inscription is visible. "Love his messenger but remember he came first? I'm no one's property."

{*I'm not a messenger and you aren't property, love. It's a gift, with images and words you'd find familiar. You were brought here-*}

"I don't want to *be* here! I want to go back. Take me back. Please, Karr, make him find a way to send me back!"

{*Why? This is your home. This is where you are supposed to be-*}

"Nobody asked me! No one asked if I *wanted* to be here! I want to go back!"

{*But you wanted to be here. You told him-*}

"Yes, 'wanted'. A long time ago. Before he abandoned me there."

Karr watches the tears burn down my cheeks and seep into the damn dress and Blaze's black hair. {*You can't go back, love,*} he broaches cautiously. {*He doesn't know how. You were his anchor. He won't be able to find that place again now that you are here. And I can guarantee that there's no reason you could give that would make him send you away. It was hard enough for him to allow me to see you first.*}

[Sure it was.]

"Promise me something?"

{Anything.}

"Don't ever let him find me."

{Lira-}

"*Promise* me, Karr."

He hesitates, glancing from me to Nightmare.

"Please, Karr. You have to promise me or......or you have to go."

{Lira-} he attempts again.

[We can't force you to do something you don't feel is right. If you have to leave, we'll understand.]

{I promise,} Karr vows before the unicorn finishes speaking. *{How could you think I wouldn't? I said I'm her Guardian, more so than you, and that's what I'll be.}*

A tense silence settles between us all, forming walls that are dividing us. I can't have that. It's hard enough to struggle with their hostility toward each other, but I cannot be angry at Karr for his associations before me, and I can't let him think that I am angry with him for something out of his control. The silence stretches on, and I let it carry my anxiety away before speaking again.

"I'm sorry. I've put you in a bad place."

{No, Lira.}

"He's your friend-"

{You are suffering because of him. He's not my friend at the moment.}

"Then......please......don't bring him up ever again."

They both push their presences into my head, and I let go. Karr's presence grows stronger, outshining Nightmare's. Nightmare merely observes, ensuring my past remains unknown, keeping my darkest secrets safe and out of everyone's minds.

Karr's greater control guides me into sleep. Night becomes a warm thick blanket with sleeves, encircling me with comfort and beauty and serenity. Night. How can Night become wonderful again? Before my eyes shut completely, his wing cascades down like a great blanket over me; the deep color of his scales somehow the truer comfort, shimmering as scorched sand again. It allows my eyes to grow too heavy to remain open, and I fall asleep exhausted, the night dreamless but filled with red scales and purplish eyes. I can forbid everyone from mentioning Him, but my own mind never fails to betray me.

29

YESTERDAY, AS I'VE PUT ON SOME WEIGHT, proved that I could walk without getting dizzy, and could look towards the suns without fainting, my Guardians allowed our wandering to continue after weeks of being grounded to that spot by the pool. They'd formed somewhat of a truce in those requirements that I had nodded my head and agreed without (too much) protest. They don't need to know about the headaches or the sharp, stabbing stomach pains, the vertigo, or the times my vision wanes. Those will go away on their own as well. For the most part my Guardians have been halfway civil to each other. Within hearing, at least. And I took advantage of my week of being stationary to do nothing but tend and feed Blaze.

Once we started moving, though, I couldn't stop, and figured out quite quickly how to nurse and walk at the same time. A feat that Karr can't get over, and which upset Nightmare enough that he kept checking to make sure I was properly covered.

It's been so long since I've walked any distance that last night I wasn't in the least tired, and just kept going after Blaze and I had eaten. Amazingly, neither male had tried to prevent me. Clouds covered moon and suns so it had been unusually dark. Magically dark. It wasn't the same suffocating black that had first greeted me on the hills. It was the dark like the house at night when we'd draw all the shades and curtains. We'd light a single candle in the center of the living room floor and Mom would tell Talyn stories of here. She'd loved that.

I smile forlornly at the memory, holding Blaze and staring at the thin thread of chimney smoke as it rises over the trees into the sky; like a vein in marble, visible only because I know that a single house stands down in the little gully below. By Mom's telling, all homes here are tiny little huts clustered in tight little villages. But the one below is a good-sized square house with a pitched roof and an additional half story, most likely a loft. And it sits all alone.

We very nearly fell right onto it last night. I couldn't see a thing before me, and had foolishly decided to use the opportunity to test my other senses. Sight without the use of eyes, like sending off a call through my skin and reading the echo that came back, and I mostly knew when to veer slightly right or duck beneath the oncoming branch.

Nightmare had stopped first, and then Karr, and suddenly I found my feet at the very edge of a precipice with an immense openness before me and only black sky above, the shoulders of my cape and shirt in Karr's teeth the only thing that prevented me from falling. The earth fell away and dropped down about fifty feet to a small little valley below. The sounds of animals- a goat, possibly an ox- sharpened my attention. Then I smelled burning wood, deciphered the dark outline of a little house.

There was no other choice but to stop for the night. This morning we snuck back to the precipice to see with the aid of day. Only one old woman lives there. She was out feeding the ox.

My eyes follow the smoke down to the little house. There's a small paddock beside it housing that goat and ox. Some free-roaming chickens graze around the open front door. Karr's already scared a few too many villagers and we don't need word spreading about a rampaging dragon. Nightmare would be much less apologetic about terrifying people than the dragon.

With a pointed look at the unicorn, I volunteer myself: "I'll go. You both stay here."

{What? No. I'll go. It's all I can do for you.}

"I can care for myself, Karr."

It's nearly summer now, and though we stumble on some edible forest wares in between Karr's begging, it's not enough, and I want to have more to do with Blaze's and my survival. Going down to a house and begging for my own food is something I can do.

{You're not going alone. We have no idea who lives down there.}

"An old woman, Karr. And I'm not going alone. Blaze will be with me." I can't leave Blaze behind, no matter how much I trust Karr and Nightmare. Not having him in my sight, losing him somehow......I can't risk it. I can't set him down and turn my back again.

The dragon snorts a pop of flames that turn to black ash around me. *{The little troll doesn't quite count as you not being alone, love.}*

"You'll be near enough."

{I won't be near enough. I should go with you. I could go for you.}

"Then you'll be down there and I'll be up here. What's the difference? I'm not incapable. Tell him, Nightmare."

[Why? It's his own insecurities he's projecting.]

{Coming from a demon.}

[Controlling freak of nature.]

{Dragons are completely natural, one-sexed beast.}

[You shoot fire from your belly and somehow manage to fly. Do not tell me that either are natural.]

{I also have two horns while you're stuck with one.}

So much for the external truce. "Ok, fine, I won't go. I'll stay here and babysit the two of you and then I'll have no food and Blaze and I will starve and *die*. But then you won't have to worry about me going down to that house alone and I won't have to worry about the two of you killing each other while I'm gone. Sound good?"

{No,} Karr pouts. *{Lira.}*

"Karr," I challenge back, silencing him completely.

Blaze finishes his breakfast just as the suns take their morning positions. "I'd better go now. Do not kill each other while I'm gone."

{I can't even try?}

[Try all you'd like. You are not as large or as strong as you like to think.]

"Karr, promise me?"

The dragon huffs, a small billow of smoke escaping his mouth. *{I promise to be at my utmost behavior. I cannot vouch for the unicorn, though. His kind has some rage issues.}*

[I'll stay on this side of the fire and he'll stay on that side of the fire. We'll be fine. Call if you are in trouble. We'll hear you.]

I hug him. *Who knew I'd ever love a unicorn?*

Karr snorts.

[Jealous, are we?]

"Oh, stop it." I watch the smoke trailing upward into the sky, like a waterfall turned upside down. I'm stalling, suddenly reluctant to actually follow through and walk away from them. I calculate the time of walking down to the house, speaking with whoever lives there, and making my way back to them, and feel a rising panic.

Karr changes from argumentative to supportive. *{You'll be back quickly. I'll wait right here for you. It's impossible for you to get lost: no matter which direction you take, you'll walk into us. It's all fine, love. I know you need to do this yourself. No fear.}*

I walk to the dragon and kiss his cheek, running my hand down his forehead. His eyes dive deep into mine, searching. They're swirling again, rubies and pewter and silver. "Karr, I don't think you realize just how much I love you."

{I do, love. I do.}

"I feel so silly. My first day away from the two of you. No reason for emotional good-byes. I'll be back soon."

At the precipice, I stop to look behind me. They're deep enough within the trees as to be completely concealed. This is it, my first time out alone. How ridiculous. Just like That Night, I'm nervous as a child.

It is quite a walk along the ledge till I find a place where the distance to the ground is not so great. It proves way too uncomfortable to slide down the rift in a dress, so I pick my way carefully down by foot, grabbing onto roots and using rocks as leverage with one hand, and holding Blaze secure to me with my other. At the bottom of the small canyon the grass grows short but lush. I smile, enjoying the softness, the medicine it gives to my sore, callused feet. I might just have to grit my teeth and wear the shoes Karr has been carrying around for me. I hate shoes.

The ox chews lazily on some long strands of grass, barely able to spare any energy to notice me. The goat is gone, and the chickens are too intent on catching bugs to care about me. My stomach jumps. Fresh bread, the open doors of a home, even the smells of the livestock hit me with the quick change of the wind. They affect more than my stomach. I have been roaming here like a nomad for months now and haven't thought I'd missed the things of a solid, unmoving dwelling. It makes me think painfully of Mom, sitting in her kitchen by the great hearth, regretfully thinking about how she'd told Mihn he'd never make her domestic.

If He had returned for me, Talyn would be growing and running freely under open skies, away from all Other people. Just us, secluded and isolated. Domestic. Safe. Happy. And together.

Yet, where would Blaze be if that had occurred? I check to be sure he is still safely under my cape. His dark eyes peer back up at me, as if he had been contemplating the same question. Our lips begin to tremble so I walk on, leaving my thoughts behind. The ox moos as I pass her.

The door is slightly ajar. "Hello?" I call, waiting and receiving no answer. I set my hand on the door and take a hesitant step forward, leaning in. "Hello?" The windows are covered by worn fabric, but they're drawn open. The fire is burning low in the small stone hearth. It's fairly dim inside, fairly difficult to see until my eyes adjust. It's a small place, larger than what Mom had complained about, but only about the size of the front room in our house in The Other Place.

One small table, eight chairs. Hardened earth floors. A fabric partition, tattered and horribly faded, that must hide the bed. A ladder leading to the little loft. It's warm, comforting. To whoever lives here, this is perfect. Honestly, what more do you need?

Bathroom. With a toilet. Using the ground has taken some embarrassing practice. Mom forgot to teach me that one. I also really miss my bathtub. I miss my shower. Hot water running down my back and the steam filling the room-

The goat butts the back of my thighs with the front of his horns and grabs a mouthful of the damn dress. "Knock that off!" I scold, tugging to reclaim it. After a small fight, the goat decides I'm not going to be any fun and spits the dress out. I pat her head to show forgiveness but she turns away, making sure to flip her little triangular tail up into the air at me.

When I look up, I'm met with a watery blue-eyed stare from the old woman. She is small and almost-round, wearing a gray skirt and a rust colored blouse. A worn navy blue kerchief is tied over her head and her waist-length grey hair hangs loose and nicely combed beneath it. Her too-pale blue eyes don't quite look at me. Is she blind? Her skin's perfectly flawless except for some minor wrinkles, and has a nearly translucent sheen.

"I'm sorry. I-" My feet are past her doorway and I suddenly feel like an intruder; a dirty, dishonest intruder, taking advantage of a potentially blind old woman. What was I thinking, coming in here? I don't remember how to live around people anymore. This is rude. It was selfish and presumptuous of me to come here. I should've left this to Karr.

Her face warms into a smile and she waves my awkwardness away. "Sorry for what? Paying a lonely old woman a visit? Pfft." The woman wobbles forward on stiff legs until she's before me. She fumbles for my hands. I give her the one that can be freed from holding Blaze. "What is your name?"

"My- my name is Lira. I'm sorry to come upon you this way-"

"Lira," she repeats to herself. She steps away and turns, sweeping her hand invitingly through the air. "Come in, Lira. Come sit. Sit, sit," she orders, pointing to the chair beside me.

I watch the chair warily as though it'll jump up and bite me, and hold my weight up when my rear touches the seat, somehow expecting it to crumble to dust and send Blaze and I to the floor. When it doesn't I relax, and smile at the marvel of sitting in a chair. It's been so long! I run my fingers along the rim of the seat, down the front legs, and dig my back into the back rest. The old wood groans but it was built by a sturdy, skilled hand who'd ensured it would only get stronger as it aged.

"I was about to make myself an early lunch. I'm so happy that I'll have company to share with. My sons and grandsons come by every few days, but today is an in-between day. Normally I like my days of solitude as all I have are boys yelling and tussling about! Well, men now. Ach, can't believe they're all grown. No girls in my family. Each of my boys only made boys."

It's oddly strange to be in the company of another person, to be within walls and a home again. Normal is no longer familiar. Was my life ever normal? I look down at the goat and remember mom's non-dragon lizards, the birds singing in the kitchen rafters, the opossum curled up with her babies before the hearth. The lizards would curl around Talyn, soaking in and reflecting back her heat.

It wasn't until I was older that I realized that our home was further from normal than I had already known it to be. The other girls didn't have wild animals seeking shelter and companionship in their homes. Mihn speculated that the creatures recognized my mother as a wild thing like them, who was lost and struggling, and they came to give *her* comfort. Nature coming into the walls helped her, I know it did.

I shake my head and bring myself back to where I am, in Home, in an old woman's house, sitting stiffly in a chair. I am the wild thing that's come in, but I'm not sure why.

"I have some bread from yesterday. And the hens laid remarkably this morning. I think we'll have some pudding. Would you like that, dear?"

"Yes, I would. Thank you."

"We'll have some goat cheese and some of last fall's wild berry preserves, I think. It's a little chilly still, but summer's not far. I don't keep tea. Would you like some coffee?"

"That would be lovely. Can I help you with anything?"

"Help? Absolutely not! You sit there and just rest. How long have you been traveling?"

I try to answer but falter. How long?

"A long time, I take it. What are you searching for, Lira?"

"I'm not searching for anything," I answer softly.

"Sometimes you don't know you are until you find it."

Dust floats in the suns' rays through the open door and windows and I watch, my eyes drifting across the room with more focus. Behind the small partition across from the door a wood-framed bed peeks out, covered by an old wedding quilt the goat has just nestled herself in the middle of. Chickens periodically walk inside, lazily making their way back out when they tire of being indoors.

My mind catches the tiny hidden things: the veins in the wood that make up the walls and floor, the scuff marks and knife dents in the table, the rafters overhead, the small hearth, the chipped bowls and plates. There are small, random things scattered in a pattern no one but the woman and her family knows: a feather; a pile of rocks; some broken, blue speckled bird's eggs set with care inside a carved wood bowl that has the remains of small, child-sized muddy handprints. There are several dried and dusty bouquets of flowers tied with ribbon and hanging in random places. Keepsakes, reminders of special moments in the woman's and her family's lives. Such a tiny house, and yet it's snug and warm and perfect.

"You have a beautiful home."

"Thank you, dear." She pours her pudding over the bread she's torn into pieces and places the pot into the stone oven built into the hearth. I remove my cape and bunch it into a cradle on the floor before setting Blaze down in its center, and then rush across the house to grab the cups of coffee my hostess has poured. She joins me at the table and the goat follows behind her, snuggling around Blaze and licking his cheek a couple times before closing her strangely pupiled eyes.

"My husband and I built this house right after we married. Would you believe that there were once unicorns in our pasture?"

She takes a sip of her coffee.

"Unicorns came here?" I ask, surprised.

"Oh yes. I opened the door one morning and there were four of them. The poor things were covered in wounds. I use to bake them sweet bread and set it on the windowsill there for them. Sometimes they'd stay for days, and other times just for a brief rest. My husband bored out a large dead tree and made sure there was always clean water for them. Poor things. It amazed me that they would come here, with my house full of boys and me no longer a maid. It made me look at my boys with pride. If creatures as pure as they felt safe with my family, then I felt confident that they would grow to be the men I'd prayed they'd become. And they have.

"I'm sorry. Us old women like to reminisce. I've been dreaming of unicorns in my fields and dragons flying overhead lately. All of a sudden."

She shakes her head and smiles apologetically. "My husband passed away last year and my sons beg me to live with them. But right this minute I'm reminded why I can never leave this place. If I had, where would that have left you today?"

I hold the cup between both my hands, unable to drink. The steam rising up is like the mist that had covered her pasture this morning. The flecks of ground root floating along the surface turn to unicorns filling the open area around her home. I glance down to check on Blaze, and then look out the window, imagining the unicorns there again. Unicorns still calm and innocent enough that they had no trouble being so near a man, boys, and a Touched Woman. The hollowed-out tree is still there, cracked and unused in decades. But there. In case they return and are thirsty.

She continues to talk, and her voice, with words spoken from human lips that move, fascinates me enough that my anxiety about being apart from my Guardians and with another person washes away.

In the Other Place, when I was little, I enjoyed going into each of girls' homes, either for a visit or when Mom went to deliver new siblings. Each home was so distinctly different. I would stand against the wall or sit in a far corner and listen to the different languages and accents that said they weren't of There, either. I felt as though I were stepping into the countries the parents had left in order to move There.

Each of them had specific color preferences, different spices they put in their food that controlled the way the homes smelled, different styles of clothes and hair, different mannerisms and customs and food and languages and furnishings. They kept different tokens to remind them of personal happinesses, just like this old woman. They had different statues and pictures of important creatures they routinely prayed to- which is what spurred Mom to paint our walls.

Their parents' souls, no matter that they'd all chosen The Other Place purposely, were forever tied to the places they were born in just as Mom's still is, and their homes reflected that just as ours did. What did they see and think when they came into our house, with Mom's overly large version of a shrine? I don't even know what she told them about us, about her.

This house here holds new combinations of smells, a different aura as well. There's no painted walls, no elaborate woodwork, no beautiful furnishings. Everything is simple, handmade by either her or someone in her family line. The colors are all in shades of wood-brown, but it's not drab with the sun streaming in through her open windows and doors.

We kept our doors locked and our windows had glass. We kept our shades drawn and tried to keep that world out, but it broke in anyway.

Aside from the baking food, herbs, and warm candle glow, her home overflows with the feel of her life, her husband's lingering presence, memories of her children. Coming into the house is being drawn into their lives, making you part of them. This is a happy place. Will I ever have a house that someone will walk into and sit in my chair and eat my food and think the same: *"This is a happy home"*?

The old woman is again by the fire, checking on her food. The smells and heat from the fire surround me, soothe me. Blaze stirs just as my breasts swell full. I pick him up before he starts to cry and with him snug and feeding, sit back in my chair to look out the window.

"Men from all around appeared here one day, speaking of wars and a stolen little girl. And dragons. Did your people ever tell you of the dragons that use to-" She stops and turns away. "That use to many things. Dragons and unicorns. Dragons in the sky. When I was very little, they were always flying to and fro from The Cliffs to The Valley, all day. Then things changed. And changed again. And again. And now- now, they're gone. Did you know there use to be dragons?" she asks me.

"Yes. I know."

"Where did they all go? Unicorns wandering the trees and Forest Girls dreaming of becoming Bound. I think they've regretted those dreams." She limps to the door and stares at her field. The late morning sunlight hits her face warm and kind, old friends. "Do you feel that?" she asks me. "Until last night I hadn't realized that I'd forgotten how the air tastes and tingles when a dragon is near, or how the earth vibrates when there's a unicorn." She looks down to her feet, and out to the trees again. "They're out there, Lira," she smiles. The smell of our food over the open flame shakes her free. "Oh dear, I'm going to burn our food with my nonsense!"

"No, let me," I plead. Blaze has finished, so I lay him back down alongside the goat and help the woman back to her seat before going to her fire. I close my eyes and breathe in the heat from the hearth. No one in the Other Place had a hearth like we did. A hearth like homes here have. They had big, noisy things called *stove* and *oven*. In the winter, Mom and I would sit in the kitchen near our hearth and drink tea and talk, soaking in the warmth from the fire and each other. You can't do that around *stove* or *oven*.

The pudding has finished, so I pull it from the flames and walk it to the table.

"The cheese, dear. Over there on that counter. Wrapped in my blue cloth. I'll go get the preserves from the cellar."

"Let me-"

"No. You are my guest. Pour us both some more coffee and sit down. When was the last time you sat in a chair and rested your feet? Yes, I knew so."

She walks through her front door and around to the side of the house. I slide my feet gently along her worn dirt floor, my hands holding her pot of coffee, her door open to the trees and air of Home, which travels through the doorway to find me, to remind me. I pause and look around the house once again, Blaze smiling and kicking on the floor. It is so quiet, so *far* from anything.

What if......?

I had grown up in a house like this, with no dragons painted on our walls because they'd be flying overhead, no locks on our doors or glass in our windows as there's no people everywhere. Can I see Mom here, in a house like this one but a house here in Home that is ours, her bare feet covered in the mud she had danced in during the night's rain? If she'd agreed to this life, with Mihn, would he still be alive? Can I see me here in Blaze's place, my childhood within walls like this?

Can I see Talyn here?

Him?

I set the coffee pot down, remembering the dangers of 'what ifs', and bring over the gourd of honey along with carved bowls and utensils. I look out the door, worried. Where did she go? Is she alright? I spot her when I take a step through her door. She's standing still, staring into the trees with her hands tightly holding her jar of berry preserves. She senses me watching and smiles nervously again, hugging the jar to her middle even tighter. "I'm sorry. I just......was hoping......"

My eyes dart to the trees, but there's neither Karr's red nor Nightmare's golden horn. "I stood out here last night and I waited to see them. I waited so long that night had nearly come and gone by the time my eyes stopped staying open. It's why I was still sleeping when you came. And still in yesterday's clothes! Shameful." Self-conscious, she laughs and smoothes out the front of her blouse and skirt. "Have you-" she begins, unable to finish.

I look through the trees, my hallways of trees, worrying suddenly that I've lost them. That I won't be able to find them, in spite of their promises. Her need mixes with my own, and my heartbeats begin to tumble over themselves. What if I'm left, waiting for them to come back to me as well? I can't do that. Not again, not anymore-

When I turn to face her, she's a step away from me. Her eyes float away behind trapped tears and her mouth trembles."You *have* seen them. It's you, isn't it? I felt them out there, close by, last night. And this morning, you appear. No coincidence. I'm not a batty old woman stuck in the past having strange dreams for no reason."

"I'm sorry. We've been walking a long time. And Karr normally gets me food. But you were here alone, and I didn't want you to be scared, and I wanted them to see I could take care of myself."

As I speak, her smile spreads. She closes her eyes, and sighs, and reaches out for my hand. She squeezes tight. "Karr is….?"

"A dragon."

"A dragon. A dragon!" she laughs. "A dragon. Back in The Trees." She looks skyward, and asks where the others are.

"I don't know. I haven't seen them yet."

"A dragon in The Trees," she whispers soothingly to herself. "You haven't seen unicorns?"

But her question, in the plural, brings up images of the ones on the hill before settling back to Nightmare. "I have."

"Oh! Unicorns! Come back inside. You talk to me while we eat!"

Blaze has fallen asleep. I lean down and wrap an edge of my cape around him and pat the goat's head before settling back into my chair. The old woman beams as she cuts slices of bread and cheese and scoops out a large serving of warm pudding onto our plates. She opens the preserves and sets it close with a spoon inside for me to choose my own amount. But suddenly, I'm not hungry. A pain pierces through my stomach and I sit and ignore it, sipping my chilled coffee and staring at Blaze and through the window.

"Where have you come from? How did you find them?" she asks eagerly, sitting straight and still, like a child waiting for a favorite story. I smile, and tell her the better parts. I skip the hills, Soldiers, the unicorn camp, and describe only the unicorns from the camp- calm and serene and beautiful. I tell her of Nightmare and him leading me into The Trees, and that Karr had found us. I do not tell her of the circumstances, of the Soldiers there again. So close to her home. Of me being attacked, poisoned, arrowed. Or about Blaze.

She begins to eat contentedly, but I drift, wondering over the greater amount of unicorns in my life. Of Soldiers, just like my mother.

"You must be so hungry. Aren't you going to eat?"

I can't answer. I want to be by Karr's side again. My only dragon amidst so many unicorns and Soldiers. In agreement, Blaze wakes and begins to cry, seeing the strange face of a goat beside him and walls all around. I reach down for him quickly, soothing his fears. "Hey, baby boy. Mama's here. Shh." I cradle him under my chin and pat his back, and he shoves his fist into his mouth and quiets.

The woman drops her spoon and it lands with a crash first onto her plate, and then ricochets to the floor.

"You have a child? He's been so quiet I didn't even notice- How can you have a child? The unicorn —" Her voice and attention drift for a moment. She pushes her unyielding joints to carry her back to me. Her hands search my face, and I wonder again if she's blind.

My body tenses up.

Her hands withdraw and she sits and thinks and I can't read her expression. I don't know what she was looking for, or what she'd found.

"I think you left some things out of your story. Daughter of Elaar."

"Wha- what did you call me?"

"Who else could travel the trees with a child, a unicorn, and a dragon? You are too young to be Elaar. But, by my guess, you're just about the age of a daughter. You said you were on the hills and I didn't even stop to think about it. Or why unicorns would come to you. Or a dragon. Dragons never paid us humans any attention before or since her. And they wouldn't leave their cliffs for another random female human. You are the Daughter of Elaar."

When I make no response, she leans over the table and stares intently through my eyes, making me wonder at the strength of her sight. "My dear child, where have you been?" she whispers. "The Hills? They took her, didn't they?" Quickly, she wipes her eyes and turns away, lifting herself from her chair and feeling around the floor for the spoon. After setting it on the table, she stands, reorganizing her mind before noting that I hadn't touched my food. Gentler, she leans towards me and takes my face into her hands.

"Daughter of Elaar, you have food before you that wishes to serve you. You've come a long way, and, I'd say, you have a long way yet to go. This food is yours. You have earned it. Enjoy it, Lira."

She carries her plate and cup to the other end of the house and begins scrubbing them quietly in a small wash basin. After a few deep breaths, I wipe the dampness from my eyes and, to please her, I try to eat. Each mouthful is a struggle, but with each one the next comes easier. My guilt and shame drown in the food, and all I'm left with is pure, simple hunger. My throat burns and my sense of taste and smell is off. I have to eat, or the males will plant me to the ground permanently. It'll go away. It'll all go away.

"This house was several times full of Forest men, Lira. Frightened, angry, good Forest men. My husband joined them easily, quickly. That whole Valley full of corrupted men were intent on destroying one little girl. But our Treed men came together to protect that same child. Your mother." She looks at me, but it's not her dwindling sight that fogs her vision. "I never saw her. But I was a new mother, and I wanted to save her. I was exceptionally proud that I'd married a man who would join a battle to save one small unknown child. My boys grew up, and they joined too. There were unicorns in our field......"

She's weeping. I hold Blaze, weeping with her though I don't know why.

"Those unicorns you spoke of, and the one you travel with: they knew you'd been Touched, but they didn't care? They did nothing against you? I was alone with only them here for a lot of the time, but I was never afraid. The changes were so slight, I pretended they weren't there. My husband would return home and he'd look at them outside our door and warn me, beg me to take the children and move deeper into the trees. There'd been rumors of them attacking Forest men without provocation. Talk of them murdering man-bound women began spreading. I saw the change slowly creeping through each new ones' eyes, but I couldn't fathom unicorns murdering, and murdering women at that. Did you know that Valley women were once wanderers? The men- before becoming Soldiers- stayed put. All of us here descend from a Valley woman, Lira. At some point in our family line. The women wandered with their unicorns, meeting with their men when it suited them, and bore their babies in the grass while the unicorns watched over them. It had been that way for centuries. What would happen to make unicorns attack any woman? Being Touched had never bothered them before.

"I walked out the door one afternoon completely carefree and he came charging from the trees. Right then, the unicorns I had been told stories of since I was a baby and had grown use to seeing outside my home no longer existed. I have never been so terrified before. I had an ox that I'd raised from a calf at the time, and she charged through her corral and got in front of me in time to stop him. My youngest ran out of the house and pulled me back inside. I'd fallen back so hard I'd broken a rib. But what hurt more than anything was to see that those beautiful, pure creatures had somehow become corrupted." Her eyes, trapped in that day, smile at me. "But you were Touched and they didn't harm you. And you have a boy-child and your unicorn stays with you. And they are back in The Trees again. And you've brought the dragons back as well. It's changing again, changing back the way it was supposed to stay."

I don't know how to respond to her. It's hard for me to understand that the dragons vanished after the Wizard sent my mother away; hard for me to see that people were affected by their absence. That I'd be known as Nightmare had said I would be.

My eyes travel out the door, worrying over the condition of the trees if my dear Protectors have lost their tempers and are engaged in an all-out war. I don't smell smoke but, again, that doesn't mean much. I've been here longer than I'd intended. What if they've decided against petty battles and went straight to just killing each other? How could I have left them alone?

"I need to go," I tell her.

She stops what she's doing and considers that, and nods. "I feel your tension and know your Others await you. The vibrations they cause are getting a little strained. They're worried."

She pulls two sacks from a cupboard before methodically going through her house with calm precision, filling the empty bags with items from drawers and cabinets and from behind the partition. She returns and holds the bulging bags out to me.

"This is for you."

"No. I can't take anything from you."

"Child, it is nothing. I think you need these more than I. Here. I'm too old to hold it out like this much longer."

I grab hold of both as her arms drop, their weight forcing me to protest further. "You give too much," my voice cracks. "I cannot cause you hardship."

"What do I need all these things for? They just sit here, collecting dust and no longer useful. Let them serve you now."

I rise from my seat and hug her, feeling a 'thank you' far too inefficient, though I say it anyway.

"Thank *you*, Lira." I pull back from the embrace, but she holds onto my arm and reaches up to my cut hair. "Something troubles you, and you are trying to run away from it. Only you've reached the end of the woods. It is time for you to change direction, and go towards what fills you with fear. It will all be well. I will always remember this day, Lira, the day the dragons' granddaughter came for lunch."

I back out of the house in a daze, wanting to say more but without any idea where to begin. The chickens run about my feet, and the ox moos me a loud, final good-bye. I clutch Blaze and the bags against me and, bewildered, head back through the field and up the incline. I scramble through the trees, my arms full of child and bags, not at all sure I am going in the right direction. With each pound of my foot, I begin to worry that I'm going the wrong way, that each step is taking me in the direction opposing where I had left them. What if I end up in The Valley? Or find myself face to face with the Soldier? Or worse, face to face with Him?

No. No, I'm not going to panic. I'm a grown woman. Stars, once I was sure of everything, and now I'm sure of nothing.

Breathe, shake it off.

I tie the bags together and loop them around the back of my neck so that each bag lays at either side, freeing my arms to carry only Blaze. I'd turned around when I left Nightmare and Karr. I only need to find the spots I had seen. I wasn't completely brainless when I began on this mission.

More focused, more coherent, I begin again, scanning above the trees as well for any plumes of smoke- from our campfire or their war, whichever. I smell a thread of smoke just as I spot an oddly shaped branch that looks vaguely familiar. Pushing through, I catch a spot of black too complete to be shadow, and then a blinding flash of red.

[Lira? Is that you?]

A few steps more, and they're standing before me. Internally I breathe a sigh of relief and congratulate myself, but with them watching, I scan them both for injuries. "Really? You were both good? No gushing wounds or missing limbs? Even the trees have made it through! I'm proud of you both!"

{You could give us a little more credit, love.}

"Yes, because you sent me away with nothing but confidence."

[You did rather well yourself, though you were gone a long time. We were getting worried.]

"I was worried about you both as well."

[We wouldn't have left you,] Nightmare murmurs, reading me far too closely. Karr's eyes shift to me sharply, that fear of mine never having crossed his mind.

I untie the bags and begin to sort through the old woman's gifts. "Let's see what we have," I sing to Blaze, naming each item I pull out. "Flour- Oh! Now maybe I can make something decent. Bread? Cake? So many things. What else would work with flour? Here's salt. Oh, now it'll have some flavor." Blaze coos. Soon he'll be smiling and laughing.

"Sugar. That'll make things sweet. Milk. Mmm. What's this?" I untie and unroll a coarse, thick brown cloth to find three large hard boiled eggs. Another similar cloth sack tied with twine holds a round of hard cheese and another a loaf of bread. There's a tin of coffee, some dried fruit.

I reach into the second bag, my fingers falling on something soft. I pull up a worn woven blanket a faded dark lavender with dark blue vines embroidered around the edge, and an intricate, large flower embroidered in the center. A long knitted gown, thick socks to cover his feet, a cap for his head, and squares of cloth for diapers.

{*Yes, please change the little hobgoblin. He smells like a troll. Well, so does your unicorn stalker, but unfortunately that can't be changed.*}

[Speaking of change—]

{*Yes, let's speak about change.*}

"Oh, stop it," I scold distractedly.

There's a patchwork blue and purple and silver cape with swaths of sage green, and a sling to carry Blaze. A small sewing kit, a pair of close-fitting, draw-string pants, a wool sweater, and an old, worn shirt designed for nursing mothers. My eyes well up. I can burn this damn dress!

[Aww. If we keep collecting stuff for Karr to carry, he won't be able to get airborne. He'll have to stay behind. It's bittersweet.]

{*No, that's when you'll actually have to prove your worth to Lira. I can't figure out what you're good for. You can't fly, you can't keep her fed or clothed, you carried her a short way and traumatized her for life, you brought her to Soldiers rather than kept her from them......you can stop me whenever.*}

I pick up two branches the same circumference as my wrist and hurl one at each of their thick male skulls. The impact makes a fascinating sort of thud and chime when it collides with the dragon's scales.

{*Lira! Ow!*}

Nightmare is a little further away, so he has just enough time to move his head so that the branch hits his horn and falls into golden ash across his mane and down his leg.

{*And on top of all your previously mentioned faults, even with gold sprinkled across you, you still aren't as pretty to look at as I am.*}

The unicorn snorts, sending the gold away on the breeze. [Fill that bag up, Lira. Please.]

30

WHEN MORNING TRIES TO ROUSE ME AWAKE, I find that I can't move. The response doesn't come from nowhere, as the sorrow never leaves me. Where is she? What are they doing to her? What have they done? It overtakes me without warning, and I can only lay like petrified wood and allow the lake within me to river up and out, and pray that there's an end to it.

I sob, as quietly as I can.

{Lira, what's wrong?} I know Karr's body is near, I see his red before me but know nothing other than that. I don't feel the warmth that usually spreads out from him, don't sense his proximity. Only sorrow. Only loss.

The unicorn's lips brush down my cheek. I know it, but don't truly feel it. He doesn't nudge or push, doesn't try to make me stop or get up, just wants me to know that he is here and that he understands.

[Go ahead, Lira. It's alright.]

With that, I lose all control and all conscious thought.

{Why isn't she responding to me? Lira? Bastard, what's happening?}

[She's fine.]

{She's not fine!}

[Leave her be. She's been through some harrowing events, as she's explained to you. They are going to haunt her. Once this passes, you will pretend it never happened.]

{I'm not agreeing to that!}

[Your only other choice is that you leave, then.]

{I'm never leaving her.}

[Your life is pretty miserable right now, isn't it?]

Sometimes it's day and sometimes it's night. My Guardians argue and I nurse Blaze, but otherwise I don't move until I emerge out of the void again. Without a word, I rise on shaky feet and resume walking as though we'd merely paused for a brief rest. I don't stop for a long while, not even after I push the tremors and the pain back down into the earth. Karr's silence is thick, and I make every effort not to look at him. I know if I do so too early, I'll tell him everything. I'm embarrassed enough over my lapse in control. My pride won't allow me to share with him the details of all my shames.

I want to move, now, anywhere, any direction, for a very long time. I'm anxious and trembling- thank the dragons for the old woman's sling. I'm afraid to trust my arms to carry Blaze even a few feet.

There's so much I don't understand, and I hadn't known until now how thoroughly unprepared my parents' preparations have rendered me. Why was nothing told to me sooner? Why'd they wait until I was too incompetent to push for more information, more answers, more directions?

I try not to think about The Valley, about our ties to it. It's too far in the past to have any true bearing, isn't it? Our roots are planted in this treed soil, not in that grassed one. I want to believe that it doesn't matter who we've come from, or the details of it, but that changes my hopes for

Talyn. If environment and the life you remember and the people currently surrounding you take precedence to your origins, where does that leave me in her life? Is there nothing of me left, have I been erased, no matter what the future may bring me? When Mom and my father find her, and bring her to the house, and try to explain to her her origins and what had happened and why I'm not there, will she care, or will she turn away and choose whatever life she's been stolen into?

What does that mean about Blaze: will his origins override what I give him?

My Guardians sense that I am still off and they stop, declaring we set up camp until tomorrow. Normally, I leave the fire-making to the magically-inclined unicorn or the natural-born fire-starter dragon. It's become the unspoken routine. They're good at it, aside from the fact that it's instantaneous from their nearly effortless effort. At the house in the Other Place, it's almost the same. Mom or I would want one, and a fire there would be. Mihn did it. I feel so lost, so blinded and sheltered. I miss my father. I'm worried about Mom. I am so afraid for Talyn.

I grab some logs and begin to pile them, with the dragon and unicorn standing bemusedly back to watch me. I need something to do, something to refocus my mind. Mihn had taught me how to make a fire. We'd sit in the back yard with a small pile of kindling, sometimes a piece of flint and a striker, sometimes his preferred way of rolling a stick down into another until it caused enough friction to spark. I was so very little when he first began teaching me.

Now, of course, nothing is working. No matter how I hit, the blade only slices through the flint, never even making a spark. Soon I am cursing, my anxiety and unease turning to rage. Eventually, I realize my lovely Guardians are laughing as discreetly as they can. From the corner of my eyes, a small light flashes. And then another, and another. I stop, curious, when the same small flashes happen on my left side.

Spaced precisely about a hand's width apart for as far as I can see, miniature little bonfires the size of my palm have sprouted like weeds. There's thousands: on the ground, on every tree branch and leaf, on every shrub and fern, and perched precariously on the tips of renegade grass. They cover everything and everywhere but the one small space I am trying to light.

Unable to hold it in anymore, the dragon and unicorn burst into laughter that ricochets through the trees, making the mini-fires waver in delighted humor. Karr falls back onto his haunches, smoke streaming from his mouth and nostrils until he's coughing. Nightmare maintains some of his rigid dignity by keeping himself on all fours, but golden tears stream from his eyes and his horn is glowing brightly.

I grab a handful of kindling and fling it at each of them, making them laugh even harder.

{I think it best you leave the fires to the males!}

Such a Mihn-thing to say. "I hate you both."

[You love us dearly.]

Just like that, the turmoil that led me here vanishes. I pull Blaze from the sling so he can see all the fires glowing like fireflies, and though I can't quite laugh outright with them, my smile is bright and genuine and grateful. Where would I drift off to without them to continually pull me back out?

*

As the old woman had stated, I've reached the end of my direction. There is no reason and no possibility to continue going north. I follow Nightmare and Karr silently as they lead me eastward. My grief ebbs down, staying behind, replaced by the protective shields of the dragon and Nightmare, consumed by the care and concern for Blaze and the daylong task of placing one foot before the other and walking and living.

Above us the moon shines full; a soft, feminine white light that reflects off everything in an ethereal glow. The Forest People, the dragons, center on the warmth of the suns and the necessity of them. But being here I am drawn more so to the solitary moon, left alone to guard the night and watch all those below her, forever isolated and separate. I empathize with her torment. The suns are so close, but it's hard to tell whether they pursue her or whether they would aide her. There's something old, something innate in my pull towards her. Is it because of the Other Place? They valued the moon There. No, it was masculine There. It was red, There. Red as Karr for that one perfect night.

The trees Here are so different in the night. With the moon as low and as bright as she is right now, the whole forest has changed hues to this gray-blue-purple. It's quieter when everything else is asleep, even the smells are changed. A thin blue mist has formed. Nightmare and Karr both call it a sign of coming rain. It weaves through the trees like a slow-moving ghost with a long-flowing tail. The beauty is captivating, interrupted only by my infrequent cough.

{You aren't getting sick again, are you?}

"No. It's just the change in climate." And me laying on the ground immobile for the last couple days.

{Would you like to stop?}

"Oh, please no! There will never be another night like this. It's not meant to be slept through."

Nightmare stretches as he walks ahead, his horn catching on a thick branch. He pulls against the tension until finally the branch bends as far forward as it can before ricocheting backward into Karr's unexpecting face. [Sorry. I didn't hurt you, did I?]

"Karr," I warn, placing my hand on his shoulder. *"Nightmare."*

Karr blows air softly from his mouth, and a small fire sprouts atop Nightmare's head. The unicorn turns. The fire is gone but it leaves a definite smell of singed hair. [Will you be leaving, *soon*?]

{When I am good and ready,} Karr retorts. Mom's family never hunted or ate when she was within sight, either. He leaves every few days, but I've stopped waiting for him, stopped rooting myself to the spot he'd last seen me in. I know he'll always return, will always find me. Maybe he returns to the cliffs to check on that dragoness of his, remind her of his existence. It must be uncomfortable for him to walk with us. I'd fly for days if I was him. Keep my wings stretched out and just soar and dive, catching stars and racing the wind. *{You could always come with, love.}* There's a smile in that question, mixed smoothly with a challenge.

I shake my head fiercely as I do every time he asks. Somehow, flying with him seems a violation. He's a friend and I love him. It's wrong to climb on his back and demand he carry me. "Mmm-mmm."

[You must be starving. Too bad there's nothing for you to hunt around here.]

"Karr," I caution, hearing his thought of fire- of *more* fire. "Nightmare, really," I scold. "Was that completely necessary?"

[Yes.]

Karr is laughing to himself. {*Night must be an awful time for you, beast. All that love and magic filling the air. Humans all around making more little goblins like this one here. How many stalkable virgins does your kind lose every night?*}

"Blessed dragons," I curse. There goes my magical night.

[How are you handling your own frustrations, dragon? Must be *torturous* to be stuck down here, with me, and so far from your golden dragoness.]

"Can you not allow me one night of peace where I don't have to hear you two fighting?" I yell. They lower their heads in a show of humiliation, but the snarl in their mouths, the smoke ebbing from Karr's, and the point of Nightmare's lowered horn cancels the gesture.

Karr's great empty belly interrupts whatever argument he wants to present. {*That's just great,*} he growls, cursing.

"Karr, you're hungry. Go get yourself some food." He makes a sound that is part growl, part moan.

[Yes, Karr. Go. Hunt elsewhere. Must satisfy that monstrous appetite.]

{*Yes. The one that's large enough to devour a whole unicorn.*} He pauses. {*Love? Not even this once? Quick trip. Get away from the demon for an hour. A day. A year? Fine. An hour.*}

"Nope."

His belly rumbles again. Quite loudly. {*Alright. Next time,*} he dismisses confidently. {*I'll return as soon as I can.*} I

wait, my breath on hold, for his take-off routine. Blaze
even stirs from his sling to watch. The rustle of Karr's
scales makes me want to close my eyes and drift off into a
dream, so comforting and amazing is the sound he makes.
He meets my eyes comically, reading my thoughts. {*What
would you like me to bring back for you?*}

"I- I don't know. There's nothing I want."

{*I don't believe that.*}

[Will you just leave already?]

Karr frowns, checking the sky. Morning is only hours
away. {*I'll be back in the afternoon. Evening at the latest?*}

"I can never tell if I'm supposed to wish you a happy
hunt. That's just gruesome."

He laughs and crouches low to the ground, his belly
touching the earth. {*If you ate meat it would so much easier to
feed you, you know.*} In one great burst, he's airborne. Once
at a decent altitude, his wings burst open and his place in
the sky is fixed. He always pauses high over the trees
when he first rises, to look back down upon me. I
reactively fall silent and return his stare. Blaze utters a
long '*Ohhhhhhh*' and begins kicking his feet into my ribs.
Three months we've had him now, and how he's grown.
Skinny little limbs now curve in healthy rolls. Eyes wide
open, no longer sunken, and so alert and eager now.

Karr circles and swoops partly down. Then his wings
pump in slow, long strides, making that unmistakable
*whoosh*ing sound that only dragons' wings are able to
make. I wave and walk back towards Nightmare, the
sound of Karr's wings brushing little strokes against my
ears.

[Hmph.]

"Jealous beast," I laugh.

[Hmph!]

I pat his neck sympathetically. "I still find you terribly amazing."

Still within range, Karr mumbles his disgust. *{Terrible is right. There is a good place to stop a few yards ahead. Beside a lake. I'll meet you there tomorrow.}*

Hands on my hips, I stare up at the vacant skies. "Isn't this *my* journey? Sometimes it feels as though the two of you are leading a little too much."

The whooshing returns, stirring up little currents all around me as Karr appears overhead again. More than a touch of sarcastic humor plays with his tone. *{You forget that I am much, much bigger than you are. If I truly wanted you to be someplace in particular, I could swoop down, carry you up into the air and drop you wherever I want. Even your demon stalker could drag you wherever he wants, if either of us chose to behave that way.}*

"That's a bunch of masculine nothing-ness." But I turn to the unicorn, frowning, trying to think lightly about my first day here. He's already dragged me where he'd wanted me to be.

[Well it continues to be a lovely thought.]

{More so on my end. But I, at least, would never cross such a line as you, barbarian jerk. In any case, Lira, I can see better than you. You're arguing with me about a lake. A great big, beautiful lake. Been a long time since you've been by something like that, hasn't it? Go sit on the beach and do nothing but bask. The little troll and Furry over there desperately need a bath- they reek.}

[Furry? At least my appearance would never be mistaken for a disease, Scaly.]

Karr dives before pulling sharply back up, a strong gust of wind eager to keep up with him topples me over into Nightmare's side. His laughter falls behind him as he flies away.

[He says I smell? He's just a larger, even more putrid male than I normally have to be around. What is so appealing about them?]

"About dragons?"

[No, men. I wish you'd stop dreaming about Him. The dragon probably sees too, you know.]

Well that was quite a turn in thought. I walk along at the unicorn's shoulder, my hands beneath the bulk of Blaze. I'm torn again, conflicted between missing Him and hating Him for leaving, for bringing me here so late, for not coming after me. Part of me wishes He'd fight through my barriers, my Guardians, and come for me. Apologize, hold me against him again, steal me away to Kholsari.

[Oh that's horrific! Stop your head, please!]

"I wish you'd stop antagonizing Karr so much," I say to change the topic.

[But he makes it so very fun. Plus, he's no good for anything else.]

I forage as we walk, stopping often to pick weeds and herbs or to dig up roots, slipping everything into a sack strung across my shoulder.

"Oh," I exclaim, stopping suddenly when the forest abruptly stops. "How beautiful! Look at the lake, Nightmare. Just like Karr said." Just ahead, the moonsuns sparkle off the surface of a small lake like millions of stars in a new ocean of sky. More light rises from the lake itself than falls from the sky above, and it floats over the surface of the water in a bright white gloss. After being under the constant canopy of trees for so long, I've forgotten what the light of stars is like. It's magical. A night of pure magic.

The trees end two dragons' widths from the shore, leaving a beach of pewter colored rocks and peach-colored sand, long green reeds and pink, white, and purple night-

blooming wildflowers growing amongst the rocks. I watch
the water sway and breathe, remembering.

THE DAY BEFORE

TALYN'S EYES CATCH MINE from where she plays on the floor. Her eyes are blatantly purple; they always catch me a little off guard. Her hair is a cross between the two of ours, the shade between blonde and brown. The ends have just reached her shoulders, except that they curl upwards, bouncing whenever she moves, so delicate that they get lifted by the slightest air.

The Year of the Dragon ended eight months ago. It's summer again, a summer that is nearly over, and his daughter is now eleven months old. I haven't seen Him in nearly two years.

Talyn's face explodes in a bright smile that chases away the thoughts in my head. "Ma-ma-ma-ma-ma," she babbles. She stretches her hand out to me, flexing her fingers several times. Her palm faces her when she waves. It's funny how she merely repeats motions, like a simple wave, as how it appears to her.

"Hey, baby girl." I wave back and slide off the couch to sit on the floor with her. Mihn had carved little dragons for me when I was her age and somehow they'd all survived. I must have known these were not to exercise new teeth on. "Dragon. Can you say dragon?" I hold my favorite one up, a dragon in mid-glide. His wings are up and partially drawn in, his arms and legs are flexed as though ready to do a quick maneuver just for the sheer thrill.

"Da!" She yells excitedly, reaching out and doing her reverse wave again. "Da!"

I smile and lift it up, pushing it through the air over her head. Right, left, down, up. She stares, captivated, dropping her arm back to her lap. "Dragons fly, Talyn. They live where your daddy does, remember? On top of the cliffs. Daddy lives in a manor called Kholsari that's built into the cliffside. If you are ever in The Trees, just go east and you'll find it. You'll find the dragons. They'll be up in the air, flying like this- back and forth, up and down. Slow, and *fast!*" I zip it down quickly towards her, making her squeal and fall backwards onto her back. "Oh!" I jump forward, but she is laughing ecstatically, trying to push her body back to a sit. She has the most infectious laugh. When she gets going, she can bring Mom, Mihn, and myself to tears. "Goofy girl!"

Her shorter laughs are just like His.

"Ma ma ma ma." She plops her hands down and crawls to me, snuggling into my lap with the dragon in her hand. She holds it up. "Da."

"Dragon."

"Da."

I paid attention to the songsbox last winter. I could feel the approach of year's end, regardless. On the eve of the new year, the last day of the Dragon, I went back to The Lake, to the spot we had been in, and sat and waited. I sat without moving, staring at the spot, waiting for him to step up from the ground and reach out for me again, waiting for that first chance to grab onto his hand and never let go. The moon was nowhere to be seen. Not a hint of red anywhere, but I waited, and I prayed.

Mom came for me in a few hours when it was time for Talyn to eat again. I followed mutely as we walked back to the house.

The year ended with nothing, not even a sign.

And now it's summer.

Talyn is struggling to walk on her own. She squeezes the blood out of my fingers with her very good grip- Mihn has plans to train her with a sword. He's already begun to carve her one. He's happy about that, passing his weapon of choice on to her. She's such a placid thing, never cries, and laughs at every little thing. She's determined, too. Although she sometimes seems to expect to fall when she takes her own steps, she then crawls back to where she began and tries again. It's how she was when she was learning to crawl. She expected to fall on her face a few times. It's amazing to watch her learn, to watch her work things out. I have to think her father is this way.

What is he doing now? I somehow know he's thinking of me. But I'm worried. What if he's not in Home? What if he did go out for a walk that morning and something happened? I have his clothes.

May's and Rani's mothers caught Mom dancing outside one day when I was young. They told her something called *arrested* and *police* would happen because of *indecent exposure*. It did knit our mothers together, though. They met regularly and taught each other their cultures' dances. I remember those days, pondering Mom in their bright clothing, her smile, and watching her move to their foreign beat, knowing that as soon as we return to the house, she'd run out to the back and dance bare, the rawness of her sadness returning.

In any case, people soon came and stole me away, citing *indecent exposure*. Indecent exposure. I still have his clothes. What if He's still here? Trapped and in trouble?

If he was here, though, I'd be able to sense it.

"Da da da da da."

I cover his daughter's hand with mine and show her how to make the dragon fly. She kicks her feet and erupts into her fit of laughing. Mihn appears before her. He tries to sign something but can't. He just sits cross legged and watches her, laughing soundlessly with her, which makes her laugh harder.

Mom walks into the room then, already smiling. Talyn's this house's own sun. Rays of light spread out from her. Since she was born, Mom's how she was when I was young. She smiles more, laughs often, doesn't drift away into her head. I hadn't remembered her being this way. Her regression had been so slight. She's trailed away so slowly over the years that I thought she'd always been that way. Watching her since Talyn was born has brought the faded memories back quite sharply. Therein lies my answer: being pregnant and having me did help her. She had been happy.

Somehow she always knew He'd come, maybe that's what caused her to begin drifting away. She also must have anticipated Him taking me with. Where, I'm afraid to wonder, would that have left her?

She always corrects me. When I say he's coming back for us, she softly says, *'You, Lira. You and Talyn.'* The conversation ends there. I think she believes she'll never see her home again. I can't wait for Him to prove her wrong.

I can't wait for Him.

"What got her going?" Mom laughs.

"I have no idea. We were playing with the dragons."

"You use to love those. But she seems to enjoy them more."

I smile and lean back, glancing out the window. It looks so beautiful out there. "I think I'm going to take a walk."

Mom and Mihn jerk back in unison. "Really?"

"I'm feeling claustrophobic. I think I'll take Talyn to The Lake. Let her get her first swim. Collect shells on the beach before summer ends."

Mom rolls her eyes playfully. "It was *torturous* dragging you away when you were young. We had to sleep on the beach a few times. The Others didn't like me doing that."

"I remember." I hand Talyn to her grandmother and stand. "I'm going to pack some food and things. You'll come with?"

"No. Make this a mother-daughter thing."

"How can the three of us together not be a mother-daughter thing?"

"You never have alone time with her."

"Mom."

"Lira, it's important to have that time alone together. It's been you and me all your life. Now it's time for you to be the mom and experience all motherhood will give you. You have to form her strongest, most important bond."

"Mom."

"Have no regrets, Lira. Don't be like me and one day think, I should have......taken her for walks more often. Once time has passed, you see all the gaps where there had been plenty of time to do all the things you had planned. Don't become me, Lira. Don't sit inside this house and wonder about how things could be, if only. He'll return when he can. You can't halt your life or Talyn's until then. Enjoy this alone time you have with her." She smiles, "Soon, you'll have to share."

*

"Talyn!"

She squeals in delight, all set to go, forgetting she can't independently walk yet. I catch her quickly before she falls face forward into the sand. She reaches out to the horizon, doing her backwards wave. *Want.* I laugh. Another water child.

I walk her into the waves. "Oh it's cold!"

But she doesn't care. She stomps her foot into the shallow water and screams what sounds like a greeting. I look up, trying to see what she does. Water, blue-green and perfectly clear, stretching on to the end of the world. I wish it was that way. Then we could just get a boat and off we'd go, and maybe once we fell off the edge of This Place, we'd land in Home.

The hundreds of people in the water and on the beach fade into the sand and waves, and it is only her and me. I take her deeper and spend the afternoon teaching her to float, to hold her breath and understand how to move her arms and legs. We play in the sand until the sky darkens. I glance up and the majority of the Others are gone.

I understand what Mom may have tried to say: it *is* going to be hard to share her! To step back and let Him discover his daughter and her to discover her dad. I had nine months to prepare and have had eleven more to know her. He'll have just a moment. Surprise! You're a dad! I should probably figure out how best to tell him.

How will I begin? I can't be so cruel as to say *Surprise!*

Dragons, I'll have to share him as well as her. How will I coordinate that?

"Come on, baby girl. Time to go." I pull her out of the sand and she screams, kicking her feet. "We'll come back tomorrow, ok? We'll bring Grandma and Grandpa. I promise. Ok?"

"Da."

"We left the dragons at the house, baby girl."

"Da. Da."

I heft her onto my hip and turn away from the water, toward the thick cluster of trees on the other edge of the sand. It's getting late, but, just one more place.

A man passes us as he heads towards the water, though he's fully clothed and shoed. He bobs his head, "Good evening. Beautiful little girl. What's her name?"

I shift her to my other hip and tighten my hold of her as I shuffle past, not answering. I turn back once we pass him, reassessing his dark uniform. *Po-lice.* Hadn't he walked past us on the sidewalk on our trip here? *He walks and moves like a Soldier. Don't trust him, Lira.*

I enter into the trees and think about the man no more. This is the first time I've brought her in here. Is that odd? Perverse? To bring her here?

I sit in the brush, several feet from the clearing. Talyn plays with leaves and I stare, waiting. The ground never moves, the earth never rumbles, the fully foliaged branches over my head emit no sound. I don't know how he arrived here, or where, or how he left. But this is the last place we were together. Maybe I'm the one who's lost, and was supposed to stay here until he found me again.

Talyn's head falls upon my chest and I startle. She'd fallen asleep. I look up and it is completely dark. I pull her blanket out from my bag and wrap it around her, and we leave the trees and make our silent, lonely way back to the house.

32

WE'VE ALL HAD OUR NOTIONS on what our lives would be that next morning, didn't we? Now we have to rethink everything and accept that plans have changed, for whatever reasons. Go on, Lira, get out of this room.

My father's words span through the worlds, through time, back into my head as though he is beside me again. I close my eyes and steady myself, and then follow Nightmare to a place close to the water's edge where we prepare a suitable space to borrow for the night. I change Blaze's diaper and feed him before settling him down into a burrow I'd dug. I wash his soiled cloth in the cool lapping waves of the lake, the water just kissing my bare toes before retreating, returning for another trepid kiss and retreating again. Oh, how I want to strip down and wade into the middle of this lake and never come out.

I slip out of my outer clothes but only stand at the edge of the lake, staring across it. The cool night air slithers over my skin, down my shoulders, my back, around my hips, through my legs and arms and hair. I lift my face into it, into the wind that comes from the east across the lake. The water pushes up onto the stony shore at my toes, wrapping itself around my feet before being pulled back in, begging me to join it and play.

This lake disappears and The Lake from the Other Place replaces it. So much larger, so much wilder. I hear Talyn's shrieks of joy and welcome echo over the surface as she squeezes the blood from my fingers. That was the last time I had visited my once favorite place, until the day, her second birthday, when I found myself following whispers and silver light back to that spot, that damn spot where I had last been entangled with Him.

You could never find the opposite shore in that other lake, no matter how clear the day. Sometimes, Mom would sneak us out into one of the light towers and we'd spend a night or two. Mom told me of the sunken ships she sensed lost beneath the depths. It amazed her. There's nothing like that here, no boats, no glorious aquatic ovoid manors with tree posts sticking straight up into the air and sails stretching against the pull of the wind. How amazing a sight that would be. How amazing to get on one and sail far away.

I had liked to be near The Lake during the winter storms, when the high winds would bring the waves arching fourteen feet or more upward and crash down over the street that ran alongside the beach. They'd shut the road down and there'd be no one, no one but Mom and me out in the middle of the storm. I loved the power, the anger, the sound.

Wind did exist There as she does Here. So many days she'd nearly knock us over, and Mom would lean inward, laughing happily, her arms thrown out and her feet threatening to lift off the ground. It wasn't her wind, but it treated her almost the same.

I turn away from the water, from the calm gentle sound so different from the one I can't erase from my head. The air rifles sympathetically through my hair, kissing my cheeks, and I no longer see that other lake. I see the glorious simplicity of this one; it's unobtrusive, undemanding beauty enveloped in my magical, black-blue night filled with stars. Tall trees rim the whole perimeter of the lake, their leaves dancing joyously in the wind. If you don't pay attention while traveling at night, you may just find yourself wet. I draw the soft *rustle*-sound of the leaves in, the feel of the tamer air, the way it smells of clean fresh water and not so much like fish. I smell the trees and the rocks, the wet soil beneath.

Quiet. Calm. Absolutely no Others. I kneel, my hands splayed over the water, and breathe the lake in through the skin of my palms, accepting it, listening to it as Mom had always told me to do. *Listen to the hum, listen to the whispers and the secrets.* It kisses my palms without touching me, and I smile. I'm Home. I'm Home.

I wash my clothes and drape them over boulders and nearby branches to dry. Nightmare begrudgingly keeps near Blaze when I leave to forage for firewood. Properly sized rocks are everywhere, I merely have to form them into a circle. All that's left is to pull out the blasted flint. This time, though, I've gathered some bark chips and dried moss to use as kindling.

[Oh, you're going to attempt again?]

"You be quiet."

[It didn't work so well for you last time.]

"Go take a bath!"

[I just might!]

Blaze coos beside me, smiling so, so sweetly. He kicks his legs and wiggles his arms. Only three months, but he's been mine for a lifetime. Having him, watching him, loving him, is almost like having his sister. He jumps again, trying to coordinate the sound of laughter.

"Ha," I agree. "We'll show them, won't we stinky boy? Mommy can set a fire better than they can. They don't have hands and fingers, but we do, don't we? Yes. Soon, you'll figure that out, and then all the things you'll do! They've grown a little full of themselves, you know, our obnoxious Guardians have. Time to balance them out."

I arrange the bark chips beneath the moss, inside a hole I chip into a narrow chunk of branch. The flint and dagger in my hands feel cool. They're humming and I'm listening. I journey through each of their layers, till we understand each other. The surface of the diamond dagger is smooth as glass; I float along the engraved words until I am in the knife's soul, glancing outward at the etched dragons flying around me, so reminiscent of the etched dragons spiraling upward on the front doors of the house.

Then I realize why I hadn't been able to start my own fires, and that neither of my wonderful Guardians had chosen to tell me what I was doing wrong. "Bastards," I curse, sheathing the dagger and digging through my sack till I find the plain, normal, utilitarian silver knife I use for chopping food. Plain, normal, and made of steel. "Bastards," I curse again.

In one swift move, I strike the two together, the steel dragging over the flint rather than slicing through it as the diamond had, casting the sparks downward into the kindling.

> *"Little fire that I spark*
> *Hit and crack and there you are*
> *Catch and keep and come to life*

Warmth to my child and me this night."

Blaze jerks again, expelling only air for a laugh. He's getting closer.

"Like that, stinky boy? Ha! I think it worked!" The spark is an orange glow, twisting and turning the moss as it eats it through. I bend down and cast some of my breath upon it in even, soft blows, adding more bark and moss until a small ember grows. I quickly grab some twigs and add them, and the fire expands until flames lick and stretch outward and up. "Showed them, didn't I? Women create, little one. *They* need either acid in their bellies or spells, but women create all on their own." He falls silent. "Sorry, my strong little man! Boys have their magic, too, don't worry. Just......don't listen to Nightmare's opinion of that."

By the time the unicorn emerges from the lake, my fire is burning steady and perfect.

"Huh. First try, unicorn."

He stares at the burning pile, stunned.

"Guess I just needed the right words. And knife."

[Figured it out, I see.]

"No thanks to either of you."

[If you weren't being so enjoyably comical, we'd have helped.]

"Sure you would've. Glad the two of you decided to finally team up on something."

He shakes, showering Blaze and me with droplets of lake water. Blaze gasps at first, then squeals in delight, kicking his chubby legs over and over.

I pick up a handful of sand and fling it at the unicorn. "Hey! Away from my fire! Away, away, away!" He shakes his head, casting his mane back and forth over his head, covering me with another flurry of rain. "Beast!"

I bring Blaze into my lap, sitting him up on my legs, and lean back against a large rock. The lake whispers in a rhythmic way, the waves upon the shore, one always followed by another. We're enveloped in a world of blues: cobalt, navy, cerulean. Turquoise at the circumference of the suns.

"Your grandpa loved the water, Blaze. I can stare and stare at this for days and days and never grow tired or hungry, just like him. It always moves, as though it breathes, and just gives me peace-" A bought of coughing breaks that thought.

Nightmare studies me intensely. [I fear that poison may have been worse than I had thought.]

"Don't be silly. People do cough here and there for no reason, unicorn."

[It's been three months, Lira. Your cough hasn't gone away.]

"It hasn't gotten worse, either. As I've told you and Karr repeatedly."

[What would I do if you were to fall ill? Again? You'd leave me to deal with your dragon?]

"I'm not sick, Nightmare. I promise. I must have swallowed a fly." I decide not to mention the headaches. The nausea. The piercing stomach pains that make me gasp and blame a non-existent rock underfoot. Or the dizzy spells I've so far been able to mask from both of them. The throat spasms.

The welts around my eyes have completely gone away. My sense of smell is normalizing. There's no longer blood mixed with my tears, and my eyes don't tear as much as they had before. The coughing, the headaches, all of it, will fade away as well. They both saved me. I won't complain about some short-term effects. Without them, I'd be worse.

The lake is fairly large for one set amidst trees. And that sound, the sound the lake makes when it's just past being merely calm, as though it's the transparent lungs of the earth and you can see and feel and hear her breathing. As soothing as a lullaby, soothing as the thrum of dragon's wings. I clap Blaze's hands together absently. "Everything began at a lake," I sing. My eyes glaze over, seeing both this one and that other one.

[Notice that I'm not complaining. I am keeping myself completely quiet.]

"I miss it. It had been a favorite place to go. Despite the masses of people. That Night, it was magical. I know my mother went there often to search for Talyn, as though the place would offer her some sort of clue. That, or she was searching for Him. Waiting for him like I had done. Why was the Lake so important, anyway? It's where she woke, it's where I took Him, it's where He left me. I went back on her birthday. I don't know why. Look where it got me. Where it led all of us.

"Mom doesn't have to worry and care for me anymore. Now she can focus on finding Talyn. I know she'll find her. I know she will." I still, gazing out across the water absently. I'm already doing it, already drifting into my own blankness. Is Mom's retreat a downcast blue-gray like mine?

I blink and force myself to look down at Blaze. The suns have fully fallen over the lake. The breeze whips up from the water, coming out to touch my face. "Mom knew that He was there, that day. She knew He would find me and knew what would come of that. It was at a lake, Nightmare. At a lake……"

[Do you wish she had warned you, given you the choice of that meeting?]

"I don't know. Once I did. But That Night gave me Talyn, and I will never trade her for anything. Certainly not for my own ease. And That Night. That Night. It *had* been beautiful, Nightmare. It wasn't the way he touched me or the way he kissed me. It was the way his eyes changed when he looked at me, the way I changed when he was near, the tone of his voice when he spoke to me. I liked who I was, I was comfortable in my own skin and with myself for the first time. I no longer saw the world I was living in as foreign and hostile. I felt whole, and safe, and happy. I felt perfect. I curled up against him and felt as though it was something I had always done. I could talk freely, not having to hide that I was different. I could speak in my own language. But it was also the silences. He let me watch the snow fall, and we lay and listened to the water. He supported me standing on that block of ice and I felt like a queen. I wanted a forever with him, doing things like that, waking up in the morning with my ear over his heartbeat. I did have a choice, and I made it. Why didn't He stay?"

The unicorn's ears perk up. He lifts his head and turns eastward.

"Nightmare, what is it? Is Karr coming? Is he alright?"

I lift Blaze and stand, waiting, relaxing only when the sound of wings echoes through the night.

[Lira, prepare yourself.]

"Why? What's wrong?"

[I'd say the dumbass got himself into a horde of trouble.]

The wing beats become louder as they push closer; the strokes are longer, the rhythm unfamiliar. I hold my breath. A dragon is coming, coming fast, but it's not Karr.

Before she is even close enough to see, I know. I know who is racing toward us. I know who'd found me at last. My fear of meeting her, my fragile belief that I could hide from her, vanishes. *How stupid*, I chide myself. *How so very stupid.*

She is Gwesana, Sana to the other dragons as well as to Aril and her family, Ama to my mother. She is my mother's mother, and her image is painted somewhere on every single wall of the house. She fills two walls in Mom's bedroom, right over the spot where Mom sleeps. My mother *loves* her mother. At the worst possible moment in her life, she was taken away from her, and was forced to face my father's murder and her pregnancy with me all alone, in a strange, unknown world. Humans, humans everywhere. Dragons- her family, her mother- nowhere.

With the perpetually full moon off to the south and west of us, it hits upon her body as she speeds into view, turning the sky and us below an astounding emerald green you'd only expect to find in the brightness of noon's sunlight. Her wingspan's amazing, twice that of Karr's. How can a body so big glide so effortlessly in the air? How can wings that look so transparent and thin hold her up?

She had flown at full speed straight towards me, and is now hovering above me, pausing to catch her bearings. She knows who I am. She knows I know who she is.

Neither of us even flinch. In that gaze, my mother's legacy and stories settle firmly into place. I am standing in the trees of Home, and my mother was thrown out a tower window in Ravery before being saved and raised and loved by the dragon landing down beside me. My grandmother is not the old woman in the little house nearly blind. She's Gwesana, the dragoness.

Ama's wings stir up a spray from the lake. The cold droplets mist over me before fingering their way down my skin, but I can't even shiver or shield myself. Nightmare bows low, backing out of her way as her feet gently meet the lakeside ground. Rocks shift, crunching and scraping and grinding; rock against rock, rock into wet sand as they sink, rearranging to support her weight. We stare at each other, my grandmother and I, an eternity, watching, studying, disbelieving in the other's presence.

"Ama—"

With that, all tension escapes from her body, and I learn that dragons cry. I bite my lip, but it continues to tremble violently. One at a time, her magnificent emerald feet lift up, precisely, mindfully, fingers curled inward to protect her talons from the rocks. The tops of her toes graze over, scrape softly across the stones. Her eyes rove over me silently, hungrily. I turn my head to follow her as she circles me. She gasps when her sensitive nose finds the combined blood of my parents and confirms that I am her daughter's daughter. So much, so much inside me threatens to explode, to come rushing out. I wish I were a child and could cry out, throw myself at her, crawl into her palm like Mom had done and beg her to take me away. Take me home.

Her feet dip into the lake, the tips of her drooping wings and her trailing tail redirecting waves and patterns, sending waves rushing towards the other shore. Emerald green on a star-filled background of differing shades of blues and silver and lavender, grays and blacks. Green eyes that match her scales don't blink. They don't even swirl. The stars and moon and distant suns reflect in every tear that falls down her cheek. She, too, wants to explode under the pressure of emotion.

{Where have you been?} Hushed and broken, her voice still has a rich, deep and powerful tune.

A sob cuts through from within me. I can't speak. Why did I want to hide from her? I should have told Nightmare immediately- *damn* Him. I should have said *Take me east, take me to my family!* Why didn't I? Why am I more afraid of Him instead of feeling more need for them?

She approaches closer still, her wings held slack up and away from her body. Her footfalls are soft, still shifting pebbles. Her neck is level with her body, holding her head low over the ground. She wants to speak more. Words tumble from her head madly, too many to catch and make a sentence from. Too many emotions too close to the surface, just as my first meeting with Karr had gone.

She can't mask the sadness in her eyes, not from me- two mothers mourning daughters. It doesn't make me cringe back with guilt. My heart breaks because it understands, because it sees how much my mother is loved by her mother. This has been passed down to me, passed down to my children. All because of her.

A dragoness ignored the rules of her society and saved and took and raised and loved a humanling- what a ripple effect she created in that one decision. Look at what she's done. Look at all the lives she has saved. Because she took my mother, my mother lived and found my father. Without either of them, without Ama showing more compassion on yet another human child and finding his only remaining family, he'd have died alone in the woods, an unknown and unimportant orphan. And I would never have been born. And Talyn would never have been born. And Blaze would have died alone in those trees.

This is a mother's gift: not entirely birth, but the love she teaches, which grows and spreads and never diminishes. Now I understand what Nightmare had tried to tell me at the Unicorn Camp: It is not the makeup of your blood or the species you were born of that binds your generations together. She has proven that.

I seek out the unicorn now, remembering that I'd yelled how I could never love a child that didn't come from me the same as I love Talyn, and that what the Bound women feel for the children that come to them could also never compare. And now I have a foundling son and am reminded of how my mother was adopted as well.

Closer still Ama circles, her head lifting as she looks down at Blaze in my arms, who watches every move she makes as though he can't quite comprehend that two dragons exist in the world.

The sky fills with the sounds of wings and he and I look up. *So much more than two exist in the world*, I think, as an array of colors flash among the stars.

...Home, where rainbows are winged, loving things.

Large draconic bodies lighter than the air they swim through begin falling down, and the water of the lake spirals up in mini hurricanes to greet them. My proud little fire twists and is gone. The lake's surface sparks alight with the reflections of the moonsuns, of my grandfather Marr, my uncles and aunts: Gref, Spirit, Ju-uh, Yetabo, Saramine, Frit. Around us all— the dragons, Nightmare, Blaze and myself— the wind circles, making herself part of this moment. Where is Karr? Where is his red?

My long-separated family surrounds me, and the night spins into twilight, into morning, as they each touch their cheeks to mine, calling me niece, calling me granddaughter, calling me theirs. In the middle of wings and scales, drenched by night, comforted by waves, I am no longer grounded, bound into tree roots and doomed to a life of living low. I am now part of their limitless air.

When I was a child, I use to sit in the center of the dark hallway leading to the kitchen and close my eyes, imagining our dragons had leapt off the walls and were flying over my head. So often I did it, yearned for it to be real so much that I eventually couldn't distinguish it as a dream.

Now it's happening, yet it feels more like an hallucination than those long-ago fantasies had.

Why did I think I'd need to hide from them? Their massiveness, their number, hangs over my head like a much needed rainstorm overdue to break. A rampage of voices is rushing through my head. Intoxicatingly lovely, wanting to know everything, but I can't speak. This can't be real. I'm dreaming.

Marr glances over his shoulder. *{I'd like for you to leave. Both of you.}*

"What?" I turn sharply around and see Karr standing quietly just within the tree line. At my grandfather's order, though, he takes a thoughtless step forward, prepared to protest.

{It is our right,} Marr growls stiffly as he advances quickly on Karr, a much smaller and lesser dragon. But Karr does not back down nor show any sign of fear or submission. My grandfather moves again, blocking me from both of them. *{She is ours, not yours.}*

"Wait. No," I begin, remembering my voice and my ability to speak. Behind me, my grandmother remains in the water. My uncle and aunt, Gref and Yetabo, come around me at both sides. I am dwarfed and tiny, imprisoned by large, impenetrable, scaled bodies, with Karr and Nightmare unreachably far away.

The unicorn dips his head. [Of course.]

You can't just leave me!

Karr takes another defiant step forward after glaring disgustedly at Nightmare. {No. *If she 'belongs' to anyone, then her tie to me is as great as her tie to you. You can't order me to walk away from her.*}

{*You'll do well to think better on your actions!*} Frit, another uncle, yells as he lands down by his father. {*How dare you not tell us she was here! She is my sister's humanling! You have no claim on her!*}

The spines on Karr's back quiver and rise, unbraiding from their resting place. His eyes narrow and the smallest thread of smoke escapes his flared nostrils. (*She is not a child that be claimed or hoarded- by anyone.*} His eyes become red streaked with dark lightning bolts of purple. This is a new color, a new emotion, and it's not at all happy. In the silence that grows, I can't tell if he is speaking to them more directly, or if he is preparing to do something incredibly stupid.

Apparently he does both, because all at once the beach explodes with angry dragons. The fury, the sorrow my family has contained since they lost my mother- twenty four years worth of it gnawing and torturing them- unleashes itself upon Karr, the more present scapegoat.

He has a habit of pissing others off at first meeting.

Their rants and accusations run one into the other, everyone screaming and yelling at once, with Karr doing his best to not be buried beneath their anger, which is unleashed from everywhere: beside, before, behind and above. My family, being decades older, are larger, heavier. They tower over him, teeth bared, sparks shooting out from their mouths. The air fills with smoke. Blaze and I begin coughing, forcing me to turn my attention away from the dragons and shield our faces so we can breathe.

{You intentionally hid her from us! Did you think we'd never find her? This world is ours, she and her mother are ours! *Not yours!}*

{I Heard her! She was attacked and I Heard! Would you have preferred I wasted time to see you before coming to her aid? Would you have listened?}

{Where is Elaar? Why is she being kept from us?}

{Where is my daughter!} Marr's bellow sets the trees shaking, makes the water's surface tremble back so that the level shrinks several inches in fear. *{You figure out how it was done, and* you *get her back to us. By the stars, I'll rip you and Him* both *to shreds!}*

{That's not how it works! He doesn't know how it happened! And threatening me will get you nothing!}

Blaze starts to wail, terrified. I pull him from the sling and press him close, feeling that I might soon be joining him. Nightmare grabs my shirt in his mouth and pulls me backward, out from under dragon bodies with fire-filling bellies and sharply taloned feet and swishing tails as they continue to berate Karr for His actions, as though my dragon had any inclusion in my being found and abandoned, found and abandoned again. I try to tell them he's been protecting me, he's been keeping me from being found, but none hear me. Bellies rumble and expand, and the temperature around us rises significantly enough to cause a fog over the lake.

{The mess you've made is astounding!}

{Senseless and stupid is what it is!}

{Did you have permission to go into human places and let them know we still exist? With Lira unprotected so close to the

Forest's edge? Were you thinking of her at all, or only you? Only Him?}

{Then how, exactly, was I supposed to find her food?}

{By bringing her home, to us!}

{And how would you have fed her? Like you did with her mother- you went into human areas and asked!}

{The fires you started- you drew the Soldiers into the trees! Now they'll hunt her down!}

{I set those fires because they were already in the trees!}

{That is your fault as well! I'll kill Him for sending her there!}

{He didn't send her to the damn Valley!}

{She is......my daughter's......daughter, Karr.} Ama sits back, full of disbelief. Her hoarsely whispered words amidst all the shouting quiets the tempers around her. {How could you be so thoughtless, so heartless?}

{There is more than you alone to consider in this,} Karr roars. {Where is your heart in that, where is the demon's? You aren't the only family who needs her.}

"I have no family," I whisper tearfully, my arms trembling around Blaze.

Nine pairs of vehement dragon eyes turn to me, the anger vanishing with the fog as their body temperatures plummet at my words. I step back a few paces, suddenly aware of myself beneath a horde of dragons, aware that I had said something that shocked them. What did I say? Did I speak out loud again?

{What did you say?} Marr queries, astounded.

{Do you not see us as family?} my grandmother asks, her face stricken.

"You didn't even know I existed. How could I mean anything to you? I asked him not to tell you, not to bring me to you. He demanded, but I refused. I did. Not Karr. I made him promise. I made them both promise. What if you turn me away? How can I just walk up to you and say that I am Elaar's daughter and you believe me? I'm not a child. You may not want me. You may not accept me. I'm here somehow without my mother. What if you blame me? I thought you'd throw me off the cliff-"

Ama's body collapses. *{Lira,}* she whispers, appalled.

"I have my mother but she's not here. My father is a-" Talyn is......is where? "I don't have a family. I don't know what that means or what that feels like or how I'm supposed to behave."

Karr shifts, and the motion, the noise he makes, draws my attention. His posture, his eyes, have changed as well, the purple bolts softening down into lavender. *{Oh, love, you do have a family. More than one.}* He looks at each of the turned-away dragon faces dividing him from me, and nods thoughtfully to himself. *{I'm going to leave you for awhile. You need to spend time with this family. I owe that to all of you.}*

"No. *No*, Karr. You can't leave me-"

{Nothing will make me leave you, not even them.}

{I don't think you have the power to make such a declaration, dragon,} Spirit snarls.

[Daring him is not a good idea,] Nightmare mumbles under his breath, no one but myself hearing.

{Yes. I do,} Karr snaps, a dark cloud of black smoke escaping his lips and cascading down his neck. *{But after what she said, I'll back down. I am not heartless, or thoughtless, or selfish. She needs you, and I know you need her. I'll go as you've asked, but I will not be leaving her.}*

He can sense my panic- my grandfather and uncles are barring the way and making it clear that he will not come any closer to say good-bye.

{Do not worry about me, love. I'm still hungry, so I'm going to go get something to eat while you relax and spend time getting to know them. Your worst fears have just been put to rest. They'd have never denied you or thrown you off any cliff. That goes for all who love you, Lira. All.}

<u>33</u>

{*I THINK I MAY LIKE HIM,*} Gref mumbles, watching the space where Karr had been. {*He doesn't back down easily.*}

{*Well, I* don't *like him. Mihn would have-*} Frit cuts himself off after receiving pointed glares from his parents.

"He told me to watch for him," I say, angry at their attack of him, panicking that both my Guardians had assented to the dragons' order and left. "He told me to go directly to him when I came here. But I didn't." In my haste to defend Karr, I'd forgotten to watch my words, which are being met with startled silence by all. Above me, Saramine and Ju-uh almost collide.

{*Lira, your father died here, before you were born. I saw him, I saw him dead,*} Gref stammers. {*With your mother in my arms, I set his body on fire. I* did. *He was my best friend-*}

"I know Mihn's dead, Gref. But he *told* me to search for Karr, from the time I was born."

The dragons gawk at me with eyes that no longer swirl, their jaws slack as they question my sanity. "My mother didn't know it, but he was there with us. Even if I didn't promise Mihn, I *need* Karr. Please, don't keep them away. He saved my life and he only did what I asked. Both of them. I was afraid, it's not their fault, but I need them. I need him."

{There is nothing we could truly do to prevent him from being with you,} Ama answers as she recovers from her initial shock. *{But he is not a part of this reunion. He can return when we say so. You can't control fear or what you don't know, Lira. But he knew better.}*

{We could take Karr cliff jumping,} Spirit suggests. *{That would be very fun. How do you think he'll do, Gref?}*

But Gref doesn't answer. He is staring, unblinking at me, his jaw loose in his mouth. I return his gaze softly, understanding the questions he doesn't know how to ask. Gref is my mother's brother, the ever-protective, always-there older brother. Her bond with her other siblings was strong, but not so strong as theirs. But my father and he had been best friends as well. And Gref had been the one to set his body on fire and turn his back, fly away with my mother screaming in his grasp.

{Terrible,} Ju-uh answers for him. *{He'd die and Lira would never speak to us again.}*

{But if Lira is like her mother......} Frit ponders.

From above us, Saramine laughs. *{Karr would kill you both if she even tried.}*

Frit scoffs. *{That's funny, Meen.}*

{I side with Sara,} Yetabo adds. *{Remember the scorched patches of trees we've found? Karr could out-flame you both.}*

{We are not discussing a flame match, Tabo, we're discussing a cliff jump over the canyon, no wings allowed. He does not possess the strength nor the courage to pass that. And he can't out-flame either of us!}

{He possesses something neither of you have,} Ju-uh interjects. *{Put him through your tests. Let's see what else he's capable of.}*

{I don't think your dragon understands what he's won with their change of mind,} Marr rumbles.

Saramine and Ju-uh descend from the sky. They walk carefully along the rocky bank, their feet making the ground crunch and creak below them. When their feet lift, they make the popping sound of being freed from mud. Water fills their footprints. I can sit inside them like a bath- *Oh, a bath!* Once we leave this spot, the lake will have a completely different look than when I'd first arrived.

They press closer, each of my mother's siblings, until they are as close as they can be without being on top of me. Their bodies tower over me, their heads low as they all study and smell. Ama remains standing furthest back, still in the water. Maybe the water is what has kept her temper and emotions more in check. But they're there, swimming just below her skin. Marr circles around his brood and settles nearer his mate.

They shine, this family of mine. I'm grateful that I've met them at nightfall and my eyes have been allowed to adjust to their brilliance slowly with rise of day.

{You have your father's color,} Saramine murmurs. Her own scales are a brilliant turquoise; her sister Yetabo is a sleek, dark copper; Ju-uh is a dark, nearly matte grey blue; Gref is a lovely dark purple; Frit is a rich jade; and Spirit is a pale, pale bronze (something he was- at least when he was younger- very defensive about). Marr's deep, comforting cobalt and Ama's emerald. Weaving faint and elusive in-between them all while catching a ride on the wind, I catch a brief glimpse of that ghost-like white, draconic body.

As the suns begin to descend, my mother's family burrows their bodies into the rocks and curls their tails around themselves, taking turns plying me with questions.

They want to know where my mother is, her life since being taken from here, and how I came here. I answer them the best I can, picking through my words carefully. I can't tell them the truth about the damage the exile and Mihn's loss have done to her, how she sits beneath Ama's portrait and cries and cries. I can't mention how she sits and forgets where she is sometimes, and waits hours and hours other times to hear her siblings coming to fetch her as they'd always done.

She'd come out of that state just before Talyn was born. His arrival had given her a more tangible hope to hang onto, and Talyn's presence had made it all the more real. I don't tell them any of that, either. About Him, about my daughter. I don't remember much after Talyn was taken, almost nothing before walking out of my room that day and waking up here. What state is my mother in now? Her granddaughter stolen and her daughter missing? What if she believes They came and got me? What if she doesn't know that I am here? Would it make any difference? She's alone. She's completely alone.

I can't tell them any of that. Maybe, I try to tell myself as I have been quite often, maybe, hopefully, my father has come out of his hiding and shown her that she isn't nearly as alone as she has believed.

Oh, she'd kill him.

The dragons hold their faces over my head, taking long, deep breaths as though drinking me in. I think they are. Is it my smell, or is it the mix of my parents' smells? I hope there is a trace of them in me, something the dragons can taste, something I can give back to them. I can see, can almost smell as strongly as they, the magnitude of their loss and anguish. It's never left them either.

They stare at me harder than I can return. Their colors become blinding, and it's hard to look at them at such close range, when they are all clustered together and their scales are reflecting everyone else's. They bring their noses right up against Blaze and gaze intently at him, their eyes right there against his body. He holds so still, and follows their every movement. I want to touch them, run my hands along their necks and bodies, throw my arms around each of them and hug them, and I think they wish they were physically capable of doing the same.

It comforts the dragons, to be able to speak of my parents, and it sooths me, to hear the shift of their tones as they speak and remember. Their stories are more than just stories; their words tighten the link between us, to show me that I am theirs and I am family.

After I eat lunch and tend to Blaze, I tell them about the walls in our house, about what the Wizard had told my mother about Karr and me; again leaving out Him, leaving out *Two Lives, One Breath, Three*. I tell Ama about the bowl of apples my mom keeps. Before she took her, Ama would leave perfectly red apples in Ravery so my mother would have something to eat.

{*Come home with us, niece,*} Saramine pleads as night creeps through the sky once again. Where had last night and today gone? {*This is not where you belong, on this low land. You belong with us.*}

The others are silent, waiting for my reply. I instinctively look past them, scanning the trees. I don't know where I belong. My parents loved it down here, as much as my mom loved it on the cliffs with them. I need to know this place. They'd expect that of me. And I'm not ready to say goodbye to Nightmare or Karr. But I don't want my family to leave me. How do I say that?

Marr intervenes before I need to. *{No, Saramine. Not yet. Lira, I'd like nothing more than to hold you in my hand and carry you with us. But I concur with Karr's shocking wisdom: you need to know and feel that you are of this earth and sky as much as your parents are, as much as we are. You need to know that you are a part of us, and that we want you. That many want you. If you come with us now, I don't think any of that will happen.}*

{Besides,} Frit interjects, a sardonic edge to his voice. *{If we take you home with us now, your dragon will never have the opportunity to redeem himself. And I am so looking forward to him trying.}*

I look sharply over his shoulder, immediately spotting Karr's tell-tale red just within the trees.

{Frit, be nice,} Yetabo scolds. *{He's earned it by keeping watch over her while she's been here.}*

{Mmm-hmm. Are you forgetting that we learned she was here by accident? How much longer until he'd have remembered to tell us?}

I can feel Karr seething silently from wherever he's standing. The shadows have shifted and devoured him again.

{We'll return tomorrow,} Ama interrupts, stretching out and pressing her nose to my face. *{Lira, Lira, Lira,}* she whispers, just for the relief of being able to speak my name.

As quickly as they had come down, they return into the air one by one, Gref the last, my father's burning body and my mother's screams still haunting him. The wind trails along, a light airy breeze, twirling carefree and happy just behind. The smooth sounds of their wings beating the air holds me spellbound, carrying me along with them as they disappear.

My head is spinning. I close my eyes and wait for the spell to pass. Behind me, the rocks groan, the air swirls around Karr's body as he walks towards me. I open my eyes and turn to him. "Why didn't you warn me?"

{This wasn't planned!}

[Of course it wasn't. That's why they were all so happy with you.]

{I ran into her- I flew into her. She knocked me out of the sky —}

Nightmare laughs heartily. [How is that not surprising?]

The dragon frowns but ignores him. *{She was angry that I had not informed her of your presence here.}*

[Being banished is such an inconvenience.]

The dragon snarls over my head.

"Banished?" I interrupt.

Karr stretches out his tail as he circles but Nightmare doesn't budge, daring him to strike out, even though it was he to say that daring him is unwise. Karr's tension from my family's reaction to him continues to slice through the night. His anger at the unicorn's betrayal of his secret could be all that's needed for him to lose his temper completely.

{My family was banished from The Cliffs many years ago, for an offense we were held accountable for. I……he……} The dragon stops, heaving a sharp exhale before beginning again. His words are carefully chosen, and he starts slow, trying it out first in his head before letting it spill out to me.

{When you arrived in The Valley, the one you will not speak of came to me, asking my help to take you from the beast. Your man- don't argue- may have needed the help of a dragon, but I, myself alone, **Heard** *you scream across the distance. I Heard*

you, I Felt you, love. And so I am here. In my rush to you, I did not tell your grandmother that you were here. And when I found you, I, simply, forgot that I should. I know they're angry, and they'll probably still never forgive us.}

"Am I your means of redemption for your family? Is that what Frit meant? Is that why He sought you out and not my family?"

Karr rushes to me so quickly I almost back away. His eyes are blaring ruby once more, lightning flashes of indiscernible color streaking through his irises. Sometimes I swear they're like that damn dress, almost purple in one glance but then becoming indecipherable between that or silver or some shade of blue, or all at once. Right now, though, level with mine, they're so solidly red that I think I must have been crazy before to think they'd had any other streaks of color. They're hypnotic, always vanquishing my anger. I regret my question instantly, and turn to back away. "No, I'm sorry, Karr. I'm just all turned around."

{No, Lira, I'll answer you. But I need you to face me.}

Nightmare threateningly shifts weight between his front hooves.

{Back off!} Karr growls, lashing his head toward the unicorn. *{You were an unbelievable amount of help with them.}*

He turns back to me, softer, his nose almost touching mine. *{At first, I think I did. I thought that if I were the one to find you, my family's honor would be restored. But my reasons quickly changed when I found you. He and I are alike in that way. I stay for you alone, not for me, not for any other's benefit. You need only whisper you want to return to the Cliffs and I'll take you there. You want to seek out the one who brought you here, I'll do that for you too. You want a place to forever hide, I'll guard that place for you. If you wish me to leave you, as impossible as that would be, I'll do whatever you bid. If I'm* *forever bound to exile, I can live with that. My family's issues have nothing to do with you, Lira, of my tie to you. As I swore to you months ago, I am your Guardian first and foremost. Everything else will wait.}*

He sighs, his body losing its tension, his voice losing its fiery bite all at once. He retreats back a couple steps and sits down, looking exhausted, leaving me a little bewildered at his intensity moments before. *{It was good to see them finally, wasn't it? As bad as you feared? I'm certainly glad it's happened.}*

Behind him, the suns are falling. In a way, it's as if the suns and moon bounce excruciatingly slow, the suns always a day behind her, whom they perpetually pursue. Night is V-ing up from where she glows white, but day remains prominent. The place where Karr stands is directly under the moon, as if night actually spreads out from his thoughts and day is made from his body.

{Here, I've brought you another gift.}

"Wh-what?"

{A gift. You know, that thing humans do as an act of good will or just because or for love or whatever.} He reaches under a fold of his wing and pulls something out, which he keeps hidden in his giant hand.

"If you keep this up, I'll have to settle down somewhere just to store all your gifts!"

{It's the Curse of the Dragons— can't help but to collect things. Would settling down be so bad, anyway?} he stretches his open hand out before me.

"A tea kettle!" I shout, snatching it from him in greedy excitement. Inside is a matching clay mug, and inside that are two packages of dried leaves. I chuckle almost insanely. Delightfully, insanely, greedily, before going into another fit of coughing. I've been brewing tea in cups placed near the fire. Not too near. Wood cups catch fire and make the boiling liquid inside explode outward. Tin ones become so hot you can't touch them.

{Now you can have decently hot tea, to soothe that cough. Are you sure you're not ill?}

"It's just a cough, Karr! I can't believe the two of you! I feel fine, I promise. I feel better than I have in a very long time."

{I'm not talking about the coughing only, Lira.}

The pre-night air is so wonderful, smells so fresh, so new, so clean. A cool thread is weaving its way through the breeze, and it's lovely. I haven't slept in two days, I realize, but I'm not a bit tired. I am deeply settled within myself.

I look back to Karr, my head askew as I process......so very many things. "Every room of the house my mother and I lived in was covered with everything and everyone of here. I know you all so well because of her and how desperately she made sure I could recognize all of you. Except there was never *you*. The Wizard spoke of you, though, something she only recently revealed to me. His words- those words he had told her of me- I think they've kept her going.

"Mom was always so confused, because she knew no red dragon, but the Wizard told her you lived and you would come and she trusted him enough to not ever question it. But you were banished, and now it all makes sense. I wish I could finally explain to her that he was right. You exist."

Karr doesn't speak and it doesn't matter. I hadn't spoken to get a response. I turn away from him, glancing out over the lake. Ama came to find me. Seeing her has reinforced my longing for her, for that tie that had been severed. I wish she had stayed longer. I wish I had gone with her. She is the part of me I always needed to know. She's brought me hope, hope that I'll have this same type of reunion with Talyn. Only when she gets close enough for me to touch, I *will* whisk her away and never let her free again.

The lake beckons me stronger than the desire to run to the cliffs. Nothing will welcome the night and end the day better than a swim in this lake. I settle Blaze down and peel out of my clothes, walking naked into the living blue mist and the cool water. *Savor*, I smile.

With night just breaking, I swim away towards the center of the water where I can be alone and where it's quiet, and regard the world from the change in perspective as I float. Water is life and medicine. Supportive, replenishing, healing. I've seen my grandmother, whose image I had played and cried and begged under since I was a little child, and she accepted me, and she loves me as her own. One of my worst fears has been put to rest.

It makes all the difference, that I was missing but have been found. *I am wanted. I was made in love, and I am surrounded by love.*

34

IN THE MEADOW IT IS WARM, and this time I feel the complete strength and warmth of double suns. The grass grows light green and to my knees. They ripple in rows and swirls according to the breeze, changing their hue depending on whether they bow away or to me.

This morning was also the first time I'd woken before dawn (something that shocked my Guardians). We watched the day fall over us together, and it was a breathtaking sight. Soon after that, Karr flew off with my uncles and aunts. All the dragons seem to have settled their initial disputes and have quickly ventured past tolerance and into genuine regard- aside from constant challenges for show of strength and endurance and flight and fire......What have they dared him to do this time? Nightmare, however, is reverent to them in a way he will never be with Karr.

I close my eyes and tilt my head back, letting the shine of the suns bleed through my closed eyes and wash down the inside of my skin while the suns themselves tumble down the outside...

...Home, where only my suns can keep me warm.

The wind flits through the thin reeds of grass, making them rustle and whirl, and unconsciously, I am aware that I am swaying with them.

......I don't dance!
What a horrible lie......

After Karr had left earlier, I was overcome by the need to shed my clothes down to the thin little shift he had brought back to me awhile ago. He may not have understood the power of clothing, but he instantly picked up on the upset it ignited in Nightmare, which gave him greater satisfaction than any reaction I could have given. Except that as much as I wanted to show my pleasure and intrigue at the little thing- a fancy and impractical little luxury given the way I'm living- I couldn't help but feel skepticism about its true origins. Though I'm sure Karr would never lie to me- if it came from Him, he'd tell me. I hope. A village woman could have lied to Karr, though. He could have given it to someone else to give to Karr to give to me-

Stars, Nightmare is right. I am pathetically paranoid.

Even so, as inconspicuously as I could, I had run my hands over the silk, checking for seams (which there were), just to be sure before I could smile and sincerely accept it. The dragon had raised a ridged brow, but didn't comment. He kept silent when I ripped it in two, as well. Having a separate top and bottom makes it easier to feed Blaze, but also, with the newly-made skirt now hanging off my hips and exposing my middle, I can feel more air, more suns.

The breeze lifts and plays with the hem of the barely-there slip as it caresses up my legs. Grass bunches up between my toes, and I move them just to feel it. Not for pain, only pleasure, joy. The air on my exposed skin makes me shiver but also smile. I am my mother's child. One day, maybe I'll find the nerve to run entirely bare. For right now, I like the transparent feel of this fabric, the way it feels as it moves against my skin.

Blaze is asleep, nestled atop his sling. The grasses waving over his head and humming to him ensure he'll sleep a good long while, and wake just as smooth and serenely. I turn around happy, thinking of him, but for the briefest of moments I re-experience the terror of turning around to check on Talyn hidden safely behind me only to find her in that man's arms. I stare at the moving grass until the room, the front room of that house so very far away is gone, That Day is gone, and I am back in the clearing. The grass parts just enough for me to catch sight of Blaze's head of black hair mixed among the green, the wind hugs my shoulders until the tension and panic flee, and the grasses close like a curtain in a nursery back over my sleeping, safe, son. Every part of this world does what the other had refused to do.

I think of life as he knows it, and smile brighter. No walls, no roof, no people. Just trees and grass and open skies, wind and rain and moon and suns. Dragons and me and a unicorn. Everything I should have provided to Talyn.

What is life as she knows it?

A dragon's smile feels like the sun has been born into your mind- a wonderful feeling of brightness and warmth and their overwhelming amount of love. With humans you have to guess at their true feelings for you; not so with dragons. They somehow fill you with it as easily as they speak into your head.

Ama's smile as she watches me warms me quicker from the inside out than the suns are doing from the outside in, driving out the taunting panic and grief and fear until I once again relax and bask. My skin's probably going to burn, and I'll be miserable for the next couple weeks, but I can't stop. I can't open my eyes, put on my clothes, and walk away.

I spread my palms over the tops of the grasses and let them tickle the undersides of my hands. I scrunch my toes-the spaces in-between each packed with stalks- again and again. The earth is still slightly damp from this morning's dew, but warmth is spreading down the stems like slow-moving rain. They're surprisingly stiff and sturdy for such tiny things.

Can the same be said of me? Am I truly not as frail and weak as I feel? What would He say?

The inside of my head sways, spots bringing haze to my vision while a sharp pain stabs from my temple to the back of my head and sideways to my ears. Too much suns, maybe. I turn away and return to Blaze, sitting down quickly beside him as my body starts to tremble. Blaze immediately wakes bright and lively, and the episode drifts away. Propped up with my clothes arranged around him, he babbles to himself as he reaches towards the suns. Every now and then, a loud, quick burst of laughter escapes him before he settles down to stare again. I cannot wait for him to talk, to be able to talk to him.

I look out over the meadow, remembering that a meadow is where my father is buried. Is this that meadow? Would I know?

"Can you tell me about Anin?" I ask the dragons. "Why was she so insistent on killing my mother?"

Marr and Yetabo regard Ama as she wonders how to answer. Seeing Yetabo, I worry again over Karr and the dares the rest are throwing on him. She's his supporter. The mediating voice of reason. But she's here.

"Is she dead?"

{I don't know if she has died. There's been no sign of her or Soldiers since your mother-}

When she doesn't continue, I speak again. "A Soldier followed me into the trees."

Marr responds, {We are aware. Nightmare told us that the Soldier had been following you on the hills since you arrived, but because you are a female human, not because he knew who you were.}

So no one mentioned to them that I had revealed who I was to the Soldier, all by myself. "Why did Anin hate her?"

{We should seek Aril, The Wizard's wife, to explain that to you.}

"No," I reply overly forceful, so stern and quick that a flash of gold signals that my response had been heard by Nightmare, who keeps himself at a distance when the dragons come down.

{You have no desire to see her? Did Elaar not tell you about her?}

"She did, Ama. I do want to see her. But-" I am not liking where this is heading. "I can't. I won't."

{Why? She loved Elaar. She'd want to meet you, Lira. You should realize by now there's no need to fear anyone, us and least of all her. She would be better able to answer your questions. I haven't seen her since......since it happened.}

I study the dragons' faces, completely forgetting my own torment and wondering over theirs. Over everyone's. They haven't spoken to Aril in (how old am I?) almost twenty five years?

{*We need to see her, Lira. We should go tomorrow. We'll carry you and Blaze.*}

"No, Ama. I can't go that way."

There is silence while they wonder and wait. I reach for my son and pull him into my arms, kissing his head and just holding him. He squeals and laughs.

{*Lira, you need to explain. If she'd done something to Elaar—*}

I shake my head. "No, Ama, she's done nothing. She has a son."

{*Yes.*} Ama answers. {*A daughter as well.*}

I wish I can convey what I feel in just a look. No words, not even a thought. Just a look and it'll be over. Nightmare can read images as I think or dream them, Karr can even read the change in my emotions. Can't I just touch them and transfer everything without speaking or thinking? "Her son brought me here, Ama."

{*So Karr has told us.*}

"Did Karr tell you that He'd found me long before that? He found me There, in The Other Place where my mother and I had been living. I have a daughter, Ama," I whisper brokenly. "*His* daughter." I want to hug Blaze closer, but I can't move. I turn my head away from all of them. "I had a daughter."

Tears burn. I keep forgetting how hotly they burn. As painful as the bullet, which is throbbing once again. Knowing I can't leave it at that, knowing for a long time that I need to tell them, I take a breath and tell. I shake as I speak. It's the first time I've ever detailed it out loud: how deeply I fell in love with Him, how strongly I believed in him, how much more I fell in love with our daughter, and how broken I became with both of them gone. Just gone. And then everything that happened here. I hadn't been this honest with Karr. I haven't needed to be this descriptive with Nightmare, and he doesn't like hearing most of it anyway.

{Lira,} Ama's voice is surprisingly firm. *{You need to speak to him. You can't hold this in-}*

"No."

{Lira,} my grandfather begins.

"I can't, Marr. I won't. Why would he care? Where is he now? Where was he then? He left me there. He won't help me, Marr. And I won't beg for his refusal."

{Lira, Karr knows where he is. If you tell him what you told us, he'll help-}

[Karr has already agreed he wouldn't.]

I turn my head, grateful for the unicorn's interruption.

My grandmother balks. *{Why would he do that, Nightmare?}*

[Because Lira requested it. She can't see Him now, and we will not force her. When she is able to, she will.]

It faintly sounds like a prediction, rather than a reiteration of the present. I frown, wanting to argue the likelihood. I am too surprised by the fact that the dragons argue no further, as shaken as Ama is. Did she beg The Wizard to bring her daughter back? If so, he never did, did he? Why would his son do any different?

My eyes filling, I plead, plead for my life. "Please. I can't. Don't ask me again. I can't." My heart springs loose and feels like it's bouncing off the walls of my chest while beating too quick and sporadic. Yet one more route that can tell him what I don't know how to say. *Surprise, you have a daughter. And I let her be snatched from my arms.*

{Lira, if you hold all this in, it will tear you apart,} Ama warns. But I remain adamant. I have no control over myself or anything or anyone else, but I can control this one thing.

*

{Lira. Lira, wake up. Are you awake? Do you hear me? You're having nightmares again.}

All I see is red, and at first it scares me. But it's not the moon, it's not a warning. As comforting as Mom's hair, it's Karr's wing, hanging over me like a blanket. I shake off the disorientation lingering from the dream and roll over. "Karr?"

{I'm right here. Are you awake?}

"When did you get back?"

{Not too long ago. There's a village very close by. I think we should all go there. I think you should go there. Speak to people, eat some real food. Makes better sense than me begging and carrying stuff back for you. Plus, I think your family is going to start doing the same. You will very soon be bogged down with so much stuff we won't be able to move. How about you beat them to it?}

I crawl over Blaze and push to my feet, forcing Karr to lift his wing and let me walk away.

{What were you dreaming about?}

I throw some logs unnecessarily into the fire and spin in circles until I spot the bag hiding in the grass. Karr watches me and Nightmare wakes, followed shortly by Blaze. I cough a few times, wipe the tears that linger from my dreams, and ignore the stomach pains that now accompany most mornings. All the poison's effects will go away eventually.

The tea kettle is on the top of the pile inside the bag. I forage for the leaves and the gourd of water, and set to heating it up while I nurse Blaze.

[What's the plan for today?] Nightmare inquires, his eyes darting to Karr's.

{She's going to the village about half a day's walk from here, per her grandparents.}

"They can't foster me off. I'm not a child. I've had a lifetime of people. I can choose that the rest of my life should be completely void of more."

{They worry that you see your world the same way your mother did. Surely you've encountered some good with your own species. Even just one?}

I look at him hard, wondering what else they'd told him, but he doesn't make a motion of knowing more than he is saying.

{I find that hard to believe. You had no one in the Other Place? No friends?}

"How could I call anyone a friend? Or myself a friend to them? I lied to them. I lied to them every day. There was no way they'd have understood the truth about us. None of this- this world, your kind, Nightmare's, my parents' lives- none of you exist in their comprehension."

{But it does for the people here. There's no reason for you to isolate yourself.}

I turn away from him, stare mindlessly through the trees. The hallway of trees. Blaze sits in my lap, slapping his little hands down on my upturned palm, his new fascination, but I barely feel it. A hallway of trees.

[Your water's going to be too hot to drink.]

I pull my eyes from the trees, return to the fire and, by pushing a long thick branch through the handle of the kettle, lift it up and away from the flames. Setting it down in the dirt to cool down, I return to the dragon's side and curl up against him, shivering and cold.

{Love, you're not alright, are you?}

I shake my head no. "I dreamt of Blaze's mother. She held onto my hands tightly and thanked me over and over again, and told me He'd lead me out of the dark, but she wasn't referring to Blaze. I was in Kholsari and He was searching for me. He kept calling my name and I could hear him pacing the halls looking for me, but I stayed where I was and closed my eyes, praying he wouldn't find me. And he didn't."

[Lira?]

Blaze slaps his hands against his reflection in Karr's scales. I turn from the dragon to empty the kettle onto the fire, never thirsty to begin with, sighing when it sizzles, as though the steam and smoke it produces is a sign that my dreams have been vanquished. If only it were that easy. I quickly wipe my cheeks dry and turn to see what Blaze is squealing about. His little hands are curled tightly around Karr's nostrils and he has risen to his feet to stare into the dragon's eyes.

{Ow. For such little hands, he has the grip of death.} With a gentle push of his head, Karr guides Blaze back to his bottom. He blows smoke out of his nostrils, sending Blaze into an hysterical fit of laughter.

Nightmare walks closer, wrinkling his nose. [I don't see what you two see. Smells too much like male to be anything other than that.]

Blaze falls onto his side and rolls onto his stomach, babbling and stretching his arms out for the unicorn's nearest golden hoof, pushing his feet out excitedly behind him so that he propels himself forward and flat onto his belly. He hasn't coordinated with his arms yet, but he'll be crawling soon. She entered into a phase where she hated being held. She wanted to move herself. What will I do when we reach that stage? Karr loves to joke about me needing to settle down with every new gift he brings, and that will certainly give him more fuel for his teasing. How will I coordinate wandering when Blaze won't be held still but isn't strong enough to wander on his own feet with us? I can't stay still. As soon as I stop, He'll come.

[Lira?]

I give the unicorn a saddened smile. "The way he was laughing, I was just......You're a liar. You love him and you know it." I grab Blaze by his middle, lifting him into the air upside down. He laughs, laughs harder when I hold him higher and blow kisses onto his belly before turning him head up.

Maybe today I do need the noise and distraction of a village of people. "Fine, we'll go to the village."

{What?} The question of 'Why?' stirs into my head though he doesn't come right out and ask it. I wait, daring him to ask a question I don't want to answer. Maybe part of me wants him to force it out of me, make it impossible for me to hide any longer. *Don't dare him*, Nightmare had warned.

[We may as well leave now. Get you there in time for a decent breakfast. Right, Karr?]

The possibility shatters. Karr blinks and nods, turning his head to flick his nose south, behind me. {That way.}

I inhale deeply, my heart pounding. What was I thinking? My family had hoped that by their absence today, that maybe I'd do what they think I need to do, say what I need to say. If not to Him, then to his closest link, to the only one who can find him. I just came very close to destroying everything. I don't need to go to the village for food or companionship, but for distance. To distract everyone away from me, because if anyone were to ask me right now, I'd say yes, yes please tell Him I need to be found. I'm drowning in my dark.

*

Karr and Nightmare have only been able to force me into a couple villages since my visit with the old woman. The people were always happy and active, and each was overwhelmingly noisy. Well, to me, as I've been isolated from civilization for blessedly long spans of time.

Like all the others, this village is noisy, so bursting with life and pulsing with energy that I stand within the shadow of the trees in an attempt to figure out why it feels different than the other villages.

It's fascinating, watching the bright, large smiles; hearing the high pitched, excited tones, the easy laughter; following the children as they run around and play; watching the hugs and quick kisses on the cheek as neighbors greet each other. Venturing closer to hear their words, I eventually catch upon the reason for their undertone of excitement: dragons. Plural. *My* dragons. They haven't flown in over two decades, but since finding me several weeks ago, they've not been hiding their presence. They fly during all hours of the day or night, sometimes high, sometimes just over the treetops. Frit, my uncle with a more comical approach to life, winked as he passed over them a couple days ago, which made them explode into this excited frenzy: Dragons exist. They've returned.

I smile to myself, envisioning them flying over the old woman's house, and the peace of mind that will finally give her.

So many of the people Here have never seen them, have thought them mythical legends their parents and grandparents used for some unknown allegorical lesson. Somehow, seeing them, seeing that they are in fact real, has made them see their world, their lives, as beautiful. Magical. Powerful. Something worth celebrating.

{I'm jealous. I stop in a village with a sincere request for assistance and everyone's terrified. The other dragons fly in a sudden unannounced swarm overhead and everyone's celebrating. I don't see the fairness.}

I peel my attention from the people to smile at Karr, standing behind me. Do I see my world, my life, as beautiful, magical, powerful because he is beside me? In comparison to where I was and how I was before here and him, the answer is unquestionably yes.

{What are you staring at?}

"You."

He rolls his eyes mockingly. *{Don't take them so seriously. I'm just a dragon. These people are the sort who were already always happy. It doesn't take much more for them to find something to celebrate. And should dragons ever fade from their sight again, they'll continue happily as they always do.}*

"No, Karr. Maybe sometimes people are originally happy and healthy, and then their life and perceptions become enriched by the unexpected addition of another, who made them happier and fuller than they ever imagined. Everyone has the power to make another's life that much better without even doing anything outrageous, but when they disappeared, they took everything good and secure about my life with them."

Karr's eyes narrow and his face lowers closer. *{What are you talking about now, love? You started off speaking general, and then it became personal.}*

"I'm not a happy person, Karr. I was not raised in security and bright joy." My eyes burn with shame, but I do not turn away. "But you, and Nightmare, and Blaze, you fill my life with......so much. How could it matter if you were already happy when something comes and makes you better? I'll be devastated beyond description if any of you left me. It *killed* me, Karr, killed me when-

"Every day I feel like I'm dying. Then I go to bed, and in the morning it begins all over again. Look at them, Karr," I add quickly, needing to look away right then to contain myself. "There's humbleness, and there's arrogance. But then there's the serene pleasure knowing that your presence truly does bring joy into someone else's life. You have done that to mine as well as theirs. Don't diminish it by saying they'd be the same whether you were here or not, or whether you stay or not. That's cruel."

{That's not what I meant, love. I refuse to fathom life without you. Or the little troll boy. Nightmare, I dream about losing him all day long, every damn day.}

[It's mutual.]

{But I want to know what you are trying so hard not to say to me. What hurt you?}

[You are indescribably dense. I think we've both made it pretty clear.]

{No you haven't. I need for her to tell me without you constantly interfering. Who are you protecting?}

[I'm protecting *her*, genius.]

{By forcing her to swallow whatever burden she's carrying? I am larger than you, Lira. Let me help you.}

[We're being watched.]

Just a few feet away stands a little girl of maybe five years. Her index finger pulls down the corner of her mouth as she deliberates on what she should do next. She's so little, so beautiful and somehow so fragile. She tries to brush her thick, messy dark brown hair three times from her bright, earth-colored eyes before giving in and allowing it to lay where it wishes. No longer bothered, she redirects her entire focus solidly and solely on Karr.

She guts my breath. She's not Talyn, doesn't look like her, isn't her age. Maybe it's the way the light frames her, maybe it's only my grief and my haunting dreams, or the sight of her feet, small and bare and dirty. I take a step toward her, wanting to protect her, or just bask in the light that glows around her. But before I can move, she makes her decision and walks purposefully to Karr.

He smiles, his eyes becoming lazy slits as he brings his head down to press his nose into her outstretched palm. She laughs a high, happy giggle.

"I see my face in your skin! Can you breathe fire?"

{Only for you.} He lifts his face to the sky and blows out a thin, crackling stream, making her jump in ecstasy and clap her hands.

"That's mean," she scolds Nightmare. He shrugs off my unspoken question. "Why are you hiding here?"

{I don't really know. Lira, my beautiful companion over there with the troll-boy humanling, seems a little afraid of your village's happiness. Frown at me all you like, love, you're only proving my statement.}

"That doesn't make sense," she admonishes me, with a laughable amount of adult reasoning and wisdom.

From behind me, the girl's mother's voice breaks above the village's constant noise. The panic, the consuming terror.

"The dragon's being silly, sweetie. But your mama's going to be very frightened if she can't find you. I'll walk you back?" I reach out my hand instinctively, feeling a rushing need to reunite her with her mother, quickly, quickly, before that sudden dreadful question comes unanswerably into her head: *where is she?* Only when the girl's fingers slip into my palm and my fingers close over them, does the pain hit me again. I swallow the sorrow and move away from my Guardians.

She gives Nightmare a happy wave and smile as we pass him.

{Don't do that, or he'll steal you away!}

I whip my head back. "Stop that, Karr! You'll scare her!"

{Well, someone needs to keep the little ones safe from his kind. Besides, Illie knows I'm kidding. Slightly.}

Her hand squeezes mine. She's grinning. "They're silly. Nightmare told me the dragon is going to swallow me whole! But I didn't listen because Karr showed me a picture of him swallowing Nightmare instead, and then he rolled over and patted his huge tummy before burping, and it was so funny! So I walked right up to him. He showed me fire! Did you see?"

"I did."

"It was made of thousands of little unicorns, which Nightmare didn't think was funny, so he- Mama!" She tugs her hand from mine and breaks off running toward her pale-faced mother. We'd left the trees without my being very aware, drawn as I was by her voice, her chatter- what exactly had gone on between her and my companions in those few minutes of what I thought was silence?

At our appearance, I am startled by a bombardment of cheers and clapping and exasperated sighs of relief from the whole village. It shocks me, one entire community so in tune with one solitary, tiny other. I had heard their voices, their tones changing as we'd walked closer to them, knew that they'd all picked up on the missing child, but I hadn't anticipated seeing the genuine shared fear and concern on all their faces. Is this real? Is it possible for a collection of humans to be so devoted to each other? At the cheers and renewing laughter, men are running in from the trees at all pathways. They'd all gone out looking for her. Why didn't we have this?

Her mother snatches her right away into her arms, hugging her tightly. Blaze makes a noise, and the other mother's eyes part just enough to see me, to remember me, remember that I'd come from the forest holding her daughter's hand. I can't help but feel guilty, as though I'd done something wrong, as though it was I to cause another mother unnecessary pain and grief. She gives me a fretted, angst-ridden smile that releases my feelings of guilt. Relief and gratitude flood off her in waves thick enough to float through. When your emotions become that strong, you don't need to be a dragon to make others understand you. I feel so frail and pitiful while she's so enviously strong and happy and whole. I pat Blaze's back to distract myself. To soothe myself.

"Thank you, thank you so much. Where did you find her?"

"In the trees. Not far in."

The other mother presses her hands on either side of her daughter's face. "You can't go off like that, Illie! Do you know how terrified I was?"

"Mama, I had to say hello to Karr!"

"Who's Karr?" she asks, her voice suddenly cautious, frightened, hardened.

"Lira's dragon! They were hiding in the trees and I wanted to go say hello. His scales are red and they sparkle and I could see my reflection in them better than in water!"

Most of the fear leaves the mother's face at the word 'dragon', being replaced instead by confusion. The villagers' voices mute and then die while the mother's eyes widen; Karr and Nightmare have just emerged behind me.

"See, Mama!" Illie points to them excitedly. "That's Karr! And that's Nightmare, the unicorn. They came with Lira and Blaze. Karr is Lira's Guardian and Nightmare is just stalking her. Blaze is Lira's baby, but the dragon calls him a troll. Isn't that silly?"

I throw my hands on my hips and face 'my' dragon. *You used the word 'stalking' before a child?*

{I can only speak the truth. Anyway, the villagers appreciate it. Do you not notice how squirmy the men become when your demon stalker shows his ugly self? When the details come from a child's mouth, they relax a little. The demon's not after their women and children. Or are you?}

Nightmare snorts, slamming his hoof into the ground. In fact, the villagers are chuckling to themselves. He'd said that last bit aloud.

The crowd draws closer in, but then breaks apart at my right. I wait stiffly, knowing what is to come next. Two Elders are led to my side. The woman touches my cheek with thin, long fingers. Her hair is still brunette, not a hint of grey or white, but the lines on her face, her gauntness, show her age.

"I am Chan. It's because of you, isn't it?"

"What is?" I ask, knowing, of course, what she is asking.

"They wouldn't show themselves like this after so long for just any human. You're her daughter, aren't you? You're their granddaughter. The daughter of Elaar."

A murmur travels through the people like a hum. Illie is smiling while her mother looks even more shocked. My guardians are silent. Blaze reaches through the sling and pulls at the woman's sleeve.

"There's been a rumor," the man beside her, the other Elder, a short, rounder person of the same age, speaks. "But we didn't believe it. When we first started noticing them a couple days ago, we didn't even connect the two. And you show up days after they do, with a dragon and a unicorn in tow. Is it true? Are you Elaar's daughter?"

I glance at my Guardians and slowly nod.

"What is your name, Daughter of Elaar?"

It always takes me off-guard, the recognition. Nightmare had said that people will know me, no matter where I go, and I hadn't believed him. Even now, after it's happened at the old woman's and at every village they drag me into, I still haven't gotten use to it.

When I'm silent too long, Karr answers for me. *{Becoming fearful of your own species, love? Her name is Lira.}*

The Elders chuckle.

{Stop frowning at me. I think your family is right- too much isolation from your own is bad. You forget who you are.}

[That's quite ironic, you know.]

Karr growls.

35

LOWERING MYSELF INTO THE STEAMING TUB made of wood set in the center of the tiny back room of Illie's mother's house, I sigh loudly. It hadn't been meant to be so audible, though. Mortified, I throw my hands over my mouth, very stupidly releasing my supporting grip on either side of the tub. I slide across the bottom of the bath, my face going under, before my feet hit the other side and push me backward. My saving push to keep my head above the surface lacks the grace and silence I'd intended, though, and a lot of water splashes out by my over-correction.

"Are you alright?"

[Are you alright?]

{Are you alright?} I am asked at once from Nalee, Illie's mother, just outside the curtain, and Nightmare and Karr inside my head from wherever they are waiting.

"Just a little slip. I'm fine!"

I soak for awhile, relishing the water, the heat and the steam, the silence and solitude, the clean. Oh, being clean! My eyes catch on the scar on my thigh, the one on my shoulder, and then the one across my palm and how they each look under water. The diamond blade He had left for me had cut my skin smoothly, and it had healed smoothly.

The scar is now so pale it is almost silver. The skin there is tighter than it had been. All I need to do is stretch my fingers slightly and the answering tension keeps me reminded. I cup my hand loosely against my collar bone and look away from the water, at the wall where there's nothing, trying to pull myself free and back to Home, back to the Trees and Blaze and my Guardians, back to this village and this house and this tub full of cooling water.

Before the water turns chilly, I intentionally slip (graceful and quiet) all the way under and hold myself there, there in the silence beneath the surface where I can allow myself to believe for a few lazy heartbeats that I am cocooned and separate from everything else.

I push myself reluctantly up with a curse when I remember I need air, and wonder how this morning seems so long ago. Watching the village, finding Illie, coming into the village. After the shock and added excitement of my parentage withered down, the Elders demanded I stay for however long I needed, and asked that someone take Blaze and I in. Illie had grabbed onto my hand and begged me to stay with them, with her mother's sincere agreement that she would love it if we did. After breakfast, Nalee had kindly (and discretely) asked if I'd like a bath. I pumped water into the tub for Blaze first, and let him splash and play for most of the morning with Nalee sitting in a chair beside us, chatting easily and Illie bringing Blaze all sorts of toys to sink and throw around in the tub. Once Blaze was dried and clothed and settled down for a nap on the floor near the tub, it was my turn. Nalee had even found me a comb to detangle my hair.

I reach for the soap she had set aside for me, which smells of rosemary. Rosemary is the plant for remembrance and love, and I struggle to fill my head with only Nalee's words and nothing more. She'd said her husband had brought some sprigs back after his last visit to his family in the lowlands- the narrow region that bridges the trees and the cliffs- just before he'd fallen ill and died two winters ago.

The light hitting the window shifts, the sounds filtering in from outside have dulled. I blink and look around, wondering how long I had been drifting. My skin is covered in chill-bumps and I'm shivering. It's time to get out.

Nalee finishes slicing a loaf of bread as Blaze and I emerge from the curtain partition at the back of her home. She smiles brightly. "Was beginning to think you'd fallen asleep! Baths medicate the soul more than they clean the body, my mother use to say. You look exactly like what she meant by that."

"I'm sorry I was so long-"

"Nah," Nalee shakes her head, making a motion with her hand to follow her outside. "I remember those days. I'm not from this village. Illie's father and I wandered some for awhile before we decided to settle here. That first bath after days or weeks out in the earth, it was nearly magical. I use to tell him it was more magical than sex- because that taunt always brought on some *outstanding* moments." Her smile is broad and her eyes sparkling, though not with tears. She winks at my shocked expression, and I smile in turn.

"Now I have neither magical baths nor those magical moments with him. The way you looked when you came out helped me remember. Those were very good days. Brought me Illie, who has run off to play with your Guardians. The dragon insisted it was alright but-" she laughs, a short, nervous laugh. "Let's go save them from her." She winds her arm through mine and walks against my side. I envy her ease, her ability to just grab a hold of someone and it be normal. I've always felt that I'd be thrown off for the same motion.

My attention wanders, pulling my gaze towards the trees though I am thinking of the Other Place, of the girls I'd grown up with, how they'd always hugged and held onto each other, but I was never an instigator. I always stood back but allowed.

"A couple days ago everything was as it's always been. And then......now......there's dragons all over. The first several people who came running breathless and shouting 'Dragon! Dragon!' were laughed off as temporarily insane. And then more people were proclaiming the same. A person from the east of here came storming in just two days ago to say that they'd been spotted flying over her village. And then, right when she stopped speaking and before anyone could call her insane, five passed overhead.

"Now, today, my daughter wanders into the trees to talk to a dragon, who is now relaxing inside the village. It was once unfathomable, it sounds almost comical, but now it's real. It's happening and everyone has just kind of shrugged and gone on almost as before, as though nothing's completely changed. But you grew up with them, so it's nothing."

I shake my head. "I didn't grow up with them, Nalee. Not really. I had stories and pictures and my mother's word. But as I grew older, and they never came and found us, I began to doubt they were real. Until Karr found me. I felt the same then as you do now. I want to hold onto the surprise and the shock, the unbelievableness, because then I can more keenly remember how it was before him and never take him or any of them for granted. He believes that were he to leave, it would make no difference in anyone's life. And that terrifies me. I was so relieved, so relieved when he came, that he was real. There was so much before him-"

She pulls me closer and bends her head against mine. "Those of us who've known grief can spot it in others, Lira. As though our souls and hearts will forever be marked as having been broken. Shattered?"

I nod. A hug- how so very human. How so very powerful. A hug, empathy, and mutual human understanding, to somehow make things feel smaller.

She squeezes my arm. "Dragons," she curses lightly. But the joke is more in her tone, as though it is something everyone commonly says: *Oh, you know how silly those dragons can be.*

{I heard that.}

Get out of my head!

"It helps, though," she continues, "to see that for all their size and the fact that they could most likely devour us, that they instead can display such devotion and tenderness. Dragons are no longer the stuff of legends from our preceding generations. Your parents aren't...... myths. Our world's been turned on our heads and it's all for good, even if it does feel that I haven't quite caught my breath before something else happens- like my child climbing onto your dragon's head. Illie!" She releases me and jogs toward a newly cleared area large enough for my pair and a few more dragons at the western edge of town. The men are happily hauling away the felled trees and stacking them far out of sight and out of the way, and by their demeanors, I gather that my pair had just earned their keep.

I stop walking and smile at the rest my Guardians are not being given. All the village children have swarmed onto them- well, namely only Karr. Some are making faces into his scales, one little girl is counting his talons, a couple boys are on his back investigating his wings, and Illie- already proven to be the bolder of the younger children- has climbed up his neck and is sitting joyously atop his head. Her little legs are wrapped under his horns and alongside his skull just behind his eyes, and her laughter abruptly hushes when she notices all the things she can see from his vantage point. This is a child who will no longer be content while earthbound.

The few teens in the village hold further back, with the pretense of watching their younger siblings, although the envy in their eyes shows their wish to be so open and easy. One braver boy is speaking with Karr, with a forced air of adultness, while the quietest teenage girl is approaching Nightmare with an earnest look of need. She reaches out a hand to touch his muzzle, and Karr sprays a thin little stream of fire at her behind, making her jump and scream while all the children and watching adults explode in laughter.

"No, no!" a burly man, obviously her father, yells. "Us fathers of daughters prefer that they bind themselves to a unicorn! You sting her little behind when she goes *their* way!" he indicates the boys standing nearer Karr.

"Dad!" she yells, mortified.

{That hardly seems fair. These are good boys. Especially this one here, who refuses to admit how much he likes your daughter.}

The poor boy whom Karr had exposed turns a shade near to his, making everyone, even the girl's father, erupt in new laughter.

"You and I are going to have a talk," the father bellows, squaring his shoulders and sucking his middle in.

That was mean, Karr, telling on him like that! I laugh.

{Well he was never going to speak up. Things like that should never be hidden.}

Nalee stops beside Karr and shield's her eyes from the suns' and his glare. "Illie, get down off his head! That's rude!"

"Mama, I can see the whole world from up here," Illie whispers, still awed. I don't think she heard any of what had happened below her.

I walk toward Nightmare and drop my face into his mane as greeting.

[You smell like trees. Feel better?]

I do.

{Illie, tell Lira how spectacular it is. She won't fly with me and it makes me sad.}

"Can you take me flying?" she screams, standing quickly in her excitement.

"Illie!" her mother screams. "Sit down now!"

"Can you? Can I fly with you?"

{Only if Lira does first.}

"Please, Lira? Please? Please fly with him so he can take me?"

"That is so unfair, Karr! Enlisting a child to make me fly!"

{You're not going to say no now, are you? Look at her eyes, love.}

The others all around clap and cheer, encouraging me or just exasperated that I hadn't. Nalee motions again for her daughter. "Illie, come down off Karr's face please. It's time for dinner."

Illie plops back down to her bottom and pouts. "Oh, all right." Karr, however, brings his head down to the ground quickly, making her shriek one last time so that she leaves him happy. She throws her arms around his neck (which doesn't make it an eighth of the way around) and kisses his cheek before running immediately to me. She grabs my hand tightly. "Will you go? Right now? I really want to fly with him, Lira. Auntie Lira. Please, please say you'll go?"

I frown over my shoulder at him as I follow Nalee back to her house, exasperated over his absolute nerve. But he feigns innocence, giving a shrug and a big dragon smirk.

"Illie," Nalee chides, "eat first and then you can harass the dragon and Lira further."

After dinner, we leave the dishes on the table and lounge outside the house, chatting easily. I set Blaze on the ground and hold myself back while Illie becomes determined to be the one to teach him how to crawl. She keeps his middle supported and speaks in a high pitched voice to encourage him to move, but he is just too pleased to have her there, and collapses to his belly to smile up at her. So she crawls, and falls, and rolls. No matter what she does, he laughs, encouraging her to get sillier.

I feel broken, hearing their laughter, remembering what infectious means but not quite reaching it. I turn to study Nalee's reaction. She is leaning forward, trying to muffle her laughter with a hand over her mouth and tears in her eyes.

"How do you manage?" I ask without thinking, feeling something from the pit of my stomach tug at my nerves, my whole being, threatening to unravel me at the seams again.

Nalee regards me for a moment, not needing clarification of what I'd asked. Would I have had easy, mind-settling moments with the girls in the Other Place had I allowed them in, had I attempted to trust them? Maybe I would have built this community around us, and had their support, their safety.

"He filled our days with so much life and happiness, that to allow myself to sink into my loss would be an insult to him and to Illie. I can't do that to her. These people swallowed us up and wouldn't allow it either, and I'm grateful. Grateful to him, mostly. I allowed myself to feel the pain, to grieve, because that's normal and needed and allowed, but you have to then step out of it and return to life. I enjoy it for him, too. It's the only way I can honor him, and it's the better way to remember him. Where are you now, Lira?"

"I don't know."

"Did he know about Blaze?"

"No," I whisper. She takes my hand and holds it.

{Who wants to fly?}

Illie jumps up immediately. "I do I do!"

Her mother looks through the air. "That's amazing. It's like his voice travels on the air. Where is he?"

"Where we left him. Trust me though, they can become pretty intrusive."

{I'm not intrusive!}

Illie tugs on our hands, pulling us to our feet. "Can I, mama?"

She turns to me. "Is it safe?"

"I trust Karr with my life and Blaze's."

{Well then. Remember our deal. You first.}

I never agreed to anything! "Illie, Karr says he'll take *all* the children for a flight. Why don't you round them up?"

"Alright!"

{That is not what I said!}

No using children to manipulate me, Karr!

The offer spreads extremely fast. Though we aren't far from Karr and Nightmare, by the time we reach them Karr is covered in children once again. This happens in every village we are in. The adults are typically reserved and terrified, but the children see them for what they are and need to be close and touching. He's never flown them, though. Was I mistaken in offering?

{You have only succeeded in making this a full out war. I'll get you to fly with me, love. You'll see.}

The villagers swarm around us as Karr begins teasing the children over who will go first. A handful of girls- from barely walking to nearly adult- wander over to Nightmare instead. He lowers himself down and nuzzles the youngest tenderly. The change in both beasts is astounding. To see them become so gentle, so patient. Three boys became brave and tentatively head towards the unicorn. He bares his teeth but they ignore his weak attempt at a threat and quietly sit down facing him.

I study the faces around me. We're changing these people's ingrained beliefs and fears, altering the courses of their lives, of our lives, by the three of us- Karr and Nightmare mainly- being before them together, by boys being allowed to touch a unicorn and no longer fear him. Their parents may no longer remember dragons, but these children will now. They'll always remember Karr, and the taste of flight he's about to share with them.

Karr scoops the smallest into his hands and merely opens up his wings to let the air carry them upward and level with the tops of the trees. The older they are, the higher he drifts, always slow and controlled. For those who beg and whose parents nod trusting consent, he glides over the village in a wide circle. With the teens, especially the boys, he flies faster, higher, and the boys began to challenge each other on who'd take the longest time and the most frightening maneuvers before screaming.

Grounded, encompassed by adults, I let myself sink into being human. I still my nerves, my desire to retreat back into the trees. They stand close to me as we watch their children, their arms and sides pressed up to mine, hands on my arms, my shoulder or back. They pet Blaze's head and chatter sweetly to him, and I don't feel threatened, don't feel as though I am suffocating in Others. No one questions me further about my parents. They ask about my Guardians, they join Karr's cause and tease me about not flying with him, and some mothers touch Nightmare's face with tears running down their cheeks. They ask where we'd been, ask after their family or distant friends I may have met on my journey before arriving here.

When their questions have been asked, they allow me to stand and watch their children in silence with them. I drift off into wondering- how different things could have been in The Other Place. What if it was like this? What if the people surrounding me then had been like the people surrounding me now? I think of the girls I'd grown up with, and realize with a shock how hard they had tried to include me, to pull me into their circle. I had been so afraid of them, afraid of becoming like them that I kept several thick solid barriers between us.

When That Woman tried to take us, when my mother brought me back, there was my parents drilling me with fighting and May suddenly drilling me with *Uh-mare-eh-can* customs and beliefs and traditions. All of those girls had found a way to balance happily within their two worlds, while we existed almost solely in our own, which was somewhere between Here and There and neither and nowhere.

Is that why May thought we were taken? Because our parents weren't born in that place? All of her efforts yet That Woman's motive had less to do with us being children of immigrants, and everything to do with us being fatherless. Her father left before she was born, unable to handle the responsibility of being husband and father.

Karr's eyes are changing from red to slate to purple as he watches me brooding. Maybe He didn't have enough time to fill me with an unshakable outpouring of happiness and life, but Karr and Nightmare and Blaze are now. I give Karr a weak smile but stay where I am, bundled tightly amidst people I can never call Others.

Karr continues to pick on the shy teenage couple, and my emotions vary as I watch their every glance. The grain of Something Growing surrounds them, brimming out of their awkwardness, shooting from their embarrassed looks, seeping through their nervous smiles. The memory of themselves at that stage plays across the faces of their parents. Oh, that initial unease, the easy, thrilling nervousness, and then that moment when it's just no longer there and you suddenly feel powerful and free.

Karr struggles to both watch me and the toddler he is cupping in his hands. I can see how much it bothers him to not know what I am thinking about. It scares him when I slip so far into my thoughts that he can't find me. I wonder what my face is saying to him.

I twist my ankles to feel my feet sink deeper into the dirt, making sure I am properly anchored and won't run to his side. My thoughts are my own tonight.

I remember the moment the awkwardness left, and all I wanted was *more*. More of Him. To be closer to Him. The frantic urgency from inside the club had vanished as soon as we stood under the moon and snow, and from there everything had slowed down. We wandered, we talked. I slipped my hand into his and he didn't let go until he was gone. It's actually true, that all it took was my hand in his, like Mom and Mihn.

I had thrown snow balls at him and he had tried to hold his balance on one of the massive chunks of ice floating on The Lake. He'd held out his hand and I accepted and stepped onto another one, with him assuring me he wouldn't let me fall in. I didn't merely believe him, I knew without a doubt that he wouldn't. I want to swim in his aura again, to feel that night all over again. We had packed a lot into the time we had. Did we know it could only be temporary? That no one can ever feel happiness like that forever.

If He were to appear now, I wouldn't berate him, scream until my throat clamps shut. I'd cut his teasing off with silence and just wrap my arms around him and hold on, pressing myself into him so tightly that all he will be able to do is keep me from falling as I carry my loss to him. He'll know how much I've missed him, how much I had needed him after he left, and maybe time will reverse, and he won't leave at all.

Nightmare creeps up beside me and nudges me with his muzzle. I wrap my arm under his neck and press my forehead to his cheek, closing my eyes and breathing in the unicorn's smell, dissipating the other smell that has begun to envelop me. I know He's near, I feel him reaching out for me. I press myself closer to the unicorn, waiting for

Nightmare's presence to force Him to admit defeat and back away.

"I was wrong, Nightmare."

[Dare I ask?]

"About the girls in the Other Place. My *friends*. They were my friends, Nightmare, and I didn't understand it."

Somehow while we'd watched Karr play with the children, the suns had fallen and it is night. A woman starts singing, at first a slow, sad peal of lost love to get everyone's attention. When the children and their parents have gathered around her and her song ends, the village's musicians begin to play a livelier tune and everyone yells out and begins to dance. Nightmare and I trot quickly out of the way to Karr's side and I hold Blaze so that he can see.

As the evening stretches into night and the suns began to sigh in their descent, villagers start to retreat back to their own homes and I am faced with an alarming decision: return to the trees with my trio of males, or stay in the company of these new friends.

{Stay, Lira. Sleep in a bed, under a roof for a change.}

"I am not like my mother, Karr. I know about living in a house and being confined between walls."

{Yet like your mother, you don't know how to identify people with good things. Or see a house as a home and not a prison.}

"I don't need to-"

Nightmare rolls his eyes. [You understand that she'll argue with whatever you or even I say to her, no matter how she truly feels.]

"I will not."

They both fix me with a good long sardonic stare until satisfied that it had sunken in. I suck my lips into my mouth and turn away.

"Fine. Nalee has already invited us to stay. Maybe......maybe I will. Just for tonight." In truth, my head is pounding fire into my skull and eyes and down the sides of my neck. Very tiny spots in my vision are fuzzy gray. My thoughts from the night have also subdued me to a dangerous vulnerability. I look at the trees with wariness; not wariness of them or even Who hides among them, but of me. I'd let down walls I'm not ready to have breeched.

36

"KARR! KARR!"

I shoot up from somewhere distant and dense, sweating and frantic, reaching. *Reaching.* My mind is caught between the house in The Other Place and trees. But my familiar earth-borne scents and the sounds of tree branches swaying over my head, the feel of cool soil and the comfort of Karr or Nightmare around my body has all been replaced by the odd foreboding dark that lives only in unfamiliar enclosed spaces. My hysteria amplifies.

"Nightmare!"

Blaze starts screaming beside me and I throw myself into a shield around him, the sound of a bullet echoing in my ears and my shoulder reverberating the feel of being shot with each repetitive *pop!*. A hand falls down on my burning shoulder and I scream, grabbing Blaze and propelling myself backward into a wall.

{Lira! Lira what's wrong?} The ground starts thumping with large footsteps that throw me back toward the galloping earthquake the unicorns on the hills had created.

"Lira, it's me, Nalee. You're having a nightmare, sweetie. You're in my house, remember? You found my daughter in the trees while you stood there with your dragon and unicorn. Remember? And you brought Illie back to me and I brought you to my house, and you took a nice long bath in my tub, and we ate dinner, and we watched your dragon play with the village children with my daughter Illie perched atop his head. Then at night everyone gathered and danced and sang and you watched, and you came back to my home to sleep in a bed for a change, because you've been wandering the trees for a very long time. So I made up Illie's bed for you and Blaze, and Illie and I are sleeping in the next room in my bed, and your Others are on the other side of my door threatening to tear my house down because you had a nightmare and were screaming, but you're fine. You're fine."

By the time she is done speaking, I am coherent enough to think. I let my head fall back onto the wall and all the air escapes out of my lungs. As I breathe more even, so does Blaze. The gloomy dark inside the house clears and I see Nalee's outline before me, as well as Illie's terrified face from the wall she has anchored herself to.

The thumping ground stops and Karr and Nightmare bellow for me outside, demanding Nalee open the door.

"They *are* pretty damn intrusive, aren't they?" Even in the dark, I can see her roll her eyes and smile. "I'll go settle the little boys down while you sit there and wake up a little better. Illie's going to light a candle, isn't she? Because why?"

"Because nightmares are so fragile, even a small candle's light is strong enough to banish them away." Saying that ends the child's fear and she smiles at me before turning back into her mother's room for a candle. She returns and sets the lit candle on the floor beside the bed and sits down beside me. She brushes the hair from my face and runs her thumbs over my temple slow and constant in an easy rhythmic pattern.

"First a light and then a touch, and troubled dreams lose their clutch. First a light and then a touch, and troubled dreams lose their clutch. First a light and then a touch, and troubled dreams lose their clutch," she whispers. "Better?" she asks hopefully. I nod, fitting on an appropriate smile.

Nalee returns and kisses her daughter's head. "Perfectly done, Illie. You are now a champion nightmare vanquisher."

{Oh thank the stars! When can she start working on the big one?}

Illie meets my eyes in the dim glow of candlelight and giggles into her hand. "He's so funny! But it's not nice to talk about Nightmare like that. It's not his fault that's his name."

"You're right, sweetie. I'll yell at Karr later."

{Yell at me now so I know you're alright. What were you dreaming about that made you scream like that, love?}

"Illie, now that you've cured Lira of her bad dream, give her a hug and go back to bed."

She hugs me, Blaze, and her mother before proclaiming she has to go outside and hug Nightmare as Karr had hurt his feelings, and Karr because she still loves him even if he is mean to her other friend. As soon as she is out of sight, I cradle my head in my hands. The pounding from earlier this evening has only grown.

"I'll just sit here with you now that it's quiet. Both Illie and I have endured our time of bad dreams, and silence and nearness can be as medicinal as shedding the pain." Though her words are sincere and meant for me, it works like Illie's nightmare charm and silences the beasts outside. I can only give a slight nod of my head to show her my appreciation while I concentrate on letting the images fade back to where they'd come from.

The house settles back into its mid-night silence. Nothing moves outside, not even wind, and the infrequent sounds on the inside of the house is Blaze nursing, Illie sleeping in the next room, and Nalee just sitting beside me. Silence, it seems, paints a picture according to density. I can go through it and see the layout of Nalee's house, see her daughter dwarfed and safe on her bed, see Karr laying outside the door and Nightmare standing still as a statue waiting. I can see Blaze, and Nalee beside me, all by the degree of silence and shadow. It reminds me of when Mom and Mihn had sat at my side day and night after......

I start to cry and Nalee gets up, returning with a worn grey cloth. "Lira," she speaks softly. Her tone is a little off. "Your eyes are bleeding."

[What?] both males exclaim, Karr lifting his head up sharply from where they are watching- through the door they'd kept open after Illie had returned inside- and he hits his head on the lintel above, rattling the house with his force. Something somewhere clatters to the floor and shatters.

"Mama?" Illie calls, sounding frightened again.

"Dragon, you're destroying my house and scaring my child."

[I don't think she likes you anymore, *dragon*.]

{*No, when I'm referred to by my species, it's affectionate. When Lira or I or anyone else calls you beast or demon or unicorn, it is because we really truly hate you.*}

[She loves me now.]

{*She's always loved me.*}

"Mama!"

Nalee scolds the two as she heads to her room, "Neither of you are allowed to stand outside my home and bicker like children. One more insult and I'm shutting that door, understand?"

She returns with Illie in her arms, the child's head upon her mother's shoulder and her arms and legs wrapped tightly around her. "I'm sorry, Lira, I'd heat up some tea if there was a fire." Summer has arrived in the trees, and the last few days have been bright and sunny and too warm for fires. But she'd made one for me this morning for Blaze's and my bath, and might have kept the flames going had the rest of the day not interrupted her. All that lay in wait are embers burned down. Somewhere inside, they might still be hungry, but not enough to ignite.

There is a low roar, like water, running down the inside of her chimney, and then a small fire bursts aflame on the morning's old kindling. Small enough to boil some water, and small enough not to add any heat to the summer night.

"Dragons," Nalee exclaims, clutching Illie and spinning around when the sudden burst makes her jump. She is rewarded by Karr's answering chuckle.

"He was being helpful, Mama."

"Scaring me is not helpful."

I take a deep breath, my eyes closed, my body stilled. Though my head rolls like The Lake during a violent winter storm, my back is sturdy as trees in the same storm, and holds me up. I look at the cloth in my hand, the drops of blood jumping out against the soft grey of the threads with the twinkling light of the candle. "Nalee," I begin, unsure how to finish. "Thank you. I'm so sorry."

"There's nothing to be sorry for, Lira. We can't control our dreams."

"I was poisoned," I blurt, still looking at the drops of my red.

Nalee's and Illie's eyes are large in the dimness as they take that in. "I think your nightmares require much more than one candle," Nalee reasons.

I smile. I laugh and the remaining threads of my dreams untie and return to wherever they'd come from. "I have to leave. I can't stay- these walls. Roof."

I'd looked at the old woman's house and Nalee's as warm and inviting during the day. But the darkness in Nalee's house has become smothering and the walls and roof are closing down around me. I was trapped in that room. There had been no escape, no safe place to hide. But in the open, in the trees......

My life in the Other Place was nearly hermitic. I'd kept myself segregated from choice before she was gone, and kept myself imprisoned after. I couldn't move, couldn't breathe, but now I can't stop moving. I *can't* stop moving.

Something of my thoughts must have flashed across my face because she nods in complete understanding.

"Lira, of course you can leave if you need to. But know that you don't have to. I'll keep you for however long you'd want."

"And I'll keep Karr!"

{*Absolutely!*}

"I'm not leaving. I just need some air. I need to sleep outside." My head's still pounding and I'm nauseous as though I haven't slept in days.

"And stars. Stars are brighter than candles," Illie declares, earning a hug and kiss from her mother before being returned to her feet.

"Here, take some blankets with you."

I shake my head and grin, "Thank you, but I have a Karr. He radiates warmth when he's not destroying people's homes."

{*Lira's more cold-blooded than dragons. Keeping her warm isn't easy.*}

"So a dragon actually has more use than just teasing teenagers and scaring house-dwellers?" Nalee ponders.

[Lira, you need to keep her as a friend.]

{*Very funny. And yes, I do have other purposes in life. Terrorizing humans and unicorns and are just bonuses.*}

"Mama, that wasn't nice."

"Oh, I was being nice. He threatened to tear my roof off, tripped my heart, and scared you awake when he slammed his giant skull into my doorframe, which I'm very attached to."

{*I think I prefer when villagers were terrified of me. She's being a little mean.*}

"Karr, people have bad dreams and wake screaming. It's normal. You can't threaten to shred the house of the person who graciously offered me a bed for the night."

{*I will argue that dream being normal for as long as you can stand, love, because it wasn't. It didn't feel like a dream to me, but a memory.*}

He drops his voice, but a change in his depth, an increase, an acute denseness to his voice, tells me he is speaking to only me: {*It kills me that you don't trust me enough to tell me.*}

I trust you, Karr. But there's things about me I don't want you to know.

He's come to know when I'm done speaking, and he's never pressed me for anything I won't offer willingly. I know that he hasn't abandoned his interest or that he forgot, but that, for awhile more, my secrets are secrets that will remain mine.

{*Nalee,*} his focus expands to include everyone once again. The sudden inclusion opens like an explosion through my skull, and I have to sit down again. I wince and clutch my head, praying the migraine will end soon. I send both 'boys' a sharp *I'm fine!*, knowing they are about to ask. {*Nalee, I'm sorry I threatened your house and scared you with a little fire and my giant skull. How can I make it up to you?*}

I pull my hand away from my face to see what Nalee will do. Her head is tilted as she weighs his offer, her mouth puckering out. "I will get back to you on that," she replies.

Instead of discouraging him, his eyes flash moonlight with the promise of a dare. What a dragon. {*Make it a good request.*}

"Oh, I will."

{*Good.*}

I let my eyelids fall closed, but the heat of four non-human eyes attacks my skin. To get to them, I need to walk through the echo of my screams bouncing off the hallway walls, off these walls. I force myself to my feet. "Nalee......" I can't finish. I have to get back to them immediately. I make it to them in a couple rushed strides, but stop when I stand both inside the house and out. I clutch the doorjamb and turn back to Nalee. My rambling thoughts from earlier come tangling around us, stealing into the open door and bouncing off the walls, sparking candlelight when it hits Nalee and Illie. "Come with us," I invite. "Would you like to?"

"Sleep outside?" Nalee asks, almost confused.

"Mama, can we? Can we please?"

A faraway smile tugs at the other mother's mouth. "It's right there, isn't it? Right outside my own door. I look at 'outside' all day long and forgot when we built the house what being outside meant. I would love to sleep outside with you and the boys tonight."

[I don't really like being called a 'boy'. Or lumped into the same terminology as *him*.]

"You threatened to burst through my door, too. You don't get a say-so in what I call you."

{Lira, keep her as a friend.}

37

NALEE SPREADS THE BLANKETS she'd brought and makes herself and Illie a bed for what remains of the night, as Karr scrapes out a place for a fire and I fill it with fallen branches. Illie comes close to him and crouches down, blowing with all her might as he is about to set the wood on fire. His face near hers, he casts lavender-flecked eyes down upon her and blows softly, a steady orange stream of flames that root into the kindling quickly. Illie jumps up and claps her hands, believing in the way only children do that she'd breathed fire and not the dragon.

Nightmare curls around me and presses me into his side with his head. [How are you?]

"Tired," I answer, leaning my throbbing head against his.

[Alright,] he responds, leaving it there. He walks closer to where our new companions have already settled down and descends to the ground, tucking his legs beneath his body, snug as a cat. I retrieve Blaze from where I'd set him and lower myself gratefully down beside Karr. I nestle my head down into the earth, trying to breathe the tightness away. Closing my eyes brings up images I don't want to relive again, so I open them to stare into the fire.

But the light is sharp and I shift my gaze down away from the glare toward Nightmare, and find Nalee sitting up close to him, her legs laying relaxed on her left. She reaches out tentatively at first, but when her fingers feel his skin beneath them, they flatten with more confidence until she is running her hand down his face again and again. In the moon and starlight, I spot a few tears traveling from her eyes into her smile.

I've seen that in most of the women we've come across-the effect he has. What is it about unicorns that turns women sad and happy all at once? How can they remind us of who we were when we were girls and free of the troubles of being women?

I was not as immune to him as I may have believed. My day had been the day before we'd found Blaze and he and I had run and run through the trees. That moment when I turned to him and buried my head into his neck, he had ceased being a beast, a demon, and especially a nightmare.

Karr wraps his tail around me, pulling me close. *{Will you talk to me now, out here?}*

Why is it so important for you to know what I dream about?

{Because your screams have woken me up on many nights but neither you nor the demon tell me why. Your screams, love......}

I don't want you to know my nightmares. I don't want you to know what happened to me before you found me. With you, I remember what I use to feel like, and I can almost believe that life is good. I can pretend that you don't see me as damaged or as broken as everyone else does.

{Love, I care about you. You aren't damaged or broken and no one views you that way. But something is hurting you, and I want to be able to find a way to stop it. I want to do my

damndest to help you feel safe and certain that life is good regardless of our nightmares. I'm tolerating that other one fairly well, aren't I? Even though he follows me in the day as well.}

It's not the same.

{I know it's not. But it doesn't change what I-}

It's not your responsibility to banish my stains away, Karr. I love that you want to, but I'm not going to let you.

{It's not my 'responsibility', which is an absurd way to term it by the way, but you need to accept that when others do things to help you, it's out of love. So let me love you.}

I let my tears fall to the earth, unable to answer. *{If you won't share your nightmares, share your dreams}*, he suggests lightly, trying to change the mood.

Dreams.....are only dreams. Nightmares-

{Don't exist right now. Right now, you're going to dream. Of someplace you feel safe. Someplace where you are unquestionably happy. And let it grow so strong that it follows you into day and every night.}

Dreams to follow into day.

Immediately, I think of where I am right now- with him. How can anything haunt me with a dragon by my side? I think of the trees overhead and Nightmare and new friends sleeping close by. I think of the wind stirring around Karr's scales before spreading his warmth over me, and the gentle sound of Blaze snoring beside me. And red, red all around me, changing the black that normally fills closed eyes into a comforting maroon.

As I drift further into sleep and my headache loosens its hold, I dream of the red moonglow on snow, and the waves rocking like a lullaby.

> *The damn dress is on me again, only this time it's the color of Karr's scales. His black cape is draped*

over me, and I lay in His arms bathed in both of my Guardians' colors.

He shifts in his sleep and curls His arm around me, pulling me back in tight, whispering to me to keep dreaming. Dreams are what reality is made of, while nightmares are only of things past, things that no longer are real, that are so fragile, that sunslight, even candlelight or a child's touch is strong enough to vanquish them. If so fragile with these little things, how much more insignificant do they become with Him there to guard me?

But he is also so fragile that a single sun can vanquish him. I begin to pull away from him while he pleads: This dream can follow into day. As I pull from him, His fingers trail down my side until they stop at my waist. He holds me still and kneels up with me, sliding his arms around me and pulling me to him smooth and fluid as smoke. I focus on the shape and strength of his hands- one curled around my hip and the other around my shoulder, and the way he and his surrounding human maleness is so much more calming than Karr's and Nightmare's constant need for dominance is. But I pull away, my eyes on the coming sun, and his body snaps away into air, the air raging on the Hills, where two suns prove even stronger than one, keeping us far apart. The Soldiers on the unicorns racing toward me are now the men who'd invaded my home-

-and I shoot awake with the same propulsion and sound as their gun, sweating and panting until

the trees and fire and Blaze and Karr's red wing
come back into view.

{Dear love,} Karr murmurs, sounding shocked.

Afraid laying down will bring Him back again, I sit up
and curl my legs up against my chest and turn into the
dragon's body, my head on my knees, my right hand
clutching my left shoulder to keep it from exploding.

*What are candle lights, suns, or faulty dreams when I have
your red?* I ask him softly. Even while I'm trying to
convince myself of that, He's raining down around me,
and I'm certain that should I open my eyes and turn my
head from Karr, I'll see Him standing there behind me.

*

The pain in my head doesn't lessen with the day. Rather,
the sunlight makes it worse, sending it down into my
teeth, confusing my eyes so that it doesn't know what it is
seeing or where to place things. My body is stiff and sore
as though I'd slept too long. Nalee walks me to the village
Healer after breakfast proves impossible to accomplish.

The Healer asks me to lay down, and I eye her bed
with a large amount of nervousness. Not so much the bed,
but the walls and roof and solid floor encasing it.

"Here, Lira, let me take Blaze outside and you get
yourself seen to."

I tighten my hold on him and turn him sharply out of
their reach. "No. No, when I let her go......" My eyes well
up, realizing what I'd released, knowing there is no way to
take it back. "We're fine. He can stay with me."

Both Nalee and the Healer stare at me, trying to read into my words.

"Yes, dear, the baby can stay. Would you like a basket for him to sleep in, or do you prefer he lay with you? All I'm going to do is spread a salve on your forehead to draw the ache away, although now I suspect this migraine stems from something else, doesn't it?"

"She said she had been poisoned," Nalee offers. "And she woke up screaming last night."

"Yes, I heard. We all did. We came out running afraid the Soldiers- but your Guardians told us to go back to bed."

"I'm sorry." I bite my lip, agonizing over being heard by so many-

They feared Soldiers had found me?

"Sit down, Lira, and tell me about this poison. It could be related, or nothing at all. But it will help me know what to prepare for you."

"It was a powder. She blew it into my face- but I'm feeling better. It doesn't happen as often anymore."

"What doesn't happen as often?"

"The headaches. The nausea. The cramps. The blackouts and the dizziness. The nightmares have been better since Karr found us."

"But last night you slept away from the dragon?"

I nod.

"He guards more than just your person then, doesn't he? Who poisoned you?"

"A Healer. A Seer. She was Unicorn. But then Nightmare saved me and he drugged my water. Karr came when the Soldiers-" I cut myself off again. I don't want those things known.

"And the other thing," she asks gently. "Who did you let go?"

I shift Blaze in my arms and peer into his large black eyes. *He will lead you out of the dark, love.*

"That's alright. I think I know what we can try. Nalee, open the doors and the windows and let the suns in for her. And then come back after lunch."

Nalee smiles and waves reassuringly as she obeys the other woman and leaves. The Healer, Lapta, helps me lay down and tucks Blaze securely at my side nearest her wall. I listen to the sounds she makes as she moves around her house and grinds up whatever she's chosen to use. The smells that greet my nose are like mint and lemon, and something earthy, and something that makes me think of fire. She spreads a warm, grainy mixture over my forehead and tells me to lie there until it dries, which may be awhile, and then she walks away, taking a seat somewhere by the door. The heavier smells fade as the paste cools, and I fall asleep.

She wakes me later with just a small tug on my shoulder and washes her medicine away. "You slept. How do you feel?"

I smile. "Much better. Thank you."

She holds up a blue pouch. "Mix this with your water or your food at night and it should help with the stomach aches. And this one," she holds up her other palm to show a black pouch before dropping both into my hand, "should help with pain. You've been clutching your shoulder since Nalee brought you."

Nalee walks in and waits with Illie's hand in hers. Lapta hugs us both and gives Illie a little treat and Blaze a small toy before we leave.

"Nalee, please, don't tell Karr or Nightmare anything I said."

She has a more thoughtful look on her face than she'd had when she'd dropped me off. "There are things we've experienced no one has a right to know the details of. But I'm worried about you, Lira. I worry about what you are afraid to let them know. However, I have noticed how overly protective they are of you. I've seen how they reacted to you having a bad dream. I don't want to know how they'd respond to you being even a little bit sick. I think your humanness scares them. It makes them feel vulnerable because they can't protect you from the internal things that haunt you. I know what that feels like, too."

I am in a better spirit when night finds us still there. The Healer's magic has worked enough to make smiling, light, and noise bearable. I'd never before slept at any of the villages, always ensuring we were out before dinner was offered. This not only makes the first time I'd slept in a village, but the first time I'd stayed for a second day, going now into a third. I can't return to walls for fears of last night's repeat, but Nalee and Illie join us outside once again......as well as the majority of the village, and my aunt, Saramine, who'd crammed herself into the only remaining open space.

Karr is doing something a little on the sneaky side with the children. They keep disappearing and returning with candles he has them set in the ground. The adults whisper to each other and shrug, laughing curiously but otherwise either watchful or helpful according to the children's instructions. Soon there's candles in every conceivable space within the open area to the west of the village my pair had helped clear two days ago. Saramine sits with her side leaning against several trees, making them bend a little deeper into the forest while she watches. While my aunt is gentle and friendly, she is not the sort of dragon that behaves like a children's playground as Karr does, so none are even asking to climb or to have a flight. The older girls not involved with the candles are especially drawn to her more feminine grace, though, and all sit calmly around her, the poor teen Karr had been teasing giving me a shy smile as she joins them.

The candles are all set in perfect time with the last streak of day transforming to night, and the village falls into that fascinating sort of dark. You can only make out the brightness of a few clothes, some smiling teeth, and the moon and stars shimmering off the dragons' scales and Nightmare's firefly-encased golden horn. I settle myself near Saramine to feed Blaze his last feeding of the day.

Karr blows a small thread of fire, making all the villager's eyes big as suns and their faces open and glowing as moons. One by one, the candles light in a sort of wave; somehow, even the ones his flame can't have possibly reached without scorching some people. The effect is very much like the little bonfires that had sprouted during my first attempt at fire-making. No one elicits a sound, not even a sigh or an 'Ohhh'.

Karr frowns, looking from the candles to the children to Illie to Nightmare, and finally back to Illie. *{Illie, it's not vanquishing my nightmare.}*

The unicorn whips his head around and growls, and the night erupts in such laughter when Karr's joke is understood that the candles are momentarily blown out. I try really hard not to laugh. Karr turns to me and shrugs his giant dragon shoulders, and I remember how hard the unicorn had been laughing at me during that fire-making episode, and I laugh with ease along with everyone else until my breath is lost and my eyes can't see through the mirth-filled tears.

The village soon quiets down and multiple conversations begin, a candlelight of voices to match the little lights the people are re-lighting by hand. The girls sitting around Saramine turn to Blaze, who's been a fascination for them. The youngest child in the village is just beginning to walk and none of the women are currently pregnant. A baby is suddenly more of a rarity than a dragon or a unicorn in their eyes. They want to hold him and play, they beg to change his diaper for me. But I can't let him leave my hands, so they play peek-a-boo, take turns waving so he learns. As he's learned where his eyes, nose, and toes are, they call each out to quiz him and he claps and laughs when he keeps getting it right- while he sits in my lap.

Saramine is fascinated with him as well. My mother was a toddler when she came to them, and, I learn, none of them had seen the other children my mother had had. The dragons are bewildered by how tiny a human youngling is. He's no longer the starving newborn that I had found. What would their impression have been if they'd seen him that day? His body now rolls in lovely chunky curves, he smiles and holds his head up, shoves his whole hand into his mouth, and he laughs and shrieks when he sees any of the dragons.

It's as though That Place doesn't exist. I look around me, surrounded by Home's people, with Home's tree pressing her bark into my back and tangling on my hair, with a child of Home in my arms whom I call mine, and my dragon before me, and my aunt beside, and my unicorn pouting in the trees; and the Other Place is a faint tug in my mind, and it's frightening.

Nalee sits down near me but my thoughts keep rolling.

Saramine turns her head down toward me. *{Yes, love. Why don't you fly with any of us?}*

I blink. What?

All eyes pin me where I sit, and Karr's chuckle fills my head- I'm blushing, of course. My eyes dart a glare his way.

"What did you say to them?"

{My plight. How I'll be forever tormented until you get over your fear of heights.}

"Tormented," I snort. My uncles have been unrelenting in their challenge of him Cliff Jumping. I see the thrill of actually taking them on exploding in his eyes, but he decided to twist things against himself and state that he would accept only after I fly with him.

"You seriously think I'm afraid of heights?" I'm a teen once again, having a sleep-over with the girls at Inez's house and retreating to the corner while the rest played Truth or Dare. The other girls were never allowed to back out, but they pretended that I played when I never did. Were they as afraid to ask for my truths as I was to tell them?

"Are you?" one of the girls asks impatiently.

{If you're not afraid of heights, then why?}

"I have Blaze."

Karr roars with laughter. *{I'm being called a coward for allegedly 'hiding' behind you, but you're actually using the little troll-boy as a shield. For shame, love. The demon or anyone here can watch over him for you.}*

{He's so little! I'd love to care for him,} Saramine offers. *{You go play with Karr.}* I frown at the laugh in her eyes, and the fact that she'd ineffably inflated Karr's confidence.

{I would prefer that,} Karr says. Nightmare snarls. *{The demon might turn him into a girl. Or you can throw the youngling into your sling and bring him with.}*

"I won't do that!"

{Ah, so you don't trust me.*}*

"I do trust you-"

{Mmm-hmm. It's such a beautiful night, don't you agree Sara?}

{Every night is beautiful.}

{Oh, so very true. Let's go, love, and then I can shut your uncles up about Cliff Jumping.}

"It feels wrong."

{How is flying wrong?} Saramine asks, shocked at the thought.

By now, all of the villagers are listening to the conversation, their heads swinging from each of the dragons to me. Now, though, everyone's waiting for me to answer.

{Now you're insulting your very own family, love.}

"I am not! And you both know that. I can't declare you carry me. I can't just climb onto you and demand......demand......" I am doing a lousy job rationalizing to them, and I know it, but I can't explain. If he was human, I wouldn't demand he carry me. And why would I agree to it if he did? Yes, carry me because......you're bigger? Taller than me? Stronger? Male?

{I'm a dragon, and you're not demanding anything as presumptuous as you seem to take it. I'll carry you because I can fly and you can't.}

"That still-"

{If I was human, by the way, I'd just pick you up and carry you off-}

"Stop reading-" I cut myself off sooner than he had. The stars are sparkling in his eyes- a skyfull of red stars- and I can just about see his brain turning, and I am not liking the way it's going. *Do not dare him.* "I can't fly with you, Karr. Any of the dragons. It feels wrong. I have my own two feet and will carry myself."

My aunt shrugs. *{You're both doing a lousy job convincing each other.}*

{Well, I'll have to work on changing that. Or......}

{People......they do this, Niece. They gather around at the end of their day and they talk and they share. Dragons fly, Lira. We fly together. That is how we bond. And you are part of us. It's not about size or strength or gender. We want you with us and as you don't have wings of your own, we'll use ours to carry you.}

38

MORNING WAKES QUIET, with everyone rising at about the same time and going back to their homes to start on their daily tasks. Saramine leaves as well, and Nalee, Illie, my Guardians and I eat a quiet breakfast out by the trees. Villagers- friends- return with gifts of clothing and food, intuitively knowing that I can't stay any longer.

They give me fierce hugs that render me shaken and tearful, and each kiss the top of Blaze's head and give Karr a companionable yet still awed pat on his gleaming shoulder; to Nightmare, a respectful bow of their heads.

{Nalee,} Karr calls. I turn around, not realizing he had left with the waves of people swirling us. He hops to us from the trees on only three legs. At first I worry he'd injured his right front arm, but then see that it's holding something. Nalee's mouth is trembling in an expectant smile. Her eyes are tearing and she quickly covers her mouth with her hands. Illie is jumping up and down, tugging excitedly on her mother's shirt.

Before he opens his hand, I know what he holds- I can smell it. His movement is sending the shrub's oil into the air, and everyone around takes a deep collective inhale, exhaling with a sigh. Rosemary.

{As I promised,} he bows and presents a young but full and hardy rosemary whose roots are carefully wrapped in a red cloth that almost shimmers. I tilt my head and ponder it before realizing why it is strange. My eyes shoot to the dragon's placid pewter-rimmed red ones. He didn't wrap its roots with his huge, talon-tipped dragon fingers. And the red cloth is like the damn dress- it wasn't made in the normal way. It shimmers red and the way it's wrapped around the root ball, it looks like the moon did That Night. Rosemary is for remembrance, as well as love and loyalty.

"Karr, when did you do this?"

{While you were tending Lira yesterday. I found the patch easily with your directions, and returned before either of you knew I'd been gone.}

"Our first house had these nearby," Nalee murmurs, though I'm sure she must have told Karr that already. This must be the thing she was going to demand in retribution for his banging his head on her door frame and threatening to destroy her house after my nightmare.

The smell is overwhelming and I can't help but feel there's a message for me wrapped up in its arrival. "Back in the lowlands- the 'lovelands', we use to say because that's where Illie's father and I lived and fell in love before we got the itch to wander this way. Every summer we'd go back to see our family and we'd bring back a branch. I haven't made the journey since he......"

Nalee laughs nervously, hugging the rosemary and grabbing me in the same embrace. "Your legs and soul are itching to keep mobile, aren't they? I remember, so I won't keep you with my nostalgia. Thank you, Lira. Thank you for returning Illie to me.

"I hope you'll bring her back this way soon and often," she tells Karr. "I want to see you."

I can only smile, knowing so little of my future to promise such a thing.

{I promise.}

As much as our presence may have altered their courses, so too has my time with them altered mine.

*

"I need to sit down for a bit, Nightmare, that's all." Dusk is instead, dust, misting across the sky slowly, turning the blue into shades of lilac and pink and grey. We hadn't stopped for lunch and my body's yelling at me for it. Karr sets down a handful of branches before I can go about collecting them. I sit meekly back and watch the fire, nursing Blaze and biting slow chunks from some bread the village had gifted me.

{You need more than bread, Lira.}

"I think I was wrong, Karr. What if I could have told them the truth about us?"

{Told who the truth about who?}

"May was always trying to make me more of That Place than I wanted to be. I didn't understand her obsession with trying to change my clothes and hair, makeup, trying to teach me That Place's history and mannerisms, their music and their talk to eliminate the accent she said I had. She'd drag me shopping and to movies and make me pour through magazines and I allowed it all without paying any attention or letting anything sink in. They were all almost like us- their parents had fled their homelands for various reasons and settled There. She insisted we were *im-a-grants* just like the rest of them. But unlike me, the girls all adapted and could live in both their parents' distant homes as well as that place we were born in. I was afraid to.

"But the more I watch the people in these villages you drag me into-"

{I don't drag. Ok, not physically.}

"You're not trying to change me or try to get me to forget myself, are you?"

{No, love.}

"She was trying to protect me, I think. She chose to forget that Those People had come for her as well as me. Neither of us could change the circumstances of our mothers' lives, but she could change how she fit into her family's adopted country.

"They saw it as unforgivable, Those People; it was reprehensible that women would bear children without a father to oversee it, or that they believed themselves to be capable of raising us alone. Why was that such a threat? Her father......her father......" my voice cracks, no longer speaking of May.

[Lira.]

{I don't understand what you're saying, Lira.}

"We were children. But it made me cling harder to the fact that we didn't belong there, while it made her try harder to fade into the place, to make me fade into the place as well. It wasn't only me, either. She was older than all of us and she watched us all like a dragon mother. Maybe I should have told her."

[Are you sure she didn't already know?] Nightmare asks.

"What? How could she know such a thing? That we were from another world? That the dragons my mother painted and the stories she would tell them were all true?

She was so furious with me for That Night. I think she was scared that They'd come back and taken me away. And I didn't see that. I should have told her the truth but I was so wrapped up in myself I didn't think that her mind needed to be eased just as much. She was there when I was......when she was......"

{Lira-}

[She's saying that she was targeted There, rockbrain. She stood out and was punished for it. They tried to take her from her mother when Lira was young, but Elaar was able to find where they'd taken her and get her back. They had tried to take this friend of hers, but Lira fought them so she could get away.]

{Were you there?} the dragon demands angrily, smoke trailing from his mouth down to me, making Blaze cough a little.

[Of course not.]

{Then why can't you let her answer?}

[She's not able to, is she? Do you want to know or not? Does it change what happened if you hear it from me instead of her? You demand she go into these villages where she stands out once again. Now you know why that's threatening to her.]

{Oh don't make it sound like I'm the bad one. You're demanding she go just as much as everyone else.

{And I've yet to resort to dragging you, just so we're clear on that. But love, what you're speaking of happened a long time ago in a different place among different people. You do stand out- look at who you travel with. But look at the reaction you receive. It's not the same. And regardless, you've got the both of us now. No one will threaten you, I promise.}

"It's not that at all, Karr. I was wrong. The girls and their families were our village, but I could only classify them as Others."

39

IT'S RAINED NON-STOP THE LAST THREE DAYS. None of my fires will keep, but Karr's do, so I've regretfully fallen back to allowing him to set them. He's wisely kept his thoughts about masculine and draconic superiority to himself. Blaze is bundled, dry and warm inside his sling, further covered inside the patchwork quilt given to me by the old woman. Whose name I never asked for. Again.

The rain washes down my face, warm and steady. Coming from both sky and trees, it's heavier than it probably originally is. I like it. It's a change from sun and blue skies. It makes everything smell wonderful. My pants are soaked to my knees and I want to throw off my cape and dance. I *want* to *dance.*

The rain is nothing, Blaze and I are both enjoying it, but Karr's been upset about it all morning, insisting Blaze and I go into a village somewhere nearby until it stops.

"Why do you keep arguing with me? I'm not going!" I yell again, my upper body leaning forward to establish my resolution. "I am no more possessed by a dragon than I am a unicorn. You cannot force me to do what you want me to only because you are male, or dragon, or bigger than I am.

If I want to stand out in the rain, I'm standing out in the rain!"

Karr is fuming mad, trying so hard to keep from snarling that the counter-tenseness in his lips makes him grimace. Smoke puffs from his nose and his belly rumbles, but I hold my ground. Nightmare rather enjoys that I am arguing with the dragon, and sits himself out, remarkably quiet, watching amusedly.

{Yes, you are*! You need to. Nightmare agrees.}*

[This is not my battle. I'm wise enough to know when not to throw my overly-glorified weight around.]

{You self-serving demonic bastard. She's drenched! You're going to stand stupid on your dainty little feet and not tell her she needs some new, dry clothes and some food? Nuts and berries and what I can scrounge up for her is not adequate!}

[Then maybe you need to work on scrounging up some better options. Dragon.]

"I ate rather well this morning," I interrupt irritably, if they care to remember I am still here. Fire cakes and fried potatoes, with cheese and fruit on the side, and tea flavored with wild raspberries.

I wait tensely for Karr's rebuttal, unsure of what he may have noticed. Aside from the usual cough and headaches, I woke with an odd feeling of over-fullness and was slightly disoriented. To drown it out, I'd prepared all the food we had, making myself a feast. I'd devoured it all without any problem, and the unsettling feeling was washed away with the food. My perception righted itself, but I know that I was quieter than usual while trying to decide whether or not to be concerned, hoping neither of the pair had noticed anything was amiss.

{I've never seen you eat so much.}

"I was hungry."

{Well, I enjoyed seeing you eat like that, and I want to see you feast all the time, but this morning's breakfast was just one meal out of hundreds, Lira. It doesn't amount to anything, especially since, now, there's nothing for the rest of the day. You have to go to a village. Why not stay in a house for a few days again, rest, be with people, get out of the rain while you're there?}

"No."

{The village is a half day's journey away. The rain will be over by then, you won't have to stay long.}

"Then why go? You can fly there and back with a fresh pack of food and clothing before the suns move at all. I'll be dry by then, too."

He growls, which is both funny and quite alarming, as he's never growled at me before. *{You spent three days in Nalee's village. Suddenly it's bad again? It's what your parents did!}*

"Yes, I know it's what my parents did, which makes it all the more unnerving: everyone staring at me, asking where they are. I don't want to be reminded that I'm here and she's not! I hate having to tell everyone over and over that my father is dead. He was never dead to me before, Karr! Here, I feel him murdered again and again. I want to hide. I want to stay like this, with no people. That's *also* what my parents did."

Hidden by the cloak, I am, of course, trembling. *No, no, no.* My body wobbles, as though filling and turning completely into water. Blaze's weight is grinding into my shoulders, making the nerves from there up to my head throb. I'm sweating and both cold and hot. If I collapse, Karr will have won. The food I'd gorged myself on a few hours ago is churning in my stomach, threatening to reappear.

I cannot faint. I've kept this from them long enough that I cannot let them know how much besides that cough I've been hiding from them, especially not right now.

As nonchalantly as I can, I pull off my cape and let it slide to the ground. Turning from Karr, I walk to the unicorn and take Blaze and his sling off of my shoulders and set him down at the unicorn's hooves. I feel lighter, and not completely light-headed. Blaze reaches out through the unicorn's Shield to touch the rain falling just away from him. "You can't make me go, so leave it at that."

[Oh no.]

Silence. *Do not dare him.*

I abruptly cease shaking, remembering quite clearly what he'd said at Nalee's: {*If I was human, by the way, I'd just pick you up and carry you off-*}

Very, very slowly, I turn from the unicorn to face the dragon, finding Karr smiling so broadly I swear he's making himself glow.

{*I can't* make *you?*} he asks, his whole being just about humming with excitement. {*I* can't *make you?*} he repeats for the simple joy or rephrasing his emphasis. Whatever had barred him from doing so in the past is now completely gone.

He walks a few well placed steps away from me. I look up, for the first time aware that we're standing under a perfect patch of nothing. When I look to Karr again, he is hurrying to me.

{*Don't move.*}

He leaps, and as he sails towards me, he grabs me in his hands and shoots upwards.

"Karr!"

{You dared me, love. Remember, I'm bigger. I warned you that I could snatch you up into the sky and set you down wherever I wanted to, didn't I?}

I twist around to try and grasp him around the neck, but his scales are slick with rain and would have been slick regardless. Pressed tightly one upon the other, they're smooth as glass. My arms aren't able to hug around him, anyway.

We burst over the trees and it's not raining at all. All the water in my clothes and hair is blown out from Karr's speed. I can see for miles on every side, my face pressed against his chest. Trees are odd hills colored a darker shade of green. From above, The Forest rolls like waves, though it doesn't seem so tumultuous when on the ground. It goes on for so far that I can't see The Valley at all. I can see the Cliffs, though. Closer than I had thought they were.

Karr whips back westward. Trees forever and ever are so much better than hills going on and on. He rises higher and it's warm. *{Climb to my back. Sit on my neck.}*

It takes more concentration and effort than I had ever imagined to speak and breathe against the force of the air.

Are you crazy! I shoot into his head instead. No wonder dragons don't physically speak. What good would it do when they fly like this?

He slows, bringing his body level. His arms move, pushing me upward. I grab onto the ridge on his back, eyeing it warily. *I can't sit on those!*

{They won't hurt you, I promise.}

The trees are small little shrubs below my feet. The height distorts my perception. I shut my eyes and shake my head, feeling dizzy and nauseous. *Do not faint. Do not fall.* My right foot pulls up and steps into the inside of his elbow. His wings rise and fall in long swoops, but the lullaby they make while I'm grounded is masked in the force and roar of the wind as we soar through at Karr's exhilarating speed. His wings stop and stretch out completely, and he soars on a glide. I push my weight down and pull myself up, using his arm and the ridge on his back and his right wing for leverage and support.

True to his promise, his ridge softens down. My leg slides over his spine, my knees press against his neck, my feet curl under: I am sitting on my dragon's back and we're flying miles above the surface of the earth.

His wings begin to move again, deliberate up and downward strokes. I never realized how great a wingspan he has. Ama had made him seem small, and then Marr came and Karr seemed tiny. But up here, with no one else around, he's just perfect. His wings stretch from one sun to the other and in turn, the suns' light creeps up the thin skin stretched between his wing bones. Red. The sky is red today, yet there's no fear or threat of Him.

I face forward, the whole world stretched out before me, mine to explore. My mouth falls open.

{What do you think?}

I can't answer, but that is the exact response he had wanted. We soar through rain and then out. In again. Out and in, cutting through storms like parting a curtain. He swoops side to side for the fun of it, to see if I'd scream or shriek. My insides follow my body only after he shifts the other way, but I enjoy the rush, the height, he and I alone. I am drenched and then dried by the suns just before diving back into more rain.

My body forgets its tension, and I release my arms from around his neck, begin to sit up, slowly, slowly, letting my fingers slide away till they don't touch him anymore. I inhale, and sit up completely, straighter and surer than when I'm sitting on solid ground.

He weaves and rocks, his body sometimes tipping on either side. My breath stays in the center of my chest. He dives, gliding down and then lifting sharply up to soar just over the trees. Branches tickle the tops of my feet and my chest contracts, freeing my air to let me smile and laugh. I turn my head to look behind us, my hair dancing wildly in my eyes. The Forest falls away, trees and trees and more trees, so clustered together you can't pull one from the other. Trees and trees and more trees, only it isn't like on The Valley- hills and hills and hills. So dense and full, it's no longer a hallway leading straight to me.

Ours is a place of endless possibilities, of this journey I don't ever want to end. Why go into a village? Why be pulled in and tempted to not leave? Why trade this for that? Why do I need people, why did Mom? Isn't us living this way enough for everyone else? Trees and trees and more trees. No need to ever stop.

Karr's tail sails over the tree tops, still distorted in my sight by the height. Focusing on trees makes it look one way, focusing on his tail makes distance appear another way. If I try too hard, it makes me dizzy and stings my eyes. So I stop. His tail does not merely trail behind us, but works as a rudder, carefully directing his body and steadying his balance.

Forward again and the rain is gone. The height no longer bothers me, nor does his slippery-smooth body. We're one. Without realizing it, my body has begun to predict his movements and adjusts to match. My thighs to contract, my back bowing or leaning, my feet tucking or relaxing as he rises or dives. Only my lower body holds me to him, and it's surprising how effortless it is. My arms remain free this way, so I spread them out, palms up to catch the rain, down to merely soar, forward to feel the air go through my fingers. Air the dragon and I create together.

Pulling upward, the trees vanish and there is only sky. And more soft, warm rain. My head cascades back, my face relaxes, eyes close, and I greet and acknowledge each drop of rain that lands and slips off my skin.

The moon is so close I reach out to her. A sun touches my spine, sending a line of heat down my back. I laugh again.

He rises higher, picking up his pace. I spread my arms out wider to match his wings. I am so incredibly stupid. What was I afraid of, to keep refusing him? There is nothing insulting about this, only beauty, only us.

He turns his head to catch my eye and I smile before shifting my gaze to look at everything else- at the entire world he's sharing with me.

From here, I can see everything. I see how he does, almost the way he does. Small gaps in the trees reveal villages. There aren't many, and they're typically spread quite far from each other. Months of travel plotted out in one spark of sight. He's the one plotting our wanderings, which aren't wanderings at all, as I've believed this whole time, but well-concealed directions from one chosen place to another, and all the while I'm left thinking I've been directing where we go.

He flies towards one village just to goad me and then arcs gracefully away before I can yell at him, his right side lifting significantly higher while his left side dips low, bringing my right thigh against my ribs in an attempt to keep myself attached to him and balanced. He levels and glides. Ahead of us are The Cliffs, completely visible, a great stone wall whose top is cut off by clouds. They seem to spread completely from north to south, from one end of the world to the other. They fill my awareness, my sight. Is he taking me there? The Cliffs, The Cliffs......

And then it all goes away.

I gulp, choke. I drop forward and frantically try to grab hold of his neck, his spines, anything, but my hands slip across his scales no matter where I set them. "Karr! Karr, I can't see! Karr! I can't see! Go down! Go down!" I scream, not knowing if he can hear me over the wind.

Trees are gone. Villages and threads of smoke, mountains and moon and suns. Abruptly gone, replaced by an impassive level blue. My body shivers in chills. Blue. Only blue.

And then I am sliding back. My ankles slip over Karr's shoulders, his wing hits my wrist, and my body falls off the tip of his tail and into the blue......

SEAMLESS

"LIRA!" MAY DROPS HERSELF into the chair before me with such force that it slides a couple inches. Anywhere else, the sound of the metal feet scraping across the stone floor would have been an excruciating sound and her sudden appearance might have made me startle, but both reactions are swallowed up and devoured in the roar and constant bounce of the place we are in. It has a name......

"Lira!" she shouts across the table again, interrupting my attempt at remembering. "I didn't bring you here so you could sit and hide at a table!"

"I'm fine!" I scream back, loud enough to shatter my ability to ever speak again.

She pats my hand. "I'm gonna find you a guy."

"May-"

But she is gone again. *Find a guy who'll knock your panties off!*, is the phrase she'd accidentally used before my parents.

I frown, the night's deeper agitation returning. It's not the club, it's not the Others, it's not May. Everything else is *wrong*: the season, the weather, the moon, the air. There's something in the air. It's so full I feel it like foam in my mouth and in my nose, feel it outside my skin, weighed down and sinking around me.

Club, that's where we are. What was I thinking?

I carefully lift the glass of water to my lips, using both my hands in an attempt to quell the violent shaking that is a permanent resident in this whatever place. The tremors stem from the thumping music as much as from the rhythm of the masses of people dancing on the floor below me. Rani makes a brief appearance, jumping up and down to catch my attention. She laughs dismissively when we spot each other, and allows herself to be consumed once again into the horde of dancers. I fall back into my chair and grumble at myself some more. I don't dance. I don't like being among so many Others. Why did I agree to come here? The air is drugged.

In the hours before arriving at the club, I'd blamed the air, blamed my parents, blamed the orange moon for the apprehension I'd been feeling. But sitting here now, I don't think it's any of those things.

The chair jumps with the floor and pushes me forward again and again until I give in and sit forward, touching neither table nor chair back. I am never going to be able to hear, or speak, or have a normal heart rhythm ever again.

I go from hot to cold quickly here, in the outfit all of them had forced me into in the parking lot outside this place. I pull May's jacket off and throw it back on the chair beside me. The shirt I'm wearing is tight, cropped, just barely reaching my waist. I'd frozen in horror when they'd danced it before my eyes. The fabric's thin and stretchy and shimmers a beautiful deep blue, like my grandfather Marr's scales. The front of the shirt dips very low and- added to the tightness over my chest- makes me feel very exposed.

I grab the jacket and put it back on.

The......what did they call them? Dragons, I can never remember......jeans are so tight, I'm still amazed I can sit, though the seams go in places I don't think they should go. I had to bounce myself into them, admittedly surprised at their softness and give. But......my chest is hanging out and my middle is showing. When I stand, it feels as though my rear is on display.

I find myself wishing for those seamless frocks the wizards use to pride themselves on- stupid useless garments that would be at least more forgiving when you are forced to sit for long periods of time. How can they dance in these things? I feel that if I move, the seams on everything I'm wearing will burst and my clothes will all fall off.

A breeze lightly touches the back of my neck, a soft touch of nearly human fingers that travels down my exposed spine. I gasp, a shiver following the touch. When the sensation leaves, I lift my eyes and find a man before me.

"Hey. Hi. May sent me. I'm Ben."

I glance over my shoulder, but the fingers and the body they belong to are nowhere in sight.

Ben ignores my warning glare. "May sent me," he repeats emphatically. "Come on," he jerks his head towards the Others dancing on the floor. "We should dance."

I sit back, folding the jacket over my chest. "I'm......I'm waiting for someone."

He laughs. "You've been sitting here staring for the last couple hours. He ain't coming, dear. So come dance with me."

I shoot him a glare that can rival a dragon's, making him blanch and swallow hard.

"I'll take that as a 'no thank you'," he mumbles, ducking his head and slithering away.

I wait, wait for the chill air to touch me again, to return, to say something, but nothing arrives. I scan again for a window. I want to go outside. I want to see the moon. What color is he now?

The moon was subtly red when I left my room tonight. The color didn't affect me as it had when it was orange. I was afraid when it was orange, even pulling out of its reach. But just as I finished getting dressed (in the clothes the girls then stripped me out of outside), the moon was almost red, and I was compelled to creep back inside my room, into the center of the red as I bid the candles and the songsbox to stay unlit and off. Give me the red moonglow in silence. The glow surrounded me, washing over every surface of a room I would have said moments before that I knew, and had made me shiver.

Absently, I realize my fingers are strangling the dragon charm dangling off my necklace. I release it and force some more water down my throat. There's a girl on the floor with bright green hair somehow frozen atop her head in impressively tall spikes. No matter how hard she bounces her head or how energetically she dances, they don't move.

"Lira! Benjamin De-Something was a perfectly good specimen of a man! Shame on you!" May pulls the chair around the table and slides a little more gracefully down into it.

"I'm fine, May! I'm not interested in meeting anyone!" I scream into the air.

"You are a lost cause, I think." May shakes her head and rolls her eyes, sighing in exasperation as she turns away. The music abruptly stops but the noise only amplifies when a man jumps onto the stage.

"Hey *CHICAGOOOOOO!*" he yells. My ears and chest threaten to burst with the explosion of noise reverberating dangerously inside me: the pounding of feet on the floor, the screaming Others, and the drums from the band on the stage.

"In five more minutes we'll begin the countdown to the end of 1999 and the start of the year two-zero-zero-zero!"

Dragons, when's the drummer going to stop?

The balance in the room shifts again as everyone roars and stomps their feet or hands upon the tables around them. Now I can't hear right. I sip some water, helping my ears pop and relieve the pressure, and sit back. I fidget with the glass.

Rani charges through the crowd and bursts toward the table, sweating, her face flushed, her nearly black eyes bright and lively. The flashing lights make the tiny stone in her nostril sparkle. "Come on, you two! They'll be starting the countdown soon, and if you don't get down there now, you never will!"

"Countdown?" I ask.

"New Year's, Lira! Year 2000! The Year of the *Dragon*! We count down the seconds towards the approach!" May, returning to her usual exuberant self, shouts excitedly into my ear. "I explained all of this to you on the way here!"

The Year of the Dragon. She'd used that phrase at the house. That's what made Mom so withdrawn, so insistent I come here with them tonight. May's explanation of her culture's beliefs- how she and I and some of the girls with us tonight were born in the year of the horse- didn't even sway her. And Mom *hates* all things remotely similar to unicorns.

"Come on!" Rani grabs onto May's hand as well as mine. "Don't forget to think up a New Year's wish!" she calls over her shoulder to me as she pulls us. Her grip on me is weak, though, and my hand slips from hers as she and May run off. The mass of people swarm around me and cut me off from them as they push their way to the stairs. Panicked, I push against the swarm until I am back at the table.

What do I do? Out of breath and disoriented, I look over the balcony but can't spot Inez or Agnes, either. I watch the stairs, but see neither May nor Rani making their way down. Suddenly anxious and edgy, I remove the jacket once again and sit. My leg bounces nervously as my eyes dart. I don't know what I'm anticipating.

The Year of the Dragon.

On the car ride here, the girls had argued about something called 'Why Two Kay' crashing, the world ending, and I'd relaxed into my seat, soothed by that very thought. Is that what it'll take for us to return Home? The destruction of this place?

I will gladly count down the moments until our year comes. I'm so tired of waiting. New Year's wish......will this be the year we leave? The year we're remembered and brought back Home? The Year of the Dragon. How appropriate. I grab the jacket off the chair, deciding to go downstairs and be a part of their countdown.

Another breeze, soft and warm as present breath, passes across my skin, igniting my necklace. "Ow!" The jacket falls from my hands as I bring the burning charm off my chest and into my fingers. I plunge my hand into my glass of water and rub my collarbone where the necklace has burned. Leaning forward to keep it off my skin, I plunge my other hand in the water as well, cooling it first before closing my hand over the charm, which sizzles upon contact. What's wrong with it?

The whisper is so close to my ear, I can feel the lips that form them: *"May I have this dance, my lady?"*

I jump, whirling around too quickly and nearly colliding with the man who watches my reaction with both shock and amusement. My balance thrown, I fall backward, but he reaches forward and has both my elbows in his hands, holding me steady. A warm, wondrously enthralling smile skips slowly across his face, making my heart backtrack foolishly.

"That's not the way you were supposed to react," he confides in a teasing whisper. Despite the noise that makes the girls and I shout in order to hear each other, I can hear his soft tone perfectly. His alarming amethyst eyes dance wildly, brightly. Absolutely intoxicatingly.

"I'm sorry?" I stammer, out of breath suddenly.

"Dance," he smiles. "You know, that thing men and women do when music is playing. First, you-"

"I know what dancing is, smart-ass. But I think you're a little late. The music's ended," I retort wryly.

He laughs. "Mmm. I guess I should have adapted my opening, then. Took me all night to think of it. I'm going to let you go now. You won't fall?" he grins.

Something in his eyes stops my retort. The lights in the club are dim, and it's filled with smoke that is playing around him. But his eyes, his eyes are an unusual lavender color that jumps out against the grayness of......where are we?

A barrage of images floods into me, so fast and sinking so deep, they spread roots through my bones. The most incredible of places. Brief, lightning quick images with the most intense of details: trees and trees and more wondrous trees; a lake in a black night with the moon and a million stars shining brilliantly overhead, making the water below glitter as it breathes; the top of some crest, some hill overlooking a forest that rolls on and on, and he's somewhere close beside me, and I'm filled with a sense of overwhelming peace and contentment; sitting beside a river bed with him and I'm so relieved, so relieved he's there; standing on a mountain top overlooking an ocean, with his arms encircling me from behind; standing face to face, mist swirling around us and our breath white on the air, with trees towering tall and close around us; a dark room with a balcony, and a sheer multicolored curtain waving in and out; my back against a tree and the whole length of his body pressing along mine, and I'm pouring myself into his kiss. And trees. And more trees. And endless more.

Don't fall? "I'm not so sure I can guarantee that."

"Then maybe I won't let go just yet."

The images last seconds, but I smell the earth, feel the heat from the suns above. Even now, the sound the river made as it lapped up on the small pebbled beach echoes in my ears; I taste the salt of the ocean on my tongue and feel the earth in my flimsy slippers and the coolness of that stone room; I smell the trees and earth and feel the wildness of the wind whipping through the crowded club. And him, him encircling me with his body.

Distantly, I realize that every word he's spoken has been in our language- my parents' and mine. The language of Home. And by the bewildered look in his amethyst eyes, the places we both just saw are not places of Home where he's already been, but places the two of us will see together. I relive the feel of him and the strength of the bond we'll have in that future, and am stunned speechless.

His eyes sparkle and shine in the dim light, as though lit from within. I search their depths, their odd, precious color. Everything is perfectly clear: *I'm going to go with him, and life with him will be marvelous and beautiful.*

Music so vaguely familiar, faint, as though coming from inside me, or him, fortifies the tight space we struggle to maintain as private. My eyes pass over his face, his brown hair, his alarming eyes, his very dangerous smile.

I search, but all my alarms have curled up as secure as Mom's non-dragon lizards sunning themselves beneath the window. *Make a wish*, Rani had said. A New Year's wish. A wish to bring me into The Year of the Dragon. A year to bring me into him. I glance again at the space between his arms, and want nothing more than to be there, tucked in beneath his cape. A gentleness encircles him, an openness that charms me, puts me at ease. I know him, somehow, as though he's been seared into my soul. He has been the oddity in the air, why it can't snow, why the moon changed its color, why my parents were odder than normal.

"I've had this all planned, but now I can't remember a thing I had intended to say to you. Is it safe to let you go?"

"No."

"Guess you'll have to dance with me, then. We've already discussed it, remember?"

"Remind me how it's done."

He pulls me into that desired space, seamlessly granting my wish. His warmth surrounds me, and I thank May heavily for making me wear her scrap of a shirt.

I panic, though, when he starts to move. "I don't dance!"

"Such a horrible lie."

My body is moving with his easily, to a song so strange, so slow. I'm in his arms, against his body, one hand lightly caressing the back of his neck and the other tenderly held in his. The wait, the tension, the uncertainty of the night withers away.

"I'm sorry for scaring you. I didn't know how to approach you."

"I think it fair to say you've been following me for a good long while. What took you so long?"

"I got here as soon as I could."

I laugh. "Now who's a liar?"

Embarrassed, he turns his head. "Fine. I got *Here* as soon as I could. Approaching you became a completely different endeavor than I had anticipated. I was not at all prepared."

"Why are you here?"

"I am alive because of your mother. I want to show my gratitude, so I'm bringing you both back home. I'm taking you Home, Lira, daughter of Elaar," he repeats softly, turning it more personal, more intimate.

"You're from Home." I say it just to hear it. It doesn't sound plausible. This feels like a dream. Someone from Home other than my parents and myself. I want to burst into tears. It's over? It's finally over? Just like this, just so sudden? We're leaving Here? The Year of the Dragon. It is perfectly fitting.

Home, we're going Home, but he smells so wonderful. I relax, I surrender, I fall. *The red moon is a good thing. Reach out to it.* That's what Mom had whispered to me as I left this evening. She *had* noticed the moon was changing. They knew he was coming.

I should find it frightening, strange that I've accepted this man so smoothly. Only it feels so right, he feels so right, so fitting.

But the Others are everywhere. "I don't want to be here."

He releases my waist, keeping my hand secure in his, and leads me through the crowd. Everyone is jumping in unison as they count down. *Ten, nine, eight......* as we push our way down the stairs. Their voices are mute to our ears even as the ground shakes with their stamping feet, with the finality of each number as they near the inevitable end. *Five......four......three......* to the door. Their world passes on a different dimension than us. *Two......* We see it, but we aren't a part of it, it doesn't affect us.

One......

The front door bursts open before us, sending a burst of cold fresh air upon us. But it's not the same bitter cold I'd known earlier. His cape's around me. I stop, take a deep breath while he watches me with a smile.

Snowflakes fall down, thick and soft and heavy. It's snowing. It's finally snowing. He's been the one to hold it back. And his presence is the event to set it free. Underneath our feet and on every outside thing lay a thick carpet of pure white snow; pure white snow eerily accented in red. The heat we radiate makes the flakes melt quickly.

The moon, the full, completely red moon hangs so low I can reach out and touch it. The man holding my hand and future whispers, "The sorcerer's moon."

I drink him in, this beautiful man I'm going to hold onto, tracing the outline of his face now that we are under the combined glare of the streetlights and the snow. "Doesn't it bother you?" The way my hand feels in his. The way it feels to stand beside him. The way I feel when he looks at me.

He pretends to not understand. "The red is alarming."

I love the way his voice fills me. I love his sound. I want to keep him talking as much as I want to stop all words. "No. Not the moon."

That I am so far away from him, just our hands touching, bothers me greatly. He's taking me Home, but Home can wait.

41

"*NO!*"

[Lira? Lira, can you hear me? Can you see me? Sit down, sit down! Don't move so quickly.]

"Nightmare?" Where did He leave me this time?

I shield my eyes from the suns, hold my weight up with my other arm. My head is reeling, as though I'd been spinning madly and stopped but it can't stop. My wrist *hurts*.

[What happened?]

"I don't know. I feel dizzy. I had the best dream, though. Karr had taken me for a flight. I think it was a dream. Wasn't it a dream? How could anything real be so exquisite?"

[He did take you for a flight. You dared him, remember? But then something happened: you told him you couldn't see, and then you lost consciousness. You fell off him but he caught you and brought you back down.]

"What? I fell?"

Blaze sits behind Nightmare, holding his arms out to me. I inhale, my head still a little foggy, and motion for him to come to me. He plants his hands down before him and crawls beneath the unicorn. I pick him up and place him on my lap.

Trees conceal the sky and from here, I can't fathom how high up we had been. Very, that I am sure of. And it was beautiful. Raining ever so gently, and Karr just gliding, just as softly. Well, and diving, and racing. Soaring. I hadn't dreamt it, but it seems so hazy. I fell? From up there? I shiver. I can't remember it. But he caught me and brought me back down.

Oh no- "Where's Karr?"

Nightmare throws his head over his shoulder.

{Over there,} Ama answers. I spin around at Ama's voice. Oh, that was very unwise. *{Hello, love. We were on our way to visit you when we saw you fall. You gave us all a horrible fright, you know. Your Karr has been recreating the terrain. I'm not certain this is the proper place for a canyon, though.}*

Karr is pacing madly back and forth, hanging his head and so distraught he can't hear me speaking. It looks as though he'd lashed out at a few trees, slicing them through with a whip of his tail.

"You're killing my trees," I say.

Karr stops his pacing and comes charging at me. The whites of his eyes are red. *{Lira? I'm sorry. I'm so sorry. I shouldn't have-}*

I rise to my feet with Blaze in my arms. My body is numb and tingly. The return of sensation stings and my legs tremble, but I walk nearer to him anyway, ordering my body to obey. "Karr, no. It wasn't your fault. I just got dizzy. Karr, flying with you was amazing. I don't know why I never went with you before. Thank you. I don't know what happened, it was so sudden, but it wasn't your fault."

{This all began because you refused to go to a village?} Marr asks, laying beside Ama with his body snaking uncomfortably between trees, shaking his head at me as though I'm a wayward child.

Huh. This isn't the place we had started from with that silly argument. I'm not so completely incoherent. Where are we?

{Seems Karr was right,} my grandfather continues. *{Will you go now?}*

I frown. "No."

Karr drops his head to shake it, chuckling. *{You are so stubborn. Fine. I'll go.* Again. *Stay here and just rest. Will you comply with me in that at least?}*

The urge to challenge him is quelled by a stronger urge to heave, which will only empower him. I assent with a dip of my heavy head. My hands are trembling oddly, so I hide them around Blaze.

Karr shakes his head again, grumbling, and turns. *{I'll be back shortly. Make sure she behaves herself,}* he adds stupidly, circling in his pre-launch preparation. I pick up a branch and launch it at him, hitting his shoulder. *{Are you daring me again?}* he taunts.

"Go away! Get me some food!"

{Don't think that type of attitude is going to be ignored. I'll do as you wish this time since you've nearly plummeted to your death and are maybe slightly out of your right mind, but you may have to earn my generosity next time.} Then he speaks so only I can hear, *{Don't ever scare me like that again. Do you promise?}*

I nod. *I promise. I'm sorry.*

{It was my fault, love. I shouldn't have flown like that with you. Not on the first flight.}

"Wait. You plan on more?"

{Definitely. Just not today. Stay right there and don't move until I get back.}

"Stay. Right here. Until you say otherwise," I repeat. He immediately catches the mock in my tone and sits back, inclining his head in wait. In challenge. He's picked me up and carried me off without any real retaliation. At this moment, his former reservations are gone, making him pretty damn cocky. He's craving the slightest excuse to do it again, now that he knows that Nightmare really can't do anything about it.

Nightmare turns to my grandparents. [Did you never tell him that dragons are supposed to be intelligent? He's set on getting us right back where we began.]

Karr laughs, still looking at me. {He just realized something he does not like.}

I don't back down from our battle of stares, even if he did steal that thought out of my head.

[Yes. That you're a greater moron than previously assumed. Dropping her to her death once already isn't enough? You're eager to risk her more effectively a second time?]

Karr breaks eye-contact with me and rises to his feet. {It was a request I'd have thought you, with all your brilliance, would agree with. She fainted, for no plausible reason, and so she shouldn't just start walking as though it didn't happen. Her grandparents, and I presumed even you, beast, would also think my request was sound. I'm assuming?}

"Oh, so I lose you to get additional sitters?"

{You'll never lose me.}

[We can always hope.]

A deep rumbling erupts from Karr's throat as he turns away. A spring and he is free, back in his air and clouds.

Blaze holds out his hands to him, clenching and releasing his fingers. "Da. Da." Dragon. Just like Talyn. *{I should come down and drop you into that village anyway,}* Karr mumbles before disappearing. As soon as he is out of sight and out of hearing distance, I collapse at everyone's feet, unable to contain the shakes within my body any longer. Every place I look, I see red coating the trees, the dragons, my skin, clothes, the unicorn, the ground. Red threads everywhere.

{Lira?} the concern erupts from all sides.

The only thing I can do is lie. "Don't tell Karr, but I'm not my mother. I loved it, but flying does not love me."

42

KARR TURNS HIS BACK ON ME and sets fire to the trees. They disintegrate into ash around me and are replaced by green and gold grass that reach to my waist. I look around, but he is gone. Where's Blaze?

I wade through the stalks, pushing each foot through to move. I spread the grass with my hands and call out for him, but the wind whips up from the west and shreds my words into the air. Where's my son?

My shoulder is grabbed from behind, and He appears before me. I am yanked to the side and thrown to the ground. I look up and it is Nightmare. Ealin fastens a rusted muzzle over his mouth. The unicorn's eyes are going vacant. The neck brace's pointed tips are cutting into his skin just under his jaw, adding his blood to the layers of old rusted unicorns' blood already adorning the ancient metal.

I turn back to Him and scream, fighting to go forward as Soldiers come and grab me by each arm. Blaze is in His hands! He's holding him out in anger, in malice. I lost his daughter, He'll steal my son.

I scream, and the grass around us shatters as the windows had done long ago. He sneers, dangling Blaze by the collar of his shirt, and Blaze is screaming and screaming for me, reaching out and all I have to do is take his hand back into mine-

I scream, howl, and hear the sound of the bullet again, feel it propel into my back this time. An arrow protrudes from my shoulder with the bullet now displayed on its tip.

Soldiers are dragging me buckward, back to Ravery, and Nightmare's in chains. Tossed aside throughout the valley are the bloodied bodies of the dragons, my only family. But He's walking away, taking my son. I scream and scream and scream.

The sound of my despair echoing down the hall and through the grass thrusts me out of sleep. I rise onto my knees, staring intently forward through the doorway with the etched dragons, seeing The Valley just beyond, but He and Blaze are nowhere to be seen.

I scream and scream and scream. Nightmare steps in front of me and is speaking, but all I see are his metal restraints and the vacancy in his eyes turning to belligerence. I grab my shoulder, trying to keep the blood inside, trying to claw out the arrow and bullet that are burning me from the inside.

{Lira! Lira stop!}

Blaze is screaming, calling for me, but I can't see him. Want. *NEED*. What do our children become without us? What do we become without them?

[Lira. Lira, look at me. You're dreaming. You were dreaming.]

Karr pushes Nightmare aside. *{Lira, look at me-}*

I lunge, throwing my whole body at the dragon and hitting at him with balled fists. "You turned your back on me! You let Him take my son!"

{You're still dreaming, love. Open your eyes. Blaze is asleep behind you, right where you set him. I didn't turn my back on you. I'd never do such a thing. I left for food, remember? That's all. It was a dream. A nightmare. But it's over. Love, it's over.}

The doors blink here and gone, here and gone. The Valley grows trees, shrinks to grass, trees again. Tall, dark, closely clustered trees. The fire in its pit is smoking. Had I run through it to attack Karr?

I don't want to, don't trust him, but I turn anyway and cry out in relief when I see that Blaze is where the dragon had said he'd be. I drop my head to the ground, trying to distinguish real from false, reality from dream. I feel as though something's taken over my head, my body.

{I'm not leaving again,} Karr is arguing with Nightmare.

[If you want to stick close on her heels from now on, fine. I'll enjoy watching your slow agonizing death as you starve.]

{I can't wait to be rid of you.}

[It's not going to happen any time soon.]

{But it's a given. One day, you'll be gone and I'll still be here with her. Doesn't sit so well with you, does it?}

I focus on the sound of the unicorn grinding his teeth in irritation, the curses falling from his head, the sound of Karr breathing, shifting his weight and making his scales scrape over each other. Nightmare reaches out to me and I recoil back.

[Lira, you're safe. It was a dream.]

{It was not!}

Blaze is screaming and I am looking helplessly at him. There's no such place as safe. I can't move, and I cannot be touched. I cannot touch. My skin is crawling and burning and I can't stop shaking. Karr sees and nudges Blaze with his nose, curling around him. *{Mommy's fine. She's fine little troll. Come here.}* Blaze turns and crawls into the space between his arms, watching me from a cave of red scales, hiccoughing his sobs back.

I'm fine. I'm fine. It was just a dream. Karr would never do something so hurtful. I've been so afraid since talking with my family that they'd tell him, that the dragon would tell Him. The panic seeped into my dreams. I'm fine.

Karr, I'm sorry. I'm sorry I'm sorry.

{Love, come here. Come back by me and I'll keep you warm. You don't have to sleep. Come back by Blaze.}

"No. Can we go? I don't want to stay here. I don't want to fall asleep here again. Let's move? Let's walk? I'm going to be sick," I say before averting my head to vomit.

{We're leaving!}

Only he doesn't mean the same 'leaving' as I'd asked for. How many times has he threatened to pick me up and plop me where he wants me? "No! No, Karr!"

He's on his feet, towering over me. *{Why won't you tell me what's wrong? I can't keep doing this anymore! You're going to The Cliffs, to Aril, to Him-}*

"*You can't!*" I cry, falling back and crawling away from him. "You can't-" and then I'm crying, painful, wrenching sobs.

{I'll break my promise, love. I'll bring Him here myself. I'm not going to watch you be destroyed when He's able to help you!}

I pull the diamond blade from my belt and hold it out before me. "No!" Blaze is on the wrong side of my knife. I'm thrown back in that dream, but it's Karr who has my son and not Him. "Give me my son!"

Nightmare comes to stand over me. [Stop,] he tells Karr. I lower my knife and look up at his chest, stunned. Stop? No yelling, no threats or names or insults, just a simple, polite 'stop'? [Breathe, Lira. Put down your knife. No one's taking you anywhere. Not this moment, right, Karr?]

{Yes. Yes, that's right. Come here, love. It's me. It's Karr. Come here. I haven't taken Blaze. He's just sitting here waiting for you. See? Come here. We won't go anywhere you don't want. Just, please come here.}

I crawl, and it's like that night on the hills outside Ravery, when I'd dug my elbows into the grass with my wrists bound and moved closer to Nightmare. My body feels as heavy and immobile as it had then. But Nightmare is at my side walking slow with me, and I focus on Karr and Blaze, desperate to return to them. The Void is swaying in my head, gaining purchase, but I don't want to sink again.

Before I reach him, Karr reaches out his arm and pulls me into him, holding Blaze and me tightly. I grab onto my son and curl around him.

{This has to stop, Nightmare,} I hear Karr say before I do what I don't want to, and fall back to sleep.

43

AUTUMN IS CLOSE TO DOUSING THE TREES with vibrant color. The earth is like Mom and her painting, drowning the walls with a flick of her wrist, a pour of her soul.

Already, the leaves are quaking on their stems, beginning to dry, aware that change is coming. Do caterpillars fear their cocoon? Do they fear the transformation they have to take, of what it'll turn them into? Do they know they'll emerge and fly away on beautifully painted feathered wings?

Autumn's coming and I need to open my eyes and watch it. Day is on my face and I need to greet it. Blaze is wobbling away towards Karr and I need to revel in his accomplishments.

But I can't will my body to move. My eyes are heavy and inflamed. So, so tired. Sometimes, I wake in the morning and still think I have been dreaming everything. Even when I look around and Karr's eyes meet mine, and Nightmare and Blaze are beside me, I'm still not completely sure. Sometimes I want to scream and ask why. Other times I look at Karr and Nightmare and my son— *my son*— and am completely awestruck. How did this happen? How did I get to this place? I always always, every morning, instinctively reach beside me, knowing as I do so that I still sleep alone. He's not there. Even though

I'm usually snug against the dragon and am greeted by the sight of Nightmare, I don't think they realize who I continually reach for.

And then there's those other times when I look just past Blaze, lost in that world of wordless loss.

I can't shake the Void. I inhale, trying to dispel the thickness that has rooted in my head and the rolling in my stomach that hasn't let me eat much the last few weeks, and nothing the last few days without retching it all back up. I've fought the signs for so long, adamant to Karr and Nightmare and myself that I am not sick. The cough and the headaches are from the change in the air, the dizzy spells are from rising too soon, the loss of appetite really isn't that serious. I routinely don't eat as much in the summer as I do in the winter......so many excuses.

"Mama," Blaze pleads. Time places his grip at odd moments. He's getting so big. Won't be a baby for much longer. Seven months old and already talking. He'll be walking so very soon. I never got to see her walk.

I push myself up to sit, and my empty body reels in protest. My head turns light and fuzzy, creating small gray dots that scramble my sight. Oh......

I push myself the rest of the way up and fall back against a tree. I'd layered all my collected clothes over each other, beginning with the tattered pants, shirt and sweater from the old woman, clothes from Nalee, the slip, and then two wool skirts Karr had recently procured for me, and then the capes draped tightly around all that. I am still freezing and am trying hard not to let anyone else notice how badly I'm shivering. My jaws hurt from clenching them so tight to prevent my teeth from chattering.

Blaze has grown so suddenly, and somehow I haven't been paying enough attention. I should've. Should've held onto each moment that's passed, done more to embed them into my head. Maybe Nightmare is right. It's that poison. Am I poisoning Blaze by nursing him? Stars, why hadn't that occurred to me? What if something happens to him? What have I done?

The trees spin in concentric circles. My head pounds and throbs. I shut my eyes but the pain only worsens.

[Lira, you *are* sick—]

"I am NOT sick! I'm not getting enough sleep. I'm fine." My voice is no longer as certain of my words. I fight the need to cough, almost making myself retch. So tired. I want to just lie down and sleep forever. That's all I need. Sleep. I'm not sick, just......so tired. All this walking. This wandering. How could Mom have lived this way?

My vision blurs and everything is spinning. I force my eyes quickly shut and grasp my forehead. My head's going to explode! Nightmare and Karr try to enter, try to get my attention, almost shouting for me, but my head is pounding too painfully and there's no room for them inside. Closing my eyes makes me more dizzy, more nauseous. But opening them brings in the sharp sunslight.

{*Lira, love, let me take you to the dragons. Let me take you to the Wizard's wife. Let me take you to someone!*}

I want to speak, but can't. I remember the fear in his voice when he'd threatened to fly me away, or fly Him to me. This time, though, I don't think Nightmare will intercede.

I don't want them to see me like this. I am The Daughter of Elaar! So angry with myself, so ashamed with how I am presenting myself. Weak. I can't be sick. I never get sick. Never.

Except when I was shot. The first poison, creeping under my skin, sneaking into my veins, turning my own blood toxic.

Blaze is calling for me and I have to go to him. I have to walk to prove to them I am fine. I take a step, pulling my body from the tree, and the world is ripped away. The Void has won after all.

Falling, slowly, like a feather- everything passing so slowly. My barriers shatter, all my ghosts rush me, pouncing upon the newly reinstated vulnerability.

His face. Angry. Ashamed of me. I had given up on him. I hadn't waited long enough, fought hard enough, like I should have. I had failed the honor of being mother of his child and had let her be taken. Turned my back on how he made me feel. Convinced myself I'd never loved him and he'd never loved me.

Her, faceless, no longer a baby. Blessed moon, look how much she's grown! Look how beautiful and perfect she is! And accusing, and so very angry. I abandoned her. Ran away, to Here. I failed her. I should've fought harder for her. Ripped out the throats of those that took her from me. I should've just stolen her back. Found where they kept her and stolen her back. Given them each an arrow in the chest in return. She is mine. How could I have just given up so easily? I should've been able to ignore what that bullet did to me. Got to my feet, ignored it, and searched for her.

I should've demanded to be returned There. I should've let Karr take me to the dragons, the Wizard, *Him*. Forced Him to see what he'd done and demanded he repair it all. Someone could've helped.

What kind of daughter am I? How could I have come from her? If this had happened to Mom— she would never have allowed it to go this far. She didn't. That's why they hadn't been able to take me from her.

I'm not as strong as any of them. I shame her name, the title of mother, the honor of being the dragons' descendant, His love, Nightmare's time by being so weak, by falling.

And Blaze, my little boy who needs me so much right now—

Their angry faces swarm around me, screaming, crying, yelling. I failed. I'm weak. I let myself get poisoned.

Falling. So slowly......

Blaze's cries break slightly through the haze, briefly rising loud before fading away. All their faces go mute and die away.

I wait for the hard ground, knowing I deserve it.

Yet I fall into arms. Strong, loving, human arms that cradle me close to a familiar chest with a pounding heart whose beat I know, and my breath catches and I want to wake. Him.

Home, we're Home, and He smells so wonderful; like earth and trees, mist and mountains. I relax, I surrender, I fall.

HE'S FOUND ME AT LAST.

Book Two of
Ravery's Daughters
coming soon!

Visit
www.MidnightTomorrowBooks.com
for author L. Nahay's insights, social media
links, updates, and more!

www.ingramcontent.com/pod-product-compliance
Lightning Source LLC
Chambersburg PA
CBHW020247030726
47499CB00001B/97